ALLAHU AKBAR

EDWARD NASH

SMYRNA PRESS

©1988 by Smyrna Press

Illustrations by Bob Fink

Cover illustration by Cindy Reiman from a design by
the author

ISBN 0-918266-20-3 (paperback)

ISBN 0-918266-21-1 (hardback)

Manufactured in the United States of America
Second Edition

To The Martyrs

"WAYNAK YA ALLAH?"
(O God, where are you?)
Cry of woman mourning at Sabra-Shatila mass grave.

NEW YORK

1

Samuel Shames squeezed Basil's bicep and steered him toward the two bureaucrats standing with drinks in hand, respectfully awaiting the introduction. "Will ya lookit this guy? They grow them big in Israel! Basil . . . Morrie Davidson, special assistant to hizzoner the Mayor, and our good friend Al Prezzobono, State Rep from Staten Island." Basil extended his hand to the two men and uttered the obligatory phrases of introduction. He was accustomed to Shames calling attention to his size, accepting it as an expression of affection and pride. They were disparate physical types, his six feet of brawn juxtaposed to Shames' five foot five runtiness. The difference commanded a lively admiration from the older, smaller man. Basil had never heard of the two men he had just met, but he assumed they wouldn't be there unless they were of some consequence in the scheme of things — that is, in Samuel Shames' scheme of things. He really hadn't wanted this going-away party. But after making the proper motions of objection and protest and being duly overruled, he went along with the program. His two and a half years with the firm had taught him the importance of the social element in Shames' *modus operandi*. Because the ultimate beneficiary of the evening's doings was the firm of Shames, Garfield & Chase, the entity that Samuel Shames had led into the promised land of megabuck success. Other New York architectural firms were bigger, better known, richer. But it was the intangible element of "hustle" — as personified by Shames — that distinguished Shames, Garfield & Chase, even from those enjoying greater national and international reputations, the ones Shames referred to as the "Gentile firms". If the "Gentiles" led in reputation, the gap was narrowing in gross receipts, an area where the firm had recently made powerful

3

surges. By garnering a lion's share of commissions, public and private, of the 80's building boom, making timely investments in three construction companies and undertaking an ambitious program of land acquisition, both improved and unimproved, the firm was bidding to become a growth industry. The credit for this growth belonged to Shames. His vision and patient laboring had laid its foundation. The afternoon's cocktail party was a typical Shames creation, a stage where contacts could be renewed, established clientele refreshed, and new prospects attracted. For Shames was an impresario, a macher, a man whose style and personality had always been too big for the drawing board (an activity delegated to subordinates while he came up with the "big picture"). To those who accused him of mixing architecture with Broadway and Madison Avenue, he responded by suggesting that Wall Street's present monopoly of the art was abnormal, and that it was he, Shames, who was working toward an architecture combining all three streets, reviving a synthesis that had died more than half a century ago in the Great Depression. Whatever the truth of the matter, the fact was that the process was creating the fastest growing architectural firm in the city. "The balance sheet, read the balance sheet!", was his answer to the naysayers. To Shames, it was a lot of sour grapes to be appropriately mashed underfoot.

A lesser, but perhaps equally essential player, was Fanny Rivlin, the firm's social secretary. In addition to performing the ordinary tasks expected of a New York social secretary, such as insuring that the firm always had a sufficient stock of tickets to musicals, plays, concerts, sports events, etc., Fanny was charged with the management of office parties, from cocktail to Christmas. With 23 years experience and an unlimited expense account, her department was known for quality productions. Her tables were always supplied with the best and the freshest, with even the bread baked to order (the usual morning bread was considered not fresh enough). Under her direction the humble sandwich was transformed into a memorable event. The beverage category was no less exalted, the freshly squeezed juices making drinks uniquely intoxicating. Fanny's prodigious memory for names and faces was backed up by three or four file cabinets filled with biographical data on the firm's clients and social and political allies. She resisted computerization believing such would be in bad taste if not invasive of privacy. As children she and Shames were in the grades together. It was even rumored she was an old girl-friend. But friendship ended where duty began. If there was one indispensable person in the firm, that person was Fanny Rivlin. Even Samuel Shames would admit as much.

The firm's parties usually began at · 3:30. The early starting time had originally evolved to accommodate guests in the entertainment business, the Broadway Joes and Janes whose day began at night. As the fame of the parties grew and more entrepreneurs, politicians and self-made became guests, people in the 9 to 5 category were progressively by-passed and outclassed. Because it was social attraction, more than any combination of food and drink, that brought the social lions to the 37th floor of the Woolworth Building. Like glutted lions gorged with the finest of life's offerings, only the extraordinary moved them. The attraction that afternoon was a party where leos could roar in each others' face and lionesses bare enameled talons. The scene in the large drafting room called for the skill and experience of a *National Geographic* photographer. Perhaps only that august publication could do justice to this urbane gathering of prides. Nevertheless, the other press, the specialists in social vulture journalism, were present in force. To be sure, for the stalker of big name there was good hunting. Yet, outside of the natural history element, there was little that was quota-ble, even big people talked small. Happily, amid the chatter, there would be a few *bon mots* for attribution. Dashed like pepper through an article, they gave fantasy journalism a degree of verisimilitude.

Beyond the purely promotional, there was a subtler, more personal motive behind the parties, one that emanated from Shames' own social nature. Few of the old rich ever attended the parties. They had their own society, one in which Shames had never felt comfortable. He preferred people who were interesting for themselves, for what they were or did. Of course, if they were rich so much the better, but wealth per se was never a criterion for an invitation. For many, mere involvement in the arts was enough. Among aspiring artists an invitation to a Shames, Garfield & Chase affair was considered a plum, an opportunity to debut their personas to prospective patrons. Shames considered artists his natural peers, often declaring that architecture was the mother of the arts, a concept, which in spite of all his calculation, he really believed. Over these assemblages of human achievement, like some high priest, hovered Samuel Shames, the Gothic majesty of the Woolworth Building his temple. If the scenario tended to the grandiose, it was not accidental.

". . . yes, you have to admire the spunk of those people," said Morrie Davidson. "Yeah, it's a great country," seconded Al Prezzobono, the bureaucrat and politician unanimous that Basil was a natural for a successful career there. It was the least they could say to the Israel-bound individual, and not surprisingly, they said it.

"Say, Sam," said Davidson, suddenly shifting the conversation away from Basil and Israel, "the Mayor wanted me to be sure and relay his regret at not being here tonight. The Associated Police Chiefs of America are in town and he's speaking at their banquet on the city's efforts to reduce the crime rate." To the city's beleaguered denizens crime was *the* issue, perhaps the issue of the century. It certainly took precedence over a party, even one given for someone going to Israel. "That's alright," responded the seemingly unconcerned Shames, "we'll get him next time. With a job like his he can't be Plastic Man and be in two places at the same time, he's got to go where the action is . . . not that there isn't any action here." Shames made an upward nod of his chin toward a clump of girls standing by the bar table waiting for drinks, secretaries from other offices in the building. A firm believer in the boy meets girl routine, Shames liked his parties to have a fair proportion of the opposite sex — appropriately young, pretty and unmarried. Not that he had a reputation for womanizing. His own married life was a model of regularity and as far as anyone knew, he was a dutiful husband. Matchmaking was another manifestation of his social philosophy — the "altruistic" aspect. Shames placed his hands upon the shoulders of the two men and adroitly launched them toward the girlish congregation at the opposite end of the room, declaring, "You boys look like you could use another drink. This is a free country, don't let me hold you back from the possibility of some beautiful memories." Then turning to Basil, Shames said, "What's wrong, kid? You make hay while the sun shines. C'mon, they're not going to come to you, you gotta show some initiative! You're the guest of honor. Go ahead, do them a favor!" For a moment Basil was nonplussed by Shames' forwardness. He had struck a sensitive chord. How did one answer a man who believed the mating game governed by the rules of an ordinary business transaction? There was no denying he would have liked to walk over and grab one. He had a nodding acquaintance with some of them, having seen them in elevators and nearby eateries. And he had already undressed them in his imagination. Generally that was the extent of it. With the secretarial set there was always a problem of what to talk about. He found himself running out of words rather quickly. He had never developed a line of chatter, nor that peculiar aura of self-confidence bordering on the vainglorious so irresistible to women. But this was no time to play Hamlet. The party was his, it was his name that was painted in large, red letters on the banner stretched across the wall above the bar.

"GOOD LUCK BASIL!" it proclaimed, with "come back soon" below. He owed it to himself to seize the opportunity. Certainly, nothing like this was waiting for him in Israel. Striving for all appearances to look like a man in search of a drink, he strode toward the bar. Suddenly, materializing before him and barring his way, was a knot of reporters and photographers. "Mr. Primchek!", called out one of them, a woman with thick, gray hair, "I'm Lorna Ballinger of the *Times*. We've been told you're the reason for this party."

The experience of a half-dozen or so persons milling about and demanding his attention was unnerving. His previous encounter with the press had been limited to an interview with a reporter from the *Architectural Times* subsequent to the firm's receiving a first prize from the New York Architects Guild for his design of town houses in Brooklyn Heights. "Yes," he said, composing himself, "I suppose you could say that."

"Well, would you tell us something about your background, where you went to school, how long you've worked for the firm, your . . . ah . . . specialty, and why you're leaving the firm at this time?"

"I attended Brandeis and Columbia, receiving a master's in architecture from Columbia. After obtaining my baccalaureate from Brandeis, I joined the firm for a special journeyman program. During that time I attended Columbia, gaining a master's the following year. I should mention that I was the recipient of a full scholarship from the Samuel Shames Foundation after I graduated from the Technion in Israel . . ."

The mention of Israel provoked a veritable eruption of questioning — "Israel? You're from Israel?," piped a short, chubby-faced young woman. "Then you're a Samuel Shames protégé? Do you plan on returning to Israel . . .?" What had been a relatively organized group with a single spokesperson was now a jumble of journalists frenetic at the unanticipated development of an Israeli connection. Suddenly, a tall, dark-

8

haired man appeared. Interposing himself and raising his hands, he calmed the group with a commanding, "OK, ladies and gentlemen, one question at a time. Mr. Primchek is not a computer." It was Mark Lerner, Basil's friend and roommate at college.

"And who are you?," demanded the chubby-faced reporter, taken aback at the intervener's effrontery.

"I'm Mr. Primchek's attorney," responded Mark, "here to insure that he is not unduly harassed at this party in his honor." Mark's mock seriousness temporarily intimidated the gaggle of journalists. Sensing the bewilderment, Basil explained their relationship and in a hurry to extricate himself from besiegement, condensed into a two minute narrative his Israeli origins and plans for repatriation. A couple flashes of light and the interview ended, the journalists dispersed to other parts, leaving only the chubby-faced reporter who lingering behind, let go a tentative smile. Embarrassed by the presumption, Basil thanked her and wished her luck. It was the nicest way he could think of to get rid of her.

Mark drew Basil toward a wall, away from the other celebrants. Earlier he had telephoned reporting on his wife's inability to obtain a baby-sitter. Now his urgent manner suggested he had something weightier than domestic relations to disgorge. "I got the job!", he cried, his voice mixing relief and excitement. "My uncle called this morning and told me to report to Senator Maudlin's office Monday morning!"

"Say, that's great. Maybe we should have a coming-out party for you now."

"I'm on my way, baby. What a relief to leave that law firm and all those dunderheads. They made me sick walking around with a pole up their ass all day. I've taken mine out and now I'm banging them over the head with it!"

"Does the job come with a title? What do we call you now?"

9

"Administrative assistant, US Senate. Forty-seven g's and a non-abusive expense account. But they can shove the money, I'd do it for the satisfaction."

Memories of their days together at Brandeis flashed through Basil's brain. Mark had majored in political science . . . "poly sci" they called it. No issue had been beyond his involvement — war, peace, civil rights, the environment, poverty, medicare, that endless stream of unfinished business assuring the perpetuation of government. Originally, Basil's knowledge of the American political system had been rudimentary. Like his own country he knew it was a democracy, except that the president was elected by a complicated system based on popular vote. Prior to meeting Mark he viewed politics as the actions of remote and important people, the statesmen and politicians who determined the world's destiny. It was all very amorphous. In contrast, Mark believed that politics was too important to leave to politicians, somewhere in the process supervision was necessary. Compared to the approach of his patron, Samuel Shames, Basil found Mark's theory on intervention too late and too low. The advantage was with the man exercising leverage at the top. The military and the church were based on that hierarchical principle. Simple enough to be grasped by fools, it has served them well. He was indulging himself, he didn't know the answers to the questions his mind was posing, or even if there were answers. His friend had gotten a job in the political hierarchy. He was glad for him; he hoped he would be in a position to influence events. But he doubted it.

Mark motioned to the person he had brought to the party. Basil noticed the mustard oozing from the fellow's sandwich was causing some difficulty, a dollop of it had besmirched his cream colored cravat rather badly. Seeing Mark's signal he came over, a look of frustration on his black face. "Damn! I had a little accident. Excuse me while I wipe my hands from this mustard."

10

"Didn't I tell you you wouldn't find a better sandwich anywhere in town?," exclaimed Mark. "You're just not used to Jewish soul food, that's all."

"That's where you're wrong. We lived near a deli in Brooklyn. My mother was always sending us out for sandwiches when she didn't feel like making a feed for the hungry five. With all my practice I am profoundly humiliated!"

He had the unlikely name of Worthington T. Carter. He was also an administrative assistant to Senator Maudlin, and like Mark, an attorney. He had telephoned Mark after receiving word of his appointment, a courtesy call. Mark had invited him to the party. He was very impressed with the quality of the food and drink, declaring that it had to be the finest cocktail party in his more than six months of cocktail party hopping in Washington and New York. A recent graduate of Harvard Law School, Carter had been recommended by a former university colleague of Maudlin's. He was making contacts that would be of benefit in the future — he hoped to run for congress after serving an apprenticeship in public service. A commendable ambition thought Basil, knowing a seat in Congress was also Mark's ambition. It would make a great story were the two to compete head to head for the same seat — "Worthington Carter challenged by Hymie". The joke was too tacky for the situation. Having only just met the fellow, there was no telling what kind of Pandora's box would be opened by some "tasteless" ethnic baiting, even in jest. While humor was his first line of defense, one man's defense was another's offense. Blacks and Jews could be super-sensitive to supposed slurs upon their respective kind. He would never forget the flap over a facetious remark made to the sister of a black friend. He had been asked to pick up a rug from the sister's apartment in a New York high-rise. Hoisting the roll to his shoulders he had remarked, "Any cockroaches in this rug?", a not unreasonable precaution given the

11

insect's infamous success in saturating the city. As far as is presently known, cockroaches are no respecters of persons. At most the remark was an indiscretion, yet it was taken as an insult, earning him a "racist" tag and terminating a friendship. The incident was symbolic of current Black-Jewish tension which, like a fire in a peatbog, could be whipped into flame by any kind of an ill wind.

Here he was, a candidate for no office, in a few weeks leaving job and country, giving up the opportunity for a laugh at a friend's expense. It was altruism triumphant over egoism. He congratulated himself on his self-control in obeying the first rule of politics — offend no one. Poor Mark, he would never be able to remove that pole from his ass. Only upon reaching the top of the political dunghill was there a dispensation from the "public" to relax and be human. And that was accorded to few in public life.

At the food table he ordered sandwiches of tongue and prosciutto, projecting later selections of hot pastrami and corned beef. He stood chewing, listening to Mark and Carter discuss world affairs. Finally, tiring of their talk, he looked around and saw Elliot Chase and son Darwin sitting at a table together. Elliot Chase was his mentor, the person he relied on to suggest solutions to his architectural stumbling blocks. A natural teacher, Chase had been an instructor in architecture prior to Shames' recruiting him for the firm. His son Darwin was the only offspring of the partners to follow the profession. Twenty-six years old, he was seeking to establish himself as something more than "Elliot Chase's son".

No sooner had he joined the Chases at their table than Shames and Garfield walked over. Something was up, Shames was whispering into Chase's ear. The three partners motioned for Basil to accompany them to the center of the room. Mounting a chair, Shames raised his hands in an appeal for quiet. "Ladies and gentlemen: before we get further along this evening, I'd like to say a few words about

12

the person whose future we're celebrating here today. His name is Basil Primchek and he's our man from Israel, our sister democracy across the sea. I've known Basil since he won a scholarship to study architecture at Brandeis. It's not often we can follow our scholars all the way from the halls of academia to our workshop here, but Basil blazed a trail of excellence so dazzling that we really had no choice but to insist he work for us. We are grateful that he accepted, and in the short time with us, he brought both honor and profit to the firm. Now he has decided to return to his country to pursue his architectural career . . . and if what he accomplished in his short time here is any indicator, the future is his. Our loss is Israel's gain! Ladies and gentlemen, friends and colleagues, I propose a toast to Basil Primchek, master architect!"

The three partners simultaneously raised their glasses high while Shames cried out "li chaim" and "mazel tov". Picking up the "mazel tov" refrain, colleagues and guests descended upon him to shake his hand and wish him well. Women planted noisy kisses on his lips and cheeks. He had never been the object of so much attention by so many people. Shames' words and infectious delivery seemed to invest the guests with a special zest. He was sweating now, embarrassed by the scene's show-business aspect. Shouts of "Speech! Speech!" issued from the crowd. He saw Mark gesturing and felt a pushing on his back. Finally, he realized he was expected to make a response. It would have to be short, Shames was a tough act to follow. He glanced at his watch, it wasn't even 5:30 yet.

"I would like to express my appreciation for all your good wishes to me here this afternoon. My special thanks to my colleagues for their patience with a novice, and my special gratitude to Misters Samuel Shames, Hilton Garfield and Elliot Chase for giving me the opportunity to work and learn as a member of the firm. Thank you all very much!"

Conscious of his redundancy, he knew when to stop. A

13

burst of clapping followed. As it tailed off, he was relieved that the worst was over. He and everybody else could get back to the business of eating. It might be years before he would encounter such superb bread and meat again. But before he could rejoin Mark and the others, he spotted Shames leading a tall blonde in an indigo knit dress. Shames was holding her hand, advancing directly toward him. "Where the hell had she come from?," he asked himself, he would have to be blind to have missed her.

"Basil, I'd like you to meet our friend, Alison Cleveland. She hosts Channel Thirteen's "Speaking of New York". Alison's rather an expert on architecture and has helped us explain some of our projects to the public. I know you two will have a lot to talk about." Shames' eyes made an arc of silent exclamation a la Groucho at Alison's breasts, prominent under the clinging knit. Shaking Basil's hand, Alison held it affectionately as she spoke, "Sam, you're super! . . . Sam has this knack for giving me undue credit. Actually, he was a terrific help with the documentation for our production on Gotham Towers. I really could not have done it without him."

"Alison, you are a real kibitzuh! You know neither of us can afford to be modest in our business." Then looking at Basil, Shames asked rhetorically, "Would you hide this under a bushel? Whattaya think of her, kid? Not bad, eh? She's an actress, hardly a year out of drama school and already on every TV producer's comer list. Barbara Walinsky, you're taking early retirement! And here she comes on like Little Miss Modesty."

Alison had released Basil's hand and was beaming down at the little man at her side, a look of admiring amusement on her face. Shames' performance brought to mind a phrase from Sportin' Life's song in *Porgy and Bess,* "little David, but o my". Here he was, knocking over this amazon like nothing, his exotic repertory of gestures fascinating the child-woman in her. "Super Sam."

Unknowingly Alison had hit the mark. It would have made a great nickname were it not so devastatingly accurate. He would surely resent it.

"I'm leaving you in good hands, Alison," said Shames as he backed away wagging a playful finger at the radiant TV ingenue. "I hope you'll make the most of it." Basil's mind was whirring at full throttle. He was racking it for the bits and pieces dropped during the brief conversation, the perfect diction larded with colloquialisms suggesting a calculated chatty effect, the reference to training in dramatics indicating artifice. He was seeking to construct a synthesis, a guide, something that could take him to the next level with her. The physical devices were obvious — the dark, clinging dress; fluffed out blonded hair; crimson fingernails; professionally dramatized eyes; all on a florid body. The impression was one of overkill. But Shames was right, she was one of those creatures that should not be hidden under a bushel. He expected his brain to digest all the data his senses were feeding it, and like a computer, throw out a plan of attack, a tack, an approach, anything. Of course, it did nothing, failing him in crisis.

Neither spoke. He watched as she coyly folded her arms in front of her, delicately stroking the stem of her martini glass with long, classic fingers. She was enjoying the tension, imitating the panoply of Garbo mannerisms probably learned viewing late night TV. Her eyes were dreamily looking at and through his. She was good, very good. He suppressed an impulse to offer his compliments — that would be Sam's schtick, not his. It might be construed as sarcasm, at this stage of the game probably fatal. He was testing her, trying to go as far as he might with the unsaid, reaching toward some crazy ideal of wordless rapport. It was a risk, one determined by circumstances. She could walk away, dismissing him as some crude macho expecting women to swoon from the mere scent of his armpits. Most women would have. But she wasn't most women.

15

"So tell me, where did you get the name Basil?"

"My mother. She was an admirer of Basil Rathbone."

"I think she chose well. She could have given you one of those funny Israeli names like Uri, Uzi, Zeev . . . or even Matatyahu. And you do have a villainous cast about you. I think you are one . . . are you?"

"You've got the wrong movie. I follow the Holmes tradition, straight-up and straight-out."

"Elementary?"

"No . . . elemental."

Alison turned and walked to a nearby window, leaning on her elbows against the sill. He followed, stopping reverently behind to view her dorsal aspect. Perhaps it was a matter of aesthetics, his preference for fundamental women. But as a rationale, aesthetics left off where the curve of Alison's rear began. It was about as useful in explaining the power of those saliences as theology in describing heaven. A humbling power, it reduced him to his knees, worshipful devotee to the intimate world of She.

"You've got a nice view of the Brooklyn Bridge," she said, "I love that bridge."

"Everybody does. Perhaps that justifies the suffering it took to build it. What better monument to mortal sacrifice than a beautiful structure?"

"That sounds so pharoanic. You're not Egyptian are you? I thought you were a Hebrew?"

"When they got power, they went Egyptian too. Building on the grand scale, temples. The ancient world had this colonial mentality *vis-a-vis* Egypt. History teaches otherwise but today you can substitute America for Egypt and watch the cycle repeat itself — except for the technological variables."

"But history is bunk . . . Henry Ford said so."

"He could afford to say anything — and he did — he changed the world."

"Did you ever think what you would do if you were

16

fabulously rich . . . I know it's not the most productive type of fantasy?"

"Sure, I'd change the world. But you're right, fat chance of that. I much prefer the fantasy . . . "

"Excuse me, but tell me how you would change the world, I'm interested."

"Are you sure you don't want another drink? Now you're getting into my philosophy of architecture — 'Abandon hope all ye who enter here'. This conversation reminds me of the Delphic Oracle. My answer is that I'd change the world back. Now figure that out."

They were face to face, standing by the windows' light, each exhilirated by the excitement of meeting a kindred spirit, a situation neither would have dared contemplate just 15 minutes ago. He was as close to her glistening, fruity lips as he dared permit, close enough to detect what seemed to him her body electric. He had begun by depreciating her as merely another filly in the stable of the TV hustlers, but now, convinced by a social miracle, he was discovering in her the rarer virtues, virtues incorporating what the Italians call *La Femmina,* a quality best defined as "womanliness". The sensation was uncanny, bewitching, almost levitating. He was fain to throw off his clothes, embrace her, kiss her. But convention screamed "stop!", robbing him of an experience, that as far as he knew, occurred only in dreams.

She must have sensed the tension, because she broke it, almost brutally, by resuming the conversation, "What kind of architecture does Israel have?"

"Derivative."

"Is that good or bad?"

"Bad, wrong derivation."

"Basil, I know we've just met, but I have something that I'd like you to consider." She paused to assess his reaction before continuing, "How long will it be before you leave for Israel?"

It was a question he had prepared for from the moment

of their introduction, "I really can't say. At the earliest it would be weeks, perhaps four to six, but it could be months since I'm really under no pressure to wind up my affairs here. Also, I've been considering a trip to San Francisco, maybe do some camping now that the weather is warming up."

"Then I'd like you to do a show with me. I think it would be fascinating. Your being from Israel would make it a natural for our audience. We could tape it in the morning or afternoon, your convenience. You'd have full editing rights in case anything too personal or embarrassing emerges that you decide you don't want divulged. And don't worry about the topic, our little conversation has convinced me that will be my problem, not yours. How about it?"

He had expected her to suggest they continue the conversation in a social setting, perhaps at lunch or dinner. Despite the flattering nature of her proposal he felt disappointed. During his years at Brandeis he had been solicited by a number of Jewish organizations and rabbis to speak about life in Israel. His response had been an invariable "Thanks, but no thanks". There were always the others, those Israeli students eager to promote Eretz Yisrael. The expectation that he should see the world through "Jewish eyes" irked him, as if he were some Talmudic scholar with a Teutonic *Judenweltenshaung*. The matter was complicated by his having turned down a request from Shames himself, to come and address his temple's congregation. This was shortly after he began working for the firm when Shames, flush with paternal pride, was showing him off at every opportunity. He recalled the hemming and hawing he had gone through in avoiding that request. Shames had been sympathetic, attributing the reticence to shyness. What would Shames think now? That he had outgrown his shyness? His hesitation prompted Alison to speak, only now there was an importuning quality to her voice, "Look, if there is any problem . . . if you'd tell me . . . Basil?"

18

He reached for her hand, holding it. Then, pausing for effect, he began speaking, slowly, like one given to long and serious consideration, "Alison . . . pardon me . . . but I'm rather flattered that on such . . . such short acquaintance, you would consider me topical enough for your show. You know I would do anything . . . to help you. But first . . . let me clear this with Sam. There are a lot of trade secrets, pending deals . . . things going on, that he may not want aired at this time. I'm sure he'll have no objection. But just let me clear it with him and the other partners."

"Of course, I understand. Let me give you my card." Fetching her purse from a table, she reached inside and plucked a card from an elegant wallet of ostrich skin. Scrutinizing it, he noted the raised blue letters on a beige background. The art deco border of diminishing lines and triangles was unusual for a business card.

"Alison Cleveland, Telecaster," he said, reading aloud from the card face. "I like it. Your own design?"

"Yes, I like to think there is more to me than the actress."

"I believe it. But can you bake a cherry pie?"

"I don't know, but I could try." Alison glanced at her wrist, a signal the interview was over. He resolved to press his suit another day even as she made it obvious that for the present, time was up. "I wish I could stay longer but I really can't," she said. It's almost six and I have a seven o'clock dinner engagement. I've enjoyed our little encounter . . ."

"Before you go, I'd like you to meet my friend, Mark Lerner. We were roommates at college. He's an attorney and he just took a position as *aide de camp* to Senator Maudlin."

"Senator Maudlin! Really? I did a show with him a few months ago. I was just starting out then. He was so kind. He's a charmer."

"Yeah, it'll only take a few minutes. You'll have time to spare."

"I want to say goodbye to Sam too. He's been a dear."

19

Basil spotted Mark and Worthington T. Carter in discussion with a group of men. Leaving Alison, he walked briskly over and excusing himself, pulled Mark from the circle. "What's up, Romeo?," Mark asked, piqued by his friend's urgent brusqueness, "I saw you making time with that bird of paradise. Who is she?" Basil was pulling Mark by the arm and striding toward Alison, cooly standing where he had left her, arms crossed, a pose he found defiantly sexual. "Patience, my son, you'll soon find out . . . Here he is, Alison, just as I promised, Brooklyn Heights' own Mark Lerner. Mark . . . Alison Cleveland."

"Alison Cleveland! I didn't recognize you! Maybe my glasses . . . Pardon me, but I've never seen you in person. I wanna tell you my wife watches your show religiously!" Alison extended her hand to the evidently pleasantly surprised individual before her. "I guess we all look alike," she quipped. "Basil tells me you're working with Senator Maudlin. Would you please give him my regards, he's one of my favorite people."

"I'll make it my first order of business with the senator . . ."

"Excuse me, Mark," Basil interjected, "but I promised Miss Cleveland we wouldn't interfere with her schedule. She has a seven o'clock appointment."

Basil placed his hand on Alison's elbow and pointing across the room, directed her to Shames. He watched, as head up, she made her way through the crowd.

She reminded him of the Arabians he had seen as a child at a horse show in Beersheba. They were beautiful, almost too beautiful to ride. Graceful, slender legs supported great round bellies and asses. Who is it that does not love a horse's ass? Even their excrement was done in the round, the memory of its invigorating scent on that day in the compound had never left him. Enchanted, he had asked his mother if he might have one. She had replied reassuringly that he could indeed have a horse if he wished, but he must

20

first grow up. He never did get his horse though he was convinced that in beauty of form, it was the most excellent of nature's creatures. That is until he saw his first nude. At that a whole new world — albeit a two-dimensional one — wondrous and forbidden, opened to his eyes. At the time he was more fascinated by the aesthetics of the discovery than the rather dreary orthodoxy prescribed for the act by his peers. He realized he was a sucker for the voluptuous. Like any sucker, he was very vulnerable.

"Do I detect baited breath or do you always breathe that way?," Mark asked after Alison's exit.

"Only under water. There goes nothing."

" 'Nothing'? You didn't drag me over here to meet 'nothing'! You could have eaten her alive you were so close to her and I wouldn't begrudge you one bite. What happened?"

"I told you — 'nothing'. She wants to do one of her programs with me, that's all."

"Hey! That's great! You'll get a hundred thousand dollars of free publicity."

"Yeah, real great. I'm not running for office you know. The publicity will be deflected to the firm. Sam's worked with her on PR gimmicks, I'll have to talk to him."

"C'mon Basil, out with it, what else happened? . . . She rebuffed you, didn't she?"

He was trying to cover his tracks but without much effect, his furtiveness the result of a humiliating "affair". Although several months had elapsed, the events stuck in his throat like a piece of dry chicken. He had met her at a party in Manhattan. One of those fresh creatures from the interior whose ambition, sexiness, talent and flashing feet propel them inexorably to the stages of Broadway. She impressed him as naive and charming, a child of nature. Aroused, he had gone for it. However, she had other plans. Auditions, rehearsals, dental work, so the excuses went, for months. Through it all only the true believer could have kept faith.

21

When they did meet, and that was infrequently, it was for dinner; early, so she could digest it before going out and dancing her beautiful ass off. For a girl from the provinces she had remarkably good taste.

New York was a city where a girl, depending on her appetite, could acquire an appreciation for the finer things in life rather quickly. She had a way about her, of promising everything and giving nothing, that kept him on a long leash for the longest period of time. He admitted to attending more than one performance of the musical in which she danced. Called "O Daddy", it was not one of the season's better productions. He tolerated its boredom in the hope of gaining loyalty points. The exercise in creative sadism was finally terminated after he ran into her boyfriend — a fellow dancer from the cast — emerging from her apartment one late afternoon. Mark had told him it was a lost cause after the second week.

"Rebuff me? How could she rebuff me?," he answered defensively, "I never gave her the opportunity. Still, there was a moment when I thought I had it . . . " Mark placed his hand on his friend's shoulder, trying to reconcile what he heard with what he thought he had seen, "I take it back. Think of it as a silent rebuff . . . But then it doesn't make sense she would rebuff you by inviting you to appear on her show. No, something else is operating here. What the hell did you tell her that turned her on to your brilliant wit so summarily?"

"I don't know. All conversations should be so inconclusive. It was like conversing in fairy tales, very airy. Maybe she picked up on the architecture theme to get out of a tight spot . . . You saw me, I was bearing down on her."

"Yeah, I saw that she was apparently undaunted by the garlic in those fresh dills. That's not the usual reaction of the public person. But let's face it, Basil, you can be a charming sonofabitch — especially to the right woman. My advice is to follow this through, it has possibilities. But remember, take nothing for granted and don't come on too hard and too fast with this one. She's a queen bee, she'll have to give you the buzz."

He was encouraged by Mark's analysis yet refused to consider himself a prospect for anything more than the commercial. Having just gone through one manic-depressive episode, he wanted to avoid lapsing into another. Sometimes a man's imagination could be his worst enemy.

Shames had returned from seeing Alison Cleveland to the elevators, his face wearing a bright look of expectation. "Didn't I tell ya she was something? Didja get her number?," he exclaimed, hardly able to contain his excitement at the presumed success of his matchmaking.

"No," answered Basil, never failing to be amazed at Shames' sense of confidence, "just her business card. She wants to interview me for her show. I told her I'd talk to you about it. What do you think?"

"What do I think? I think it's a great idea! It could be worth a million in future business . . ."

"That's what I've been trying to tell him," chimed in Mark.

"Yeah, that girl's got a head on her. I knew she'd know a good thing when she saw it. Go ahead. And don't be afraid to toot your horn. Sometimes your modesty can be self-defeating. Now that you're going out on your own, old Sam won't be around to fill in the gaps for the public. Sure . . . good idea, good idea. Give it to her straight. It'll be a good experience for you. And she's great to work with, got a real gift for words — you know she's an actress. But come on, all that time and all you talked about was business . . .? Listen, there's a real chotchke. Built for relaxation. I'll bet she'd give you something to think about on that flight to Israel. Seventh heaven."

Shames made a downward jerking motion with his right fist at his side, emphasizing the gesture with a hard-eyed lothario look. Word and deed were very close for him

23

— saying it was doing it. It was part of his persona, one of the intangibles leading him to command and others follow. Basil realized Shames meant well but resented his facile attitude. It was inappropriate and vulgar, even in her absence an affront to dignity. But then who the hell had appointed him her protector? He realized he was being hypocritical. He had similar, if not "worse" thoughts about the beautiful creature whose virtue he had been so ready to defend. If that was a burden of being beautiful, it was the only one. She hardly needed his "protection". With that body and face she was writing her own ticket. The brains put her in a class by herself, making her a one-of-a-kind to the filthy rich collectors who would bid heaven and earth to possess her. That body in some Louis Quatorze bedroom, better than any piece of jade, porcelain or painting on earth. His mistake was in wanting to believe that whom a woman gave her body to was on a different plane than the winning of some grubby contract or the cutting of some deal. Shames was right. His opinions and manner of expression were outrageous, but they carried the ring of truth. And he had no right to object to the truth — she would make a fine lay for some lucky bastard. Would that it were he.

"Sam, you've got a great imagination and a real gift for presumption, but don't you think a girl like her has got to have at least ten suitors vying for her at all times? What chance do I have against that kind of phalanx?"

"Push 'em aside! What do you think you got those muscles and good looks for? I wouldn't have introduced her to you if I didn't think you were good enough for her. With that kind of attitude you're bound to be odd man out. I say go for it!"

Mark, who had been listening with some bemusement, spoke up, "Sam, I'd be glad to volunteer for this mission if your first choice here gets cold feet."

"Listen you, you're a family man now and if you know what's good for you, you'll forget about this playing around business."

"Just kidding, Sam, just kidding. I'm only into 16 year old virgins anyway."

The intensity of Shames' reaction to Mark's facetiousness surprised Basil. He hadn't realized Shames held such strong moral opinions. He tried changing the subject, telling Shames about Mark's appointment, hoping in the process to rehabilitate Mark with Shames. However, Shames' conceit proved intractable. Wrong-headed as it was, its maintenance apparently served some hidden moral reservoir. "Maudlin, eh? Good man, one of the best. You'll be in Washington most of the time so you better resolve now to forego temptation, because brother, that place is loaded with young secretaries just looking for a mark like you. Any power broker will do! And you can't blame 'em, they outnumber men five to one there. If you do succumb, for heaven's sake be discreet. Your wife is from a good family, a powerful family, remember that. And if you keep your nose clean, and when you're ready, I'll see that you get party backing for a congressional seat."

Although it was 6:30 the party was by no means over. Guests were still arriving and the assemblage appeared to have lost none of its zest. He glanced at the food tables checking the stock. Some items had undergone thinning, yet he couldn't imagine anyone leaving hungry. Everything still looked appetizing yet his stomach signalled full. Too much had happened since those first two sandwiches. Food, even the delights of Fanny Rivlin's last salute to him, assumed a secondary, superfluous status. His body was still running on the excitement of the encounter, his psychic and physical engine racing at high rpm. So when Mark suggested they go to a bar and unwind he was ready. Excusing himself, he made for the lavatory where he vigorously washed his face and hands. The effect was restorative, as only washing can be. He recalled watching the Arabs perform their ablutions outside the mosques in Jerusalem, the methodical way they washed hands, faces, feet. Perhaps they had something, the Mohammedans, the refreshment of water preparing the believer for the dreary duty of prayer. He wondered if Moslems prayed for the likes of an Alison Cleveland. Or would they be content to meet her above as heavenly houri? Poor devils, they would only have a glimpse of that face to go on, the rest of her a voluminous bag of forbidden fruit. Or was he the poor devil, tormented by the sight of that form and its fleshy promise beneath the clinging covering? To see her disrobe in some inner chamber of a Damascene palazzo, the room's fountain softly bubbling, the flames from the hanging oil glasses making a play of light and shadow over her torso . . . He saw his reflection in the lavatory mirror. He was smiling. He looked around, he was alone.

Returning to the party he found Mark standing with Worthington T. Carter. A petite, dark-haired girl was speaking with them. It was Miriam Scheine, Hilton Garfield's secretary. He and Miriam had been friends since his first days with the firm. She had held his interest briefly only to fade with time and familiarity. There was a gentility about Miriam that made her instantly likable. She was one of those women who found their highest calling in the service of a man, preferably a great one. The relationship was unequal, had been from the beginning, but at this late date the friendship was too well established to succumb to such a frivolous contradiction. There was little one could do about sexual attraction, it was present or it was not. It was one of those things one accepted, like the color of one's skin or eyes. Like her, respect her, find her company stimulating, more than any other woman he had met — but lust after her he did not. The problem was his idealist conceits. As if in all the world's couplings passion was the rule rather than the exception.

Miriam was the first to speak, "Hi, Basil. We were just discussing how really nice the party turned out. Your apprehensions were unjustified."

"Yeah, well fortunately I didn't have much to do with it. It was all Fanny's doing. But it's gratifying to get a good report."

"I saw the press with you. Tomorrow's *Times* should feature it on the society page."

"Yeah, 'all the news that's fit to print', my coming out party. The public will wonder where I've been all these years . . . uh, Miriam, we were just getting ready to leave so I'll say goodbye until tomorrow." He saw the sadness in her eyes. What had he done to feel guilty?

Out on the street, Worthington T. Carter hailed a cab while he and Mark went directly to a nearby bar. "You think she saw the drama between you and Alison Cleveland . . . that she might be a little jealous?," Mark asked.

"A little. I could have raped her on the floor and I'd still be her boy. She knows I'm no virgin."

"How do you do it? If Joy saw me with that I'd never hear the end of it."

"I guess I'm just a nice guy. As for you, adopt the Russian system. Have your wife bring your boots and knout to the foot of the bed every night . . . and don't hesitate to use them. It does wonders for wifely discipline."

"Oy vay! The 'nice guy' reveals himself."

The bar was deserted except for a couple of barflies. They chose a table in the rear relatively remote from the static of human interference. A barmaid took their order for two beers on tap. He realized this might be his last time alone with Mark. They had met in his second year at Brandeis, almost seven years ago. They got on together immediately, taking an apartment in town where they roomed until both graduated three years later. Mark had spent two summers in Israel on a kibbutz in the Galilee. Being friends with an Israeli acted as a recapitulation of the experience as well as a nourishment of his self-esteem. Although Basil's junior by a pair of years, he assumed a fraternal responsibility for the welfare of his friend. During

27

one summer the two travelled throughout the western United States and Canada, camping and backpacking in various wilderness regions and parks. Other than his army bivouac training — episodes better forgotten — it was Basil's first introduction and close contact with the great outdoors.

Physically the two were as varied as in personality. Mark, whose dark Hungarian visage and conjoined brows had earned him the nickname "Dracula," was tall, lean, even menacing — although a few minutes in his presence were sufficient to dispel any impressions of the bloodsucking count. Outgoing and ingratiating, he served as a useful foil for his reserved companion. A joiner, he had belonged to campus groups as diverse as Hillel and Jazzophile Society. As a budding politico, it was never too early to begin building one's constituency. By contrast, Basil's sturdy build and wavy, teak-colored hair confirmed his Russo-Romanian heritage. A strong nose and trim moustache gave the face an earthy roguishness, belying the general seriousness of his person.

He half-listened while Mark previewed his new role as an administrative assistant to a United States senator, how he was going to be "close to the action in DC." In Basil's lexicon DC stood for Department of Cretinism. Actor presidents, flag-waving factory workers, ubiquitous John Kennedy imitators with their blow-dried nobrow look, plastic TV "anchors", American politics was too absurd to take seriously. Mark was mad to find fulfillment in that world.

He supposed the process of maturation was inevitable. They were no longer roommates, hadn't been for years. America, Israel — geography wasn't the issue, they could have lived on the same block. The unifying element of common struggle, the bond originally bringing them together and molding their friendship, was gone. "This beer is wretched!," he cried, suddenly realizing he couldn't bear to finish the liquid in his glass.

28

"I know," said Mark, "but think of it this way — it may be bad but it's American."

"Then America be damned! Imagine saying that in a speech at your local American Legion chapter! You'd be ruined for life, that is if you had any left. I once saw a World War II film where Errol Flynn uttered a 'damn Canada!', but remember, it was an American film."

"An insidious Nazi plot. There was this biography of Flynn claiming he was a Nazi spy and a fag. Hitler himself wouldn't have had the cheek to utter such nonsense."

"Heil to our patron saint, a man devoted to the Reich, the family, and Eva Braun, and vice-versa."

"The vice-versa is what frightens me."

"Mark, I hate to change the subject, but you remember those Scands we met in Oregon?"

"How could I forget? On the beach at Seaside, Oregon."

"You know what I think? I think that may have been the best two weeks of my life. At the time I didn't realize it . . . What I would give for a second chance at that."

"Do you realize the odds against a repeat of that idyll? We could do that tour a thousand times and not run into the equal of those two. That was just dumb luck . . . helped, of course, by my silver tongue."

"All great romance is founded on luck."

"What's that, some kind of law of fortuity? By the way, did you ever hear from Tess of the tall timber again?"

"I told you she never answered my letters. I wrote twice. I think if she'd have answered I might have gone out there and married her."

"You're crazy! What the hell did you have in common other than sex? You know sex isn't everything."

"Yeah, tell me about it. What does anybody have in common with anybody other than sex, blood, or some kind of work?"

"Why don't you ask her about that? Don't you think

the fact that she didn't answer your letters indicated that she wasn't interested, you high-minded, eastern exotic. You were just a pleasant interlude to her. She probably went home and married some local lug."

"Yeah, probably . . . but if I'd have married her I would have lived out there too. Remember that one campsite we had by the waterfall in the Cascades? I was going to send her prints of the photos we took."

"They always seem better from a distance. You know from nothing about those girls. With your tastes she would have driven you out of the house. You would have gone mad from the disco and country western blasting out of her state of the art speakers."

"Separate rooms would have taken care of that."

"Yeah, I've been in places where that stuff has gone through two floors and still it was enough to send one up the wall. What would you do when riding in a car, cut it in half?"

"Who is to say she would always be at that level?"

"The sow's ear, my boy, the sow's ear! You artist idealists are all alike. You have this delusion that you can remake the world in your image. Hey! You're dealing with people here, not some pile of stone that you can arrange at will. You want a mistress, not a wife. She'd never make it. She was congenitally unsuited for the role. And what would you do out there — cut wood, or maybe design motels?"

"Why not? Who is there that doesn't like a well-designed, comfortable motel to ball in? What about vacation homes? I've seen drawings of some done by a Finnish architect — fantastic, Wagnerian structures. I'd even stoop to designing churches."

"Oh boy! Primchek, the shabbes goy of the forest. You know, you've become Americanized, programmed by an experience with two seventeen year old high school girls. It's spoiled you for everything that's come after. It's all anti-climax to you."

"But those girls were different. They had a naturalness, like farm girls."

"You just got off the boat. Lemme tell you something — there are no more farm girls. They're no different than any bitch you might meet on Sixth Avenue any Saturday night. This isn't 1920 when the Model T ruled the road and when you got back into the bush they had never seen your likes before. Hollywood, TV, this country has been penetrated to its remotest corner. Even the grizzlies are rebelling from the pressure."

"That reminds me . . . remember you told me not to tell them we were Jews."

"So what? They could have been Germans, you don't know. I got us laid, didn't I? Don't be a hypocrite and complain after the fact."

"Who's complaining? They probably never saw a Jew. Wouldn't know one if they saw one. They thought we were Italians."

"Yeah, that's always been my strategy, when in Rome do as the Romans. Thanks to the popularity of circumcision we can now pass."

"Lately, I've had this urge to go back and find her . . . Roseburg, Oregon. I wonder what she's doing now."

"Same thing she was doing when she met us — with one important change. Let's see . . . that was four years ago. So you arrive in Roseburg. After some discreet inquiries, you find her little frame house near one of the lumber mills. You go up to the door, heart fluttering with anxiety and hope, and knock — there is no bell. The door opens and some bearded brute of a lumberjack asks who you're looking for. You can hear the bawling of brats from the kitchen — who knows how many she's had since you left her, legit or illegit? Through the open door, she's holding one tow-headed tot in one arm and another's hanging onto her skirt. Above the din you hear her yell, 'Whoizzit, Bruce?'. Well brother, lemme tell you, you better have a pair of dark glasses and suitcase full of Fuller brushes with you, or you better get out of there fast. And I guarantee that you will have the most depressing plane flight back you can imagine! Had enough of nostalgia for tonight?"

"Yeah, I get the message. She's got to be married. She was too good to be overlooked. I suppose that's why I never dared act on my urge."

"I'll bet she got married as soon as she graduated from high school — *had* to get married. Thoses western girls not only mature faster than the eastern variety but start their sex lives in the sixth, seventh and eighth grades. I don't know, maybe it's those miles and miles of forests and the kiss of the sea. They just don't leave a good thing under wraps. When the apple is ripe, pick it. Besides, if you know anything about apples, and I know damn well you do, there is nothing like a slightly green apple for firmness and crunchiness."

"I stand convinced. But then what about you? You're well on the way to becoming a grandfather."

"I know. It's depressing isn't it? But don't worry about me, I'll grow old gracefully. It's you we have to watch out for. It's time you quit drooling over every tight-assed wait-ress you see and play in your own league. You're not in college anymore, you go for the big fish now. Raise your sights. I agree with Sam, it wouldn't hurt to make a play for Alison Cleveland, she's your type — and the feeling may be mutual. But remember, be cool with this woman. Keep your ace in the hole until she shows her hand. Who knows . . . you may marry her instead of that overworked timber widow who probably forgot you ever existed . . . holy hell! It's 25 to 9. The bottom line is that I told Joy I'd be home by nine o'clock. I didn't realize we talked so long."

They walked to the parking garage, Mark insisting on dropping off Basil at his apartment despite protests that the subway was handy. On the way Mark spoke of a trip to Israel that he hoped to make, perhaps a junket with the

Senator and members of his staff. He could show them places off the official track, a sort of personal Lerner tour. He invited Basil's collaboration. Having a sabra and architect as tour guide would impress his colleagues and could also benefit Basil — in the event of investment or contracts from this end of the pipeline. You never know, he said, having a friend, a good friend, in the Senate, was like buried gold, always there and always valuable.

Emerging from the car he was greeted by the doorman with a "Good evening, Mr. Primchek!". Inside, he decided he needed the exercise and took the stairs, running up the nine flights to his apartment. As apartments go it was a good one, across from Central Park between 76 and 77th streets. The rent, around $1500 monthly, was paid by the firm. Shames explained it as some kind of tax advantage. The result was an annual subsidy of nearly $20,000 with the added advantage of being only a subway ride away from work.

The apartment's interior reflected the Japanese and Arab style, styles which maximized interior space, compensating in openness of environment for a lack of material trappings. Supplementing the museum posters were his own architectural drawings and water colors. Miriam had given him a fine old Kazak rug for the living room. She wouldn't tell him what she had paid for it, but it must have been thousands. He tried to get her to take the money for it but she refused. It was one of those gestures that defying reciprocity, forces the recipient to relax and be overwhelmed. It seemed appropriate to the nomadic existence he had led since leaving Israel, living as he had, out of suitcases and old dressers. As his most valuable possession, he wondered about carrying it on board the plane. If string players could carry their Stradivari and Guarneri on board, he could do no less with his Kazak.

He had been too hard on Mark. If their careers had forced them apart that was life. The bonds uniting people were, at most, temporary — like the Oregonian. He tried to analyze why he had invested so much fantasy in her. The experience had been delightful, but his regret in not going back and reclaiming her, that was insane. As if one could bottle bliss and preserve it like jam. He thought of Kathryn Dunlow-Burke, the housewife he met in the building's coffee shop. For weeks she gave him the eye, until one day, tired of the stand-off, he went over and sat down at her table. It was a case of instant attraction. The deliciously sexual face and iron grayness of hair made her a study in incongruence. In rapid order they exchanged names and office telephone numbers and she agreed to meet him at his apartment for a "drink". The following day, at the appointed time, she was at his door. He recalled her entrance, the way she curiously looked around then grabbed his hand and instinctively led him to the bedroom. He had watched her peel down, hands behind back unhooking her brassiere, spilling the wide breasts; the graceful, balletic drawing of each leg up and out of the panties, tossing them with a flick of the wrist over her shoulder. It was all so natural.

The fact that she was married to an accountant for one of the big insurance companies, had two teenage children and lived in a house in Westchester was no obstacle, the affair went on for months. Late afternoons were taken off from work (she worked for a shipping firm in the building), and two or three Saturdays a month were spent in town "shopping with girlfriends". There were days when she left his apartment worn out. But return she did, seemingly revulcanized, never a day missed nor excuse offered, the passionate soldier of love.

He never got to know her, there wasn't time. But in some ways that was preferable. Mark was right, women were like impressionist painting, better from a distance. Yet up close her figure was amazing. She was a spa person and keeping fit was part of the program, the main support for her wandering eyes. He dubbed her "Olay", short for "Oil

34

of Olay". She enjoyed the triple pun. She was 38 years old but when she took off her clothes she was ageless. Her breasts, by some miracle of genetics, still managed to look and feel round. In profile they reminded him of a baroque volute. Her back was elegantly sensual, like a tulip lily. After she realized his fascination with her body she would prance before him, running fingers over the inner part of her thighs, teasily stroking him with her breasts. Her secret wish was to have been a burlesque queen, a profession that would have allowed her to act out her exhibitionist fantasies to their naked limit.

He wished they had met twenty years before. He would have been a lad of seven, she a maid of seventeen, yet in the world of wish time was immaterial. He had invited her to speculate where he would have begun, confronted by her body at that age. The breasts, she said, the part of the female anatomy most fascinating to little boys. She would have guided him, assuring he wouldn't always remain a little boy. Had he grown wiser or just hungrier? But then, does anyone have to tell one how to devour a chicken?

The affair ended almost as quickly as it began. Her husband was suddenly transferred to Kansas City, Kansas. Not long after she left he received a letter with a return box number inviting him for a visit. He would have gone were it not for Mark who accused him of hounding the husband half-way across the country. They still corresponded, although he hadn't received a letter in months. She had probably given up on him, or replaced him — although that seemed unlikely. As Mark said, all he knew was what she told him. Still, there was nothing wrong with keeping in touch, she was too rare a friend to consign to oblivion. One never knew when one would be passing through Kansas City.

The next morning he opened the *Times* to the society page. "Shames, Garfield & Chase Say Au Revoir With Style to One of Their Own" read the headline over the article.

There was a photograph of Hilton Garfield chatting with Michele Valentine, the Met mezzo, and Peter Barrett, the designer, as well as two of Shames with various guests. The fact that he didn't rate a print didn't bother him, society editors of necessity had to be discriminating. Scanning the article he found his name in the last column, in the next to last paragraph, "The party's object, the young Israeli architect, Basil Primchek, was wished a hearty mazel tov in a toast led by Samuel Shames. Mr. Primchek, a recipient of a Shames architectural scholarship, received undergraduate and graduate degrees from Brandeis and Columbia Universities respectively. Due shortly to leave the firm where he served his apprenticeship, he will return to his native Israel where he plans to enter private practice. Among the other guests present and accounted for were Tony Sable, Janet . . ." He refolded the newspaper and inserted it in his briefcase. The "private practice" report was off the mark, nevertheless, it sounded good. He would send the article to his father.

Entering his office he found two more copies of the *Times* on his desk. Accompanying them was a note from Miriam. He picked up his telephone and pressed her extension, "What are you trying to do, rub it in?" he asked.

"I'll bet you have a whole stack of *Times,*" she said, "your vanity knows no end."

"You're wrong, I bought one copy. As for my vanity, the article was hardly calculated to satisfy it. I think they mentioned me as an afterthought."

"Honorable mention is better than no mention. You can save one copy for your scrapbook and send the other to your father. He'll be pleased to learn you made the society pages."

"Scrapbook is right. But now I have an extra. Who should I honor with that one?"

"Send it to your girlfriend. You do have a girlfriend?"

"I used to but I think she's given me the gate."

"You've also got no end of chutzpah. The closer you

come to leaving the less we see of you. Is this some kind of rationing policy or are you just being your usual sadistic self?"

"Oh the latter of course. Since coming to your tempest-tossed shores I've had a lot of experience in that area. To hear you talk one would think you need a good beating, I've been too good to you. How about 11:30 lunch? It'll give you a chance to ventilate."

"Look who's talking about ventilating. That's all you've been doing lately, Mister Gasser. If I weren't such a masochist I'd say no to lunch and that beating. But because I'm starved for your company I'll say yes to both, it's better than nothing."

He slowly put the receiver back on hook. She had witnessed the episode with Alison Cleveland, or enough of it to make the proper conclusions. He had heard this kind of verbal sparring before. It was jealousy but controlled jealousy, socialized and witty like a Noel Coward play. Perhaps it was the influence of years of analysis, its jargon and labyrinthine rationalizations rolled off her tongue with an easy fluency. At 31 she had three years on him and probably knew more too. Yet, no one had asked her to carry his cross, she was strictly a volunteer.

At lunch she asked if she would be seeing him that evening, adding with characteristic deference, "that is if you haven't anything to do". He was due to spend the weekend at Shames' estate in Connecticut and was planning to get an early start in the morning. So they agreed to meet for dinner in the coming week at the Chinese restaurant they had read about in the *Times'* food section. She would tell her parents, they wanted to see him before he left. Her father, a retired garment worker, was a fascinating conversationalist. Miriam was a loyal daughter, regularly picking up her parent's travelling expenses to faraway places, places she urged them to visit.

Originally her ambition was to teach, she had a master's in English literature from New York University. But they assigned her to a combat zone. Two semesters of the monsters were enough. Suffering from shell-shock she came close to breakdown. Her psychiatrist, a friend of Hilton Garfield, sent her to see him about a possible job. Garfield, who was looking for a competent secretary at the time, hired her. She never looked back. It was an escape from Sodom.

2

During his first months in New York he had been a frequent weekend guest at the Shames mansion, Sam and Myra Shames assuming the role of surrogate parents to their "resident scholar" and protégé, the Shames children having long since grown up and left the homestead. The son was some kind of computer whiz who had migrated to California and started his own computer company. Other than citing its remarkable growth, Shames didn't speak much of his son. Both daughters were married, one to a publisher, the other to a doctor. So it was just Sam and Myra and the servants who now presided over the twenty-two rooms and eight baths of the English Tudor structure. Yet it was a rare Saturday night that the house wasn't host to a musicale or fundraising soirée for some cause or other. From lieder singers to big bands playing the classics of the twenties and thirties, Shames had them all.

Shames liked to promote the idea he was of humble origins. Actually, his father had been a relatively wealthy manufacturer of children's wear and his father before him a clothier. But if the patriarch of the tribe had started with a pushcart on the Lower East Side as Shames was wont to maintain, there was little evidence to support the assertion other than an old sepia photograph hanging in Shames' office, showing his bearded grandfather standing behind a counter of his clothing store, attended on each side by two young, bright-eyed female clerks. Whatever the case, Ben Shames, Workman's Outfitter, had started something in the New World. Three generations later, Ben's simple adding machine had been replaced by a computer and several accounting firms. The tallying of the year's receipts had become a business in itself. There *was* gold in the streets, the trick was in knowing how to extract it. The rude village of the Russian Pale had been forgotten forever as belonging to a humiliating and impoverished past. The real Zion was here. They had proven that — by any criterion.

Consistent with this surplus of wealth was the impulse to charity. The Shames' public benefaction was organized on a two tier basis. The first tier was local and focused on the culture and lifestyle of Manhattan. Objects of this charity ranged from the musical and performing arts, the major museums (Shames was on the board of the Metropolitan), to the horticultural, the last the special interest of Myra Shames. Indeed, the Samuel and Myra Shames Foundation bore the major credit for the flowers now gracing Central and many of the city's lesser parks. The idea was to emulate the parks of England and the Continent. Although the scheme was probably inherently over-ambitious, everyone agreed the present was a great improvement over the auster-ity of the seventies when even a bed of marigolds was considered a prodigal extravagance.

The second tier extended to the State of Israel. In addition to the Samuel Shames Scholarship Fund for Archi-tecture, largesse took the form of such charities as the Samuel and Myra Shames Fund for the Aged, the Samuel and Myra Shames Memorial Forest, a Samuel and Myra

Shames gallery in the National Musuem, and a Samuel and Myra Shames Fund for Immigrant Relief. Shames referred to these Israeli commitments as "keeping the faith".

Basil pulled into the drive leading to "The Cotswolds," the name given the Shames' estate. Originally the property of a sugar baron, the residence dated from the early twenties. The drive was lined with chestnut trees, an arboreal allée part of the original landscape plan, its interlocking limbs confirming an age of six to seven decades. Chestnuts grew slowly, like most trees too slowly to mature in a lifetime. A mistake of creation? Or was mankind's inability to adapt itself to the chronology of that ancient and universal rhythm a genetic flaw?

As he emerged from the tunnel of trees the house and its great slate roof came into view. The exterior was an amalgam of many materials — stone, wood, brick, metal, artfully and harmoniously blended. He stopped to admire the textures before proceeding to the rear of the house where he parked the car by a grove of large oaks. It was obvious they were never part of a landscape plan. Remnants of the original forest, the oaks were survivors of colonial land-clearing and lumbering. Perhaps they sheltered a pioneer homestead . . he heard someone calling his name. It was Shames supervising two men in the planting of three small trees. He inquired whether they were dogwood. *"Cornus kousa chinensis,* Chinese dogwood," Shames replied. "They have the dogwood leaf but flower about a month later. Also they're hardier, but that's not a concern in this area, we've got plenty of the pink planted around. Myra wants them grouped . . " Shames turned, hollering to the gardeners to watch out for daffodils underfoot. Sensing his redundancy, Basil made a circuit of the mansion, taking in the early tulips and daffodils blooming in the surrounding beds. Coming up between the stems of the early tulips were the late bloomers, presaging the spring garden's finale when, like an orchestral tutti, whole sections of tulips bloom together,

40

forming successive swatches of color. He had seen the garden when it was so arrayed the previous year. Like no other private garden he had ever seen, it was a veritable chromatic fantasy.

Estates containing similarly large and imposing mansions adjoined "The Cotswalds". Like so many pocket baronies, imitation French chateaux, Italian villas and English manors dotted the rural Connecticut countryside, recreating little pieces of Europe for American *nouveaux riches*. This was a gentry royal in all but name, supported by income the envy of the world. He would never make that kind of money in Israel — not as an architect. If he had stayed on with the firm — and he could have — he might draw an equally impressive income, but only if he were a partner. While Garfield and Chase had hinted at the possibiltiy, Shames had not. He suspected Shames considered it his duty to return to Israel. Although never expressing himself in exactly that fashion, Shames didn't have to, the outlines of his Zionism were clear enough. There were no hard feelings, Shames had been good to him, from the beginning. The man had a right to his Jewish soul, God knew there was cause enough for that. He was a throwback, in contrast to Garfield and Chase who were ripe for Unitarianism. Chase had a Gentile wife and claimed he hadn't been in a synagogue since he learned to walk. His religious irreverence carried over to the political; some said he was red. As near as Basil could determine the charge was founded on the fact that a maternal uncle had been a low-level functionary in the Party.

Garfield was the youngest of the partners at fifty-one. The firm's diplomatist, he played the role of swing-man, arbitrating disputes that, for whatever reason, tended to arise between the other two. Soothing and personable, Garfield's division handled bids and contracts with the firm's clients and sub-contractors. Though theoretically an equal, in actuality he functioned as Shames' right hand man.

41

He walked for almost an hour before orienting himself back toward the house. He had gone around the perimeter of the estate and passed through three or four others in the process. As he emerged from the woods he noticed a white Mercedes convertible parked next to his car. A figure in a trenchcoat and Bogart fedora was waving to him. He waved back. As he drew closer he saw it was Lester Kayam, the owner of "Best's", a chain of cut-rate drugstores. He knew Kayam from the office, he and Shames had business dealings together. He also knew he did not like him. A natty dresser, Kayam combed his remaining hair back to front, reminding one of a degenerate Roman emperor. He was standing by his car, hands in the pockets of his trenchcoat, face frozen in a half-grin. Kayam had a habit of punctuating his assertions with a forced, ingratiating laugh. "Mister Primchek! Mister Primchek, I presume. How are you?"

"Well enough, Mr. Kayam."

"Sam tells me you'll be going back to Israel soon."

"That's right."

"Good, good. Ya know I've been there a few times myself, my wife and I, we love it. Where do you think you'll be settling there?"

"Probably Jerusalem."

"Great. Beautiful city. I'm sure you'll do well there. Ya know I'm on the board of the American Israel Public Affairs Committee. You familiar with that organization?"

"No, but I've heard of it."

"Well, ya know we do a lot of lobbying and public relations. We were pretty busy last year with the war and all that but these days things are a lot slower. It's looking good for a real peace in the region now that the Russians have been set back again. At least that's the way we see it. What's the word from your side heh heh of the pond?"

"About the same as yours, Mr. Kayam, peace is just around the corner." He wished Kayam would cease, his stereotypical questions stretched the limits of tolerance. But he was Shames' guest and the obligation to be polite took precedence over a natural inclination to walk away. "Ah Mr. Primchek," Kayam continued, "I've talked to a lot of people from Israel about this and some of them have some pretty strong feelings on the subject, ya know this demographic problem Israel faces. It seems heh those Arabs are pretty good in bed heh heh, or they spend an abnormal amount of time there heh heh. Our committee has been doing some studies of the situation and the long term trend favours the Arabs . . . There are some other studies that point the other way but we think they're a bit on the optimistic side. What's your opinion on the subject . . . if you don't mind telling me?"

"Not at all, Mr. Kayam. I really haven't given it much consideration, too busy with my architectural studies to pay too much attention to maternal events . . . I'm looking forward to that concert of string quartets tonight, how about you?"

"Oh yeah, the music, my wife thinks it's great. Ya know I used to play the violin . . . but I was never a Heifitz heh heh. But don't get me wrong, I can appreciate the classics with the best of 'em. My wife, she's the expert, she knows who wrote what and when, I just bring home the heh heh bacon. No offense heh heh."

Basil affected a look of disapproval at Kayam's little joke, using the hiatus to excuse himself to clean up for dinner. Dinner was at least three hours away but it was as good an excuse as any, perhaps too good for Kayam, preoccupied as he was with matching his wits against the devilishly clever Arab plot of winning in the bedroom what they could not win on the battlefield. The poor have been doing that for ages yet the rich have usually managed to control them without too much effort. He would have liked to have told him to leave the "demographic problem" to soldiers, police and jailers and stick to mustard plasters and hemorrhoid remedies, excessive worry can cause baldness.

Dinner was a splendid affair at "The Cotswolds". The baronial expanse of the oak-paneled, candlelit dining room invested the humblest course with a mystique of its own. Nevertheless, the food that issued from the Shames kitchen required no special atmospheric magic to enhance its savor, it was as fine as anything served up at any stellar, New York, name restaurant. The evening's entree was rack of lamb, served to order, the racks delivered to the table sizzling from the oven's heat. Except for Lester Kayam, the guests were all strangers to him. Prior to the dinner sitting there had been a flurry of introductions, but in the confusion he had forgotten most of them. In this instance the men should have worn name tags. Of the older generation, they could have been so many gnomes — except of course, Lester Kayam. The assorted plumage of the women seemed designed to compensate for their mates' boardroom uniformity. Over-painted and over-coiffed, they glittered with the portable baggage of wealth. Meanwhile, with the clearing of the table in preparation for the service of coffee and dessert, the first serious attempts at after dinner conversation were getting under way, some of the men lighting up Havanas that had been passed around. The musical program — quartets by Ravel, Debussy and Haydn — was scheduled to begin at nine, contingent upon the musicians' timely arrival. Shames was explaining why he hadn't invited the group for dinner, " . . .anybody who knows anything about music knows that it should be performed on an empty stomach. That rule is absolute for singers and brass and woodwind players, especially the hornmen, they need all the breath they can muster. Of course strings are different, but now you take an ensemble where every player has to be right on point with the other, one of them might be popping a couple Alka-seltzers — and that's no reflection on our cook — he may have a bad stomach. Another might be out from too much food and wine, I'd have to use a club on them to get them to play because although making music may be

44

pleasant business, it's still work. And before a man's going to work he's got to be hungry, or else he's not going to work very well—and why should he? But we always feed them after the gig. Don't worry, they don't go home hungry, not from here."

A woman seated near Shames asked his opinion of the businessman's lunch. "As a rule I don't eat lunch, that is unless I've missed breakfast and then I might take a light one. But suppose I'm entertaining a client . . . it wouldn't look good not to join them. You know eating is a ritual in itself and some of our three star restaurants are just secular temples with an altar at every table. Then I might order a salad or a few pieces of lox. Don't forget, I have to go back to work too."

During Shames' reply the questioner was seen prodding her obviously overweight mate, evoking from the fellow a blush of embarrassment. Alert to her guest's discomfort, Myra Shames quickly changed the subject to the Metropolitan Opera's latest production of *La Bohême* as sung by the new Italian tenor sensation, Ferrucio Bossuto. For Mrs. Lester Kayam it was an opportunity to enter the discussion, an opportunity she did not let pass. "Well I thought he was simply marvelous and the really strange thing was that I read Damon Herlihy's review the next day in the Times and I couldn't believe he and I attended the same performance. There were things like he sang a B flat when the score called for a B and that he was off key in *Che gelida manina*. Why the man sang his heart out. I haven't heard the final *Mimi! Mimi!* sung with such anguish since Richard Tucker."

"He does seem to be mean-spirited at times," commented the woman seated across the table from Basil, Mrs. Daniel Ballin, wife of Prof. Daniel Ballin, Harvard luminary and advisor to presidents. Basil was unsure of the discipline, whether it was economics, history or sociology, but he knew Ballin was big. Rather distinguished looking with thick, wavy, gray hair, a trifle jowlish, Ballin had gone

45

through dinner saying little, now and then gravely nodding his head in apparent agreement with this or that conversation. Now puffing contentedly on a pipe, he gave the impression of one habituated to having the last word on a subject. Indeed, a mine of such proven wisdom could not long exist without some attempt at exploitation. Rushing to be first in an appeal to the authority conveniently at hand was Mrs. Kayam, "I'd like to hear what your husband, a writer and intellectual, has to say on the subject. Professor Ballin, how much weight should we give reviews, and tell us if you think there is any tenor singing today who is above review." Fragrant bursts of Sobranie smoke issued from the bowl of Ballin's Holmesian Savanelli. For a long moment it was uncertain whether he would even answer the request. Then, to the relief of those present unfamiliar with the ways of the wise, he began speaking, "Being neither reviewer nor singer, my ability to speak with any authority on the matter must be somewhat less than first-hand. With that as caveat I submit that the operative maxim here is *de gustibus non est disputandem.* Of course, as suggested in my qualification, that presupposes a knowledge or expertise sufficient to support an opinion on the matter subject to review . . . And on that note I believe I should rest because I'm a little out of my line." There was a puff of polite laughter from some of the musically knowledgeable present, the professor's brilliant pun providing relief to the ponderous gravity of his introduction. Even Lester Kayam knew, or pretended to know, enough to add his heh heh to the chorus of ha has. Wearing the expression of one pleased with himself, Ballin smiled appreciatively at his friends around the table. In the interim his pipe had gone out and he proceeded to occupy himself with the ritual of relighting.

"Oh come on, Professor," pressed Mrs. Kayam, "you're not going to let this little coterie of confirmed opera devotees go home believing that there isn't one tenor out there that doesn't sometimes raise your hackles just a little

46

bit?" Raising his eyes from his pipe bowl to a level with his interrogator's, Ballin replied, "Well then (puff) I think (puff puff) I'd have to go with the fellow with the American Express card."

"Luciano Pavarotti!" cried a woman, overjoyed by the reinforcement from one of such reputable eminence. At the mention of the great Pavarotti a murmur of voices arose, like a sudden rush of wind, some disputing, some agreeing with the judgment pronounced. Basil paid silent tribute to Mrs. Kayam for knowing her audience — that on her first effort she should invent an issue arousing such earnest passion among them. Indeed, what began as an orderly exchange of opinion was breaking down into something indistinguishable from any vulgar argument. It was an intolerable situation, a situation that called for a moderator. Over the din and disputation came the resonant voice of Samuel Shames, "you can argue until doomsday but you'll never reach an agreement this way . . . " Shames waited for the disputants to fall into silence before continuing, "Our friend, Professor Ballin, in his characteristic way, put his finger on the problem. All of us are too close to the situation to be in a position to make a judgment."

"What are you getting at, Sam?," someone asked.

"I suggest we look at this scientifically," said Shames. "There are plenty of good tenors around today, but I'll tell you who the greatest was . . . and I tell my Italian friends the same thing I'm telling you, they think the sun rose and set on Caruso and Gigli. The greatest was . . .," Shames paused again before triumphantly announcing, "Gerson Serota, probably the greatest tenor and singer of the century."

"Never heard of 'im," remarked someone at the rear of the table. Nor had Basil. He wondered if Sam had gone off his rocker, but seeing a couple of the men nod their heads suggested the claim had something going for it. Shames continued, "Rabbi Gerson Scrota, of the Great Synagogue of

Warsaw, my grandfather heard 'im, unforgettable! Pavarotti, Domingo, you name 'em, none of today's crop could hold a candle to him. He could take a melody, twist it, stretch it, turn it inside out and sing it in reverse, and with the voice to match, *fortissimo, pianissimo, mezza voce,* he had it all. They talk about Yossele Rosenblatt, Moshe Koussevitsky, the other cantors . . . sure, they were good, but nobody could do with the human voice what Serota could, and I've got his records to prove it. He was one of the miracles of the century. Lest we forget, he died in a concentration camp, another victim of the Holocaust. So you people who never heard of him, next time someone tells you Jews are always promoting their own, ask him if that's the case, how is it that I never heard of the greatest tenor and singer of the century, Rabbi Gerson Serota, of the Great Synagogue of Warsaw? That ought to squelch the bastard. And remember, you heard it at the house of Shames." Shames leaned back in his chair and smiled, gratified at the interest aroused by this revelation of a neglected bit of esoterica Judaica. Indeed, the story itself was remarkable. Shames had not finished however, "I don't think anyone would give you an argument that we've dominated the violin and piano fields. In my opinion, you can add the tenor voice to that list. The greatest three or four tenor voices of the century, including but not excluding Caruso in that company, were Jews. The aforementioned Gerson Serota, Richard Tauber for the German repertory, and Jan Peerce. Him I include for voice and durability — he sang with gusto into his eighties. And remember, he was Toscanini's favorite tenor — and for an Italian that's the highest compliment."

Basil, heretofore a respectful auditor of the dinner's conversation, could not resist commenting on Shames' claim for Tauber, "Sam, in regard to Richard Tauber, you're aware aren't you, that only his father was Jewish, so by official reckoning he would not be considered a Jew?"

"Ladies and gentlemen," declared Shames in all good

humor, "my Jewish expert from Jerusalem, Israel — Basil Primcheck! Sure, I knew that only his father was Jewish. But you can throw that Jewish mother rule out the window, that should have gone out with matriarchy. I won't buy that Orthodox baloney. There's not a man in this room who wouldn't deem his child by a non-Jew Jewish. Tauber was Jewish enough for Hitler to kick out of Germany, and that, my boy, is damn well good enough for me."

"The point is well-taken," replied Basil, "but are you familiar with Jussi Bjoerling?" Someone suggested Al Jolson.

"Sure, a great singer. You want to add him to the list with Jolson? Go ahead."

"No, I want to add him to your list, he was Jewish."

"Bjoerling a Jew? He was a Swede!"

"But there are Jews all over, Sam, even in Palestine."

A perceptible chill settled over the table. There was none of the fluffy laughter that followed the professor's pun. But going for laughs had never been his intention. If it was a joke it was at their expense. They were smart enough to understand that, even Lester Kayam knew not to laugh. Basil faced directly ahead, eyes focused on the inscrutable blues of Professor Ballin, visible through a screen of Sobranie. By affecting the pose of a noble savage, stolidly ignorant of his transgression, he was denying his self-appointed jury the satisfaction of a guilty verdict. Nevertheless, he had committed a *faux pas,* in the context, the French to be translated as a "kick in the collective pants."

Again it was Myra Shames to the rescue, breaking the ensuing silence with a one-woman pacification effort, "As some of you already know, Basil will soon be leaving us to return to Israel to continue his career in architecture. We're all very proud of him and, I might add, quite confident about his future." Then craning her head for an unobstructed view of him, she exclaimed, "Now Basil, I don't want to see too much time pass before we receive that wedding invitation. That's a part of your future too."

"Don't listen to her, Basil," said one of the more glittering of the guests, throwing a wink in Basil's direction, "Take your time. You strike me as someone still very busy sowing his wild oats. Am I right?"

"Oh no ma'am," he replied, going along with the absurdity of the situation, "I'd very much like to get married and have children."

"Make sure she's Jewish," cracked a wag.

"Any particular number?," asked Mrs. Kayam, her position as mistress of controversy firmly established.

"I'm hoping for at least six . . . "

"Six!," cried some of the women in surprise and indignation. "Will your wife have anything to say about the matter?"

"Oh yes," said Basil, "it's a situation involving mutual responsibility. Some of you may not be aware . . .," he turned toward Lester Kayam, swelling in his seat from the unexpected recognition accorded his crusade, "I'm grateful to Mr. Kayam here for alerting me to the seriousness of the situation. We may be losing the ultimate battle of destiny — the battle of demography. You'll pardon me, but I would not want to see the Arabs win that one by default."

There were times when self-interest had to give way before the greater good. All seemed to agree this was one of those times. All save Professor Daniel Ballin, who, like some pipe-puffing Buddha, was fixing Basil with that same immutable look of stoic passivity. Was he wise? The answer to the question might never be determined as the conversation was abruptly terminated by the announcement that the musicians had arrived.

3

On Monday morning he found the memo in his box. The message read, "Alison Cleveland, 9:10, Important." She was serious about her proposal to interview him. Being skeptical of others' claims — especially if they promised one benefit — was a good rule to follow. But he hadn't doubted her sincerity, only her resolution. The fact that she was following through on her announced intention was gratifying. He felt good in being right about her. He checked the clock on the wall — it was 9:40. He walked into his office, sat down at his desk and dialed her number.

"Alison Cleveland speaking."

"Basil Primchek returning your call."

"Oh hi! How are you?"

"Fine, I just got back from spending the weekend at Sam's estate in Connecticut."

"Well then, I hope you remembered to discuss our proposal with him, and that he agreed to it."

"Sure, he said go ahead. In fact, he put me at your disposal. When do I start?"

"Can you make it tomorrow — morning or afternoon, your convenience?"

"The morning's fine with me. Is ten o'clock alright?"

"Super. I hope you don't mind but I've done some research on your work, primarily the town houses and the Turner building in New Rochelle. I'd like you to bring your sketches for those projects and any photrographs you have of them — especially the lobby of the Turner building with its oriental motifs."

"Sketches and photographs we have. Anything else I should bring?"

"Just your best pedagogical manner. I'll need some

instruction in the design elements and construction materials before we commence interviewing, it helps if I know what I'm asking about. Also, is there anything you would suggest I look at to get a better understanding of what I should be focusing on in the interview? Nothing too elaborate or complicated . . . perhaps some standard reference or source book, preferably something with pictures. Keep in mind I'm the tyro, you're the architect. I'll be relying on you to provide the comprehensive expertise."

"In that case, read *Aphrodite,* by Pierre Louys. Are you familiar with it?"

"No, my ignorance is quite wide-ranging. How do you spell that last name?"

"Louys, L-o-u-y-s. At least I think it's spelled that way. You know the French, they're worse than the English for spelling. Don't try to find it in a bookstore, it's a classic. You'll have to get it from the library. It may give you a feel for the situation . . . allegorically. You and the book's title appear to have a lot in common."

"You're very kind, but I don't think I'll be giving anything away by confessing to being a mere mortal born of woman. Wasn't Aphrodite created from a seashell or a wave?"

"I don't know, but the first time I saw you I could have sworn you jumped out of a cake."

"Really? Fully clothed and fully blown, a bowdlerized Botticelli. As an artist, weren't you a bit disappointed in being denied the bare reality?"

"Only a bit. I was provoked into letting my imagination run rampant. Of course, there's nothing like the bare reality . . .

"Excuse me, Basil," she interrupted, "but I have another call on the line. Can we say goodbye until tomorrow?"

"Of course . . . until tomorrow."

He slowly put down the receiver, experiencing a brief

flush of anger at the short shrift he felt he had gotten, then as quickly dismissing it as a paranoid reaction. She obviously had more important things to do than gab over the telephone with him. He wondered if he had said the right thing. The cake scenario — that was a little gratuitous. However, she didn't sound at all offended, letting it roll off her back. He looked ahead to the morrow's interview, he wanted to show what he could do.

He was halfway through the morning *Times* when Shames poked his head in the doorway and asked to see him in his office at eleven, he wanted to talk to him. Probably interested in hearing more on his impressions of Gerson Serota or other aspects of the weekend, he thought. Shames was like that, solicitous of the opinions of his peers, interested in their reactions to ideas and events. It mattered that people agreed with him, he could be relentless in that regard.

"Mr. Shames will be back momentarily," said the secretary. "He requested that you wait in his office." Basil entered the solemn and somber room, known in the firm as the "inner sanctum". Sunlight issuing through mullioned windows formed bright patterns of color over the room's oriental carpets, one of which, a long, silken runner, led the eye to the Italian Renaissance desk at the far end of the room. The desk's spacious top was clear except for a Tiffany favrile desk set and small, silver, Liberty clock. Rising fifteen feet to a gilded coffered ceiling, were interior walls of panelled walnut. The product of Shames' staging genius, the room's Mussolinian grandeur was designed to awe and humble, its noble dimensions making all men equal. No one was more aware of these effects than the room's runty creator, who standing behind the huge desk, greeted the visitor.

Basil approached the desk to better examine the spotlighted bronze relief of Vladimir Jabotinsky. It was the Jabotinsky Prize, Shames' proudest possession. He had won it the year before for distinguishing himself in the defense of "the rights of the Jewish people". Jabotinsky was shown unidealized, wearing goggle-like glasses, brows furrowed, jaw and lips set determinedly. Jabotinsky had died before Basil was born, before Israel was born, but he had studied Jabotinsky's contributions in school — admittedly no place to receive the unvarnished truth about national heroes. It seemed the sculptor had ignored the official mythology and captured the real Jabotinsky; because the face was that of a man to fear, not to love, a man of his times. In any case, Shames swore by him. It was best not to beard the lion in his den.

Flanking the Jabotinsky medallion were framed photographs of Shames with the late and great of politics, many autographed with the usual cliches. Basil had scrutinized them before and had been duly impressed by the collection, men of power, great power. Ben Gurion, Johnson, Begin, Carter, Senator Maudlin, Nixon, Shultz, Haig, Republicans, Democrats, party affiliation was immaterial. He paused at a photograph showing Senator Humphrey broadly smiling, so many smiling faces. Hubert Horatio, a man before his time but a great friend of Israel nevertheless. There was a park in Tel Aviv named for him, and a forest too somewhere. Israel did not forget its friends.

Basil turned to the sound at his right. Bounding past him, Shames threw himself into the leather embrace of his Maloof desk chair. "Getting an education in the political arts, kid?," he asked the still gazing Basil, eyes fixed on the black and white images in the photographs on the wall. "Yeah . . . fascinating, it's always fascinated me how one man not a professional politician could know so many in the political arena. Sam, did you ever think of running for president?"

"Nah! I'm too smart to be president. We leave that to the dummies, they're better qualified. This country isn't ready for a Jewish president, they're still smarting over us controlling the country, wearing both hats would bring on a pogrom. We need the insulation. That way they have nobody but themselves to blame."

"Sam, in all these pictures there is one glaring omission — there's none of you with Reagan."

"That sonofabitch! I'll show you our lake in the Adirondacks, sixty years in the family. Not a fish in it, they can't live in that stew of battery acid. He doesn't believe in pollution, only communism. Nicaragua, El Salvador . . . don't get me started." Shames tapped the top of his desk with the knuckle of his middle finger. "But I didn't call you here to discuss politics, I wanna talk about you, maybe give you some advice, sit down."

Basil pulled a chair up to the desk and sat down. It had been some time since he and Shames had talked man to man. "I've been thinking about your leaving . . . not so much about the loss of a good man, an asset to the firm, that goes without saying. What I mean is that you're going into a situation that's a great opportunity . . . for you and for Israel. You're young, you've got talent, two things the country needs at this time, at any time, but especially now when the doomsayers are ready to write off Israel as an economic basket case. I've seen this before, even a country as rich as this has cycles, but they snap back stronger than ever. The Bible calls it the seven years of feast and famine. You put away your surplus for those lean years, it's in the nature of things. The industrial revolution didn't change nature, it just made bigger and better warehouses . . .

"The bleeding hearts will tell you some of Israel's methods are too harsh, too rough. Well, ask 'em what happened to the Indians. Now that they're pacified and exterminated you don't hear a peep out of 'em, but let's face it, at one time they owned every inch of this country. Does it make it any less cruel that they're not around to complain? No country started with more strikes against it than Israel, fighting the British Empire and twenty Arab nations, sometimes with their bare hands, clawing their way to victory. We learned the hard way from pogrom to pogrom, but it was the Holocaust that finally taught us that *strength* is the only insurance for a people's survival."

Upon the word "strength," Shames' right hand became a fist. Wheeling the seat of his chair around, he gazed up at the face of Vladimir Jabotinsky angrily staring into the void and exclaimed, "That was Zeev's great contribution to our people. He was a Judah Maccabeus, a prophet with as much legitimacy as a Jeremiah or David, who never lived to see the tree he planted bear fruit. Oh he had to knock some heads together, no question about that. But he forged a people and a will and today there is a nation where he left off, pound for pound the strongest nation in the world, perhaps in history. But it has to be with a hundred million fanatics poised on its borders to wipe it off the face of the earth. So put that in the equation and add to it the fact that essentially Israel is a poor country with the result that there is very little surplus to go around. That's where we come in, we, the Jews of the Galut, committed to the survival of Israel come hell or high water. Because as long as there is an Israel the survival of the Jewish people is assured. The Holocaust taught us that a pogrom can occur in the least likely of places. All those smart German Jews who thought it could never happen to them — where are they now? I'm not saying we're in danger of an imminent pogrom here, I'm not *that* paranoid. But who knows what's down the road twenty, thirty years hence? Another Hitler? Maybe not, they only come once in a thousand years thank God. But maybe something more sophisticated, insidious, discrimination . . . it still ends up being persecution. So where do we go? We already know nobody wants us, sure as hell not as penniless refugees, the shirts stripped off our backs by the Goyim. That, my friend, is the reason for Israel. I know they tell you God set the land aside and it's a democracy, a bulwark against communist expansion into the oil fields . . . by the way, you read *Commentary?*" Basil shook his head. "I didn't think so, who does? But anyway these intellectuals like to spin all these reasons why Israel is important to America but if you ask me they're all transparent. The converse puts the proposition correctly: Why America is important to Israel. Sure the Goyim think they're using us to control the Arabs. I say let 'em think that all they want. We're presently in a situation of mutuality. In the present circumstances we need a base, a support. That would have been Jabotinsky's program. He was for a supporting territory, a resource base . . .

"What I'm saying is that both of us, you there and me here, we're both important. It's a partnership only now you're the senior partner, we here can only be junior. You know, politics is the art of the *quid pro quo,* the politican and his constituency, each wants something from the other without which neither could prosper. The one wants support and the other favors, it's the natural symbiosis of government. What would be the use of supporting someone who couldn't or wouldn't do anything for you? You asked me before if I ever thought of running for president. Now I know you were kidding but I never aspired to public office, but I know more about politics than any of these politicians. And you want me to tell you what my secret weapon is for getting results? . . . I'll tell you, it's guilt. I make 'em feel guilty if they don't come across like menschen. Because this is a business based on man to man contact. Like all professionals we provide service, we're not out selling widgets to the public, we're selling ourselves. After our friends know we're interested in something they're going to do some hard thinking before they turn us down or give the job to someone else. But don't think we created this network of contacts overnight. It was many years of patient groundwork that got us to this plateau . . .

"Now when I talk about partnership I don't mean it exclusively in political terms. With this country drawing closer to Israel with each passing day there'll be more and more opportunity for bilateral cooperation between the private sectors of both economies. In fact, I see it as a model for future international relations. They gave Europe the Marshall Plan, I don't see why a similar plan appropriately scaled down couldn't be implemented for Israel. I've been giving the proposition a lot of thought lately and I concluded that there is no reason why the big multinationals like Bechtel, Brown and Root and Morrison-Knudson should get all the business. With a sufficient capital investment we could jump into the niche in no time at all. There's no doubt in my mind our bank consortium would be forthcoming with the necessary capital. We could also go public and float a stock issue. Naturally, we'll need a partner over there. Now who do you think that will be . . .? Now I can't promise anything yet. Let's just say I've been thinking about it, it's still only a gleam in my eye."

Shames looked at the timepiece on his desk, suddenly realizing how long he had held forth. "I hope you weren't hungry. I forgot that not everyone is like me and can skip lunch. You big guys need more nourishment to keep that powerhouse going strong. Sometimes I think I'm too spiritual," Shames laughed at the absurdity of his remark. "But I'm in the prophetic tradition, small of stature but great of spirit."

Rising from his chair he joined Basil in front of the desk, put his arm around his shoulder and slowly walked him toward the door. A postscript was in order. "Now Basil my boy, I don't want that you should think that I'm ending on a down note, but before you go I want you to know that if you should run into any problems over there, and they should become uh . . . insurmountable, and you just can't hack it, there'll always be a place for you at Shames, Garfield and Chase. Remember that. Not that I have the slightest doubt that you'll make it in spades, I just wanted you to know how we feel about you."

"Thanks, Sam," said Basil, standing with Shames at the door, "I really appreciate the advice and support but I wouldn't be going back unless I thought the chances of making a significant contribution were in my favor. I think I'll be skipping lunch today too, you've given me more than enough food for thought."

Walking back to his office Basil ruminated upon the experience. Shames had offered advice before but never to such an extent. It was as if he had been saving it for the occasion, a private valediction with the master passing to his apprentice secrets accumulated from a lifetime of merchant experience. As such it was relatively free of the hortatory claptrap common to the addresses given graduating students, which revealed no secrets, and surely no guile, but was really only another form of socially sanctioned child abuse. Shames' offer of the business insurance, whatever it was worth in the long run, was a decent gesture. He didn't anticipate failing but he did have his bouts of anxiety over the move. He knew he wasn't walking into a rose garden, life in Israel was lived on the front lines, the country had a manic quality to it. Yet, if one could believe the statistics, a person had a greater probability of meeting a violent end in the United States than in Israel. So which was crazier?

Shames' reference to Indians brought back memories of his trip out West, when he and Mark visited some of the reservations. His own idea of the Indian was formed by the photographic studies of Curtis. Yet he knew that the "studies" were often staged by the photographer using props from his collection or those supplied by his subjects. Thus, most of the photographs were post-mortem. He recalled Mark conversing with the inhabitants of the reservation shantytowns, self-importantly, as if by his concern he had some power to alter their condition. In contrast, Shames' question showed insight into a tragedy of history. Complain? To whom? Nothing was going to change, the Jabotinskys of the world understood that. They and Shames were realists, brutal, nevertheless realists. The most one could hope for was that things would remain reasonably tolerable, tolerable for him in his country of residence. The rest of the world could go to hell, there was nothing he could do about it.

4

He arrived at the building housing the television channel's offices at twenty minutes before ten. He was early but not obviously so. The receptionist welcomed him by name, "How do you do, Mr. Primchek? Will you follow me please?" He followed her down a corridor until she halted at an open door and motioned him to enter. Alison rose to meet him. She shook his hand affectionately, in a manner recalling their introduction. He heard her voice, she was greeting him. His response was automatic, he was too absorbed to realize he was staring. She returned the stare, exclaiming in a mockingly pathetic tone, "What's wrong, Basil? Don't you remember? It's me, Alison, the TV lady. I'm going to interview you today."

"Of course, that's it!," he said. "I knew I'd met you somewhere before. Pardon me, but you look different today."

"Maybe it's because my hair is up and I'm wearing my work clothes." The reference was to the white T-shirt and scarlet flannel overalls with the two big mother-of-pearl buttons coquettishly sited over each breast. The outfit was probably her idea of celebrity chic. Striking a little girl pose, she tipped her pelvis forward and clasped her hands over her pubes, moving her shoulders to and fro. She seemed to enjoy the effect she was having on her wide-eyed audience.

Amidst the files and clutter of the narrow room her playfulness carried a suggestion of intimacy. Light from the window reflected off the hairs on the back of her neck. Moving to her desk, she invited him to sit down, she had some last minute preparations to attend to. She apologized for not being ready but he had been a little early — or did he know that? But that was fine, she appreciated his promptness, it was she who was behind. She was up late during the night, partly because of the book he suggested she read, Louys' *Aphrodite*. She had read half of it but still could not understand how it applied to the interview. His answer was that the book was more for atmospherics than specifics, his intent being to give her a feeling for the past. It was a prelude to what he hoped to accomplish in architecture. He judged her complaint about the book disingenuous. One didn't have to read it half through to realize it wasn't a treatise on architecture. A few pages would have enabled her to intuit his motive in asking her to read it. She was playing dumb.

Alison stepped in front of him to one of the file cases and pulled out its middle drawer to its furthest extension. Leaning over the drawer's steel face, her fingers riffled through the drawer's papers. On a line from his face she was about three feet away. Among naturalists of the African plain it was known as "flight distance", the distance the swift-footed ungulates maintained between themselves and the powerful, but quickly fading charge of their main predator, the lion. Her flight distance with him was arm's length, a distance she had been careful to maintain — unlike their first encounter when only a thin vapor of breath separated them. Now she was giving him her haunches knowing any charge he might make could, with one twist of scarlet, be deflected away. Pausing in her search, she turned her head and looked down at him over her left shoulder exclaiming, "Basil, do you mind if you're asked some personal questions? You can always refuse to answer them."

"Thanks, I'll do that."

"Oh no, the reason I want to get personal is that I think you have a tendency to talk over the heads of your audience. I'm only trying to humanize you for general consumption. You are human aren't you?," she asked, still looking over her shoulder from her obviously inhuman position at the tormented creature behind her. "Human, all too human," he answered monotonously, giving her a dubious look as she pushed the file drawer closed and turned to face him. "I thought so," she said. "I knew you wouldn't let me down. Now you'll have to excuse me for a few minutes. I have to change into my camera clothes for the interview." She reached over and picked up a book from the pile of materials on her desk. Handing it to him she said, "While I'm gone why don't you refresh your memory with my copy of *Aphrodite?* You might want to *bone up* on some things."

His eyes followed her as she strode purposefully from the room. By the rules of fencing he had already lost. He had underestimated her, she was no piece of cake to be won with a few minutes of enchantment. Before he would gore her, much blood would be shed. Seated there, alone in her office, he had no way of knowing how prophetic those words would prove to be.

She returned five minutes later dazzling in an ivory-colored suit, its jacket faced with an inverted triangle of sky blue sequins. Blue, Italian high-heeled pumps modishly completed the ensemble. Hands on hips, she made a semi-pirouette in a caricature of a mannequin before exclaiming, "That's show biz!," then demanding in mock Shames, "Would you hide this under a bushel?"

"Yeah," he said, "it gives you authority. But can you wear it again? Wait! You're in luck, the Israeli independence day parade is coming up."

"Maybe we'll have to do a sequel of you. Actually, I give all my used rags to my younger sister. She's not as uh . . . 'heavy-set' as I am — don't you just love that word? — but with time all things are possible, like a little less tennis and a lot more caviar. She's still in the light-heavy category . . . but feel the material." Alison extended her right forearm to him, "It's really a lovely cashmere, don't you think so?"

He toyed with the impulse of grabbing her arm, pulling her down to him. That was what she wanted, the ultimate humiliation. The corner of his eye sought the fastest route to defenestration, there wouldn't be time to put a gun to his head and blow his insane brains out. Before he could get his hands on one he might change his mind. "Yes, very nice," he said, lightly stroking the sleeve with his fingertips. Raising his eyes from the proffered material, he asked, "Alison, have you ever done any modeling?"

"Yes, but only for charity. It's such a demeaning proposition, I mean flashing the ivory in front of a lens all day, doing the peahen strut for women who can't wear what they see anyway — and not because they can't afford it. I'd rather take it all off for the derelicts on 42nd Street, they'd at least appreciate it."

"I can imagine. But it's very easy work, and the money is good — especially for the few at the top."

"But mindless work. As far as compensation . . . do you know what they pay me here, and I've only been at this hardly more than six months?"

"No, and don't tell me, I might be intimidated. You want that interview to take place today, don't you."

"Alright, I won't. The wardrobe goes with the job. Generally I get anything I want, they pay. But I have this gown of midnight blue sequins. By now you ought to know I love sequins. It's worn with nothing underneath, like a snake, very slithery," she made a snake-like movement of her body, "I couldn't wear it here, it's too, too *outré* for this city. I really bought it for a party I'm going to in L.A."

"So you're a jetsetter, eh? How often do you go out

that way?"

"Say, who's interviewing whom here? . . . We better get going, they're waiting for us in the studio."

Alison picked up the telephone to alert the studio crew. She asked if he had remembered to bring the drawings and photographs she had requested. He withdrew them from his briefcase, pointing out the significance of each. As they walked to the studio she briefly explained the procedure. There was really nothing special about it. He should relax, imagine himself in his own living room and not worry about looking at the camera, the cameramen would be responsible for the angles, she did most of her own editing, and that was about it. Did he have any questions? No? Good, then they could begin.

The interview went well. She was practiced in asking the "right" questions, penetrating appearances, cutting to the core of an issue. She provided the leads and he followed, endeavoring to avoid the tendency to pedantry she had faulted. The drawings and photographs proved useful in demonstrating the layout and lighting of the rooms in the townhouse complex. Particular emphasis was given the elaborate, arabesque lobby of the Turner Building. A conception that had been both praised and condemned, he nevertheless considered it his finest accomplishment. He openly admitted a bias for the style, believing it brought together both utility and splendor.

As an illustration of site suitability, he referred to the work of Yusuf Kilmi, an Egyptian architect who constructed whole villages in the traditional idiom using local materials, in his case Nilotic mud for adobe. He hoped to be able to do the same with his local material, the ubiquitous stone of Palestine. Additional examples of his debt to international culture were the tile and tilesetters for the Turner Building's lobby. Both had come from Italy. The imported craftsmen were necessary to fashion the complex stalactites and niches set in the lobby's ceiling and walls. He conceded that the cost was greater than the typical contemporary interior, but believed the resulting social benefits were incalculable.

Following the architectural discussion, the topic shifted to life in Israel. The questions were posed in personal terms but phrased so as to make him merely the agency for reportage. Her questioning demonstrated an unusual awareness of the issues. She had given an inkling of that at the party — the familiarity exhibited with Israeli given names, he suspected there was more to it. Either she had been around, or done some heavy reading — something beyond the Leon Uris variety. Her inquiries touched on his army duty, his contact with Arabs, his opinion of government policy — whether he could see any "light at the end of the tunnel". Not one to mince words, she put her questions cleanly and directly. He supposed that was one of the keys to her popularity, being provocative and controversial without giving the impression of being partisan. She used him like a pig in a minefield but he welcomed it, glad for a chance to show himself unafraid of opinion, outspoken, a man who could and would take the heat for her. He had prefaced his statements with the fact of his seven year absence, self-deprecatingly pointing out that under American law absence for that length of time gave rise to a presumption of death. Thus, while his authority to speak as a first-hand witness to recent events was somewhat diminished, nothing had fundamentally changed from the day he left more than seven years ago. Moreover, events in Israel received extensive press coverage in the States, far out of proportion to the country's numbers. Asked to explain the significance of the remark, he joked that if China got the same news coverage there wouldn't be enough trees to supply the necessary pulp. Facetiously, she asked him if the remark could be construed as "anti-Semitic". "No," he retorted, "anti-Sinetic."

"Alright, enough is enough already," she said with a

65

trace of weariness, rising from her chair and stretching, "I think both of us are becoming a little punch-drunk. I won't be programming that last exchange I can assure you. It's enough to get us both run out of town on a rail." Although they had been at it for over three hours, he had no awareness of time passing. She reached for the tiny microphone attached to his shirt and disconnected it saying, "Do you remember what you said or do you think you'd like the opportunity to review the complete tape?"

"That won't be necessary. Feel free to quote me."

"Alright, but some of it might arouse controversy. Think you can handle it?"

"Sure, what have I got to lose? If things get too hot, I can always leave town."

"OK, I'm running it . . . but I'll ask you one more time — are you sure you don't want to review the tape? It's for your protection, not mine."

"No, no, I don't think I could bear to hear myself so soon after my spiel. I'm more curious to see what you select out of that morass of opinion. I leave the editing to you, you're the expert. Go ahead, surprise me."

They returned to her office where she reached into a file, drew out two pieces of oversized legal paper printed on both sides, and handed them to him. "This is a release of liability for the broadcasting of the interview. Please read and sign both copies."

"C'mon, I hate legalities, what's it say?"

"It authorizes the station to air the interview and prevents you from suing the station or myself for any alleged libel . . . "

"Is that all? Alison, the only libel I'd ever sue you for is blood libel, but I don't think you'd ever give me the chance."

For the first time he could recall she had no comeback. Her expression betrayed her puzzlement, but she was too proud to ask for an explanation. It was comforting to know that her knowledge of Judaica had limits. In the context that really should be his speciality.

Alison picked up her telephone, tapping the numerals, "Hello, Gordon . . . Gordon, I want to preempt the Sheila Ashley interview this week with the Primchek . . . Why? Because I think it could be dynamite and the last two shows I've hosted women and I'd like a change . . . Yeah, he's very sexy . . . Thanks, Gordon, you're a dear. I knew you'd see it my way."

"That was my producer. We're running your interview Thursday, this week. Usually there's a week's lead time, but I'm making an exception in your case. The flame on your candle is so bright it's burning a hole in my bushel."

"Thank you, I hope I fulfill my promise." His manner was cold, rebuking. Believing she was making light of him, he began shutting down his emotions, raising his defenses. His dignity was now involved, and that had to be protected from manipulation, from the way she manipulated her audience, dazzling them with color and light along with the obvious, her beauty. These were the tested theatrical devices and she was ruthless in their exploitation. She called it right — "show-biz" — and he was on the wrong side of the footlights again, gone from participant to audience, another vicarious spectator suckered by a crazy, unrealizable dream.

She immediately picked up on his laconic response. She had offended, something she had no intention of doing, not with him. People of her breeding didn't do that, not to their peers, certainly not to their superiors. "Oh now, Basil," she said, in the pleading, ingratiating tone that recalled her effort to enlist him for the show, "I'm serious. I would never have moved you up a week if I didn't think your interview deserved it. You were wonderful, you really were! Please don't think I'm trying to flatter you when I say that. The interview has depth, interest, controversy . . . would you believe me if I said it was my best to date? And . . . and I wanted to be sure you'd still be here to see it. I was afraid you might fly off to Israel without reaping your kudos."

He was tempted to say "You really mean that?" but realized the matter had gone far enough. His sarcasm had hurt her, she really had been trying to please him. More sarcasm, however light-headed in intent, would be unseemly. He was surprised by the exposure, relating it to her vulnerability at the party. Inside that bravura breast of hers beat the heart of a little girl. He probably could have made her cry without too much effort. "I'm sorry, Alison, I don't mean to be ungrateful. I appreciate the consideration. I'm not so modest as to claim I wouldn't enjoy seeing myself on TV, especially in the pose of expert. I'll also be looking forward to seeing you, you know I've never seen you either. I must say I was impressed by your style of questioning. I won't ask where you acquired your expertise because of the implications — I mean what's a pretty girl doing with a head full of knowledge? — but your grasp of the issues is rather remarkable. In fact, my impression is that you know a lot more than you let on, but I suppose that's in the nature of interviewing, making the interviewees sound good. Having now seen you in action I'm not at all surprised by your popularity. It's not just because of those big blue eyes . . . wait a minute," pausing, he moved forward in his chair for a closer look, "what color *are* your eyes?"

"Blue-green, some people say teal."

She slouched down in her chair kicking off her pumps. His little speech of praise had relaxed her, massaged her feelings, drawn off the tension, and reassured. Her standing in his eyes was repaired. She extended her legs, crossed them at the ankles and wiggled her toes. It was very strong body language, bespeaking her feelings of ease with him, of comfort. For a moment her eyes closed, then opening them, she began speaking, softly, sincerely, "Basil, I like talking with you. You're very easy to talk to, I won't say 'interesting', that's such a cliché . . . but you of all persons should know what I mean. You know, anyone hearing us talk would think we've formed a mutual admiration society. But I think I like you . . . " Suddenly bounding to her feet, she pointed a finger in his face and exclaimed, "but only a little bit, do you understand?"

"Sure, Alison, sure" he replied with bemusement, "I understand."

"I hate having to be rude but I rally must get back to work if you want your interview shown this Thursday. You're holding up the operation my dear man."

She accompanied him to the outer office, introducing him to the receptionist as her discovery, a new star in the firmament, who after an unprecedented debut performance, was giving it all up and going back to his sheep ranch in Israel. Then, suspending her jocular romance, she turned and dashed back to her office, returning straightaway holding a copy of the liability release. "Here," she said, "I forgot to give you your copy."

"What should I do with it?"

"Take it. It's proof you were forewarned — Elena is my witness — in case you decide to sue after all."

He was out on the avenue and walking fast. Although the office was some thirty blocks distant he wore seven league boots, or so it seemed from his lightness of foot and heart. The turn of events was amazing, for a time he had almost been ready to chuck it. He concluded he was too easily discouraged, the slightest adversity and he gave up, pronouncing his own doom. "Audacity! Audacity! Audacity!" Was it Danton who said that? He lost his head, a risk any self-respecting revolutionary or romantic took as a matter of course. He started to imagine her under his hands but dismissed it as idle speculation, the first embrace promised to revise anything he could imagine. He preferred to leave it a mystery. And he had already imagined unto the limit of imagination the topography of her body, leaving only the raw flesh to be discovered, upon which he would fall like a hungry wolf.

His face bore a subtle smile as he waited at a corner for traffic to abate. A smile of one, who having taken a fine and delicate meal, was left with a pervasive feeling of contentment. Going uptown he had hardly noticed the blurred creatures passing fore and aft on the sidewalk. Now he was aware of an old couple, their faces hoary with years of togetherness. They seemed to await their deaths with a stolid equanimity. The Indian in sari with a red spot on her forehead, did they love and lust too? The obese lady with the shopping bag of groceries, rocking on tiny-heeled shoes, their sides splitting from breadth of foot, she had to be somebody's mother. Too numerous to note, coming, going, each with its minor destiny, they made up a river of anonymity, like the anonymous hands that fit the stones of the ancient temples erected to provide answers to the dumb strivings of the human breast. Morphological configurations, they were his public, yet only a handful would ever see him. Seeing them, he thought he finally understood the difference between a humanitarian and a humanist.

"Hold it!", Basil recognized Shames' voice calling from the other side of the lobby. He pressed the hold button and put his hand against the edge of the elevator door. Shames hurried into the car and grabbing the left lapel of Basil's jacket, loudly declaimed, "Basil my boy, I cannot thank you enough!"

"I'd do it for anyone . . .," but Shames wasn't listening.

"That Bjoerling! Wotta voice! Where was I? Where was I?," Shames exclaimed, releasing Basil's lapel and striking his forehead with the palm of his hand. "I used to hear him on the Firestone Hour but I never realized it until I played *Turandot* yesterday. I never heard it that way, tremendous!" "Excuse me, Mr. Shames," said a middle-aged woman getting out on the seventh floor. "Oh yeah, sorry . . . ," said Shames, stepping to the rear of the elevator with Basil. "The voice soars, soars, not a seam in it. I called Al Goldman's and had them send up all his records in stock, I

70

can go through 'em at home. Man, lucky for Pavo he's not around today, he'd cast a hell of a shadow!"

Basil glanced furtively at the car's two other passengers. Both were smiling politely out of respect for the loud little man seemingly oblivious to their presence. In another setting there might have been cause for some embarrassment. But not here, this home away from home, Shames' castle overlooking the Hudson. Everybody in the Woolworth Building knew Shames. A prince of a fellow — no, a king, and everybody knew a king could do no wrong. "Coming from lunch?," Shames asked. "No," Basil replied quietly, hoping that Shames' volume would modulate proportionately, "as a matter of fact I'm just coming from the interview with Alison Cleveland."

"Already? Boy, that girl doesn't waste any time. When she wants something she goes after it!" Basil was relieved to see the two remaining passengers, a man and woman, leave at the nineteenth floor. "Who socked it to whom or was it a draw?"

"Oh nothing like that, just a rather sedate *tete-a-tete*. We discussed some of our architectural projects, life in Israel, and I threw in a plug or two for myself like you told me. She's running it this week so stay tuned for 'Alison Cleveland meets Primchek'."

"Wouldn't miss it for the world, my boy," said Shames, as the door of the elevator opened on the 37th floor lobby of Shames, Garfield & Chase. "I'll have Tatiana put up a notice on the bulletin board. That's Thursday at eight, right?"

"Yeah, two hours of New York's finest entertainment."

Stopping in the lavatory to drain the bladder and wash, he decided he had better inform Miriam about the interview before she heard it from someone else. He didn't feel right about watching it with her. He'd tell her it was too embarrassing, that he'd rather watch it alone. They were going out with her parents on the following night, and since he planned to spend the weekend with her he deemed it adequate propitiation. Now that his other matter was settled he could function. Going more than ten days without sex was a strain, frequency was clearly addictive. He didn't know how the astronauts did it, months at a time up in those shitty diapers. "Duty to country" — they could shove it. Both the Russians and Americans were crazy to spend so much time in the sky. He supposed that was why they were training woman astronauts, for those longer and longer trips into the void. He wondered which system, communism or capitalism, would have the balls to proclaim itself first in the firmament. One would think it would be the Russians, they were first at everything else. Maybe they had already done it, to be revealed with a yawn when the Americans finally stake their claim — "But comrades, we did that twenty year ago, is natural thing to do." — and then drag out an enormous mass of data on the effects of weightlessness and skyhighing on sexual performance. If the Americans were behind in this aspect of the space race, it was a matter of priorities. The solution to the problem of transferring the flush toilet to the weightless environment of space came first.

5

The program's credits had not yet run their course before his telephone began ringing. It was Miriam, she wanted to be the first to congratulate him, saying that it was exciting seeing him on the screen like that. He declined an invitation to come over to her place, stating in mock militarese that he better stand by to take incoming calls.

A few minutes later the telephone rang again. The caller was Darwin Chase. He offered his congratulations for a "very interesting presentation", singling out for special praise the "penetrating political analysis, something all too rare for the media." Basil thanked him, saying it was gratifying to receive positive feedback from a colleague. Darwin expressed a desire to discuss some of the issues raised in greater detail, perhaps over dinner. He hadn't thought Darwin the type to be concerned with such issues but supposed that with a father like Elliot, something was bound to rub off. He regretted not taking the initiative to get to know Darwin better earlier. Unfortunately, lives usually passed before most people realized their affinity for each other. He wondered if other viewers had been as impressed as Darwin, whose opinion, unlike Miriam's, he had no reason to doubt. She would have been thrilled to hear him recite nursery rhyme.

He still had not received the call he was waiting for. Perhaps she was waiting to call him herself, allowing the calls from his friends to abate first. She was bound to call, if only as a courtesy. She would also want to follow up on his and others' reaction to the program, that was the minimum for professionalism. If Darwin's reaction was any indication, she would be getting equally appreciative reports. It all added up to an enhanced standing for him.

It wasn't until after eleven that the telephone rang again. That was her, he told himself, the others would have called by now. He lifted the receiver on the third ring, "Hello."

"Basil?" It was Shames. His voice had an edge to it, as if it were bottled or controlled.

"Hello, Sam. Well, what did you think, was it alright?"

"That's why I'm calling . . . You know the Mayor called me tonight."

"That's interesting. What was on Hizzoner's mind?"

"He saw the show. He didn't like it. He said you sounded 'spineless', he called you a 'nebech'."

"The Mayor's a pile of shit!" He was angry, he had never used such a tone with Shames.

"Well, I had to agree with 'im. Now what's that make me?"

"Misguided, Sam, just misguided" he replied, roaring with laughter, laughter Shames did not find infectious. "Would the Mayor feel any better if I were a casualty of the next Arab-Israeli war? I'll bet he wouldn't even say he was sorry."

"That's not the issue," Shames continued, trying to remain calm but clearly failing, "Ya know, you should have never brought up that atomic war business, that wasn't very smart . . ."

"C'mon Sam, we all read the *New York Times*. Every-one knows Israel has a nuclear potential."

"Yeah, but 'potential' is a lot different than using it, a lot different!"

"Well what do you think they have it for . . . to make pattycakes?"

"Look!" Shames snapped, now audibly acid, "We don't talk about such things, understand?"

"I think I do, but I don't agree. If that's the only issue separating us then . . ."

"What about that crap about the IDF? There's more, a lot more . . . but I don't want to get into it over the phone. All I can say is that we got this far by being the best . . . I'm disappointed, Basil, disappointed. I didn't know you felt that way."

"Maybe you should have asked me. But I really don't think we're that far apart . . ." He realized the argument was out of control, that he had better say something conciliatory while there was yet time. But Shames wasn't listening, "I'm disappointed, very disappointed."

"I'm sorry you feel that . . ." Basil heard the click of a receiver. Shames had hung up.

Now he was more than sorry, he was angry. Not at the insults — they were laughable — but at their source, the Mayor, that self-appointed prosecutor of Jewish honor and history, the nearest thing to a Jewish tyrant outside of Israel. Calling his employer was typical of his style, he wouldn't have dared call him directly, he wasn't interested in winning debating points, that was for sophomores. His method was the oblique thrust, dropping his poison where it would work the most hurt, using the network of economic relationship to isolate resistance, the classic way of the weak wielding power. Hizzoner knew the ways of power; he would give him that. He was fuming but he wasn't going to let it get to him, that would be self-defeating. They wanted him to wear a hairshirt for a few days then come in, head bent low, begging forgiveness. But he hadn't exposed himself to play the sycophant. That kind of cautious sterility wouldn't even have been worth his self-respect, and if he hadn't that he had nothing. If Shames wished to be a bedfellow of the Mayor's that was his problem. He was not about to apologize for anything. They were only deluding themselves if they thought they could bully him. They could go to hell, he was going to bed.

The following morning he was surprised to find Miriam seated in his office. "Hi, Basilio!," she cried, standing up and saluting him briskly, "one of your loyal subjects couldn't wait to offer her homage to your Majesty. I thought you were great!"

"Then you must be the only one," replied Basil with a tone of resignation, tossing his briefcase onto the desk and settling into his chair. "Guess whose displeasure I incurred last night? This will amuse you."

"Sam's." She answered without hesitation.

"Very good! How did you know?"

"I watched the program too you know. You didn't

think he was going to give it any gold stars? Did you see him this morning?"

"No, he called last night, after eleven. But hark! The plot is thicker than that . . . three guesses who called him to complain."

"Let's see . . . somebody from the ADL checking on your credentials?"

"No . . ."

"Sidney Falk?"

"No! Since you only have one guess remaining I'll give you a hint . . . Now think, the most obnoxious person in New York, who is it?"

"The *Mayor?*"

"Yes, yes, the *Mayor!*"

"Whatever did he say?"

He described the telephone conversation, his indignation over the affair, and finally his resolve not to invest it with any more significance than it deserved — two old men blowing off steam at a whippersnapper challenging jealously held beliefs.

"What did Alison Cleveland have to say about it?"

"I don't know."

"She didn't call?"

"No, why should she? Am I her keeper?" He was being disingenuous, too disingenuous.

"No . . . but you'd like to be."

"Maybe I would. But I can live without it. Let's let it ride until dinner tonight. When I came in Tatyana gave me a message from Elliot, probably about the interview. I better call him now . . . call me around four."

Lifting his telephone, he dialed Chase's extension.

"Basil," asked Chase, "are you going to be in your office for the next few minutes?"

"Sure, 'there's nowhere I'm agoin',' " he said, repeating the lyrics of a favorite song.

"Good, I'd like to talk to you. Nothing serious, proba-

76

bly more comic than tragic."

Chase walked in and immediately sat down, "First, allow me to say that I watched the show and cheered. But that's not what I want to talk about. I guess you know Sam is upset over the opinions you expressed."

"Yeah, he uh . . . left me with that impression last night. He called after the show. He and the Mayor seemed to have decided that I had violated my oath as a Jew."

Chase smiled, "Well, I'm encouraged by your attitude . . . What I wanted to tell you is that you shouldn't let this incident affect your relationship with Sam. I'm sure he'll get over it. I don't want to tell you the times he and I have locked horns on the issue . . . but that was a long time ago. Eventually I decided that it wasn't worth it. We weren't proving a damn thing and the result was hard feelings — harder for him obviously. He has very strong feelings on the subject, sincere feelings. Nothing is going to change his mind, he's literally dug in. And now you — I'm sure you're aware of the basis of your relationship — it was a kind of shock. Right now he's in grief. He's lost something that he can't rely on anymore, in the ideological sense that is. That means something to him. You and I, we can say 'so what?', but he can't, he's too emotionally involved. It's like jealousy, only the lover can appreciate what all the fuss is about. And the rage goes on until it burns itself out . . . naturally. So give him a few days, he'll come around. Hell, you're going home soon, I can't see him carrying a grudge over this." Chase rose, "As for you I can only say — keep it up. You're a good man, Primchek. The world needs people like you, it's in a hell of a shape."

Chase shook Basil's hand, turned and left the room. He was right about Chase. He was a good man too.

He and Miriam left the office early for the rendezvous with her parents. They were meeting them at Wong Low's, a restaurant near Columbia University, home to one of the city's better Schezuan kitchens. One of its chefs was said to have cooked for Chou En-Lai during the years of the Long March, when the main force of the Red Army was holed up in Yenan waiting for better days. The claim, like many of those put forward by merchants, was open to doubt. Simple calculation suggested the fellow would have been a mere boy at the time. Having eaten at the other end of the ideological table — at a restaurant claiming as its chef one who had cooked for Chaing Kai-Shek — Basil was convinced cuisine was one of the major human activities least susceptible to ideological considerations. Unless, of course, one subsumed the perennial debate between meat-eaters and vegetarians. That vegetarianism had enlisted such disparate advocates as Adolf Hitler and George Bernard Shaw suggested the influence of diet upon ideology was coincidental. Until all the evidence was in, he would continue to eat meat. Food, like sex, was still a matter of taste. Both had their dangers and their satisfactions.

Basil and Miriam arrived at the restaurant at the appointed hour of five o'clock. Harry and Sarah Scheine had preceded them and were already sitting at a table. Seeing Basil enter the Scheines rose to greet him, ignoring Miriam in their enthusiasm to congratulate him, words like "wonderful" and "brilliant" issuing from their mouths. Basil reckoned the demonstration some of the "kudos" predicted by Alison Cleveland. It was one more accolade to weigh against the previous night's criticism. Miriam had given her father an inkling of the controversy earlier in the day. Now he was anxious to hear it straight from the horse's mouth, the absolutely best source of what happened provided the reporter was not burdened by ideological considerations. Basil suggested they order before getting into the "gruesome details". That suited Harry, aware as anyone of the limitations of ideology in the satisfaction of hunger.

The late-night telephone call with its message of insult and disappointment was like a meal spiked with monosodium glutamate — who needed it? Nevertheless, the two villains of the piece, over plates of shrimp with lobster sauce and eggplant wo dai, received their own measure of criticism and denunciation for their intemperate reaction. The matter was analyzed and remarked to exhaustion so when it came time for the fortune cookies, the party was eager to address another, more salutary topic of conversation. Harry Scheine led the way, referring to the portion of Basil's interview where he questioned Israeli policy *vis-a-vis* the Palestinians, linking it to the larger question of the Jewish state's relationship with the whole of the Muslim East. "What I'd like to know is now that you've posed the question on the major issue facing the country, what do you intend to do about it when you get back?"

"What do you mean '*do* about it'?," asked Basil.

"Just what I said," said Harry, now speaking deliberately, "what do you plan to do about your criticism when you get back to Israel?"

Basil hesitated, trying to decide whether to dismiss Harry's question as impossibly naive or indulge it as a matter of courtesy, "What can I do? Who the hell am I to do anything?"

"You're a citizen of the country that's what. You have to do more than grumble before you can have any influence over events!"

"Wait a minute! You're a citizen of *this* country. How much influence did you have in stopping the war in Viet Nam?"

"That's a different situation altogether. But to avoid being diverted by long explanations I'll admit I'm nobody, just Harry Scheine, garment worker, a poor Yid. But you, Primchek, you're the elite, or you will be once you get established. Your background and ability puts you there — maybe not power elite, but nevertheless elite. You go on television there and say what you said so well here and there'll be a momentum for change. Because you're not alone, you've got people out there frantic for another way out, any way out. They are your allies! But you go back there with that do-nothing attitude of yours and you may as well give the country on a platter to the Aharonis and Eretz Yisrael bunch, because sure as hell that's where it's going to end up. You know what Edmund Burke said . . . or do I have to repeat it for you? Sometimes I forget you're a foreigner and not familiar with our great tradition. Ha! Ha!" Harry laughed heartily at the irony of the sarcasm.

"No, I don't know what he said, you better tell me."

"'*The only thing* necessary for the triumph of evil is for good men to *do nothing.*' My emphasis."

"So when do I start?," exclaimed Basil sarcastically. "Look at the harpies I called down upon my head for merely expressing an opinion — and that in a country not my own about a country not their own! Figure that one out."

"You mean Shames?," Harry made a dismissing gesture with his hand, "With all due respect to the gentleman, and I say this in front of my daughter here with whom he has been undeniably generous, you don't win the Jabotinsky Prize by promoting reconciliation. They may as well call it the war prize, Jews against all, as if they had a chance. They'll end up like the crusaders, a couple temples in Jerusalem and the rest dispersed to the four corners of the Earth; or worse, victims of another holocaust, only this one will be self-induced, no crazy fuhrer here to blame the ills of the world on the hapless Jews . . . if anything the fuhrer will be Jewish. You probably don't know this, but I'm 73 years old and I remember fighting those characters in the twenties and thirties. Obviously we lost. The Holocaust put them over the top, the big Jews went with the nationalists. They say it was the result of the Christian conscience making up for its apathy, but it was their consciences making up for their own silence before and during the war. Sometime you should ask Shames where his father was when the Holocaust was going on. For the first time in his

80

life he might be at a loss for words."

Harry paused to allow his words to sink in before continuing with his revisionist version of modern Jewish history, "And now that they've succeeded in pushing *their* solution, all they can talk is 'survival'. Because they know or should know, that history is a very fickle creature and that although Israel is the cock of the walk today, not too far down the road a bigger and tougher cock is aborning, and it doesn't pay to kick sand in its eyes. Meanwhile, from the relative safety of fortress America, people like Shames and that oaf of a mayor can egg Israel on, unable to see beyond their big Jew shnozzolas, prepared to make 'heroes' out of millions of people to satisfy some twisted chauvinism.

"Now we know what America has in store for the world. We saw it very clearly, too clearly, in Viet Nam. We're seeing it now in Central America, war no less brutal because of the lower intensity of involvement. So the question I pose to you tonight, is whether you, Basil Primchek, are going to be accomplice to a policy that makes us, the Jews, expendable, as historically we have been to the 'Christian' world . . . or, and I say this without presumption, whether you'll stand up and say 'enough is enough' and hope that out of the struggle — and there will be a struggle, a hell of a one — a better solution will prevail."

Harry sat back, forearms resting on the upper cross support of his chair. There was no response from the others, only the sound of restaurant babble all around, the dining room having filled with patrons in the meantime. Being in the nature of exhortation rather than communication, Harry's question was unanswerable. Realizing this, his afterthought was apology as well as epilogue, "I hope I didn't put a damper on the evening's festivities . . . but you know us senior citizens, we have nothing but time in the time remaining us, so naturally we like to talk. You'll forgive the ruminations of an old man, but you can't say you didn't give him cause for comment. Sarah's prodding me — there are people waiting for a table and you two probably have your own plans for the evening . . ."

Basil called for the check. Outside on the sidewalk, the party broke up with handshakes and embraces. He hailed a cab for Harry and Sarah. He would miss them, people with such opinions were all too rare.

He left Miriam's around three on Sunday afternoon, the possibility of receiving a telephone call from Alison Cleveland made him anxious to get back to his apartment. She could have called while he was out, Sunday evening was a likely time for her to try again. He was still nagged by the fact she had not called Friday. He allowed she might have gone out of town, perhaps chasing another interview. And then it being the weekend, he conceded her a social life.

Inside the building's lobby he went directly to his mail slot. There was a slim possibility she had sent a thank you note, that would have been a class thing to do. Finding nothing, he reminded himself to avoid making a straw woman of her, conforming to his own frantic image. He decided she would address anything to the office, that was the logical place of contact.

6

Tatyana, the receptionist, was surprised to see him. She was usually the first to arrive, turning on the lights and performing other early bird tasks. "Good morning!," she called, "The weekend must have agreed with you."

"Yeah . . . ," he said, preoccupied with searching the slots of the message box for a possibly mislaid memo, "twasn't bad, twasn't bad, a pity for Mondays . . . Say Tatyana, you wouldn't happen to have any messages on your desk for me by any chance?"

"No, were you expecting something, something important?"

"No . . . just wondered, trying to take care of unfinished business."

"Basil . . . I didn't get a chance to say very much to you last Friday about the program, I really enjoyed it. You know you're a very smart man . . . I mean you hide it too well. We'll miss you, Basil. I know Mr. Shames will."

"Thank you, Tatyana. And you are a very kind woman. We try, we try."

"Tell me, Basil, Alison Cleveland — I heard she came to your party but I didn't see her — is she really as beautiful in person as she looks on TV?"

"Even more beautiful, Tatyana, even more beautiful."

"I thought so. Some of these women are very heavily made up. I don't know if men notice such things, but we do. But she's young, and when you're young you've got nothing to hide."

"She wears a little makeup . . . but you're right, on her it looks good. What did you think of that costume she was wearing?"

"Oh, wasn't that marvelous? Very becoming. She's the kind of person who can wear anything. She has the height for it."

"You sound like you're a fan of hers, are you?"

"Oh, I've watched her program off and on, depending on who she has on. But after seeing you and her together I think I'll be watching her more often. You and her made a very nice pair, a very nice chemistry. She sounds very intelligent, I mean for a young woman she has so much poise. Does she really know that much about architecture? She comes across as very well informed."

"No, she's just a fast learner. I taught her everything

she knows in fifteen minutes. She's really very modest, an ordinary person, just like you and me."

"Do you think you'll be seeing her again? . . . I don't mean to be prying but she's such a beautiful woman and I . . . you know, you wonder what these people are like . . . you know, when they step out of the public's eye. I know she's not married . . ."

"I really can't answer your question, Tatyana . . . . We can only wait and see what fate holds in store for us. As usual in life, it's out of our hands. But thank you very much for your kind thoughts. I appreciate them very much."

If she was ever going to call him today would be the day. It was her responsibility to call him, any journalist would have conceded that. When she wanted him she had called. Now that she had had him would she do what those "throw away" women did, the ones who picked up men for one night stands then discarded them, a phenomenon one psychiatrist had dubbed the "Doña Juanita complex".

The image of the dancer barged into consciousness again. Everytime he started getting high on a desire the memory returned like a psychic cold shower. He picked up the morning *Times,* scanning its front page for the day's news. He had given up reading the Sunday edition, it was too short on news and too long on "culture". It was also a prodigal waste of resources — he had once read that the paper required for one Sunday's press run consumed two hundred and seventy-five acres of trees. One of the draftsmen dropped off a set of plans for his approval. The original conception called for a circular, brick structure with a terra cotta tile roof. A warehouse, offices were to have lined the building's outside circumference. But when the client saw the cost-estimate it balked, it wanted square footage, not a temple. The result was a large rectangular barn sheathed in aluminum. He had added a few designs as embellishment for the building's plain sides, designs that a good sign painter could execute in a few day's time. It was the era of the

84

bottom line and few were prepared to rise above its dismal standard. Shuffling the blueprints over the drafting table the idea came to him, a response that occurred millions of times every day at all levels — compromise. He drew her card from his wallet, picked up the telephone and dialed the number. A familiar voice answered, "Whom shall I say is calling?"

"Basil Primchek."

"Oh hello Mr. Primchek, I thought it was you. This is Elena, remember?"

"How could I forget? How are you?"

"Fine, thank you. May I say that we were all very impressed by your interview?"

"Thank you, it's good of you to say that."

"Not at all, I assure you it was meant very seriously. I hope you'll be able to interview with us again sometime soon. But I'll let you talk to Alison now . . ."

Alison was on the line, "Hello, Basil, it's nice to hear from you."

"Hello, Alison, how are you? I was getting worried. I hope the fact I didn't hear from you on Friday wasn't an indication the results were disappointing."

"On the contrary, we were delighted with the interview. You know I really must apologize for not calling, I only arrived back last night from a long weekend in Vermont. Also, this morning things have been hectic, otherwise you would have heard from me. I'm really very sorry to have left you in the lurch like that. Next time I promise to be better organized."

"That won't be necessary, there won't be a next time."

"Oh come on, don't quit while you're ahead. You're not going away forever. We're on the threshold of the 21st century, you're only a plane ride away."

"That's hardly the problem . . . the Mayor called Sam after the show. I got very bad marks from his excellency . . ."

"Is that all? He called me too."

"Is that so? What did he say?"

"It's really not worth repeating . . . the usual gripes. He wants me to offer a reply, you know, under the 'equal time' principle, as if this were some kind of a debate. I told him I'd think about it. Of course, I have no intention of letting him push me around. I don't work for City Hall."

"Alison, you are a woman after my own heart! But listen, that isn't the end of my story — Sam agreed with him. He hasn't spoken to me since he called after the show to advise me of the Mayor's displeasure."

"Really? That doesn't sound like Sam. Men, they can be such drags. But if it's any consolation the response so far from my women viewers is overwhelming in your favor. Basil, you are a hit!"

"That obviously says something for women . . ."

"Or something for you."

"Now!" he told himself, "Say, Alison, can we continue this conversation somewhere else, say the Palm Court at the Park Plaza. They serve a pretty good sacher torte there . . ."

"When are you leaving for Israel?"

"What's the difference when I'm leaving?," he replied, slightly provoked, "I'd like to see you."

"Well . . . " she was hesitating, "I am rather busy this week . . . but let me check my calendar, I think I can squeeze you in . . . How about tomorrow at two? The lunch crush should be petered out by then. I really can't stand waiting . . ."

"Very good, see you tomorrow at two." He ended the conversation abruptly, before she could change her mind. A bold stroke, it had worked, but only to a point. The "let me check my calendar" was unnerving, he thought he deserved better. Something had happened since the day of the interview. Whatever it was, he did not want to think about it.

He stayed home that night, preparing with his rudimentary kitchen equipment a rudimentary meal of fried pork chops and boiled spinach. After watching the national news he pulled out the Bunny Berrigan rendition of "I Can't Get Started" and played it over and over, soaking himself through with the song's melancholic resignation, " . . . I've got a house, a showplace, still I can't get no place with you . . . dream day and night of you . . . I scheme, just for the sight of you . . . still I'm brokenhearted, 'cause I can't get started with you." The song was a masterpiece, what the Italians called a *capolavoro,* a masterwork. He had learned some Italian from the tile and marble craftsmen imported to execute his designs for the lobby of the Turner Building. Then Umberto B, his Italian cobbler, taught him one of Mussolini's last memorable phrases — *"Meglio vivere un giorno da leone che cento anni da pecora"* (Better to live one day as a lion than a hundred years as a sheep). Upon entering Umberto's shop, he would declaim the phrase in the manner of an operatic *recitativo.* It was a password, a piece of heroic fantasy bonding them in a single existential affirmation. Irrespective of its flawed source, the statement fascinated him.

7

It had been raining heavily on and off since early morning, one of those spring downpours that brings joy to farmers, sadness to urbanites. It was slightly past one-thirty when the taxi dropped him at the Fifth Avenue entrance of the Park Plaza. Before entering its tiled magnificence he cocked his head back to take in the perspective of its ascending lines. It was a grand place designed for grand people — and small people too, provided they paid the tariff. How many, he mused, came to its precincts to live as lions for that one day of their life? He was early, almost a half hour early, but with traffic being so unpredictable there was no pinpointing travel time. He had given himself fifteen minutes and then some. He wanted to avoid even the anxiety of being late, because not only might he be late, but the concern over being late might have upset his equanimity and real lions didn't let little things like being late bother them. And then he wanted to avoid giving her an excuse to leave, which she might, even if he were only late by minutes. He didn't know whether her expressed abhorrence of waiting was a warning or merely resentment against waiting. Suddenly he realized that the circumstances of the meeting were assuming too great an importance, too much calculation was being invested into what was really a very ordinary event, occurring millions of times every day. He was treating the matter as if it were some kind of a heist, killing time by walking around the Plaza's lobby, making a circuit of the shops facing the Palm Court. He checked his watch, it was still only ten to two. He asked the hostess, or "maitresse d' ", for a table in a corner, away from the Court's entrance. The area was quieter, more intimate, less patronized. Being comfortably seated would give him a psychological advantage, she would be advancing onto his turf, he could receive her almost as a guest. Instead of waiting, he ordered coffee, that was the natural thing to do. A cup in hand looked better than thumb-twiddling. Meanwhile he kept his eye on the lobby to eliminate the possibility she might be looking for him there. That was unlikely, but everyone had their own method, their own response to a situation. He wanted to foreclose the possibility of an "I was there, where were you?". Although she really was too big to play that kind of game. But one couldn't be sure. Otherwise he could have saved the wait by leaving for the rendezvous a half hour later than he had, knowing that come what may, she would be waiting. But he wasn't at that point with her. A lion he was not, only a lion manqué.

Came two o'clock and still no Alison. He reminded himself that when she did arrive, not to admit to any disquietude over her lateness, to ignore it. Anyone could be late, New York was a big place. In the Middle East people were hours late. In fact, he had heard that was the custom in Cairo. The thought made him wonder whether it wasn't another of those jokes portraying the Egyptians in the worst light.

He looked at his watch — four minutes after. In spite of all his resolution he was beginning to feel a little nervous, thinking that perhaps he had been had, that she was sending him a message, the kind of thoughts anyone in his situation might have, and with justification. He began to speculate on how long he should legitimately wait before getting up to leave — "2:30, no, 2:40", that was a waiter's half-hour. It was better to say "more than a half hour" than "at least a half an hour". It may have started to rain again, she could have gotten a late start and to compound matters got stuck in some traffic jam somewhere. Sometimes one could walk down the avenues faster than the traffic moved. He pictured her walking fast, then running. He would have loved to see her run, nude, her breasts jangling with the pace of her gait. He fancied himself catching her in his arms and licking the sweat between her breasts, on some depopulated golf course or belvedere of a great estate, where the grass would be soft and mowed and a spreading oak would provide all the shelter necessary. His eyes did another circuit of the Court, she was nowhere to be seen. There was no possibility of missing her, she was much too distinctive, or was the word flamboyant? The face of his watch showed almost ten after. He took a deep breath, "patience," he told himself, "all things come to those who wait." Then he saw her, she was standing by the dessert table scanning the tables. He was

89

about to raise his arm when her eyes met his, she had seen him and was coming toward him. She had on a black beret tilted rakishly over her head, accenting the lightness of the hair flowing below. There were drops of water in her hair, on her face, blotches of it where it had struck the military type raincoat she was wearing buttoned to the neck. He thought she had either walked or a cloud had burst over her head. He rose to help her with the coat that she was unbuttoning as she came toward him, a signal she planned to stay awhile.

"Do you always take a shower with your clothes on?," he said as he reached to help in the removal of the coat. In contrast to their two previous meetings, her figure was concealed by layers of wool and tweed, the day's coolness making the gear weather, as well as fashion, appropriate.

"Just after the cab pulled up the heavens let loose and wouldn't you know it but I'm too dumb to come out of the rain while I'm fishing for the money to pay the cabbie. How are you? Do I need to apologize for being late? This is the second time, you probably gave up on me."

"Of course not. I was just performing my midday prayers. Naturally, you figured prominently in them." He motioned to his waiter for service.

"I hope my appearance was a sign they were answered . . . or am I being too presumptuous?"

He ordered the waiter to bring two coffees and two sacher tortes. "Make that one sacher torte, please," Alison interjected, "I'm sorry, I'll just have a bit of yours if you don't mind. I sort of overdid it over the weekend. Cross-country skiing gives one a ravenous appetite and the food made by our friends was just too good to pass up."

"I hope you don't think I brought you here to fatten you for the slaughter. I would share the very last sacher torte in the world with you. Someday you will be hungry and you'll be able to appreciate that sentiment more than you can at the present." The look in her eyes made him pause.

He didn't know whether it was a reaction to his avowal of sacrifice or to her own loss of balance from his failure to comment on the revelation of weekend pleasure in Vermont. Like much of her behavior towards him, it was ambiguous. "I learned that lesson as a child from an old Arab who worked for my father. It's from an Arabic proverb which says do not eat unless the food you eat tastes like honey, do not sleep unless the bed you lie on feels like a cloud. I never forgot that lesson . . . nor the man who taught it to me."

"Well, you look like you learned your lesson well. I don't see any flab on that frame of yours . . . or is it all in your head like most of the men I know?"

Alison smiled mischievously. It seemed she loved taunting him, to see how far she could go before eliciting a reaction, "Are you trying to get a rise out of me?," he asked.

"Are you daring me or asking me? You don't want me to answer that do you?"

The words were spoken in that adolescent, defiant manner she sometimes affected, a manner he found intensely stimulating. The arrival of the waiter bringing the coffee and torte saved him having to respond to yet another salvo of her wicked, womanly wit. She seemed to be asking for a very hard spanking, but only if he could catch her, something she still had given no indication of permitting.

"Basil, I just noticed something . . .," he braced himself for another of her good-natured insults, he supposed it was good practice for her job, no one would ever get the better of her without becoming rather bloodied himself, "your hands. They're very fine."

"All the better to fondle you with, my dear."

"Or strangle me . . .?"

"As you prefer."

"Was that the purpose of this meeting . . . I mean the fondling, you're not the type for strangling — or maybe I'm being too charitable . . .?"

"What do you think?"

91

"I'm glad you put it that way — I'll take the liberty — I think it was. Do you know how many men come on to me in this job, who want me for a weekend ego-booster? And I've interviewed some very "big" ones, some of your so-called men of the world, or rather men of parts . . . Probably not. You all play dumb when you're nailed against the wall. But I'll tell you anyway — a lot. Almost all depressingly . . . and some of them have been old enough to be my grandfather, you'd think they'd have sense enough to quit while they're ahead instead of reverting to blithering adolescents. That's one reason I took this job . . . to get away from those conceited directors, the ones who think every ambitious ingenue is stuff for sexual snacking, the little bantam roosters with their leering eyes and presumptuous manner. Besides, it pays a hell of a lot more, without, of course, the sideline. Here I can take it or leave it. And do I have to tell you I invariably leave it?

"I'm sorry if anything I've said implied that you're like the others. You are different. I knew that from the first time we met. I can tell you this because I know you can handle it, you won't suffer from hydrocephaly like the cretins . . . I'll admit I was attracted to you. You know that, it's not something I can hide from you or would. You're very attractive. But don't lock me in a room with you, I might go wild. I know you'd like that and frankly, so would I, I think. But you can't expect me just to go off for a roll in the hay with you. How do I know if it would mean anything to you? You've never even written me a sonnet to tell me how you feel. I don't know if you could even put it into words, maybe that's not your style. But I'm not interested in becoming Channel Thirteen's whore. You can understand that a person like myself has to be like Caesar's wife. Otherwise we lose all credibility. I realize it's an imperfect world."

Finally she stopped. The words had tumbled out in spurts, like ketchup from a bottle. Had he been scolded or

92

praised?

"So what can I say?," he asked, "Is this another consolation prize?"

"No. I thought you needed to be told the facts of life. Whether you realize it or not, you were putting me under pressure."

"Well, you know how we are, we can be very pushy."

"O no, you're not going to use that one on me, I won't let you! I may as well tell you now because you were bound to force it from me eventually — the person I'm involved with is one of your coreligionists."

"Zo vot you tink you should get a medal?" He was mocking her now, giving her some of her own medicine, only in larger doses. He no longer had anything to lose. She had already told him he had lost.

"No, I'm just not going to let you leave here smugly attributing your assumed rejection to anti-Semitism, implicit or explicit. That kind of sympathy ploy I will not tolerate!"

"What's the matter, can't you stand having more than one dill in the jar?"

"You know, Basil, maybe I should take back what I said about you. You're really very cruel, do you know that?"

"Look who's talking about being cruel. You're so cruel you haven't even told me who the lucky schmuck is. Don't you think I'd like to know who my better is? You can't leave me hanging like this. Redeem yourself. Tell me who it is or I strangle you right here. These hands may be fine but they're very, very strong. Don't make me any madder than I already am." He was joking but he also was angry. He had never spoken to a woman like that in his life. He hoped she deserved it.

"Alright, I will. And don't think your threats had anything to do with it . . . It's Jay Geltzer."

"Jay Geltzer!" It should have been anticlimactic but it wasn't. He almost reeled from the blow's shock. His chest

93

felt like it had been penetrated by a large, dull stake. Miraculously, there was no blood. "Jay Geltzer!," he repeated anguishedly, "Why he's the oldest eight year old in America!"

"Oh, but he's really very nice. I think you'd like him . . ."

"Don't tell me that you're a fan of his stuff, I won't believe it."

"Some of it is very clever, really. Although I must admit that it is hardly my cup of tea. The masses seem to like it though, by the millions. So who are we to judge?"

"No, no, let's not judge, that could be fatal. Let's just close our eyes and block our ears. That explains the Hollywood connection, the muddy pool becometh clear . . ."

"We don't see each other that often so one of us calls the other at least once a day . . ."

"What are you afraid of . . . that you might forget each other?"

· "No, my dear boy, they're called emotions. Maybe you don't have any. If that's the case I was right about you."

"Wait a minute! Let's not talk about emotion, I think you know I've got enough emotion to make you into a pad of melted butter. No! Let's talk money. how does it feel to roll in it with one of the world's richest schmucks? I hear the bitches find it a great turn-on, the greatest! Is it true?"

Alison stood up and reached for her coat draped over the back of a chair. The tables around them were no longer occupied, the matters discussed by the tall, elegant young woman and her Italianate looking companion would remain a secret between them and them alone. "I think we better go now," she said resignedly, "this discussion has degenerated into a dog fight. I'd like to have good memories of you so please don't say any more." Basil stood by watching while Alison placed her long, graceful arms in the sleeves of the raincoat and adjusted the beret on her head. He noticed that he hadn't touched his torte. He took out his wallet and

94

pulled a twenty, dropping it on the table, not bothering to ask for a bill. As they walked out he heard the waiter cry after him, *"Grazie, signore, grazie!"*

Neither spoke as they exited the hotel. On the sidewalk in front of the entrance Alison turned and extended her hand. There were tears in her eyes. He saw one roll down her cheek, gathering speed. He felt very bad, he couldn't speak. An involuntary gulp seized his throat. His hand was limp but she had it firmly in hers and was squeezing it very hard. "Next year in Jerusalem," she said. "Yeah, sure," was all he could manage to say. He turned and walked rapidly toward Fifth Avenue. One more second of looking into those eyes of hers and he would have blubbered like a baby.

He kept walking fast, almost running. The rain had stopped. He had planned to ask her to accompany him to the Metropolitan but that was all over. He didn't feel like looking at any art, he didn't feel like looking at anything. After walking a few blocks along the park toward the museum he hailed a passing cab.

"The El Al ticket office, you know where it is?"

"Sure buddy, you goin' to Israel?"

"Yeah . . . yeah, I'm going to Israel."

JERUSALEM

8

Basil stood up, waiting for a chance to break into line. Holding his leather handbag in one hand and the Kazak in the other, he stepped into the aisle, joining the exodus of departing passengers. His body ached from the hours of confinement in the too-small seat. It was a modern version of the stocks, punishment for the audacity of avoiding the price of a first-class ticket. He cursed the airline executives responsible, driven as they were by an almighty "bottom line". By the time he reached the smiling stewardesses and flight crew assembled at the plane's exit, he had worked himself into a small fury. In no mood to suffer the *"shaloms"* and "welcome to Israel"'s cheerily dispensed to each debarkee, he passed by the receiving line without so much as a nod, striding into the connecting tunnel, surging ahead of the slower-paced. All the *shaloms* in Israel could not atone for the torment of that seat.

Entering the baggage area, he saw two pieces of his luggage turning on the spinner. He removed them and waited for the remaining piece, a canvas and leather affair holding suits and jackets. It appeared as if people were being processed through with a minimum of harassment, the lines were moving quickly. He saw his father standing in the reception area. His aunt, his mother's sister, was with him. They had seen him too and were waving to attract his attention. He waved back, shrugging to indicate his helplessness before the routine ritual delaying their reunion. Most going through Customs appeared to be Americans, he recognized some from the plane. A cursory examination and stamping of the blue passports and they were waved through. He noticed a pair of travelers, probably Israelis, whose baggage was being examined with a thoroughness bordering on the excessive. He pushed his luggage cart ahead, he was next. He handed his passport to a seated officer who gave it a few moments of wordless scrutiny before inserting a piece of yellow paper and directing him to a table where two other customs officers stood waiting. He lifted the luggage onto the table and opened it for inspection. "What's in the package?," demanded one of the officers.

"A rug."

"Open it."

He pulled out his pocket knife and neatly cut the string and tape around the paper wrapping. "Where do you want it?," he asked.

"On the floor."

He laid the Kazak on the floor, rolling it out full length. At that, customs officers left off inspecting socks and underwear and joined colleagues who, like a swarm of moths, had suddenly gathered around the carpet. It was a bad sign. To be deemed beautiful was to be deemed valuable. He could be in for a hard time, Sephardim knew their carpets. He regretted not having sent it to his father, who was more skilled in the art of dealing with officialdom, at engaging in the petty repartee that was part flattery, part provocation. With his bespectacled Slavic face creased by age, he always passed for ordinary. If it occurred to them he was finagling, he could be excused. In the circumstances they would do the same, they were ordinary people too. They respected their own kind, the police. Others, like himself, were necessarily suspect. His distaste for police and officials was an involuntary reaction, which, of course, they read in his face and speech. In that regard they were super-literate. It was too late now to recruit his father's intervention, the leeches had already fastened onto the flesh. This was his personal "Operation Flying Carpet", the name given the undertaking that brought the Jews of Iraq, over a hundred thousand strong, to Israel after independence. Except that this carpet brought only an Ashkenazi from America.

100

They were going to sock him, a "rich Ashkenazi". It was more than racist apprehension. The sneers and leers on their Sephardi faces affirmed it.

The officer who had been asking the questions and giving the orders left the group standing around the Kazak and resumed the interrogation, "This carpet, you are declaring it for yourself?"

"Yes."

"What was its cost?"

"I don't know. It was a gift."

"A gift?," repeated the officer incredulously, his eyes narrowing, "have you a bill of sale?"

"I told you it was a gift. People that give gifts don't usually provide a bill of sale with them."

The questioning was calculated to exasperate. Responding as he did played into their hands. It was a game without rules, one of those situations where the more right you were the more wrong you were. The group admiring the Kazak was listening. Now with the sharpening of the interrogation their attention was transferred to the contest between one of theirs and the stranger, " . . . then can you secure a bill of sale from the party who bought it for you?"

He had already decided to take a chance on Customs' determination of the carpet's value, believing that the valuation would prove nominal. Now he wanted to avoid complicating the matter further by writing Miriam for a copy of the bill. There must be another method for resolution of such disputes he thought. "No," he said, "I'm afraid that would be impossible."

"Then you must leave the carpet here until our appraiser can make a valuation. Collect your luggage and follow me."

Basil pursed his lips and looked over at the barrier where his father and aunt were waiting. They did not appear unduly concerned. He raised his hand to signal a delay as the band of customsmen and airport guards drifted away. At the Customs office he was handed a form to fill out and sign, the appraiser had left for the day, he would have to leave the carpet. He asked the officer to write his badge number on the form — "just in case". "Don't worry," said the officer, "your carpet will be safe here, this is not an Arab country. The appraiser usually arrives before nine. You may pick it up anytime after the appraisal. That is all, you may go now."

A blast of superheated air hit him as he emerged from the terminal, a brutal reminder of how hot it could get in the Middle East. The air seemed to have a sere, almost crackling quality to it. Squinting in the bright sunlight, he waited with his aunt while his father and Moshe, his aunt's sixteen year old son, fetched the car. His aunt was carrying on about his moustache and how handsome he had grown since she last saw him, how she wished his mother had lived to see him this day, this way, an architect, the pride of the family. She had worried about him, wondering if he would marry an American girl and stay in the United States. So many emigrated, given the opportunity. She regretted she had not gone to the United States to visit him while he was there, but between the children and the family business there had not been time. And then she had never been across the sea, the farthest she had gone was Spain. Someday soon they hoped to make the trip. Perhaps he would show them the sights of America, especially New York where he had lived. But there would be plenty of time to talk about that later. Now that he was back he should become established in his profession. But right now he should go home, take a bath and relax, he must be very tired from jet lag. A metallic blue sedan pulled to a stop in front of them, his father at the wheel. Moshe leapt out and, with the presumption common to youth, seized two of the suitcases, straightaway depositing them in the car's trunk. As a demonstration of adolescent vigor and strength it was impressive but wasted. Basil as quickly removed the suitcases, rearranging the pieces to accommodate the remaining larger piece which he placed in first. He wondered about the car, obviously new, believing it to be leased or borrowed.

"This isn't your car, is it?," he asked his father.

"No, it's yours. I've had it for the last three months waiting for you. I wanted to be certain you'd have it when you arrived. This particular model is hard to get." He held open the driver's door inviting Basil to drive. "That way you can tell me whether I did the right thing by you."

The car was a Toyota, another example of Japanese industrial craftsmanship, the standard that gave competing international capital inferiority complexes. He maneuvered carefully between the taxis and buses clogging the terminal's entrance. A denting of the car's virginal surface on its maiden voyage would have been humiliating. Israel was classified as a developed country but its driving habits were deplorably third-world. The car was actually his first. While in America he had managed by borrowing or renting, owning an automobile in New York City was asking for trouble. But here he needed a car, any kind of car — provided it had air-conditioning. For that development in automotive comfort he was profoundly grateful. "Well," said his father after they had gone some distance, "what do you think?"

"Score one for Lev Primchek and Japanese technology. I'll take it!"

Factoring in the duty, he estimated it cost a bundle. He would have asked how much, but the recent rigamarole concerning the Kazak stopped him. Price tags were for givers, not receivers, in spite of the absurdities of Customs. "This question may be academic, but how's business — or am I driving the answer?"

"We're holding our own," replied his father matter-of-factly. "In the bread business you don't get rich overnight, but you make a good product and people will buy it, they have to, everybody needs bread. Fortunately, bread is one of those things insulated against the effects of inflation. Costs rise, our prices rise. The Maale Adumim store grosses almost as much as the bakery now . . . So we make a little more money? If I can't spend some of it on my boy — who's already made good in another country, what good am I as a father?"

Lev Primchek grabbed the back of his son's neck, stroking and kneading it between palm and fingers. After more than a decade he would have him home. Their house would resonate to more than footsteps again. A man in his circumstances had a right to be pleased. Any father would be.

They were approaching Jerusalem now, its expanse of stone and concrete shimmering under the oblique rays of the afternoon sun. He saw the monuments to the bad taste and real estate speculation in the wake of the military conquests of '67, the great block-like structures ringing the city and blotting the sky. Architects, aesthetes, and city planners the world over opposed the developments. But people powerless to prevent the erection of skyscrapers in London and Paris could hardly be taken seriously about preserving the integrity of the "city of God". They had been mouthing platitudes about Jerusalem for decades, that it should be "internationalized", etc. But Jerusalem was Jewish and Jews would indelibly stamp it so. The internationalists had their answer now — in concrete. Architecture was a cruel power. In the wrong hands it was devastating.

If the scene disturbed his fellow riders, they gave no indication. Their unawareness only confirmed his theories. Their opinions and concerns focused upon different phenomena. If this was an example of the level of sympathy, he was in for a lonely future. Except for the landscape, little had changed since he left.

They were within the city limits now. The road had narrowed and his speed had slowed accordingly. Rounding a curve, he caught sight of a car and truck ahead. The horns of the two vehicles were alternately blaring and tooting in a mock duet. "What's the problem?," demanded his aunt anxiously from her backseat vantage. "It's an Arab with a flock of sheep," said his father, "but those horns aren't helping matters." The Arab was scurrying back and forth across the road trying to herd the sheep into a manageable mass. A small boy, stationed about fifty meters up the road, was shooing the strays back to the main body of the flock. Just then came a voice yelling, *"Ya Arab! Yallah!* (Hey Arab! Let's go!) Responding to the direction of the sound Basil turned and saw Moshe standing outside the car gesticulating to the Arab and in the next instant his father's arm shooting out the open door. In one continuous motion he grabbed the boy by his shirt and rudely pulled him back into the car. Moshe's red face betrayed his surprise and embarrassment. "You should be ashamed of yourself!" admonished his uncle, "You want to be like those dogs blowing their horns? Give the man a break. His sheep were probably spooked by the noise of that truck."

"But," blurted the boy defensively, still shaken from the humiliation, "their sheep and goats strip the land of its cover causing desertification. They should be stopped!"

"Listen, Moshe," said Lev Primchek, adopting a reasonable tone, "these are poor people. Those sheep and lambs are probably all the man has. He's trying to make a living the only way he knows how — with dignity. Besides, when you eat lamb, do you worry that it might have damaged the land? I'll bet when you're digging into a piece of lamb that's the farthest thing from your mind."

"They are lazy people," responded the boy, exhibiting the one-track mentality common to adolescence. "I have seen their men ride on asses while their womenfolk walk behind. You call that dignity?"

"Moshe! That's enough! Show some respect!," ordered his aunt in a maternal show of authority, casting a glance of exasperation at the men. "Sometimes I wish that I had only

105

girls. Boys at this age give one such a headache!"

The boy's attitude both amused and provoked Basil. "Let him go," he declared, "he's telling us something. Let's send him to America where knighthood is still in flower. How about it, Moshe, want to trade places with your Arab woman and walk behind the ass?"

The boy made no response. He was smart enough to realize three against one was no contest — particularly when two were adult males. The combination of maternal authority and the taunting of the two men cowed him into a sulking silence. Almost simultaneously, the noise of the horns stopped. Basil turned to see the traffic moving in both directions — the Arabs had gotten their sheep together. He drove slowly past, waving to the Arabs. They waved back. "Hey Moshe!" he called to the petulant youth slumped in the backseat, "there go your land destroyers. You should never eat another lamb chop." His eyes momentarily met those of his father who made a quick negative shake of the head, a request for leniency Basil deemed undeserved. A look in the car's rear-view mirror showed Moshe still sulking, only now he was making a pretense of gazing out the window. "By the way," continued Basil, "those 'lazy people', they've only been working the land thousands of years. Next time you see an olive tree, an old olive tree, think about who planted it. As for 'desertification', much of this region has been desert for more thousands of years. Human activity is one factor, but the main one is simply too little rainfall. So you shouldn't blame the present for the mistakes of the past and, what's worse, for God's . . . God knows He's made enough." Then in an aside to his father, "Somebody has to tell them these things. If we don't, who the hell will?"

"Give him time," his father replied, "he's just a kid. He'll learn."

"That's what worries me."

The incident exercised a sobering influence over the

company, suppressing conversation until they pulled up to his aunt's house. Before exiting she secured his consent to return for dinner. Mercifully, for himself and the boy, Moshe was hers to take. He was one little bastard too much.

Inside his father's house nothing had changed. The main room was as he remembered, the furniture intact and in place. He noted his mother's modest collection of Syrian glass, displayed in the shelves over the bookcase, arrayed as she had left them. Light from the late afternoon sun issued through the slits of the blinds, casting grid patterns on the floors and walls. There was a timelessness about the room, like a reopened Egyptian tomb. It was another source of reassurance, of control in the face of outside chaos. Sharing the moment, his father stood behind him, instinctively silent, waiting. Basil lifted two of his suitcases and headed for his room. Like the rest of the house, it gave the impression of deliberate and careful conservation. Except for the cloths draped over his desk and drawing table, he could have left it yesterday.

"From the looks of things you still have Ayesha."

"All these years," said his father. "She'll be here tomorrow morning. Anything you want her to do?"

"No, I just wanted to make sure of some things. Let's have some tea. You can give me my reorientation."

The two men repaired to the kitchen. Basil sat down while his father went about the motions of making the tea. There was a job waiting for him in the Jerusalem Rebirth and Redevelopment Authority in downtown West Jerusalem. His father had personally delivered his application to the appropriate contacts. He had been assured his son would be appointed to the position as soon as he arrived back in Israel. Of course, he had not submitted the application cold. One of his friends, a prominent contractor who annually did untold shekels worth of business with the government, had approached the Authority's director about the job — but he shouldn't worry, he was beholden to no one. That was the way things were done, there was no harm in having all the help one could get, even if, in hindsight, it proved redundant. One couldn't know the factors involved, the number of applicants, the agency's biases, etc. True, he had excellent credentials — an American education, a Samuel Shames scholarship and subsequent experience with his firm. But good men had been passed over before. So it was only prudent to use all the influence one could bring to bear. He would find that a good rule to follow when dealing with things bureaucratic. Bureaucrats liked to take shortcuts too.

One last thing, counselled his father — he must register for his reserve duty obligation. They would ask for that information at his place of work, they needed to know the time for his unit's call-up. "Do you mean I could avoid it by being self-employed? If that's the case they can keep the job, I'll work underground." He was being facetious. He knew of no instances where able-bodied persons had avoided the obligation.

"You know you'd never get away with it," said his father, "this is too small a country. They see a strapping fellow like you driving around in that car of yours and they get envious. The only ones let off are the Arabs, but they don't have any rights anyway . . ."

"Except that one," interjected Basil.

"Listen, why don't you make it easy on yourself? Just put it in your mind that you have to do it. Until peace comes, it's an incident of life. You'll feel differently once you're assigned to a unit. There'll be fellows your age, you'll make friends, maybe some business contacts. I did. Hell, it's not so bad. I was mobilized for four wars and only saw combat once, at el Auja in Egypt. But you know that story. I spent most of my time guarding Egyptian POWs. Of course, I'm not bragging because I was lucky. But you missed the last two wars by being out of the country."

"The last two? Where do they end and where do they

begin? You've been saying kaddish overtime since that fucking war in Lebanon, the one I was lucky to miss . . . or
rather the one that missed me."

"You mean the northern front? That's under control.
It's cowboys and Indians now. They're there and we're here.
Occasionally we make a reprisal raid. Lately the staging has
been by air, so you know nobody gets hurt when they use
the air force."

"Nobody but a bunch of bloody Arabs."

"You think I like these things? I'm only your father,
not a politician. They lose too many to the terrorists on the
ground. The people won't stand for the losses. It's a cruel
world, but when you consider that there is more chance of
your dying in an automobile accident, you can better put it
in perspective. You may think that's crap, but you have to
look at these things philosophically. Otherwise you go
crazy."

"No," Basil said, "we don't want to do that. Better
we drive somebody else crazy."

"Son, we're not going to settle this over the kitchen
table. If the country says you have an obligation, you have
to do it. You served your tour, you know these things. The
country has been good for us. Defending it from its enemies is not too high a price to pay. Remember what I wrote
you? . . . I said I believed there was going to be peace, the
trend is for peace. It took them forty years but I think
they've finally realized they can't win. They won't like it,
but they'll accept it. I used to think I'd never see the
day . . ."

There was a pause. Père Primchek reached across the
table and placed his hand on his son's neck, gently rubbing
nape and hair, speaking reassuringly, "Listen, forget about
registering for the time being. There's plenty of time for
that. You just came back to a world made strange by seven
year's absence. Anybody would be a little nervous. It's a
strain. You need time to rest, readjust. Now why don't you

109

go take your bath? When you come out I'll have a little something for us to eat."

After eating, he emptied his bags and put away his clothes. Outside the door of his room he heaped a small pile of crumpled garments, Ayesha was coming in the morning. He was tired, his body's signals could no longer be ignored. There was no point resisting. He pulled down the blanket, got under the sheet and fell asleep.

Waking, his eyes caught the outside light illuminating the sides of the room's window wells. He looked at his watch. It showed 6:20 — he had forgotten to wind it. He opened the bedroom door and saw his clothes, now neatly folded and stacked where he had left them the night before. He went into the main room. The clock there showed 11:35. Evidently, Ayesha had come and gone. The room held memories. In his mind it was his mother's, he associated its space with her. It was there he remembered her most clearly — reading, at the piano, in conversation with her women friends. He raised the framed, tinted photograph from the piano, studying it, searching the eyes. Mothers were like life, taken for granted until about to be lost. Anyotrophic lateral sclerosis. He had watched her deteriorate, a wheel-chair, and finally death. Now only artifacts remained as evidence of her existence. He thought of all the swine in the world spared to live long and lusty lives. Of course it made no sense, no sense at all. Looking down at the black and white of the piano keys, he recalled her wish for him — that he learn to play the piano and well. When she died he quit. He hadn't touched her piano since. He had played some in the States, accompanying Miriam on the violin. But those had been sight reading sessions, where both had per-formed laughably. Now he seated himself on the bench, running his finger up and down the piano's keyboard. It was out of tune, apparently fifteen year's worth. He began to play *"To a Wild Rose"*. He had learned the piece well, it had been one of her favorites. That he remembered it so well amazed him. It was one more artifact.

Establishing a checking account was routine, the Bank Leumi accepted his funds with eagerness, the transaction accompanied by none of the superciliousness sometimes assumed by bank personnel in New York. They even professed gratitude for his patronage — perhaps because he was transferring dollars into shekels. His father had instructed him to leave the bulk of his savings in dollars, in an American bank. Israel was no place to lay up treasure, he said. But three thousand dollars wasn't too much to put at risk. It would provide a cushion until he began receiving a salary.

Having accomplished his lesser duty agenda — money and property — he felt better about taking on the major test — the job. He had set aside the morning to make his appearance at the Jerusalem Rebirth and Redevelopment Authority, reckoning 9:30 as a good time. By then most had recovered from the shock of waking. It was also a time well in advance of the day's problems, the accumulation of which wore down bureaucrats, prejudicing them against everybody and everything. He had once read a book purporting to define the most propitious times of day for a variety of human activities. As a theory it seemed plausible enough, although it probably was appropriated from that verse of Ecclesiastes, the one that went: "To everything there is a season and a time for every purpose under the heaven . . ." He tried to recall the rest, but at the moment the only thing his mind could dredge up was "a time to love, and a time to hate, a time of war, and a time of peace." It didn't leave much room for maneuver, yet as a shorthand chronicle of human history, it was devastating.

The office was located on the second floor of a building on Sokolov Street, near the intersection with Jabotinsky. A Jabotinsky Street return address would have been great for a letter to Shames. He would have taken it as a veritable omen. What the man lacked in religion he made up in superstition. Although he could always rent a ghost office on Jabotinsky in case a situation suddenly arose where it was necessary to impress Shames. However, after their little tiff he could consign that possibility to oblivion. He pushed open a door and climbed a flight of stairs to a large room. Three men and a woman were in a far corner chatting over cups, the aroma of freshly brewed coffee in the air. Noticing the stranger, one of the men rose from a chair. "Yessir?," said the man, more curious than helpful.

"I would like to speak to the Director, please."

"Do you have an appointment?"

"No, but I believe he may be expecting me." He thought it prudent not to reveal the visit's purpose. The group's overt curiosity put him on guard. They had set down their cups and were staring at him. "What's the name?," asked the man.

"Basil Primchek."

The man opened the door of a small inner office bounded by wood and glass and went inside. He emerged saying, "Alright, you can go in."

She was standing behind a desk, cigarette in hand, her light blond hair cut short, tribad style. A wide cincture of dark brown leather girded her midsection. Ostensibly, it was a belt; practically, it functioned to arbitrate the tension between the upper and lower portions of her torso, each portion contending for dominance. The room stank of cigarettes. His eyes, though meeting hers, took in a butt-filled ashtray on her left. Extending her hand across the desk, she introduced herself, "Olga Shalansky, Mr. Primchek. Won't you sit down?," she invited, still looking confidently into his eyes, her pleasant, some might say voluptuous, features masked in a pose of restrained hauteur. He pulled a steel and reed chair up to the desk and sat down. He noticed that the floor was unusually dusty. Or was it accumulated ash?

He took the direct approach, "Thank you. I believe you have my application for architect on file."

112

"Indeed we do. We've been waiting for you, patiently I might add, hoping you would finally come in." Her Hebrew was tinged with a heavy Russian brogue. "Let me see," she said, scrutinizing the document before her, "this application was submitted in February . . . we don't usually hold a position open for that length of time. But with your references I'm afraid we had no choice." Saying this, she raised her head, presenting the look of one expecting recognition for words well spoken, one of those cues that demanded a segue, any kind of segue. It was the engine of polite conversation, particularly as here between strangers just met.

"Thank you. My apologies for the delay in coming in, but wrapping up my obligations in the United States took longer than anticipated. I only arrived two days ago . . ."

"You needn't apologize, Mr. Primchek. A person having your qualifications is well worth waiting for, and yes, your motivation . . . Because in all frankness, one does not give up what apparently was a lucrative position with Samuel Shames to come and work for the State of Israel without some motivation other than salary, which and I trust I'm not being too personal, must be much less than the one you received in America. Mr Shames may take a well-deserved pride in the investment made in you. So much of charity is never returned you know." She paused, giving him a chance to respond. He suspected she was angling to find out the amount of his compensation with Shames.

"Thank you," he encored, "I'm looking forward to being of service to the Authority. Of course, Jerusalem is my home town and you might say I cut my architectural teeth here, so the fact that I am back is more in the nature of one returning to his roots . . . and naturally my architectural roots."

"Teeth, roots," his metaphors could have come out of a dentist's office. If only he could have squeezed denticles in somewhere. That would have made the pun really remarkable. But it was obvious he had said the right thing and that

113

she had even enjoyed the pun, the staccato nodding of her head said as much. "I'm very glad to hear that. I don't think I need remind you about our responsibility here, one that you'll be sharing with us now. I believe we are justified in looking upon our work here as a contribution toward making Jerusalem one of the greatest world capitals, truly world-class in scope, a beacon unto the nations. To that end I'm very happy you can come on board. I have a feeling you and I will get along very well, Mr. Primchek, *very well*. From your application here I already know quite a lot about your qualifications, so if you don't mind I'd like to tell you something about mine. That way you'll have an idea of where I stand, from both a professional and personal perspective. I strongly believe we professionals should be up front and open with one another. The more we know about one another, our respective strengths and weaknesses — and some of us are honest and professional enough to admit our weaknesses — the better we can work as an effective unit to perform our function."

"Oh yes, quite right."

She had immigrated to Israel with her parents five years ago. Her father was a prominent neurosurgeon in "St. Petersburg". They were from one of the more distinguished Jewish families there, enjoying the maximum the Soviet system accords its more accomplished citizens — a large apartment, car, dacha in the country. They could have gone on so indefinitely, they were under no pressure to leave. She herself was a student at "St. Petersburg's" Institute of Science and Arts, and was on the threshold of a promising career. But they applied for permission to emigrate to Israel. Why? Because only in Israel could one truly live as a Jew, free from the invisible and often insidious discrimination that all Jews living outside of the Jewish state face. Naturally, some of her Gentile friends were unable to understand the reasons for the decision to leave. Some were even hostile, as if by leaving she was betraying the country. But it was nothing to what her father endured in being denied hospital and operating privileges, and undergoing ostracism at the hands of his fellow professionals. Nevertheless, the family persisted, and when permission to emigrate was finally granted, they left with the clothes on their backs, leaving everything they didn't sell or give away to friends and relations, to be confiscated by the state. But they still had their brains and now they were using them to benefit the homeland.

Following this personal saga of exile and fulfillment her body relaxed into her chair, uttering a silent sigh. Having made her confession she was entitled to its result — relief. "So you see, Mr. Primchek, we have something in common, you and I, other than the obvious one of profession . . . Both of us have given up the lure of success to return to our homeland to be better Jews, finding compensation in things of the spirit, a compensation that all true artists must ultimately recognize as paramount. Or don't you agree?"

"Oh yes, by all means. If it were only the material that mattered I would probably be baking and selling bread today in my father's bakery. And I'd probably have made a lot more money — at least until now." He still wasn't going to tell her what he made with Shames.

"From your resume I see that you've garnered a couple of prizes. You know for the relatively short period you were employed that's very impressive. It must have been invaluable, the opportunity to work with Samuel Shames?"

"Yes, you might say I was one of the lucky ones. Of course, I'll always be grateful to Mr. Shames for both parts of my education, the theoretical and the practical. As architects, you know, we never stop learning. Myself, I approach each project as a learning experience, even the simplest. I hope this doesn't sound too pretentious, but the most important lesson I believe I learned working with the Shames' firm, if I may say so, was humility."

"You give the impression of wisdom beyond your years, Mr. Primchek. Perhaps some of that is attributable to your American experience . . . but not all Americans are alike. One of our architects is an American, you'll meet him shortly. But tell me, this name Primchek, could that be of Russian origin?"

"Yes, my father is of Russian background."

Olga Shalansky brought her cigarette to her lips, holding it between thumb and forefinger. She took a long drag, exhaling the smoke through slightly flared nostrils, a half smile of satisfaction subtly visible behind the haze. "We're going to get on well, Mr. Primchek," she pronounced, "In fact, I am almost certain of it." She stood up, closed the cover of his file, then suddenly threw up her hand, "Mr. Primchek, excuse me, but I forgot to ask your IDF reserve unit designation. You do have one I trust?"

"No, I'm sorry but I haven't really had the chance to register and be assigned since I returned."

"Well, I suppose in your circumstances that's understandable. But you will report that information to me as soon as you're assigned, won't you? We're not supposed to hire without that information, they are very strict about that you know. But in your case we make an exception, we do what they call in Russia the 'blind eye'. By the way . . . when do you wish to start?"

"I can start tomorrow if that's alright with you."

"Excellent," she exclaimed. "I see you are a man of decisive temperament. I like that. I think you are going to be a shot in the arm to this organization." She was still holding her cigarette between right thumb and forefinger as she waved her hand in the air, waxing enthusiastic over the projected contribution of her new hireling, "And do we ever need one. Come, let me introduce you to your colleagues."

As she stepped out from behind the desk he got his first look at her legs. They were encased up to the knees in glove-leather buccaneer boots that matched her belt. The

116

get-up had a flamboyance verging on the sexually perverse. The freewheeling impression given by the boots clashed with that of the immigrant hungering for religious freedom. However, it was deceptive to judge people by the cut of their clothes. Particularly women, who beneath the provocative wildness of their wrappings, generally possessed souls of the dullest regularity. The demands of modern consumerism, masquerading as style, had the power to convert the most conservative to a worshipful acceptance of the newest mode. Unlike thought, which was free and private, resistance to the tyranny of style revealed one's treason for the witness of all.

Everyone rose when their chief came out. They must have been eavesdropping, or heard enough to proceed to the next step without prompting. Intuiting their interest, she related just enough biographical information about him to temporarily stay their respective curiosities. Following this, she proceeded to identify the four by name and job category, beginning with the one woman, and ending with a tall, lank, flour-faced individual wearing thick, horn-rim glasses and yarmulke, and possessing an extraordinary spreading beard formed of tiny, dark red curls. Pausing dramatically, she announced, "And lastly, a compatriot of yours, Eliezar Ben-Judah, architect, formerly of Pennsylvania, America . . ." "Philadelphia, Pennsylvania!" shouted the rabbi-like man in correction. Olga, ignoring the vehemence of the reaction, turned blithely to Basil, calmly explaining, "The former Irving Dikstein if you have trouble matching name and country of origin as I do." Basil's ritual handshake had no visible effect on the fury flashing in Ben-Judah's eyes. Between the two, the she and the he, it was obvious no love was lost.

He left with a generally positive impression of his new "superior". For a woman of authority she was not bad. A little wacko perhaps, but then so were most of the immigrants from Russia. If they weren't, they would still be in

117

old St. Pete strolling up and down the canals. The sane ones left for America as soon as they could get a plane out.

Her references to "St. Petersburg" struck him as particularly quaint. She reminded him of a female character from a Pudovkin film — fossils in white gowns or cloche hats, creatures sure of the past and unconscious of the present. But changes of name could be traumatic, especially if they involved political change — like waking up one morning and finding that your country was no longer Russia but the Union of Soviet Socialist Republics, or Israel instead of Palestine. Mesopotamia, Persia, Palestine, Armenia — names that now appear in books or antiquarian maps — victims of war, revolution, and the men in pinstripes who sat around tables playing Monopoly with countries. Sometimes the process was mercifully quick, as when Churchill created Jordan with the aid of a road map and a bottle of brandy. At other times it was painfully slow, as when England decided Jews should have a "home" in Palestine under the tutelage of "His Majesty's government".

Lod was busy. He walked through the terminal to the customs office. Plucking the receipt for the Kazak from his wallet, he unfolded it and laid it on the counter before the woman customs officer. She checked its number then produced the original with the appraiser's notations. He glimpsed the figure of $4,000.

"Pardon me," he asked, "that $4,000, that's not the duty is it?"

"Oh no, that's appraised value," replied the officer. "Wait . . . let me show you the tariffs here." The officer opened a large black book and pointed to the tariff for oriental rugs "45%".

"But that's $1,800! Are you sure that's right?"

"Oh yes, that's been the tariff for years now on oriental rugs. But you know if you pay in dollars you're entitled to a 25 percent discount."

"That seems unduly favorable to the American

exporter."

"I suppose it does, but in that case I guess one hand washes the other. The government wants the dollars, everybody does. Can you pay in dollars? It's a big saving."

It still was a lot of money. A little honey in a draught of vinegar. Yet it all seemed above board — the appraisal (a thousand here, a thousand there), the tariff. He decided to pay and be done. He was carrying a couple of credit cards, would she accept them? Yes, but had he other identification? He showed her his temporary driver's permit. What about his military ID, did he have that on him? No, he explained, he hadn't yet registered. She hesitated. It was her responsibility if the item was released and the tariff proved uncollectible. It was a big item. She couldn't take the risk, too much money was involved.

"Look," he pleaded, "I've just been hired on by a government agency. I start tomorrow. Can you ring the office? It's the Jerusalem Rebirth and Redevelopment Authority. Call information, they'll give you the number. Ask for Olga Shalansky, she's the director. She'll confirm my status."

The officer took down the names and went to her desk to make the calls. He watched while she made the connection. He heard the officer identify herself and the circumstances, saw her nod her head and smile. When she returned to the counter she told him, "Your director said to give you every possible courtesy, that if she were present she would sign as security."

Somewhere between Lod and Jerusalem he left the main road and headed north. He had repossessed the Kazak, and with the car's air-conditioning working like a charm, he opted for the slower pace of a drive through the countryside. A military convoy on maneuvers passed going in the opposite direction. Men driving trucks, some towing 155mm howitzers, to take a position somewhere against an A, B or C force. War games. A lark compared to patrolling West Bank villages and towns, places where he did most of his active duty. One got used to the hostile stares. Generally they were manifestations of youth and inexperience, those too young to remember past occupations — the Jordanian, English, Turkish. The old timers, they couldn't help remembering, they had never known anything else. For them occupation was a condition of life. Some occupations were lighter, some heavier. That this one was heavier seemed to have no significant effect upon their attitude, they had been conditioned not to resist. They knew if they minded their business and obeyed, the occupation would go easy upon them. At times the rules worked hardship, but that was in the nature of things. Twenty years without deliverance was the strongest argument for accommodation. The refugees, the homeless, the driven out — they were the implacable ones. He recalled their blank expressions, expressions an occupier saddled with guilt and anxiety could read anything into, and did.

He had crossed the Green Line now, he was in the occupied West Bank, the cluster of stone dwellings and uneven roof line on his left one of the typical Arab villages in the area. A sign on the road in Hebrew carried a warning — "DANGER - STONETHROWERS" — he was approaching Jeisheh, one of the refugee camps. Not a soul to be seen, not at this time of day. He slowed to get a better look at the makeshift town looming above the roadbed on his right. The camp entrance was sealed off by a wall of concrete-filled barrels stacked three high. Steel rods jutting from the earth, rocks, and assorted trash gave the entrance the appearance of a fumarole spiked with rock and earth. It reminded him of those monuments to the Holocaust that were prized for their ugliness. He had had enough. He shifted into gear and began pulling away when a terrific bang reverberated through the car's right door. Almost simultaneously, a pattern of shattering concentric lines raced radially across the right half of the windshield. The noise of the attack momentarily scared him out of his wits. Roaring ahead, he cast a quick glance in the rearview mirror. It showed only the dreary, dun-colored outline of the camp's topography, stolid and silent in the glare of the sun. Getting away was more important than getting a look at the guilty. Racing down the rough dirt road, the car threw up clouds of dust. He passed an old Arab and his wife on the side of the road. Looking back, he saw them enveloped in a cloud of dust. He felt a pang of shame, wanting to tell them he was sorry, but the emotions evoked by the attack were stronger. Cursing his ambushers, he realized the ludicrousness of his position — what would he offer as an excuse? The fact his new car had suffered a stoning? They should give a damn. He kept going until they were out of sight. Then spotting a clump of trees ahead, he swung to a stop and got out to inspect the damage. The sight of the ragged, brutal dent at the juncture of right door and front fender took his breath away. The bastards! There must have been two of them, at least two who hit their target. The interval between strikes was too short for one thrower. As an act of terrorism it was admirable, nobody killed, only costly property damage, kid stuff. He was fortunate, the encounter had occurred at the elementary level. In a few years they would be graduating to grenades or RPGs. But the future could take care of itself, he had to get the car to a garage for repair. The window would be easy to replace, it was the Japanese metallic finish that concerned him, whether it could be duplicated in Israel without the telltale variation in the finish. He decided to drive directly to the dealer. He did not want his father to see or know what had happened.

The service manager at the Toyota dealership was sympathetic, but they did no collision work. He would have to take it to a nearby garage, the place where they sent all their work. While they didn't have the windshield for his model in stock, it could be ordered from Tel Aviv. The manager gave him the stock number to give the collision shop which would order it for him. The same applied for the paint. It was a new, special metallic formula and would have to come from Tel Aviv.

The collision shop was located at the end of a narrow cul-de-sac in an area of light industry and residences. Two men in soiled workclothes were standing outside the shop's open door smoking cigarettes, soft drink bottles in hand. One, a swarthy, bald-headed chap with a thick black moustache, apparently the boss, waved him toward the door, then raised his hand to halt.

"Where did you get hit?," he asked.

"By Jeisheh ca . . ."

" 'Jeisheh'!," exclaimed the man, "What the hell were you doing there? Nobody goes by there anymore."

"I was taking a drive. I guess I was a little careless."

" 'Careless'?," the man fairly shouted the word. "You've got to be crazy to drive by that place with those animals. That's why they put the new road in. Everybody takes that now." He interrupted his diatribe to toss a nod of incredulity to his cohort. "But don't get me wrong, people like you are our friends. What can we do for you?"

Basil pointed to the damaged right side and expressed his concern about the repainting problem. The bossman was confident it could be done to his satisfaction — but it would be necessary to do the whole door and fender, spotting would not do. And for the job to be guaranteed against chipping or cracking, they would have to apply an undercoat. It was a big job, much bigger than it looked. Basil asked the cost.

"Money! *Gelt, fooloos, argent!* Look at it this way, my friend, if you can afford a car like this, you can afford to fix it up right."

"Well in that case," said Basil, "I better call my insurance agent for approval."

"Save your time, they won't pay for stone damage. And with that window you sure as hell didn't run into any bird. Then you have the door on top of that . . . No, my friend, you're stuck for it."

He removed the Kazak and left the car with the garagemen, asking that they get on it as soon as the parts came in. He would tell his father the car was in for a scheduled warranty check, he didn't want to bother him with a hardship story about a couple of rocks and a car. The car was his responsibility now. It was only a matter of money.

The following morning he telephoned his insurance agent. He described the stoning and resulting damage, making sure to couch his inquiry in a positive way, "I assume I'm covered in this situation, correct?"

"Unfortunately," replied the agent, "your damage is noncompensable. Is your policy handy?"

"No, it isn't. But go ahead, you can tell me."

"Well, I refer you to Exclusion C, page three of the policy, under 'Exclusions — War, Rebellion, or Riot or Civil Insurrection'. Stone throwing is a form of civil insurrection. The courts have invariably so ruled, it's a well established principle of law. Stop in and I can show you some citations on the issue. Or, if you'd like, I can mail them out to you."

"Thank you, but that won't be necessary. I'll take your word for it."

He spent the greater part of his first day at work getting familiarized with the Authority's current and past projects. Olga had assigned the task to Ulrich Fesser, perhaps because of his age and respectability. Fesser was the kind who always wore a tie — except when bathing or sleeping. Possessed of a Teutonic exactitude, he took seriously his delegated obligation, explaining each project to his new charge in minute and tedious detail.

Everyone, save Ben-Judah, broke for lunch at the little Palestinian cafe across the street. It was at lunch that the others made their attempts to feel out the newcomer, "So you studied at Brandeis? . . . Did your practical experience include interior decoration? . . . What do you think of public architecture?" Apparently they wanted a resume, and he obliged them, colleagues had a right to consider and judge also. As they judged him, so did he them. As a group they seemed to get along well enough, no particular disagreement surfacing during this first sitting. He suspected it had been organized as a get-acquainted opportunity, for his sake as well as theirs. In any case, opposite him, at the other end of the table, sat Olga, cigarette and hand inseparable. No doubt she was the benign influence behind the gathering. While the others questioned him, she presided without comment, midwifing his acceptance.

9

Olga had asked him to remain after the others had left, she wanted to speak with him. Carrying on a conversation in the partition that enclosed her office was like trying to converse in the reading room of a library — impossible except in a whisper. He wondered what was on her mind. Not his work, she had expressed satisfaction with that too often in the two weeks he had been on the job. It was trivial, but his occasional late arrivals and early departures might have irritated his colleagues. Perhaps one of them had complained. And in such matters the complaint would not be to him but over him. He thought of Ben-Judah but decided it was out of character. He wasn't the type to complain to a woman, to a woman he obviously resented. Also, he was too direct. Anybody or anything bothering him would hear about it, unequivocally. So far he had given no particular indication of animosity. Cool, yes. But that was to be expected between persons so disparate in outlook. Correct might better describe the relationship, professionally correct.

Being without a car, he had been walking to work. He had told the others it was in the garage, but had not said for what. At this stage the incident was likely to expose him to loss of face. Although they were colleagues, they were still strangers. One was advised not to be too free in admitting one's foibles. In a crisis they had a way of returning to haunt one, becoming automatic justification for any vulgar prejudice. Leaving before quitting time was a habit too long indulged for him to abandon now. Since most of his work was done independently of others, he saw no reason to hang about until everybody made ready to leave. When he worked with Shames he was accustomed to taking off afternoons whenever it suited his pleasure. Bureaucracy was like the military, morale was essential to its functioning. His actions, autonomous as they were, could be construed as a challenge to group discipline and thus detrimental to morale.

Orlit Dalchon was the last to leave. She bid him a good evening as he bent over his drawing board pretending to pore over a blueprint. The sound of her descent merged into Olga's booted tattoo on the terrazzo floor. Turning to face her, he saw that she had already drawn up a stool.

"You will excuse the imposition, but I had to speak to you in confidence. I will come right to the point, I have a proposition for you. I believe you are the man for it. Are you familiar with Ha'itzer Bnai Azadoi Beshallim?"

"Sounds like some kind of Orthodox organization . . . no, I don't think I ever heard of it."

"Right, but now I'm telling you. It is an association of Orthodox rabbis, Talmudic scholars from the yeshivas and other overly devout Jews who are very strong on nationalism and history. It is a very fast-growing group and also very influential with the radical settlers. But I'm not taking your time because I want to give you a lecture on these people.

It's this I want to talk to you about." She flicked open a primitive flyer. He saw the boldly printed heading — 'PRIZE - 10,000 DOLLARS'. "Here, read this," she said, "then we can discuss it." It was a competition open to all Israeli architects and architectural students for the design of a prototype of the Third Temple. The prize for the winning design was ten thousand dollars. The design would be used in a worldwide campaign to promote the temple's construction. Entries would be judged by a panel of thirty, including members of the offering organization, distinguished architects, members of the Knesset, rabbis, historians and archeologists. He shook his head and handed the flyer back to Olga who responded with a "Well . . .?"

"You're not suggesting this for *me?,*" he exclaimed, pointing a finger at himself for emphasis.

"Certainly! Why not? I've seen your work, this would be a mere exercise for your talents. You are bored here, you need something to stimulate your ambition and make your professional life more interesting. And if the money isn't that alluring, think of the notoriety. And don't tell me you don't need that!"

"But these people are crazy. ' . . . thirty distinguished architects, MKs, rabbis, archeologists'. This country has archeologists in the hundreds of thousands. Every time someone stubs his toe on a stone it has historic consequences. This is a real bootstrap operation. I'll give them a prize . . . for chutzpah! Do you seriously believe I would have a chance with these people? I don't even wear a yarmulke. Give this to Ben-Judah, he'd be their boy."

"I will let you in on a secret . . . He's already entered."

"Oh, oh, the plot does thicken. I hope you're not setting up a grudge match. These intramural rivalries can be sticky . . ."

"What's wrong with a little rivalry? Come now my friend, you are not going to tell me that you didn't get where you are by not being competitive. Competition, the

126

Americans swear by it, though they honor it more in the breach. I ask you, what is wrong with the two 'Americans' squaring off in an honest to goodness competition with . . . how do you say it . . . the best man winning?"

'Olga, you've given me all the wrong reasons, now let me give you the right reasons . . . Suppose I enter this contest and the best man does not win? And from the make-up of this thing that is a very likely result . . . Wouldn't that be worse than my not entering at all?"

"No, I do not agree. The rules state that the top ten runners-up will have their designs published. I take that as assurance against the best man losing. There is no chance of your being out of that top ten unless you could point to evidence of a conspiracy against you and yet, you offer no evidence other than your secular status, which happens, as you well know, to be the majority in this country." Olga paused briefly before resuming, "I confess I would not want Ben-Judah to win. I won't pretend to deny that. I must tell you that if it were not for my position here, I would enter the competition myself to prevent him from winning. Then we could see what system is truly better, the Russian or the American!" She laughed heartily, then quickly becoming serious again, asked, "Now don't you think that I as a Russian and a woman, might have biological attributes that would prove persuasive even against an American? That is unless the jury is made up of a bunch of Orthodox patriarchs who still insist a woman's place is at the foot of the bed. But I believe they have better sense than that. I would put my trust in the memory of Golda Meir and the fact that this is an international appeal. So naturally those thirty or so men would want to show themselves in a progressive and popular light, worthy of respect. Or don't you agree?"

She was right. The rules seemed to guard against his main suspicion — that the competition was just an in-house game rigged for one of the ultranationalists' fair-bearded boys. There *was* a chance for an outsider, an outside chance, but a chance nevertheless. "And while we are in the process of adding up persuasive biographical attributes, we should not slight your own. Having studied and been employed with the Samuel Shames Company would, I am sure, carry great weight with the judges. Then there is always the physical. For promotional purposes they could do worse . . . Yes, in a way, you are right. You *are* acting as my champion. But I would not be so crass to insult you by using you for purely selfish reasons. I sincerely believe that for you this is an opportunity, an opportunity to advance your career in this country should you win. And even if you lose you shall finish in the top ten. No money, but reasonable notoriety. I am not a gambler, but I have a feeling, based on the best information — my own appreciation of your ability — that if you give it your all you will win. And I do not say this as a stimulant to your pride. I would never say this if it were not true. That would be a grave violation of our professional sense of honor. And even against my enemies I do not compromise that!"

"But what about the political ramifications of this competition?," he asked, still unconvinced of the merits of her proposal. "Where do they propose to build this temple? I wouldn't want to be part of any harebrained scheme . . ."

"What do you care for that? Do you think this band of rabbinical rabble could ever erect something so great as a temple — the *Third* Temple? I can guarantee you they will never lay one stone! No, that is not your concern. You are a professional. Leave them the politicking and fundraising. Your job is done when you deliver your idea, the design. Everyone understands that . . . So what do you think? Does what I say make sense to you? Naturally, should you decline, nothing would affect the mutual professional respect between us."

"You know, Olga, did you ever have any training as a salesperson . . . or don't they have those things in the Soviet Union?"

"No, I suppose it's just the Jew in me!," she exclaimed, again laughing heartily, swinging out her hand and poking his shoulder. He found himself smiling also, amused by her humor, one more reason not to underestimate her. "Listen my friend, do not feel obligated to decide now. How much time do you need? One, two days? I give them to you. But now you poor man, you must be hungry. I have swallowed your dinner. Let me make amends by taking you to the best Russian restaurant in Jerusalem, the Samovar. A good bowl of borscht will appease any hunger."

The offer was tempting but tonight his father was having Ayesha prepare a feast. A business friend of his father and his wife were coming to dinner, and he was expected to be present. Dinner would have to be some other time. Perhaps "after you have won the competition" was the way she put it.

Later that night, after the company had left, he broached the subject to his father. He wanted the advice of someone certain to have his best interest at heart. As expected, his father was for it, believing with Olga that only good could come of it. The problem posed by the entry of Ben-Judah he dismissed as no problem at all, provided of course, the rivalry remained friendly. And should he be lucky enough to win, the prize money was nothing to sneer at. In building a career one should not be too proud.

He hadn't told his father about the dispute with Shames, he knew who would be blamed for the resulting hard feelings. He imagined his father telling him you don't spit in the face of a man who has been good to you, that he should have been more circumspect about revealing his politics, that he was foolish to go shooting his mouth off half-cocked without expecting to pay a price. And his father would have been right. He recalled a piece of advice his father had given him — avoid putting things in writing. In a crisis, oral statements could be explained away; in extreme situations denied. Not so the written. He thought back to that day. He was still unsure of what exactly happened. Whether he had been suckered into expressing his opinions or whether, intent upon making an impression, he was hoist on his own petard? Either way she was not to blame. She had only done her job, done it well. Controversy was the bread and butter of the interview form. The experience was a fluke, unlikely to occur again. In the future he envisioned himself limited to the expression of professional opinion, ergo socially respectable opinion. He would only be submitting drawings now. Drawings were wordless, except in the pretense of critics given to finding statements in an architect's conception. He didn't foresee any of the big architectural concerns, such as Mordechai Levi Associates, entering. Risking reputation for small reward was not to their advantage. Anything. less than unqualified victory would be humiliation. Anonymity was an advantage, he had only himself and Olga to answer to. He would enter.

10

Basil arrived at the Authority as the morning coffee break was underway. After waiting three weeks for a replacement windshield he had finally been reunited with his car. Having said his "Good morning" he noticed something lacking in the group's response to the salutation. Their faces evidenced concern, for what he had no idea. The possibilities were endless. He imagined a few — a bomb had exploded with great loss of life, terrorists were holding people hostage (he hoped it was the prime minister and his cabinet), one of Israel's "elder statesmen" had given up the ghost (they would be the type to make a show of mourning). Apparently, the topic under discussion had been suspended when he entered in order that he might be properly seized of the seriousness of the concern. He looked at them, they looked at him. Suspecting a joke, he refused to be stampeded into a conventional reaction. Perhaps they were dramatizing his early arrival with a bit of cooperative theatre. Whatever they were up to did not seem to hold the promise of much humor, none of them had shown any particular gift for comedy and it was too early in the morning to laugh. Ignoring the group's expectation, he threw his briefcase on the desk. Just then he heard Shmooel Glazer call out, "Basil, haven't you heard the news?"

"What news, who died now?" he responded testily, turning to face the others who were looking at him as if he were a bit daft.

"Taufik Taufik! He was assassinated this morning near his village!"

"By a remote control bomb," elaborated Orlit Dalchon. "I heard it was an RPG," said Ben-Judah.

"Is that all?," he exclaimed, mockingly contemptuous. "From the expressions on your faces I thought it was something important. Why all the fuss? He was a Shiite. I'm sure he's happy in Shiite heaven now."

"You've been out of the country too long," remonstrated Glazer. "This thing could have serious consequences. Taufik was an adversary, but an adversary we could do business with. Under him that whole area's been quiet. He was able to keep out the terrorists while controlling his own hotheads. His removal is a challenge to the live-and-let live policy that's kept the peace there."

"It was only temporary, we knew that," asserted Ben-Judah, rising from his chair to claim the floor. "Taufik was only a stopgap. He could no more be trusted than any Arab . . . especially the Shiites, they'd cut our throats if they could. I know, I've been in those villages. You *never*

131

turn your back on those people, never, men *and* women! We may have to teach them a lesson again, the same one we gave Taufik. These people are a little thick, the guy that replaces him may not learn so fast. In that case we'll have to smash them . . . but this time with iron knuckles in our fists, no more of this powder-puff stuff. We're going to have to reclaim that area sooner or later, and I say the sooner the better because those people live and pray for the day they'll be able to destroy us. The next time we go in there, we go to stay and we do it our way!"

Ben-Judah's fist thumped the desktop, rattling his cup of coffee and causing some of it to spill over the rim.

"You call that a solution? Another war? More killing? What can it get us?" Ulrich Fesser was shaking his finger at Ben-Judah, agitated by the latter's program to the point of proposing his own, "No, the best hope for peace is to have good relations with all the Arab communities. This practice of enlisting protégés from among them is worse than mischievous, it is delusion! When the dogs tire of eating each other where do you think they will go? Your policy will eventually unite all the Shia against us, not merely the few warlords we contend with today."

"The Shia unite?," retorted Ben-Judah rhetorically, "before that happens their twelfth imam should come."

"Yes, you are confident, like some of the others whose bill we are still paying. What do you think the Americans, who are holding the mortgage on this country, will say to your plan? They will only put up with so much, you know."

"The Americans will pay for anything that involves the survival of Israel, anything," argued Ben-Judah, adopting a more rational tone. "Between us and the Arabs they made a calculated choice. Not becauuse they like us, but because they need us. *We* are the reliable ally. When they wanted Syria brought to heel, who did the job? So don't let a few more billions of dollar indebtedness seduce you into believing that support is going to be compromised, because in the final analysis that money is peanuts compared to the money we are saving them. Now if you dispute that, you know very little about geopolitics, and less about American politics. And if anyone here is qualified to speak on *that* subject, it is *this* man."

"America, Lebanon, this man gets around," remarked Basil, not letting Ben-Judah's extremism pass without comment. "Has he never considered entering politics, where he could give the country the benefit of his expertise? Of course, it must be at the top, a policy-making position, preferably prime minister."

"As a Jew in the Jewish state the ambition is not only reasonable but realizable," declared Ben-Judah. "But for the present I believe . . ."

"This 'man' prime minister? Before that happens the Messiah should come!" At the sound of Olga's voice Basil turned to see her holding a large blueprint. Apparently, she had been listening. Striding in front of a glowering Ben-Judah and exhibiting her usual disdain for his existence, she made for Fesser's desk where she unrolled the print and began questioning him on its contents. Her remark and no-nonsense manner of interruption effectively suspended the discussion. Later at lunch in the nearby Palestinian cafe, the topic suggested by Ben-Judah reemerged to vex the discussants — who needed whom more, America or Israel? The pair had developed symbiosis to a degree where separating the complex of relationships constituting the alliance required both dogged analysis and inspired wizardry. What began as a sudden impulse of two desperate lovers finding one another, had over the years matured into a typical marriage of convenience with the less than equal party experiencing the usual insecurities. This explained, or, as some maintained, justified, the occasional bouts of bitchiness from the weaker of the two. Everyone could agree on the necessity of the relationship. The dispute was over the rules governing it.

The increased use of words like "exploitation, abuse, domination, etc." by the inferior party to describe the working of the alliance, was a sign that cracks were developing in the hitherto unbroken facade of love. Marriage counsellors had a stock remedy for such tensions — "talk it out". Presumably, states operated similarly, using the normal channels of diplomacy, particularly states as closely allied as the United States and Israel. Nevertheless, the world was not static, and nations like spouses, outgrew their need for each other. Yet, no one foresaw the spats turning into a split. Thinking the unthinkable was something Jews were conditioned to do as a matter of course. But Israel without America? That was truly unthinkable. Fortunately, nothing so catastrophic was at stake, only that matters previously accepted on faith were now subject to question. Inflation, taxes, restrictions, cutbacks, all the returning chickens of incontinent governmental policies, were provoking the nation's collective outrage. People searched for a cause or culprit. The size and generosity of the United States made it a convenient scapegoat. People were loath to accept blame when another was so willing to assume it.

11

Six-thirty in the morning was an infernal time to be up and out on the street, but he was told to be early if he wanted a choice among the Arabs who gathered at Suleiman Square in the Old City, the center of the city's unofficial labor market for Arab workers, men outside the economy and Histradut union labor lists. The place was called, by both Israeli and Palestinian, the "slave market". It was one of those overdramatic designations the effect of which was more spiritual than actual, because the men who gathered there in the relative cool of the Jerusalem morning were certainly not slaves. They were men seeking wages for their labor, so that they might feed themselves and their families, and perhaps provide the small amenities that made existence more than subsistence. As such they were not much different than the millions of other wretches who in exchange for their daily bread, had nothing to offer other than strong backs and calloused hands. The mass of these day laborers originated from outside Jerusalem, from the impoverished villages of the hinterland. The city's Palestinian population was both too prosperous and small in size to provide cheap, human surplus in the abundance demanded by the metropolis' economic appetite. Thus, the majority selling their labor in Suleiman Square came from nearby towns and villages or even beyond, over the "Green Line", the line that for purposes of administration separated Israel proper from the territories, the so-called West Bank, or as the official nomenclature of the state has long had it, "Judea and Samaria". One of the administrative rules governing those Arabs who came from the other side of the Green Line was that after the day's work was done they should not tarry, but must return back beyond the Line, there to spend the night. So they arrived and left the city by truck, car, taxi and bus, spending a great part of their earnings, as well as hours of the day, in conformity to the rule. The rule was a harsh one but if complaint was made against it, the complaint was made in vain. What was one more hardship in a life of hardship? Better work under difficult conditions than no work at all. Such was the lot of those souls who placed their faith in the strength of their backs and the will of Allah. For if ever they believed in anything else, it was obvious it had long since failed them.

He came into the square as twenty to thirty Arabs were

debouching from a two and a half ton flatbed truck. No sooner had they hit ground than some converged on the driver's side of his car, vociferously hawking themselves and their skills in a babble of Arabic and Hebrew — "*Ya bey*! *Ya bey*! Here is your man! How many? How many? Take us! We are ready to go with you to the ends of the earth!" The other side of the car was as quickly besieged by a group pulling on the locked doors. He found himself pushing strenuously just to get out of the car. "*Sadati*! (gentlemen) Please!," he cried as the Arabs surged about him, grabbing at his arms and hands for attention. "Animals! Give the man his space!," shouted a dignified looking, kaffiyeh-clad Arab to his right. The remonstrance must have shamed the crowd because it backed off and the importuning hands gripping his arms released their hold. He had only to say, "I need a stonecutter . . . " and immediately two men pushed through the throng offering themselves. "No, no," he explained, waving his hand disapprovingly, "Look!" Unrolling a sketch, he held it out between his hands, raising it to give the Arabs a better look at the designs for the window mullions and fret patterns. As the Arabs became aware of what was demanded of them, they fell into an awed silence. The pair of pushy stonemasons could only shake their heads in negative resignation. "I am looking for a skilled stonemason, somebody who can execute these designs. I was told I might be able to find one here."

"Khalil Bustanji," exclaimed an Arab studying the drawings, turning and calling to a cluster of men on the opposite side of the square, ""*Ya* Khalil, *tallahoon*! (come here)."

A tall, long-shanked figure wearing a straw hat stood up and slowly advanced toward them. The pace was deliberate and unhurried, as if in contempt of the manic urgency exhibited by the others. From a distance the man's long arms ending in outsized hands resembled an anthropoid ape's. A rigid frontality of locomotion intensified the ape-like impression. As the Arab's features came into view, Basil

136

noticed the eyes, they were fixed directly upon his own, the face expressionless and devoid of conciliation. Dark, over-long hair protruding from under the hatbrim, and a trim, Islamic beard increased the impression of hostility. Standing in the glaring light of the square, surrounded by Arabs, he realized his vulnerability. The terrorist profile — was there such a thing? His better sense dismissed the concept as crassly absurd. Yet the fear center of his brain was spewing all manner of scenarios, some clearly unthinkable, the kind of thoughts one had prior to an imaginary crisis and after its routine resolution, felt shame in entertaining. Nevertheless, he braced himself for the unknown.

What followed was anticlimactic. The two Arabs, the summoner and the summoned, conversed briefly before examining the sketches together. "I can do this," said the tall Arab, looking directly at Basil. "That's fine. You see I'm an architect for JERRA, the name is Primchek," said Basil, extending his hand. The Arab flicked his left hand disdain-fully, walked to the car's passenger side and stood waiting for the door to be unlocked. Just then a contractor's truck drove into the square followed by two automobiles. With a shout the crowd of laborers rushed to surround the new prospects, repeating the same expressions of availability. It was his first experience hiring from the slave market and he had the neophyte's nervousness. But now it was done and he had his man — at least he hoped he had his man. So many of them, whether from machismo or desperation, were puffers. When it came time to show their mettle, they didn't have it. But this one was different, seeming not to care whether he got the job or not. He hadn't said a word since getting in the car — but he couldn't be blamed for that, facing the daily prospect of the slave market was not some-thing to bring out a person's amiable side. He appeared to be about his own age, probably a family man, most of them were. From the few words said he assumed the fellow spoke Hebrew. Many Arabs spoke it, especially the workers.

137

"Uh . . . Khalil, my Arabic is not very good while you seem to speak Hebrew well."

"Yes . . . you speak English don't you?"

"Yes, I speak English." The question puzzled him. Perhaps the fellow wanted to practice his English.

"Well use it with me, I'll work better."

"Of course, as you prefer," replied Basil, switching to English. "By the way, your compensation, how do you figure it, by the job or by the hour?"

"By the hour, naturally. You take the risk. The wage I leave to you, an honest Yahoodi. Naturally, I quit if the offer is inadequate."

They arrived at the job site, located in one of the newer areas of Jerusalem, an area dominated by residential flats and apartments. A quartet of Arab workmen were in the process of cutting and laying the Jerusalem stone that would comprise the clinic's walls. Basil led his newfound hireling to the small, makeshift shelter where the harder, decorative stone would be cut, meanwhile relating the special responsibility he carried for the successful completion of the building, from a technical and personal perspective. The idea he said, was not to imitate the past, that was unfeasible. Nor was it always desirable. His objective was more modest, a reflection of the past with perhaps an illumination of the future. But that was the limit of his optimism. Deeper changes would necessitate revolution, yet he knew of no modern revolution whose architecture improved upon the past. In fact, it was invariably inferior to the preceding era's, to a degree where architecture was best served by application to preservation and restoration. Thus, a skill of the past — stonecutting — was essential in fashioning the motifs that distinguished the architecture of the past. It was costly, but he was committed to its use, even if his promotion of it smacked of evangelism.

"Better fewer good buildings than more bad buildings," he declared while the Arab listened at his side. "This city is too historic, too common to too many to abide architectural shortcutting, another reason why I insist we employ these old motifs. Of course, I know it's only a small building. Compared to the megaliths around it, it may not cut much of a figure. And in the final analysis it may prove insignificant. But it's mine and I want it to be the best that it can be given the resources at hand. That's the standard I set myself and the one I assume you work by too."

The Arab made no reply. Basil gave him copies of the sketches and suggested he begin by executing one of the simpler designs. He would return tomorrow to inspect the workmanship. "I hope you can do the job. I'm counting on your skill." The Arab thrust out his hand, flexed fingers broadly splayed. The two shook hands, a handshake of agreement and conciliation.

That evening he noticed a car with two men parked in front of his house. Coming closer, he recognized them as his reserve unit mates. Although the scheduled night for the reserve meeting was two days hence, they were clearly waiting for him. He cursed as he pulled into the curb behind them. The driver, Amon Amitai, outfitted for combat, jumped from the car. "C'mon, c'mon, let's go!," he cried impatiently, "Where in the hell have you been? We called your office and they said you had left a half hour ago. We've been waiting here over ten minutes."

"Maybe I stopped to *shit* somewhere, you bastard!," exclaimed Basil, half in jest, half in anger. "Don't tell me! Don't tell me! They made a war for us!"

"I'm not telling you anything. All I know is they announced an alert and we have to report in." Amon pushed Basil toward the door of his house. "C'mon, get in there and get your gear on. We still have to pick up Yossi. Hurry! There'll be hell to pay if we're late for an alert!"

Basil raced up to the door, unlocking it and bolting inside, making for his bedroom where a closet held military gear. The compulsive urgency of the situation infuriated him. Still more infuriating was the reason for the urgency. Rushing to make an appointment with death or dismemberment was insanity. They couldn't wait to die at a walk, or even a trot, they had to be stampeded like Gadarene swine. Yet he hurried, if only because of a common obligation to Amon and the two others of his assigned reserve group. The war could be fought without him and lost too. Someday, he projected, that was going to happen anyway, bringing the madness to a screeching halt. Cursing, he threw off his pants, whipping on heavy khakis, pulling and pushing his feet into desert boots. His pack on his shoulder, he shuffled out of the room. Leaving a note for his father was unnecessary, one look at the room and he'd know. But whether a raid, preemptive strike, or full scale war, that would not be known until the morrow. Nor would he himself know until so informed by his commanders; and even they didn't know, they just followed orders too. The Arabs in the slave market, that was only ten hours ago. Now he was rushing out, perhaps to kill some of them. He was lucky, they should have torn him apart, no questions asked. With a single motion he opened and closed the door behind him. Amon was studying his wristwatch as he came stumbling out, laces dragging, battle pack hanging from his shoulder.

"Two minutes and ten seconds!," yelled Amon, looking up and seeing Basil heading for his Toyota, "Hey! We all go in my car!"

"I'm checking to make sure my car is locked, schmuck. Do you mind?," Basil yelled back.

"No, I don't mind. But that son of a whore CO will. C'mon!

He dropped his battle pack into the open trunk, jumped into the back of Amon's car and applied himself to the laces of his boots, grunting a response to the greeting from the car's other occupant, Bernard Ledderman. Ledderman, intimidated by the angry outburst, spoke tentatively, "We're sorry to rush you like this, Basil . . . We tried to reach you at your office . . . you had gone. You know how they are about late arrivals."

"No, how are they?" he snapped, temporarily interrupting his bootlacing to angrily eye the now even more intimidated Ledderman, "What do you think they'll do, send you to Auschwitz? You should have been so lucky. The worst that monkey can do is holler at you. And if he does, you can blame it all on me. Tell him I had to take a shit!"

The simian reference was to the unit's commanding officer, Dr. Julius Klug, a dentist who operated a stable of sub-dentists located in downtown central Jerusalem. Basil hated him from that first reserve meeting when Klug had drilled them like a band of recruits, his stentorian "One-two! One-two!" sounding over the clop clop of feet surly from abuse. He had left the formation shortly after the drill began, walked to the back of the compound and leaned against a tank. Later, confronted by Klug, he had put his face close to the doctor's and said, "My feet hurt, an old football injury from the States." Klug had kept his distance since then, he knew better than to pull rank on certain men, head-on confrontation with such types could be counterproductive, grudges provoked in this manner might resurface at the most unfortunate time. Discipline was the military's method to control this element. But dealing with part-time soldiers, the so-called citizen army that at full mobilization constituted the majority of Israeli forces, was a tricky business. Men who had left the military kennel were often unwilling to resubmit themselves to a dog's life of sitting and barking on command. So for motivation camaraderie was cultivated, the one for all and all for one of the game of war. Soldiers of fortune and professional soldiers both recognized its seduction, it was the love which passeth all understanding.

They picked up the fourth man, Yossi Etzion, at his jewelry shop on Balcha Street. He had been waiting ever since receiving the call for the alert. "Where have you been?," he asked, his face showing his perturbation, "I've been . . ."

"Alright, alright," said Amon cutting him off. "Don't aggravate a bad situation. You've 'been waiting for over an hour', I know. We had a communication gap. Just get in and save the zeal for the battle."

Outside the compound the parking lot was full and Amon had to drive to the far end to find a space. It was obvious they were late, the concern now was not to be latest. The four men hurriedly threw their packs on their backs and made for the gate on the run. A taxi drove up discharging a corpulent reserve soldier puffing from anxiety and haste. At the gate the men were stopped by a lieutenant and sergeant. Pieces of yellow stickum paper were slapped on their left breasts. "Orders! Leave it on," commanded the lieutenant perfunctorily. The yellow papers showed their arrival times, in large red numerals. Basil signed in, then joined the ranks of the 400 or so others standing about the assembly hall. He saw Klug seated on the dais in conversation with an officer in busdriver greens, the dress uniform of the United States Army. The gold braid on the bill of the American's cap, the stuff the Americans called "chickenshit", indicated officer status. He had difficulty placing the American in the context. Was he a liaison officer for a joint assault on a terrorist redoubt? An observer? The Americans had never participated in any of the actions Israel had staged — at least as far as he knew. Being seen with the Israelis in any capacity, observer or otherwise, would compromise the charade they maintained for the benefit of their Arab allies, the ones they styled "moderates". The object was not to hand Arab "radicals" propaganda coups on a platter. It was very Victorian but appearances had to be maintained. Besides, Israel didn't want the Americans looking over its shoulder anyway, there were things they were better off not knowing. A lieutenant called the company to attention, Captain Klug was going to address them.

"At ease, men! I have good news . . . and bad news. The good news is that you are not here this evening to be sent into battle, but to prepare for the battle of the future. Some of you, by no means the majority, have been evidencing a cavalier attitude about your military obligation, an obligation that extends not only to the nation, but to your own lives and of course, the security of your loved ones at home. In other words, when the battle is joined we want you back — *alive*. That is *our* obligation to you and to your family — to produce the finest fighting machine we can given the constraint of time. Because we can never train enough to fight a war. That is why I, with the approval of Colonel Shor sitting here, our regimental commander, called this alert today. The object was to test your response time. The bad news is . . . that your response was *too slow*. Men!, let me remind you, the race is to the swift. None of us wants to see Eretz Israel become a battleground. We must carry the fight to the enemy as always. We have been able to do that because we have always been more ready than he. I do not believe that I am giving away any military secrets by stating that sometimes the enemy was asleep at his post, permitting us to render him a knockout blow very early in the battle, or war, as the case may be. But today we face an enemy ever more fanatic, ever more determined . . . a ruthless enemy not stayed from its proclaimed goal — the annihilation of the State of Israel and its Jewish peoplehood. Now I don't know about you, but I do not want that on my conscience, never! And so this group is going to be the best damned unit as well as the best prepared unit in the whole of the IDF Reserves, ready to fight or ready to support depending on our mission and the orders of battle. That much I can pledge to you. Those of you who have served with me and under Colonel Shor here during the last several years, know we keep our word. So we expect you to keep your word with us. That should explain why most of you are wearing the blue tags. You're OK, you responded within

143

the allotted time. But you men wearing yellow tags, you're not OK, you're late. In an actual combat situation the company may have to depart without you. And the truth is, you men who came late, that some of you have essential duties, important duties, and without you we would take many more casualties than we would at full strength. Think about that, you men wearing the yellow tags, think about that the next time there is an alert and you take your time reporting in . . . that buddy of yours, a lot of buddies may not make it home because you took your time, too much time.

"Now this could be either good or bad news . . . I can't say whether we will call more of these alerts, that's up to all of you, your willingness to come up to standard. Some of you who are serious about this business should do some leaning on those who are not taking their obligations seriously. Sometimes a little friendly persuasion can work wonders. So now I want all you men who arrived on time and on the ready, those wearing blue tags, to look around the area and see for yourselves the guilty parties. And if need be, you have my permission to give them a piece of your mind."

The invitation evoked a grumbling rumble from the assembled men, a mix of recriminations, curses and complaints. Klug's speech, artfully invidious, was having the intended effect. Some of the men were fixing Basil with appropriately disapproving looks. He stared back at them, his face a blasé mask concealing the contempt and disgust within. Excepting the few who looked around out of curiosity, too embarrassed and timid to maintain eye contact, they were putty in Klug's hands. He wanted to thumb his nose at the ones gesturing at him, pointing to their blue tags on puffed-out chests. But suddenly his hand was in the air and he was calling up to the dais to Klug, now smugly surveying the scene his threat had set into motion.

"Dr. Klug!" Klug's eyes searched the area for the

offending sound before finding their man. "Dr. Klug!," repeated Basil seeing he had the officer's attention, "Some of us are not blessed with stationary jobs where we can always be reached during the day. Also I doubt whether many will sit by their telephones to wait for your call. So why doesn't the government issue us those beepers carried by doctors and other hospital workers?"

"Don't think we haven't thought of that, Primchek. But you're probably the type to forget to wear the thing. We'd probably end up planting an electrode in your head and even then we wouldn't be sure of a response."

A chorus of hoots, whistles, and jeers erupted from the loyalists among the assemblage. Their captain had blown the shirker away — and with the shirker's own gun. Klug magnanimously cut off the claque of jeers, "Alright men, we've had our little laugh over Corporal Primchek's attempt to be funny. Now let's get serious again. We have with us tonight . . .," Klug proceeded to introduce the American guest, a lieutenant colonel in US military intelligence, who, because of the alleged sensitive nature of the alliance, had to remain nameless. Those not understanding English were advised to get a summation of the colonel's remarks from their English-speaking friends.

Following along the lines of Klug, the American gave a military homily on the importance of speed and surprise in military strategy, citing as examples the Hitlerian blitzkrieg, Pearl Harbor, communist North Korea's attack on the South, and, as a nod to the home team, the Six Day War of '67. The man's drawl placed him from the American Southland, that great breeding ground of US militarists and patriots. The name of General Stonewall Jackson was invoked for an American Civil War strategic recipe for victory — "the ones that get there fustest with the mostest". Summing up, he speculated that the next war, the war of atomic missiles, would be decided in minutes, and that the heroes of the future may very well be the men in deep bunkers who would see the war only through images projected by satellite. Americans were notorious for optimistic projections on how they were going to stun the Bolshevik arsenal before it got off the ground. It was typical of the military mind that they should be concerned about heroics in a war where mere survival would be heroic.

After a few words from Colonel Shor, the regimental commander, to the effect that they should "try harder," the practice alert was over. Upon the command "Company dismissed!", there was a rush for the exits. Men making haste for the evening meal and, incidentally, to report the good news of no-war-now to the folks at home. Basil and Amon joined the columns of exiting men flowing through the doors. The hubbub of voices expressing a collective sense of relief discouraged conversation.

"You got shot down in there," said Amon outside.

"Yeah, I'm crushed," replied Basil.

"You must have impressed Julius. You're only here for four or five times and already he knows your name. You should be flattered."

"Who said I wasn't? Is that how he gets all those dogs to howl in unison? I didn't see any bones being thrown their way."

"He didn't have to, he threw you." Amon reached over and tore the yellow tag from Basil's chest, "Here, something you forgot, you won't need this anymore," he said, dropping it on the asphalt.

Conversation on the ride back was dominated by one topic — the threat of more practice alerts. When would the most likely time be for Dr. Klug to call another, limited as he was by the "cry wolf" phenomenon? Amon, who had the longest tenure with Klug, thought he was too clever to alienate his charges by simple harassment, which a policy of successive practice alerts implied. The alert was called to shake up the company. Inviting the regimental commander as a spectator suggested a desire to impress the brass. Calling

146

further practice alerts would be counterproductive — it would call into question Klug's effectiveness as a commander. "That was it for practice alerts for awhile," Amon concluded, "the next one would probably be for real."

The logic of Amon's reasoning made him feel better. Military games on a regular basis was a prospect he found intolerable. He was already entertaining visions of defiance by ignoring the practice alerts, the kind of defiance one imagines when backed into a corner on an issue. Now he could put aside such projections and concentrate on the Third Temple, the deadline for the submission of entries was only a week away. The drawings and specifications were complete, neatly set down on sheets of architectural paper, ready for the application of water color for shading and highlighting. He had surprised himself. What began on a frivolous note had developed into a cause, its momentum carrying him from inspiration to inspiration. For a joke it was a yeoman effort. He considered previewing the designs for Olga, but then decided against it. A preview might raise her expectations unduly, she might be as impressed with his conceptions as he was. He had an obligation to protect her from indiscretion, she was too involved for her own good. It was best to treat the matter as originally conceived — an architectural joke.

His first priority the next morning was to go to the job and check the Arab's level of competence. He was disturbed by the prospect of having to reject the Arab's work. The problem was not that there might be a scene — only the other Arab workers would be present — it went deeper, going to his sympathy with the man's need to be recognized in his craft. Offering him a job with the others, cutting and laying stone for the walls, would pacify him. While he might grumble, he'd take it. Still, telling a man he wasn't up to par in his profession was troubling.

When he pulled up one of the Arabs was mixing cement in the long space between buildings. He exchanged greetings and walked the plank serving as a temporary bridge over the front entrance. The one he wanted to see was in the corner of the clinic's future courtyard leaning over a rough wooden table. A dusty sheet suspended by four wooden poles was overhead, providing a makeshift sun shield. "Hello!" he called. The Arab turned, setting down his hammer and chisel, "Hello Yahoodi, I've been waiting for you." He moved aside to reveal a piece of stone upon which twisting leaves, doves and a representation of a building appeared in relief. Basil approached the stone, rubbing his fingers over the unfinished figures, as if doubting his eyes.

"This is wonderful," he exclaimed, "wonderful. The effect . . . it's almost Italian."

"Falestinian, Yahoodi, Falestinian. Italians were our teachers. Baalbek, the greatest temple of the ancient world, our ancestors built it . . . under Roman supervision of course. Compared to it, your Second Temple is an overbuilt stable."

"What do you know of the Second Temple?," responded Basil, piqued by the irony of the Arab's statement.

"No more and no less than you. It is a stone pile before which strange men of a strange sect pray to a strange god. That's g dash d. Because of it your people laid waste to half of Jerusalem."

"Come now, Khalil, don't exaggerate. Only in art is there a license to exaggerate. But mind you, I am against the destruction. That was more than twenty years ago, when the two of us were mere boys. Now you and I can do some good. I'm very impressed, very pleased with your work. I definitely want you with me on this project."

"*Inshallah* (God willing). By the way, you are a native of this city are you not?"

"Yes, why?"

"Some of your motifs, they remind me of another

native son. Have you seen the work of Boullata?"

"No, I can't say I have."

"No matter, he is in America with our oppressors. But I don't care where one goes, he will take with him this city, this country, in his blood. He cannot avoid his origins."

"Have you ever been in America, Khalil?"

"No, the furthest I have gone is Kuwait, but that is nowhere."

"Would you want to go to America?"

"You mean the 'Great Satan'? No, Yahoodi, I value my soul. But maybe you will change my mind for me . . . at the point of a bayonet of course. This country has never been big enough for both of us. A couple years ago, when I returned from Kuwait, I thought to immigrate to Canada or Australia. I know many who have gone there, and they come back rich. You know, a polyester suit and a pair of glossy Italian shoes. But then my father died and I cannot leave the family . . . Do you think I tell you this because I seek more money?"

"No, no, I understand. I'm sorry."

"Are you? We'll see *how sorry* when we discuss compensation." The Arab picked up one of the smaller chisels from his collection and resumed laboring over the stone.

Nabbing Bustanji was a coup, a great coup. A first-rate craftsman. Bitter, but he probably had a right to be. Rather a contrast to the Arab who used to work for his father, old Bakr, always one for a story or parable. He used to look forward to sitting down with the old fellow after the baking of the morning bread. It was then that Bakr would relate tales from a rustic Arabian Nights, tales of wolves, camels, vipers, of warfare between bedouin tribes and merchant princes. By conventional standards uneducated, he could call up a proverb or saying to cover any situation. Two generations separated them, Bakr and Bustanji. The latter was obviously educated — a few minutes of conversation demonstrated that — perhaps even a product of the Israeli school system, as the fluent Hebrew might indicate, Palestinians were big on education. Nonetheless, there were limits to a third world country's ability to absorb its graduates. And Israel, despite its mythology and disposition, was a third world country, if only because of its swallowing of two million Arabs. Digesting Arabs had always been a problem, but the '67 war made it an ulcer, their numbers acting as a brake on the nation's expansion. For the Jewish state, discrimination was both natural and necessary.

Except for Orlit working at her drawing board the outer office was empty. He saw Olga stand up behind her desk and motion to him, waving her hand in a come hither signal. "We haven't had a chance to talk for a while, how are things going?," she asked.

"Fine. I think I have my stonecutter for the clinic. I was . . ."

"Excuse me, I mean the competition. How are you progressing with it? You know the 10th is the last day to submit your entries."

"Yes, but I'm done. I can send them in tomorrow."

"Good. Send them registered. If you wish, you may bring them to me and I will send them."

"Thank you, but after all the time I've spent on them, mailing will be a pleasure."

"What do you think? I mean what is your opinion of the designs? Are you satisfied with them?"

She was like a nervous father in a hospital maternity waiting room. He wanted to say, "It's my baby, let me do the worrying," but it was her baby too — by proxy. "Well, I think they express what I intended, it's hard to say." He was being deliberately vague, trying to avoid the slightest expression of enthusiasm so as not to give her much to hang her hopes on. "From the start this was a fantastic project . . . so I let my imagination go, what else was there to go on? Almost everything we know about the Second Temple is from ancient sources. Although I gave some weight to the ritualistic elements, I avoided a slavish replication. At the same time I think my design is an improvement — as the third time around should be."

Olga leaned back, drawing on the butt between her fingers, blowing the inhaled smoke upward in a sustained stream, "I would ask you for a look before you send them in . . . but that might be bad luck."

That night he gave the drawings a final review before tubing them for a mailing, juxtaposing two views of the temple from a ground-level perspective, then studying them from a standing position. As fantasies go, they were impressive. After a two thousand year hiatus, a return to glory. He imagined his conception teeming with priests, working their mumbo-jumbo on the ragged and gullible Children of Israel. He wondered about the ideological issues — were they as tradition held, of the spirit, or were they a mask for the usual struggle for power? Had they devoted more effort to propitiating the Romans, there might be more of the Temple extant than a section of foundation wall. The first lesson from that disaster — ally with Rome, don't fight it — had been well absorbed. On the second — don't let the fanatics take power — consensus had not been reached.

On his desk were two unanswered letters from Miriam, now far ahead in the correspondence sweepstakes. She had the advantage of writing from New York. Her letters contained clippings and comments on articles from the *New York Times* and sometimes local trivia such as Shames suffering a fractured collarbone while driving his Mercedes near his ruraltanian spread.

The thought of a return to the big city still haunted him, the open door he could walk through in emergency or ennui, whichever occurred first. Obtaining employment at one of the first-line firms would be automatic, with or without Shames, who for all practical purposes, he had written off. Although he had been on the job for little more than two months, he was impatient with the process of

151

becoming established. His ambition was to be international, with offices in Jerusalem, New York, or London. He believed his appeal would lie in offering an alternative to the international style. It was unclear which was greater, the ambition or the underlying contradiction. Meanwhile, Miriam's suggestion of a rendezvous in Europe seemed a good idea.

12

He was sitting at his desk when he heard the sound of trudging feet ascending concrete. First to come into view was a short, stubby, black-coated graybeard, followed by three others similarly attired, beards vying in luxury. The identities of the visitors, looking like so many refugees from any of the many yeshivas in the city, were unfamiliar to him. The suddeness of their appearance, combined with the dark, medieval dignity of costuming, brought the office to a respectful halt. Visitations by such august and bizarre delegations were fairly unique events. He noticed that Olga, seated in her glassed-in preserve, wore a look of puzzlement on her face. The first thing that came to his mind was that this was a protest — a construction project threatening a last resting place, or perhaps noise disturbing the holy men's prayers. Yet, for protesters they were distinctly unangry. Particularly the stubby, elfish one, the apparent leader, the one waving the belted briefcase hither-thither in conversation with his colleagues. The group was looking in Ben-Judah's direction, perhaps seeing in him the one most likely to sympathize with their demands. Sensing their quandary, Ben-Judah approached the counter, asking solicitously, "May I be of assistance, good sirs?"

You are Basil Primchek?," declared the graybeard to Ben-Judah.

"No, sir," Ben-Judah pointed to Basil seated at the end of the room by the front windows, "that's Primchek." "*That's* not Primchek?" expostulated one of the visitors referring to Ben-Judah, as all eyes now turned in the direction indicated.

"Mr. Primchek!"

"Yes . . . ?," said Basil, standing up in acknowledgement.

"We would like to speak with you and your superior . . . together, if that is convenient."

Olga had come out and was standing by the door of her office. Apparently, neither she nor any of the others had the slightest inkling of what the visitors were about. Suddenly, it came to him — "Bustanji! They must have had a run-in with him on the job. He could have taunted or cursed them and then given them my name." It was stupid, but it was the kind of provocation he imagined the Arab capable of, some puerilely defiant act. He had made a mistake in being too open with him, in telling him how much he appreciated his work. He had also been too generous — "the more you gave them the more they held you in contempt." Now he was going to have to apologize. He hoped the rabbinical flying squad would not demand Bustanji's dismissal. In spite of the Arab's insolence, he was indispensable.

"I am in charge here. Come into my office," declared Olga peremptorily, striking an intimidating pose. Visibly surprised, the black-frocked men looked at one another, then back to their leader, the graybeard. It was clearly a situation they were unprepared for. Nevertheless, the graybeard obeyed, proceeding into the office and signaling his men to follow. It was an example of one of those flashes of aperçu characteristic of religious leaders at decisive moments. Basil stepped to one side to permit Olga to close the door of the now overburdened cubicle. Identifying herself, she officiously demanded the purpose of the visit.

"Madame Director, I am Rabbi Joel Hochmeister," bespoke the graybeard, "and these are my fellows from Ha'itzer Bnai Azadoi Beshallim. We have come to personally inform Mr. Primchek here that he is the first prize winner in our competition for the best design for the Third Temple!"

Saying this the rabbi turned to Basil and gripped his hand, shaking it vigorously, a ritual repeated seriatim by the other three. Olga, who had been impatiently standing by waiting for the formal pressing of hands to end, now jumped in with her own congratulations. "Listen to Olga! Listen to Olga!," she crowed exultantly, shaking her fist before his face. In contrast to his polite restraint, she looked as if she were about to break into a wild Cossack dance. "Gentlemen! Gentlemen!," she cried, "Let me tell you something about this man, I know he won't. Sometimes modesty can be a virtue but he does not know where to begin and where to end." She proceeded to relate how he had been a Shames scholar, taking his architectural studies in America, had remained briefly for a successful stint with the Shames' firm in New York, then returned to devote himself to his native city and the nation. She had never doubted that his ideas would prevail, as he brought not only the passion of the artist to his conceptions, but also the thoroughness and prudence of the scholar. In her opinion the judges could not have made a wiser choice, reinforcing their honor and authority by the decision. "Distinguished sirs, is this man not a Jew we can be proud of?" She was pouring it on, but he took it gracefully. After all, she was repaying a debt. The hyperbole was embarrassing but it was nonetheless appreciated, it was always better to have others tooting one's horn.

"An inspiring background indeed, Madame Director,"

commented Rabbi Joel appreciatively, "but I must tell you, we have more good news. It is a remarkable coincidence, but one of the runners-up is also an architect connected to this agency . . . Eliezar Ben-Judah by name. Is he also present today?"

"O heaven," said Olga, rolling her eyes skyward, "we are doubly blessed. This is a great day for our organization, an overwhelming day." As a performance it was marvelous, Garbo could not have made a more convincing show of sincerity. Inside, she had to be bursting with satisfaction over the sweetness of the result. Outside, the blouse of tomato-red chiffon strategically unbuttoned, highlighted the fleshy tangency of her breasts. He hadn't realized how really seductive she could be, never having thought about her that way — perhaps because he hadn't been looking at her that way. The four holy men seemed in a trance over the sight, crucified to the spot. No doubt the close quarters of the small office contributed its own share to the desire felt by the five, holy and unholy, for the expansive and vivacious *Russkaya*.

"Pardon me, I am so very happy," she resumed, now more composed. "Yes, Eliezar is here. Come, let us give him and the others the good news." The rabbis went through the motions of annunciation and congratulations with Ben-Judah, diminishing their enthusiasm proportionately, consistent with runner-up status. If Ben-Judah was disappointed, and no doubt he was, he did not show it. For her part, in the presence of the distinguished visitors, Olga treated him as a valued employee. The truce was temporary, dictated by the rules of diplomacy.

13

Hadashot, Ha'aretz, Davar, Al-Hamishmar, The Jerusalem Post — they were all calling. Would he give an interview . . . pose for pictures . . . how did he feel? Questions that ranged from the serious to the absurd, the stuff of journalistic bathos. He was hot, they were burning the wires trying to get him. The public had a legitimate interest in him, he was public property, refusing to cooperate with the press could be harmful to his career, he might need its help. So they said in response to his stock answer, "No interviews until after the award ceremony." Having learned his lesson, no sawed-off journalist was going to flatter or cajole him into relaxing the rule. Until the ten thousand dollars were in hand, he would be like a clam in the sand. The publishing of pictures, however, he welcomed. Supplicants were referred to Ha'itzer Bnai Azadoi Beshallim, the designs were its property. The ones already released had been promptly printed by the big dailies. But pictures were only part of the story they said. They needed the creator, the man behind the temple. He even received a couple calls from sexy-voiced women claiming to be freelance reporters. His response — "Send me your picture, I don't believe you", was sexist, but properly so. He thought everyone knew the Samson fable.

He wrote Miriam telling her the news, but asked that she not tell anyone at the firm. He wanted Shames to become aware of it on his own, perhaps while reading the *Jerusalem Post*, the English language weekly he subcribed to. Surprise! "Former Shames Protégé Wins Design Competition for Third Temple". That should hit him like a fish in the face. *Jerusalem Post? The New York Times!* It was their kind of story, the latest in overseas Kosher fashion. The *Times* kept a man in Jerusalem but he hadn't called — not yet. It would make a good feature article for the Arts and

156

Entertainment page, the kind they excelled at, a thorough review of the temple in Jewish religious and political history, down to the last stone. His education and apprenticeship with the Shames firm would provide an American connection. A smattering of selected quotations from Super Sam himself on the boy's talent would be more straw for the bricks. They owed him as much after the cavalier mention given him in the going-away party article, where the color of shoes worn by the wife of some big shot weighed heavier than any opinion he might have had. He had met Alison Cleveland that day. He felt sheepish in thinking about it. But the mind was inclusive, not exclusive. She had a place in it, a life tenancy no less. Would it shrink with time or, like a temple, prove indestructible — except by a force more powerful than the one creating it? She'd see the article. What would her reaction be? Regret? He realized he was reviving the fantasy by infusing it with a moral dimension. The real issue was money, tons of it, streaming in every day, hour, minute, second, the commentary he once saw printed under a check drawn by Henry Ford — "It is estimated that in the approximately two minutes Mr. Ford took to write this check, his income was two thousand dollars."

14

" . . . and so my fellow citizens, now that we possess the form of the Third Temple as given us by the genius of this young man, Basil Primchek, let us dedicate ourselves to making the ideal the reality. Let us take this man's idea, an idea most excellent and perfect in all its particulars, throughout our land, letting all behold the product of an inspiration that once beheld, shall surely become the inspiration of all. And as is true of all great ideas that may not be confined to one place or one time, it shall spread like a holy spirit over land and sea, until like the oxygen which blankets this earth with its vitality, it shall cover the world. Throughout that world Jews hunger for inspiration, inspiration that only a Jewish state can give. I say to you that they are ready to receive the message of this meeting tonight, to receive the building of this temple as a sign, a sign that at long last the Jewish People have come home, home to a permanence of eternity, never again to roam the world as strangers, as outcasts. So let us not be content with bringing only the Jews of Jerusalem, of Judea, of Samaria, of Tel Aviv, Haifa, Hebron or Qiryat Shemona into this grand scheme of rebirth. Let us go unto the four corners of the Earth, to our brethren in the Diaspora, and give them the opportunity to share equally in this, our dream. So that the dream we dream tonight here in Jerusalem shall become the reality of a universal mitzvah, a mitzvah uniting Jews of every station, every nationality, every place, toward the fulfillment of prophecy, of history, and of Israel's place among the nations — a keeper of the flame and a light unto the nations. I thank you."

Basil looked up at the distinguished guest of honor from his adjoining seat at the banquet table as the first waves of applause issued from the capacity audience below. Abraham Vir, Member of Knesset, former hero in the Battle for Independence, general of the army, ambassador to Guatemala, director of the ZIV Corporation, etc., bowed his white-fringed head in little graceful nods to the appreciative assemblage of Ha'itzer Bnai Azadoi Beshallim, their guests, members of the press and security guards. Basil lifted his hands, making the appropriate hand against hand motions.

Many in the audience were rising from their chairs in a spontaneous tribute to the old warrior. He rose with them. The small, heroic figure of Vir on his left was occupied with accepting the proffered hands of former comrades and present colleagues. It would have been presumptuous of him to shake Vir's hand. For one thing, he was too young. This was a privilege earned in the arena of common experience and struggle, a "members only" proposition. Moreover, to shake the hand of one who had just finished praising him would have been an act of self-congratulation. For the present he should stand by, clap, and watch. A banquet was essentially a platform for boredom.

Nevertheless the man was a professional, speaking extempore, with nary a note before him. Tonight was neither the first nor the last time he would make the speech. Change a few words here and some place-names there, and tomorrow it could be given in Paris, Atlanta, Los Angeles, or wherever a quorum of Jews could be assembled. It was bullshit but it was eloquent bullshit and because it was their bullshit the audience loved it. For his part he had been cautioned by his father to avoid the look of boredom that sometimes came over him unawares. "Look straight ahead with a serious expression when not looking at the speaker," he was advised. So he had. When presented with the check for ten thousand dollars his words of thanks and appreciation were warmly received. "It is indeed a great honor for one's idea to be chosen to benefit the culture and life of one's country." He had practiced uttering the phrase and made it the keystone of his brief remarks.

Making his way down from the dais to where his father was waiting, he was confronted by two reporters, recorders in hand, "Mr. Primchek, just a minute! A few questions . . ."

"Sorry," he said, making a detour around them, "it's late and I'm obligated. Some other time."

His father wanted to take another look at the mock-up

159

of the temple complex on display in the anteroom. Made of paper, it was under plexiglass, perhaps in order to protect it from the fate of its predecessors, premature destruction. Behind and above the mock-up, hanging over the doors opening to the banquet room, was a paper manifesto:

YOUR OLD MEN SHALL DREAM DREAMS
YOUR YOUNG MEN SHALL SEE VISIONS
H.B.A.B.

A crowd of about fifty men ringed the mock-up debating what some saw as the temple's good and even bad points. On Basil's approach someone cried, "Make way! Make way for the architect of the Third Temple!" Others reached for his hand, exclaiming, "magnificent . . . the country thanks you . . . glorious," while taking turns shaking it. Finally, he reached the mock-up and began describing some of the temple's features to his father, automatically gaining an attentive audience.

"Mr. Primchek, what will the outside walls be made of?," someone asked, taking advantage of a pause in the lecturer's remarks.

"Stone, marble, or tile-covered stone depending on the aesthetics and economics of the future."

"Can you tell us how much it will cost?," another asked.

"No, I don't think anyone can right now. I think the best approach to that is to consider some of Europe's famous cathedrals, the construction of which extended over a period of two or three centuries. I think in those cases one would have to conclude that money was no object."

At that the crowd burst into loud applause. Who could put a price on eternity? Deciding that this was a good note to make his departure on, he waved goodbye while making his way toward the doors, stopping to introduce his father to a visibly pleased Rabbi Joel Hochmeister, heady with the success of the evening's program.

" . . . he's a credit to the nation, Mr. Primchek. I

160

congratulate you and the mother of this boy."

"Thank you, Rabbi, we're all very proud of him."

Outside, father and son removed jackets, stopping to take the breeze. The quantity of bodies inside had overwhelmed the hall's two air-conditioners. "Mr. Primchek!" A man in a double breasted jacket and white shoes extended his hand. "Herb Portnoy, Mr. Primchek, President of Portnoy Properties, Miami Beach. Sorry to ambush you like this but there was no way I could get your attention inside. I'll make this short, Mr. Primchek . . . you see we do a lot of tourist developments . . . hotels, stores, condos, even golf courses, the whole works, strictly multimillion dollar projects. Well, we're considering a stretch of beachfront near Eilat for a really big development to draw the international tourist trade. From what I saw inside I think you could be the man we're looking for. Here's my card. If you're interested give me a ring in the next couple of days at the Jerusalem Hilton, suite 901."

"I'll do that, Mr. Portnoy, thank you."

"Fine, I'll be expecting you. Say, excuse me, but the gentleman with you . . . couldn't be your father could it?"

" Yes it is."

"Well, Mr. Primchek, sir, I don't speak Hebrew but I'd just like to offer my congratulations on your son's good fortune. And pardon me for talking business tonight. I realize this may not be the proper time or occasion for it."

"On the contrary, Mr. Portnoy," said his father, "you're talking to a couple of businessmen in Israel. Anytime is business time for us. And thank you for considering my son. I'm sure he will be in contact with you soon."

After saying goodbye to the personable American, père Primchek thumped his son vehemently on the back, exclaiming excitedly, "You're on your way! You get that commission and those ten thousand dollars you're carrying will seem like chick peas. You design that project and you'll be up there with the big ones — Shames, Eselson, Cozzo.

Those Europeans and Americans will carry your name back home with their suntans! This is the kind of thing some people spend their lives waiting for!"

"Yeah, I'll be sure to write my name on every stone so they won't forget."

"They'll know, they'll know! Do you think they'll come here, to a new resort complex, and not absorb the name of ,its architect? With all the attendant publicity and hoopla the Ministry of Tourism is going to be creating? But then never mind the publicity, take the money! By the way, this Russian girl, Olga . . . you say she's the one responsible for your entering the competition for the Temple, I want to meet her. Invite her over for dinner. I'll have Ayesha prepare a spread, make some pastries for us."

"OK, I'll tell her, but don't go overboard on this Portnoy, I haven't even talked with him yet. He could turn out to be one of those sand castle promoters."

"Don't worry, I'll call a couple friends in the Ministry tomorrow. They should be able to tell us whether he's authentic."

On the way home he drove while his father talked — about opportunity, luck, diligence, and the forging of the three elements into a successful practice. An optimistic nature prevented his father from dwelling on the past, but tonight was an exception. The circumstances of the evening made nostalgia inevitable. His mother — how his father wished she were alive to see this day.

The morning's paper gave the event full coverage, especially his statement equating the Third Temple with Europe's finest cathedrals, being cited approvingly by all. He may even have been bigger news than Abraham Vir, *Ha'aretz* publishing his and not Vir's photograph on the front page accompanying its story. Much of the article was devoted to a discussion of the international fundraising campaign launched at the award ceremony. In fact, claimed the article, one incident of the enthusiasm generated by the idea was the

162

increased popularity and standing of Ha'itzer Bnai Azadoi Beshallim, a party only two years ago not even represented in the Knesset. Political commentators were asking whether the party leadership, composed mainly of old-line, mainstream Orthodox with roots in the aggressive settler elements, had the sophistication and capacity to manage such an ambitious undertaking. It was absolutely necessary that the campaign be responsible, professional, and administered with absolute probity. Otherwise, there was the nagging apprehension the whole affair would come to naught, damaging the nation's credibility in the process. Nevertheless, one writer concluded, with that as caveat, the Ha'itzer Bnai Azadoi Beshallim had to be given credit both for the conception, and the consequent public enthusiasm generated. He was still reviewing the newspapers when the telephone rang in the kitchen.

"This is David Mindell from the *New York Times* Jerusalem bureau, Mr. Primchek. I've been trying to reach you for some time. I'd like to interview you for an article we're preparing. Any chance we can meet today . . . or perhaps tomorrow?"

"What time is convenient for you, Mr. Mindell?"

"How about 11:30 for lunch today? At Fagan's. You're familiar with the place . . .?"

"Yes, I know it."

"Good. It's a bit trendy I know, but I've found the food and the service reasonably consistent. Just ask for David Mindell's table. Is 11:30 OK?"

"Fine."

He wondered how much influence he could exert on the article's final form. Whether it would be anything on the order of the one he imagined. The local reporters who sought an interview with him, let them quote the *New York Times*, the voice of empire.

He found Olga at the cafe across from the office, sitting having a coffee with the inveterate cigarette.

163

"Mr. Primchek!," she said, waving a newspaper, "you are famous!"

"Madame Director, only in Israel, only in Israel."

"I would have liked to have been there last night," she said, "but tell me, was Ben-Judah there?"

"I didn't see him . . . but that doesn't mean he wasn't there."

"If you didn't see *him*, he wasn't there. That's good, those were his people. If he can't go with them, where shall he go?"

He was tempted to ask what this thing was between them except that it would have been prying. She would have told him by now had she been so disposed. "I don't know and I don't care," he replied, "but maybe I should thank him for where I am now. Without him you probably wouldn't have convinced me to enter the competition." He went on to relate the incident with the American, Portnoy, and the telephone call from the *New York Times* only minutes before. "As a matter of fact, my father was so hyped up by the possibilities of Portnoy's proposal that he wants you over for dinner. He wants to meet you."

"Your father wants to meet *me?*"

"Sure. Naturally I've spoken to him about you, but I think my winning the competition must have established you as something of a prophet in his mind. On the other hand, who knows? He may be looking for a bride."

"Then I must come! When shall it be?"

"We'll make it Thursday or Friday. The last supper before I report for summer camp. Think you'll be able to carry on without me?"

Olga drew on her cigarette, exhaling smoke through her nostrils with a sigh. "I suppose I'll have to," she said, shrugging her shoulders.

He had to hurry if he wanted to make the 11:30 appointment with the *New York Times*. But first he wanted to stop at the job site, he was apprehensive about how

Bustanji would take the news. He would tell Bustanji exactly what Olga told him that day in the office, that they would never lay one stone for the Temple, that he did it as a sporting proposition, as a favor for the crazy Russian, Olga, but that once he got into it he gave it a pretty good shot, and as luck would have it, he won. He felt comfortable with those reasons, because if they weren't the whole truth they were most of it. The only thing of significance omitted was the benefit to his career, something too obvious for mention.

When he arrived he found Bustanji sitting drinking a beer. There were a lot of things he could have said — in jest of course — but this was not the day.

"Hello!," he said, "Do you have one for me?"

"Help yourself," responded Bustanji, pointing to the cooler.

The Arab was getting rich off him, able to afford the luxury of cold beer on the job. Actually, he felt a little embarrassed not to have suggested the beer in the first place. But he hadn't wanted to give offense, so many of them were prohibitionists, even the young ones. And with the recent upsurge in fundamentalism, they were pouring the stuff down the drain. Now that he knew it was OK, in the future he would keep him supplied with it — and anything else he wanted.

"When do we start?," demanded Bustanji suddenly.

"Start what?"

"The Third Temple. When do we start?"

"I guess you saw the papers. Let me explain."

"There's nothing to explain, I can read. So when do we start building this great Third Temple? Or will the hands of a filthy Arab be prohibited from working on the great sacred shrine, unlike the other profane tasks you allow us?"

"Listen, this campaign is strictly politics, no one's going to build any Third Temple any place. For one thing they haven't got the money . . ."

165

". . .'haven't got the money'? You have America, you don't need money. She gives you everything and more. How much does she owe you for smashing the Syrians? Use some of that to build your temple, it's all from the same pot."

"Alright, I agree, the Americans are only interested in dead bodies, but they don't have any money left over for extraneous indulgences like temples."

"No, Yahoodi, they are smarter than you. They know that to build the Third Temple you must first destroy the Dome of the Rock . . ."

"That's crazy!," Basil replied heatedly, perhaps with more than a little guilt, "I'm absolutely opposed to that!"

"How nice, *you* are opposed. The man who draws pictures is opposed. Tell that to your Ha'itzer Bnai Azadoi Beshallim!" Bustanji laughed bitterly. "Go. Build your temple on the 'Temple Mount'. It will cause a holy war. May I live to see the day."

Basil looked at his watch. It showed almost 11:30, his beer was only half drunk. "We'll finish this soon, but right now I've got a luncheon appointment," he said, looking for a place to put the bottle.

"Here," said Bustanji, taking the bottle from Basil's hand and putting it to his lips in one motion. "This is a poor country. We do not waste, not even our blood," he declared, setting down the empty bottle.

"I'm sorry. I'll make it up by being responsible for providing the beer from now on. See you later," he called while rushing out.

He was fifteen minutes late getting to Fagan's. As promised the *New York Times* man was at his table. After the mutual introduction, Basil mentioned his acquaintance with Mindell's writing, having read his dispatches from Israel in New York. Still two months shy of completing his second year in the post, Mindell was a relative newcomer to the labyrinthine nature of Middle Eastern politics. A middle-class Jew from California, he had the requisite degrees in journalism and political science many editors preferred when assigning a reporter to the region. The Jerusalem post was considered one of the plums of the profession. One never lacked for news. If a war wasn't on, one always threatened. Hardly a day passed when someone wasn't killed or willed to be killed. Jerusalem was at the geographic center of this internecine cauldron, a place where scoops awaited discovery through aggressive reporting. Mindell had expanded the list of informants bequeathed him by his predecessor. As the recipient of a steady stream of leaks and disclosures he was expected to reciprocate the favors. Sometimes the reciprocity took the form of an exposé, or an article using the devices of "high government sources," or "not for attribution". The material given him was sometimes information, sometimes disinformation. He couldn't always be sure.

Mindell's copy exhibited a flair for imaginative writing, transcending the usual dry and spare style of conventional journalism. His articles possessed an appealing mix of history and drama, a combination that had helped him garner a Pulitzer for a series on Middle Eastern terrorism. While conceding that some of his conclusions were tendentious, Mindell understood the public wanted firm answers, a reporter couldn't leave matters hanging. His present project was to gather material for a book on the Middle East while waiting for the opportune time to spring it. Asked for an example of an "opportune time", he suggested "a general war or the wiping out of the Royal House of Saud". Of course he couldn't wait forever for such an event, he had to get a book out. Books were where the money was and being associated with the *Times* almost guaranteed success.

Mindell admitted to not giving the story much importance when he first heard about it. It wasn't until the launching of the fundraising campaign that he awoke to its significance. Like a lot of observers, Israeli and foreign, he had underestimated the sophistication of the Bnai Azadoi Beshallim party. Apparently, they had availed themselves of

167

some rather good political advice, or else secured the services of one of the better ad agencies here or in the USA. The award event and the subsequent media coverage had given a qualitative improvement to the poor image the party had been dragging around for years. He thought it intriguing that the issue of the Third Temple's site had been suppressed. It had been one of the more controversial aspects of the party's program — an unequivocal demand for the erection of the Third Temple on the Temple Mount after the necessary "purification". It didn't take a genius to conclude that purification meant the razing of the Dome along with the rest of the complex. If the world were a reasonable place, an agreement might be reached on the dismantling of the Islamic shrine and its transfer to some other place, perhaps to Jordan, the territory most amenable to a practical solution for the aspirations of Palestinian nationalism. After all, the Jewish people certainly had a historically valid pre-existing claim to the Mount, one dating back to Biblical times. But alas, Mindell ruefully concluded, the world was not a reasonable place and the dispute promised to be intractable, with the two fanaticisms, Islamic fundamentalism and Jewish messianism, squaring off for a century of strife. The most one could hope was that these fanatic manifestations could be held within reasonable bounds by reasonable men on both sides of the boundary lines. In the meantime, he was responsible for writing an article. He needed the architect's opinions on the architectural and political issues involved.

Basil began explaining, with the aid of his temple sketches, the architectonics of the temple's design to the earnest journalist. The large, lavalike, flowing buttresses that ran from the top of the walls to the base of the structure functioned as physical and aesthetic stabilizers of the massive structure, integrating it with the sere surroundings of its site. The rounded bases of the buttresses resembled giant tears, symbolic of the tears shed by the Jewish people in their years of exile and suffering. Between each buttress he placed the windows, vertical slits of stained glass in various shades of blue, which when illuminated by the sun's rays, would cast great swatches of blue over the temple's gold and white tesserated interior.

As he began describing the holy of holies, known in mellifluous Latin as the *sanctum sanctorum*, Mindell interrupted, "Excuse me . . . I'm sure our architectural writer will have a field day with these designs. I must say I find this all very impressive but what I am really after are the political ramifications . . . Now anyone looking at your drawing wouldn't have the slightest clue for the site of the future temple. Was this a deliberate omission, or is that the normal procedure in rendering an architectural drawing of this type?"

Basil answered that his conception of the temple did not include any particular site. Any land rise would do. He could not conceive anything ever supplanting the Dome of the Rock, it was symbolic of the city itself. A demand for its removal was not to be taken seriously, it was "architecturally unthinkable". Moreover, as a native Jerusalemite, he found the proposition abhorrent. His efforts were directed to preserving the past, not destroying it.

"Then let me ask you a theoretical question," said Mindell, still not satisfied, "do you have a preferred site in mind where you would like to see the Third Temple erected?"

"Yes. I would have to say the site now occupied by the Intercontinental Hotel."

"I'm sure the owners of the Intercontinental will be pleased to hear that. Well, you certainly have a knack for coming to the point, Mr. Primchek. That makes my job easier. Uh . . . one last question, you're obviously not a member of the Ha'itzer Bnai Azadoi Beshallim . . . are you a member of any political party?"

"I am an architect, not a politician."

169

"Yes . . . fortunately."

15

Upon returning to the office after the *Times* interview, he found a message from Herbert Portnoy inviting him to dinner at the Hilton. He liked Portnoy. He seemed unaffected, direct, even oddly charming. He might even be one of those rare individuals, an honest businessman. In any case he was no phony. His father had gotten the word — Herb Portnoy was as good as gold.

Dinner was a quiet affair, just himself and the Portnoy clan: Herb Portnoy, his wife Michelle, her sister Elaine, and Elaine's two grade school daughters. For Michelle and Elaine this was their maiden voyage to Israel, and like any first-time tourists, they were trying to see as much country as time allowed. Travel was stimulating and educational, especially for the children who were getting some very practical history lessons on their roots, lessons they could never get from a book. While they had pretty well toured Jerusalem and made trips to the Tel Aviv area and the Negev, because of fear of terrorism they had avoided the West Bank and its Biblical sites. Portnoy had attempted to convince them their fears were unreasonable, but since terrorism itself was not very reasonable, they had not found the argument persuasive. Also, as mothers they were charged with an additional degree of responsibility, one not so easily relaxed. Having a Sabra at the table recently come from the wilds of New York City, presented an opportunity to discuss the matter with an experienced and sympathetic source. ". . .and you say that when you walk down the street you're not worried,

170

not at all?," said Elaine, still resistant to assurances.

"I think there is a distinction to be made here," reasoned Basil, "between worry and care. One takes care when crossing the street, there are speeding automobiles. As a tourist you are as safe here as you would be in New York's Central Park . . . provided you take care to stay on the beaten track. We have our dangerous areas too, and as a Jewish American you might be a target, because our problems are more political than economic. Actually, we've lost very few tourists over the years to terrorism. But because most of our tourists tend to be American, you're more likely to hear about it. Our tourist industry has always taken a back seat to our security interest, so of course the event is further magnified. I think the threat is greater than the terrorism itself. That's one of the objectives of terrorism, to keep the enemy on edge. Given the disproportionate imbalance between the resources of the state and the terrorist, if the terrorist can only make people nervous he's accomplished the objective. Because if a state cannot protect its citizenry, what good is it? Israel has lived with terror for years and yet life goes on, deals are cut, and people fall in love. Terrorism is a fact of life here, almost an institution. In fact, we've been practicing terror for fifty years, our leaders were or are terrorists, and we now have our own second and third generation of home-grown terrorists, misguided, but 'good boys' nevertheless."

"Yes, but what about the Arabs?," Elaine asked obsessively. "I see them walking in the streets and I say to myself, 'Elaine, there's nothing to be afraid of. They're just different from you, that's all. Different clothes, customs, they're really harmless.' Sometimes their old men remind me of my grandfather. But then I see their faces on TV so full of hate and rage and I have to believe these people are out for blood . . . and I don't think I'm alone in holding those sentiments," she added, turning to her sister.

"The ones you see that remind you of your grandfather

you're probably right about, they *are* harmless. They were born under someone's heel so they're used to it. Now that they've grown old, just surviving consumes most of their energy. I suspect the ones that frighten you are the young, the ones that still believe they can change things. You should realize that there is a war on here, a war that perhaps started as a gleam in the first Zionist's eye. The Arabs of course, lost that war. They were supposed to slink away into the desert. But they didn't. Although they were defeated they never gave up, therefore the hostility. During the 19th century the United States government used exactly that concept to describe the Indians still at war with the government. They called them 'hostiles'."

"Yeah, that's right," commented Portnoy approvingly.

"I can understand what you're saying," said Michelle Portnoy, "but you've really said nothing to lessen our anxieties. If anything, you've confirmed them."

"Look," Basil responded with a shrug, "I've been living around Arabs, Palestinian Arabs, for most of my life. I spent over two years in the army playing policeman on the West Bank. Arabs are like anybody else, some are good and some bad. I don't know whether you're up to this or how important the issue is to you, it's really immaterial to me, but I have an Arab working for me now as a stonecutter on a medical clinic we're building. He's young, he's angry, he speaks English, and he probably fits the stereotype of a hostile Arab. But he's a hell of a craftsman and so far we've gotten along very well. What I'm suggesting is that I'd like you to meet him. He's got all the physical attributes for the stereotype — physical size, a black beard, piercing eyes. I really can't say how he will react to you, he's too unpredictable. If you're interested I can pick you up tomorrow morning."

Herb Portnoy thought it was a great idea. Were it not for a raft of commitments he would have taken Basil up on it himself. He was keen on his wife and sister-in-law going

172

though. This was "something to write home about", the kind of "people to people" contact that was truly spontaneous, unlike the usual cut and dried exchange of platitudes. Although intrigued by the idea, the girls were not prepared to make a decision on such short notice. Portnoy suggested the two talk it over while he and their architect guest discussed business.

Portnoy's plans for the stretch of beach were grandiose. A veritable city of vacation beach huts was envisioned, along with their support structures — restaurants, convenience stores, doctor's offices, laundries, even desalinization and sewage treatment plants to protect against environmental disaster, everything the typical vacationing beach denizen might need during the projected one to four week stay by the balmy waters of the Red Sea. There would be fishing, skin-diving, and sailing, in addition to the ubiquitous tanning factories — a year-round vacationland. A modest and tastefully integrated casino would function as the physical and social hub for the development, providing international entertainment for the expected thousands of international visitors from Scandinavia, England, France, Germany, America. With this development Israel was competing with the giants — the Rivieras of France and Spain — for the millions of travelers from the North who made the summer trek to the meridional waters of the Mediterranean Sea. Portnoy envisioned stone buildings, whitewashed and painted in gay pigments, reminiscent of the ancient architecture of the Arabian littoral. Everything was to radiate nostalgia or it was out. It should be the kind of place Sinbad the Sailor might have hove to, an Arabian Nights for the jaded travelers who thought they'd seen it all. It would be the biggest thing in Israel, the equal of anything in the world, built to accommodate five to six thousand people. The individualized "huts" would be constructed with a "state of the art" rusticity, making the place competitive with anything the Greeks or Yugos had or hoped to have. Each hut would be equipped with a small kitchen making the economy-minded traveler's stay even more affordable. Millions of dollars, pounds, and kroner — hard currency — would flow into Israel, to be spent inside Israel. Israel would be imprinted upon the European imagination, the place would be the equivalent of a thousand good-will ambassadors. "What more fitting place for the youth of the nations to congregate than Israel, the original home of the ethical imperative?" Then, as if to counter any impression he had gone off the deep end of idealism, Portnoy shifted to the mundane — fully 60 to 70 millions would be allocated as investment capital for the project. He was in the process of recruiting a consortium of investors and banks to put up the necessary cash. However, and he could not stress this too much, there was one danger — terrorism. The resort city must be invulnerable to terrorist attack. The Israeli Navy covered the sea. It was the land access that had to be secured. One car bomb and the place would be finished, "kaput for a thousand years". He was negotiating with the Israeli government for a permanent security force for the area. But that was not enough, the physical layout had to complement the military security, making the city invulnerable to all except a long-range cannonade or an Exocet type missile, the kind of weapons only another country would possess. That was war, people could accept that.

Eilat International was the name he had chosen for the place. However, if Basil could think of a better one, he was welcome to try. Everything was still very tentative, a lot depended upon his negotiations with the government, he felt it was holding out for too much money for the land. But he was confident he could "Jew them down". If not, maybe the Lebanese or the Turks might be interested. He obviously was joking about Lebanon, but he was serious about the other half of the threat. He had a soft spot in his heart for Israel but he didn't get where he was by giving money away. The United States had spoiled Israel with its generosity. It made it tough for a businessman, even a Jewish business-man, to do business. They seemed to have forgotten that business was a two-way street. These "Levantine negotia-tors" had to understand he was no Uncle Sam.

"Well, whattya say? You interested?"

"You know damn well I'm interested," answered Basil in his best Americanese.

"Good. Here's what I want. Draw up some preliminary sketches, you know black and white — it doesn't need to be fancy like those sketches you did of the Third Temple — incorporating the ideas I just sketched out. Do them for the huts, casino, support areas and . . . yeah, let me have some of your ideas on the anti-terrorism measures. I need some-thing to show the investors, they like to see pictures, they can save a lot of words. And remember what I told you about nostalgia, make that your star. If I can judge by those drawings you did for the Temple, you shouldn't have any trouble with this project. They say you have a foot in the past. I say keep it there for the duration of this project. We want to think of the place as a refuge from the atomic and computer age, 'a place where peace and joy doth reign'."

Basil asked how soon Portnoy needed the set of pre-liminary sketches, explaining that he was leaving for a thirty day stretch with his reserve unit come Sunday. "No prob-lem, we've got time. Let's plan on sixty days. If I need them sooner I'll let you know. You can be incubating the project in your head while you tool around the Negev in one of those Russian tanks. Or better yet, get out and walk, the mirages may prove inspiring. But don't forget your water. They say that sun can dry a man up in a few hours. Remember that crank who walked in there . . . what was his name?"

"You mean Bishop Pike?"

"Yeah, that's the one. What was he looking for anyway?"

"God, what else?"

175

"By the way, did they ever find his bones or did the buzzards get him?"

"I really don't remember."

"How did I get on this subject anyway? Let's go and see what the ladies have decided for tomorrow."

The sisters had decided to divide their forces. Elaine would go while Michelle would watch the girls. They were really too young "to appreciate meeting a radical Arab". Following a serving of coffee and shortbread cookies he took his leave. His father would probably be waiting for him, anxious to hear what had transpired. He had informed him about the meeting with the reporter from the *Times*. That would have been accomplishment enough for one day. But obtaining a commission for a 70 million dollar fantasy land by the sea was more than an accomplishment, it was a . . . He was unable to come up with the proper word. If he were religious he might have said "miracle". He finally settled on luck. Good or bad, it was the one concept that accommodated the unexplainable.

Elaine was standing inside the door to the lobby of the Jerusalem Hilton when he drove up promptly at nine. The broad-rimmed hat, flowered, flouncy, organdy dress, and high heels she wore were more appropriate to a tea party than a visit to a construction site. He held the car's door open, observing the way she ran her hand over the back of her dress before sitting. She was heavily made up. The rouged cheeks, rose madder lips and pale, powdered complexion reminded him of a Japanese kabuki actor. A slight sag of skin under chin betrayed the passing of a prime. Striking a compromise between truth and etiquette, he complimented her on her fragrance. "Thank you," she replied, "it's 'Fleurs de Provence', by Fallon, one of my favorites. It was one of the biggest sellers at our boutique. It's expensive but I think it's worth it . . . Do you know much about perfume?"

"Not much, other than it's made from flowers and

176

smells magnificently."

That was all Elaine needed to launch into an extensive description of perfume manufacture and distillation. France and Egypt were the two leading suppliers of floral extract. In Egypt extract was derived from jasmine while the French utilized a variety of blooms, mainly from Provence. France was the leading formulator of perfume and French fragrances were the most prestigious and priciest. Some scents had remained popular for almost a hundred years. Perfume replaced the natural pheromones, which somehow through evolution, the human race had lost. The exception was body odor, which perfume was designed to overcome. "Pardon me," interrupted Basil, "methinks there is a contradiction here. Could not body odor be the lost human pheromone? And could not our species, as it has evolved, be unique in its abhorence of its own rank smell?"

"I don't know," confessed Elaine, "maybe that's what separates us from animals."

It was a question not even scientists had answered satisfactorily. As such it was unfair. Nevertheless, it was clear the lady knew her perfumes. In less than five minutes he had learned more about scents than he could from a lifetime of riding crowded elevators. But as is the tendency of many who find a sympathetic and intelligent listener, the conversation soon shifted to the personal. She was recently divorced. Her husband, a prominent Miami attorney, had left her for a younger woman, a secretary in his firm. She supposed that was one of the perils of growing old. At the time, her husband's defection had come as something of a shock, she hadn't suspected a thing. But in the subsequent process of adjustment she had come to accept the loss "philosophically", resolving "to make the best of it". The trip to Israel was part of that resolve. After an initial period of fear and anxiety, she could now state, quite sincerely, that the life of a divorcée was not nearly as bad as she had imagined. She had her children, her family, and most of her friends. Her sister and Portnoy were singled out for a special recognition. They had done more than duty obliged and Portnoy was a "generous and kind man".

The narrative of rebirth and redevelopment was cut short by the arrival at the job site. Taking Elaine by the hand, Basil led her through and over construction obstacles into the clinic's courtyard. Bustanji, apron and shoes coated with rockdust, laid down his tools when he saw the pair approach. "Khalil! I brought a friend of mine to meet you — Elaine Korn from America." It was as much a warning as an introduction.

" 'Elaine the fair, Elaine the lovable, Elaine the lily maid of Astolot'," intoned Bustanji as he stepped down from the work area.

"Oh thank you," beamed Elaine, overwhelmed at the totally unexpected effusiveness of the Arab's response.

"Don't thank me, thank Tennyson. To whom or what do I owe the honor of this visit?"

"I thought I'd show Elaine the kind of work we do here," said Basil. "You wouldn't mind if we looked at some of the stonecuttings would you?"

Bustanji removed his apron and tossed it aside. Returning to the workshed he pointed to copies of Basil's drawings tacked to a wood strut — "Our guide," he declared. "We take this and make this," pointing to the piece of stone and then to the finished relief of a physician sitting before a row of variously afflicted patients.

Elaine marvelled at the transmutation, "It really is incredible, Mr. Bustanji, how you can do this. These should be in a museum."

"Ah, but this city is a museum," said Basil, "of the best kind — a living museum. And we are its curators and conservators."

Bustanji showed Elaine his tools, chisels of different shapes and sizes, steel and wooden mallets, then demonstrated the technique on a relief in progress. He offered her the wooden mallet, holding the chisel while she made a few dismal two-handed strikes against it. "I'm afraid I'm no Michelangelo. I just don't have the strength. Have there ever been any women sculptors?"

"Some very good ones," answered Basil, "but they tended to work in the plastic end of sculpture, molding with clay and casting in bronze. An exception was Rodin's mistress, a reasonably proficient sculptor as one might expect given the teacher. But generally working with stone has been a man's profession. Yet with women taking up weight-lifting and other previously male monopolies, we could have a Michelangela. That might be something for the East Germans to work on . . . if they're not working on it already."

After touring the building site and pointing out the significance of the architectural plan, Basil judged his charge had had enough for one morning. For the tender-handed, the transition from perfume to stone was not an easy one. "What say you now about our Arabs?," he asked when they got back to the car.

"I'm modifying my opinion . . . at least as regards your Mr. Bustanji. An interesting and talented man . . . he seemed like a person you could trust. If they were all like him, there really wouldn't be anything to worry about."

On the way back to the Jerusalem Hilton he stopped at Fagan's. It was the kind of place he thought Elaine would like, most Americans did, the place had a built-in energy about it. Noise from the kitchen mixed with the low roar of voices in conversation while the voice of Frank Sinatra issued from the sound system. The absence of drapes, table-clothes, or anything likely to deaden sound, was all part of the plan to make eating at Fagan's more than an assault upon the palate. Waiters seemed to handle the china with deliberate abandon, adding to the orchestrated din. This day the summer tourist crowd was very much in evidence, with English as the language of choice. As expected, Elaine

179

enjoyed Fagan's atmosphere, finding it a "fun place". She was going to tell her sister about it, making sure they lunch there before leaving Israel.

Back at the hotel the farewell went off without a hitch. She was grateful for his consideration and asked that he thank Bustanji for his "patience in trying to teach me something about his profession. But I think I learned more about the danger of stereotyping than anything about sculpture." She hoped they would see each other again before she left. He regretted that would probably be impossible because of his imminent military obligation. But he was glad they had met and wished her a pleasant stay for the remainder of her visit. He headed back to the job, he wanted to share his satisfaction at the turn of events with Bustanji.

"Did you think I would insult her?," asked Bustanji after Basil had explained to him the place of Elaine Korn in the Eilat International scheme, confessing the anxiety he felt over the encounter with the naive American. "That was one possibility," said Basil, "but I'm grateful you didn't. It must have been a sacrifice."

"She was your friend. Besides, she is a woman, a mother no less. Are you going to marry her?"

"Are you crazy? Where did you get that idea?"

"Well, do you want that commission . . .?," said Bustanji, eyebrows raised, a knowing expression on his face.

"I've got the commission . . ."

"Don't be so sure. Did the brother-in-law promise it to you?"

"No, but I'm sure . . ."

"You are sure of nothing! There are any number of things that can stop you from getting the commission. But if you married her, he would be bound to deal with you for this project, and any other project. He would not dare act against the interest of his wife's family."

"Brilliant. You should apply to the House of Sa'ud, they can probably use a good wazir or two. You could make a hell of a lot more money there than chipping stone."

"Suit yourself. But if you want to assure that commission, you will marry her."

Of course, until Bustanji mentioned it, he had never thought of marrying Elaine. But that was the Arab way, eminently pragmatic, where there was an opportunity worm right in. The trait was common in poorer societies where wealth, often measured in heads of livestock or wives, was scarce. The Prophet himself had married a rich widow, his followers could do no less. But the practice was hardly exclusive to Arab and tribal societies. Fortune hunting and instant wealth through marriage were practiced equally assiduously in rich and modern societies. In fact, the latter had a long history of obfuscating the issue by cloaking the baser human motives with concepts of "love".

Basil left off the uncomfortable subject and brought up the courtly manner in which Bustanji had responded to the visit of the American stranger, comparing it to the incident in the office where the rabbis of Ha'itzer Bnai Azadoi Beshallim had come to inform him of his winning the competition, when he imagined their purpose was to complain against a stone-throwing, or perhaps a cursing in Arabic from a mischievous Bustanji, "You underestimate me, Yahoodi," commented Bustanji, "I would have cursed them in Hebrew if I were going to curse them at all. But listen, have you ever paused before a wasp nest? If you keep a respectable distance the wasps will go about their business and not attack you. But disturb them and they rush out to sting anything in their path. Though wrong about me, you were right about them. They would have sought to sting me with the loss of my employment. Like wasps, their bite is painful but rarely fatal. But then who needs to be stung at all?"

"Khalil, have you ever been stung?"

"By what, wasps or flies?"

"By Jews, *Yahood.*"

"I was in a Land Day demonstration. I was sixteen years old, you know, the age of omniscience. I was carrying a Falestinian flag. Naturally the *soldaten* arrested me. My hands were handcuffed behind me and a hood put over my head. With some of my comrades I was taken to a building and ordered to stand, it seemed like hours. Suddenly, without warning, I received a blow in the groin. I fell to the floor, the pain was tremendous, I still think about it. Then my hood was removed and a little Yemeni stood over me laughing. I will never forget those faces and my anger and humiliation."

"What happened then?"

"You don't see me carrying any Falestinian flags do you? I date my education from that day, all that went before was rubbish . . . By the way, stop me if I bore you. But since you asked and it's on your time, I shall be glad to oblige. After I graduated from Bir Zeit, I took a position in Kuwait teaching English literature. After a few months, I was visited by two security men in my rooms and served with an order of expulsion. They never told me why, they just began ransacking my clothes from the closet and stuffing them into my suitcases. Naturally, this kind of attention made me feel very unwelcome. The Falestinian dog they had taken in had apparently barked too loud. Nothing serious, just enough to be thrown out of the country and my work visa revoked.

"Now I am back home and of course I still live by sufferance, your sufferance. But I have no interest in politics or politicians, Yahoodi or Falestinian. What would I prove? That I am a man? It is the Yahood who have a problem with that, as if making us sit in our own shit in their wretched jails will convince us that we are sub-human animals. You are a people obsessed with the psychology of excrement. Your army leaves its shit on ceilings, between the pages of books. Why? So you can make a toilet of the Arab nation and demonstrate your contempt of us? I will tell you why — because not even the vilest of your vile believe their racist lies about us. Thus they must perform these hate-filled rituals to exorcise the demon Arab from reality.

"Yet, compared to our Arab brothers you are humanitarians. To be arrested by the Lebanese Sureté is not to survive to complain. In their eyes our crime is that we exist. They deal with their detainees, especially the Falestinian, whom they accuse of ruining their 'Paris of the East', characteristically. After subjecting their victims to monstrous tortures, gouging of eyes and axing of heads, the bodies are dumped. The soil of Lebanon is well fertilized with thousands of victims of Israeli-Phalange collaboration.

"If the Lebanese way seems overly severe, lovers of freedom may find refuge in Syria, the home of the 'black slave', a heated skewer put up the ass. Imagine — you are strapped to a slab sweating blood as some filthy sadist of a security man is working the poker in and out, testing your pain threshhold. What do you think will be your reaction? Will you still be interested in participating in the 'political process'? After a few treatments from this sadist's dream I guarantee you will forget about politics forever . . . that is if you are unlucky enough to survive your graduate course of torture.

"The others? I retch at the thought, assassins from first to last, the flies that rise spontaneously out of the putrefying Arab body politic. I once had a discussion with one of your progressive women about this. Her answer was that it took Europe hundreds of years to develop modern political forms with protection for the rights of the individual. The obvious message was patience, be patient, it will all come to pass, even for Arabs. For the Europeans this great historical process culminated in two world wars and fascism. Were it not for the fear of Bolshevism they would still be slaughtering each other with regularity. If this is to be our destiny, what are we waiting for?"

Bustanji stood up and pulled a handkerchief from his

pocket, wiping his brow and neck of sweat and dust, the fingers and tendons of his hands alternating in rhythm as they clenched and unclenched, forming great fists. "Excuse me," said Basil, "I'm not minimizing anything you've said, but it strikes me as more rhetoric than prophetic. I'm not convinced you believe your own despair . . . 'even for Arabs'."

"You want to know what I believe?," exclaimed Bustanji brandishing his heavy steel mallet, holding it before him as if prepared to brain an imaginary enemy, "I believe in a Stalin, someone who will take these swine by the scruff of the neck and smash their heads, or put them up against a wall and finish with them. No trials! Don't insult us with your bourgeois crap, we know they're guilty, let the bleeding hearts mourn the mistakes. How many millions do these dogs slaughter in their wars and jails? Who mourns these victims? Who remembers their names when they die in their beds from American bombs? A Stalin, a son of the people, ruthless in defense of their rights, that's what we need."

Bustanji dropped his mallet and grabbed Basil's arm jerking him forward. "You see those hills, Yahoodi?" Bustanji pointed to the Judean Hills in the distance, barren and white in the midday sun. "Someday, thousands will pour over their crests. On that day all your bombs and vaunted strength will be as nothing. Once the force of the masses has been mobilized, nothing can withstand it. It will sweep you and your Third Temple into the rubble of history where it can be read by men in little hats in all the *yeshivot* of the world. You know the song, 'Give me some men who are stout-hearted men who will fight for the right they adore, Start me with ten who are stout-hearted men and I'll soon give you ten thousand more'?"

"Yes, I know it. But how do you know it?"

"I told you, you underestimate me . . . But that's alright, you can't help it."

184

16

Thursday's mail brought a letter of invitation to join the Association of Israeli Architects. They had finally become aware of his existence. That evening Mark called to congratulate him on winning the Third Temple competition, David Mindell's article had been printed in Thursday's edition of the *Times*. He hadn't expected the article to appear so quickly. He thanked Mark for taking the time to inform him of its publication. "Don't rub it in," replied Mark, "I know I'm a lousy correspondent but that doesn't mean I'm not wondering how you're doing. We've been busy as hell here. In fact, I just got back from a big fact-finding tour of South Africa with the Senator. That's where the concern is these days. Of course, a lot of it is hand-wringing, but this country has always been more comfortable with white power than black — you know, the "bulwark against communism" people. And you know how hard-headed they can be. Anyway, I'm still working on that trip to Israel. Next year the Senator's up for re-election and won't need any convincing that a trip to Israel is in order. So next year in Jerusalem for sure."

"Fine, I'll be looking forward to it."

"Yeah, now tell me about this temple. You think they'll ever build it?"

"You tell me, you're in the Diaspora. Have you seen any of them passing cans for spare change yet? You know there's no money for it at this end."

"That's what the article said. So far it seems to be a political ploy, although an inspired one. It's worked out well for you though. Have you got any commissions out of it yet?"

"One. I have to submit sketches for the project when I get back from training. It's not one hundred per cent cer-

185

tain, but I'm confident I'll get it — I'm on a first name basis with the developer and his family. Keep this to yourself, but this thing could make me. It's a sixty to seventy million dollar project."

"Seventy million! What's it for, an air base?"

"No, a vacation resort on the Gulf of Aqaba. The developer is getting a consortium together to finance it. Got a couple million you'd like to throw at it?"

"I'll pass, but I'll give you my congratulations. By the way, Elliot Chase had some good things to say about you in the article, very complimentary."

"Yeah? Good man, Elliot, reliable."

He slept in the following morning. It was Sabbath and he was tired, one of those body-weary fatigues that come upon one for no identifiable reasons. Perhaps the dread of summer camp was stalking him. The prospect of thirty days of desert heat, lousy food, and collective living was a dismal one. Sleeping was no escape, it only brought the time of departure closer. He hoped the bivouacs would be kept to a minimum. He hated sand — sand in his shoes, his food, his hair, everywhere sand, rocks and sand. For a people with as long an association with the desert as the Jews, the desert was an article of faith. Cruel and relentless, it was a place not long to be abided. These same properties made it an effective buffer between Israel and its enemies. Thus the stress on desert warfare had a logic going for it, perhaps too much of a logic. Military men, like most, had a reliance on and reverence for the past, a Maginot Line mentality. In any case, the Israeli army had always demonstrated a superiority in this area. Even in '73, when after taking heavy losses it counterattacked, trapping the entire Egyptian Third Army. Typically, Sadat sued for peace. Years later in Jerusalem, Sadat had the chutzpah to declare he had a counter-response and except for the cease-fire, would have unleashed it. His reputation for generalship was, like that of another dictator of recent memory, wholly self-generated. But what he was incapable of accomplishing on local battlefields, he performed in "Free World" diplomatic salons. Unlike his predecessor, who the Western press was wont to refer to as "Col. Nasser" long into his rule, Sadat was respectfully accorded the civil title of "president" early on, never losing it among his far-flung sycophancy. Indeed, Sadat was one of those rare leaders who when finally dispatched, was mourned more abroad than at home.

After getting up he lolled about the house reading and playing piano. Around the appointed time of five a taxi drove up, disgorging Olga minus her beloved boots. She had forsaken them for Grecian sandals, antique style, the kind whose leather thongs formed a criss-cross pattern on the ankles and lower calves. In her loosely draped, pleated linen tunic, she could have walked out of a page of antiquity. At least that was how he imagined her this summer evening, a Venus de Milo with arms — and legs of flesh and blood. An exaggeration perhaps considering Olga's oversized breasts and excessive torso, but then the Milo's torso is certainly one of the more sculpturally ample of the classical age. Yet he could have sworn Olga's torso was less than what he remembered it to be. She *was* thinner, it was not the lie of the tunic. She must have been dieting. As a matter of fact, he had noticed that she had been avoiding lunch. Whatever she was doing, it seemed to agree with her. A just-bathed look further enhanced the evidence of salubrity. After the introduction to his father, they sat in the salon where they chatted while Ayesha made ready to begin serving. Seated in a large, stuffed chair, Olga rocked a crossed leg, exposing smallish, wide feet, pedal counterparts to the plumply delicate hands that moved continuously as she spoke, complementing the energy of her prose. Responding to prompting from père Primchek, Olga reminisced about her youth in old "St. Petersburg", her school days, the family picnics in the marshes on the city's outskirts. She could have been describing the childhood of a middle class inhabitant of any of the capitalist urban centers. It was all very bourgeois, with not a trace of revolutionism or its bias. But then how does one measure "revolutionism"? By the frequency Vladimir Ilyich is cited? Her store of Russian jokes, especially the political variety, was impressive as well as genuinely amusing. If she was any criterion, the Russian sense of humor was alive and well. The Russian character, she said, like Mother Russia herself, was eternal. It would never change, never be changed. Communism was only a system, not a national character. Because it was only skin deep, if tomorrow another system were to replace it, even that of a restored capitalism, the Russian people would adapt. That was the way they were, accustomed to hierarchical rule. Superficially they exhibited obedience, but underneath a strong streak of anarchy throbbed. She pooh-poohed the efforts at reform presently underway in the Soviet Union. They would encounter widespread resistance. The reformers must know that. Nevertheless, she wished them good luck. The Russian people deserved a better life. They have suffered enough.

After dinner arak was sipped from cordial glasses. Olga pronounced the drink palpably superior to vodka. Were it not for its cost, it might challenge vodka as the Russian national drink, if, like so many other things, it were available. Then sitting down at the piano, she astonished her audience with a stupendous performance of "Bumble Boogie". Immediately following this pianistic *tour de force*, she launched into a sensitive rendering of Rubenstein's *Romance in E Flat,* a favorite of his mother. He recalled practicing but never mastering the piece. Olga apologized for stunning her hosts with her musicianship, shifting the blame to the seductiveness of the black and white keys. She couldn't resist putting a newly discovered piano to the test. She had studied piano for years, but when it came time to choose a profession she picked architecture. "Music was like love," she said, "too pleasurable to be a profession." Not having a piano in her apartment, she did her practicing at a nearby music school, inviting Basil to join her for some piano four hands. He quickly changed the subject, describing his meeting with Portnoy and the plans for the super beach resort. Delighted with the news, she amiably reminded him of her role in the matter, declaring that he would soon be in a position to consider her for a job. But she would only accept an offer based on need, not "gratitude".

Olga lived in the old part of Jerusalem, above a store specializing in olive wood carvings and other souveniers, religious and secular. She liked living among the Arabs. Markets were close by, the neighbors were friendly, and she was becoming reasonably proficient in the language. In fact, the locals sometimes referred to her as *ash-Sha'ra* (the blond) or *Bint Roosiya* (Russian girl). Getting out of the car, she repeated her invitation for dinner, "Don't forget to remind your father, and be careful when you go to the Army, they have too many accidents."

"I like that girl! She's a real humdinger!," exclaimed his father as soon as Basil walked in the door.

"I thought you would. She has a great personality."

" 'Personality'? She has everything. On top of being Russian she's smart as a whip. You know she has to come from good stock. Did you meet her family yet?"

"Hey, give the girl a break, will you? You just met her."

"If I weren't your father, I'd break your stubborn head. That girl likes you, I can tell by the way she looks at you."

"So I'm a likeable fellow, what's so unusual about that? But she should like me, I do everything she tells me."

"And you better keep on doing what she tells you. Listen, that girl has quality, you're not going to meet too many like her, I don't care where you go. You can go back to America and you won't find anything like her, American girls aren't built that way. Maybe they're good in bed, I

189

don't know, you'd know more about that than I would. But I know you. You better marry a smart girl, you won't be satisfied with anything else. You're making a mistake if you ignore this girl."

"Who's ignoring her? Maybe you can tell me if she's so smart why she smokes so much. I don't know if I could take those cigarettes of hers."

"What cigarettes? She never smoked a one here."

"Yeah . . . you're right, she didn't . . ."

"Listen, I know these young girls. They may act sophisticated, but underneath they're really lonely. It's all nerves, that's why they smoke. The day she gets you she'll toss those cigarettes in the nearest trashbasket. She'll be glad to do anything you say, giving up smoking will be the least of it. If you want my advice, I say cultivate her. What have you got to lose?"

"OK, I'll think about it. But don't get me wrong, I like Olga. When I get back from playing soldier games I'll look into it. I'm going to have to start somewhere. They say charity begins at home . . . that's the Pauline charity if you're wondering."

Lev Primchek gave his son a quizzical look. He was neither a philosopher nor a theologian.

17

Israel's military successes over seemingly insurmountable odds were summed up by the phrase, "quality over quantity". Originally, in the War of Independence, it was a guiding military idea for a relatively small number of Jews confronting a hostile Arab world. Later, newfound friends and increased sources of aid compromised the concept. The greatest of these friends, the United States, had its own formula — sort of a worst case scenario — for the maintenance of Israeli success. Simply stated, Israel was entitled to be supplied with the means to defeat any possible combination of its Arab enemies. Given this example of principled generosity, the slogan "quality over quantity" blurs into propaganda. In fact, in all of Israel's wars, the numbers of men committed to battle were superior, not inferior, to those marshalled by the Arabs. Despite the confusion of the two concepts, the idea of "quality over quantity" persisted. The slogan's modification or retirement would have meant a repudiation of the myth of numerical inferiority, ergo man for man superiority. A nation gives up such myth reluctantly. Only when beaten does it do so, and then, of course, it is too late.

The reservist was fundamental to Israeli military strategy. After compulsory three years stints in the regular army (the Israel Defense Force, the "IDF"), there was obligation for thirty more in the reserves. Normally, this meant an annual one to two months of additional and refresher training, except that in times of war or crisis, the reservist was subject to call-up for indefinite periods. From this pool of manpower, and to a lesser extent, womanpower, the standing army could at once be greatly augmented. Of course in absolute numbers the armies of the Arabs were greatly superior to Israel's forces. But because they were stationed over a vast area and under the control of disputatious despots in shifting states of alliance and enmity with each other, their potential for concerted action existed mainly on paper. The concept of Arab unity was yet another of those original myths common to a culture or group. Like the golden age of matriarchy, evidence it had ever or would ever exist was largely based on faith. Perhaps because of its own mythic origins, Israel was taking no chances. It seized upon every opportunity to encourage and abet sectarian and political divisions within the "Arab camp".

He had accompanied his reserve unit on its training mission, making a circuit from the Galilee to the Negev, much of the time riding in an armored personnel carrier, affectionately termed the "wheeled coffin" by his fellows. Generally, other than a direct hit with an RPG rocket, the armor of the personnel carrier was impervious to the light weaponry carried by roaming bands of resistance fighters. Of course, "generally" wasn't the most comforting of odds. An occupant in one of these battle wagons was torn between a false sense of security and a nagging claustrophobia. Nevertheless, being positioned behind a moving shield of armor was an advantage, particularly in aggressive operations, a standard Israeli strategy.

By the time they reached the Negev the combination of summer heat, sun, and mechanical noise had taken their toll. War was a bore, preparing for it was even more boring. An exception was the mock night battle in the desert, where the enemy was the unknown and unseen. He made sure to keep moving, trusting the thick leather of his desert boots to protect against the remote but frightening possibility of a bite from a viper or scorpion. He hadn't seen any vipers, but he had heard about them, which sometimes was worse. Scorpions he had seen, hideous, segmented, chitonous creatures that lurked under rocks. While he had never been bitten himself, he had seen someone who had. After an initial period of pain and swelling the skin turned black, creating an ugly wound. Yet, like most desert perils, the bite of the scorpion was more terrifying than terrible. Despite flies, vipers, scorpions — and even lions before they were exterminated — the Bedouin had been crossing and recrossing these wastelands for ages. The real danger areas were the Tropics, home to pest and pestilence, to the venomous of the venomous. He thought of Vietnam, to the tunnel warfare waged there, where men stooped and crawled through a subterranean network of galleries scooped from the earth beneath the enemy's feet. It seemed incredible but people actually fought and died in tunnels less than a meter in height. Men had to be tremendously motivated to crawl through those tunnels, for a cause Ho Chi Minh summed up in one word — "independence". He wouldn't have done it, not for anything.

He was something of a minor celebrity in camp — at least to those who read the papers. Officers accorded him a certain deference, some even offering congratulations. Everybody liked a celebrity, and in a place as god-forsaken and isolated as Wadi Jamil, having a celebrity had a tonic effect. Although the military liked to believe it had its own celebrities — the generals, men with stars on their collars and confetti on their chests. But how many wrote home, "Dear Mom, today I saw a general"? People wanted entertainers, real celebrities. The Americans had Bob Hope and when she was alive, Marilyn Monroe. He had hoped the authorities might bring in a klezmer band. But a folksinger and the latest movies from America were the limit of their imagination.

Dr. Klug had announced that the final two weeks of training would take place in the vicinity of the camp. It could have been worse he said, an alternative was occupation duty. With that worry out of the way, they could now "relax and enjoy the base comforts". Klug did have a sense of humor, warped as it was. Although recently he seemed subdued, his usual bluster a casualty of Wadi Jamil's blistering heat.

Either that or isolation had gotten to Amon Amitai. Since the arrival of a company of girl soldiers, his conversation had become almost obsessively sexual. He had been hanging around the girls' quarters, hoping to "catch a stray". After two days of reconnoitering the area he had amassed a store of intelligence, including their approximate dismissal time and most importantly, when the major showering activity occurred. His plan was to approach their barracks, then penetrate a break in the surrounding fence. From there the windows of the shower room were only a few steps away. However, there was a problem, the windows' height. Of the clerestory type, they were almost three meters from the ground. Two men were necessary to carry out the operation, taking turns standing on each other's shoulders or back. In the event of detection, escape was facilitated by the same factor making surveillance so difficult — window height. By the time the girls in the shower sounded the alarm, they would be long gone. "The only thing they would see would be the backs of our heads."

The plan, as described by its formulator, appeared to have a high probability of success. The elements of approach, infiltration, assault, and retreat were given due consideration in the overall scheme, all commando assaults should be so simple. Despite Amon's optimistic assessment, the strike force's other half remain unconvinced. The girls Basil had seen in the mess had left him cold. It made no sense to expend that amount of energy for "the dubious thrill of seeing an acre of fat asses soap up". The whole idea was reminiscent of a gratuitous insert in some dated Swedish film, before the legitimization of pornography made such tableaux passé. He suggested they would be better served by commandeering a jeep and driving the few kilometers to the ranches around Beersheba where they could take in the horses. The Arabian rump was manifestly superior to the ordinary human variety.

The following day provided a relief from their daily diet of heat and dust — a program of lectures and films. Most of the latter were homegrown, products of the Israeli army. Dealing with the nature of the Arab enemy, the films listed his strength in tanks, planes, guns and men. Seeing the quantities of armaments and men so arrayed, the way Israel always managed to emerge victorious was truly marvelous. An Egyptian propaganda film with the comic title

194

"Will Power", purported to show the strength of will of the Egyptian army in confronting and overcoming the defenses of the Bar-Lev Line on the Suez Canal in October 1973. As propaganda the film was laughable. However, it was shown not for comic relief, but as an example of overconfidence, a mistake that must never be repeated.

The Israeli military establishment had an ambiguous attitude towards the peace accord with Egypt. On one level it welcomed the elimination of the problem of fighting a two-front war. Yet on a deeper level, it was reluctant to put much faith in the peaceful intentions of a country only recently the nation's strongest enemy. The spectre of the *al-Ikhwan al-Muslimeen* (The Islamic Brotherhood), an Islamic fundamentalist party, haunted them. Presently undergound, the fanatic membership could surface at any time, seize power, and dragoon Egypt's fifty millions on the warpath against the Brotherhood's sworn enemy — *Israeel.* The Brotherhood or its ilk had been responsible for Sadat's assassination. Despite American and Egyptian assurances that Egypt was irrevocably committed to peace, believers were hard to find in Israel. The Egyptians suffered from a fatal and original flaw — they were Arabs like the rest.

The country targeted by Army propaganda for its severest salvos was Syria, ancient and modern enemy of Israel. Syria, intransigent, savage Syria, the region's Soviet proxy, the hand wielding the assassin's dagger, periodically plunging it into the breasts of those who would pray for peace. Syria, a country where soldier girls ate live snakes and soldier boys drank the blood of puppy dogs. Syria, primitive, barbaric, medieval, practicing torture, assassination, terrorism. It was "black propaganda", some true, some false. The difficulty lay in separating the two. Countries that exceeded the norms of "civilized behavior" opened themselves to speculative attack. What indeed was the CIA? A debating society for reformed spies and assassins?

Syria was Israel's most determined ideological enemy,

195

its people heir to a belief that Palestine was stolen from the Syrian nation. The parcelling of Syria by the Great Powers following the dissolution of the Turkish Empire still rankled. Israel's annexation of the Golan Heights was salt on a festering wound. Yet, if any group had been shortchanged, it was the Palestinians, losing both home and nation. After twenty years of occupation who could blame those who, albeit vainly, hoped for peace? The answer, of course, was Syria. If Syria could not have peace, no one would have peace. Syria was the enemy — yesterday, today and tomorrow. On that proposition the army's propaganda was accurate. History said as much.

The next session, "Enemy Psychology, Strength and Weakness", was introduced by Dr. Klug. They were "privileged to have as a lecturer one of Israel's leading experts on the Arab mind, Professor Yeckiel Toledano, distinguished academic and fellow of the Institute of Strategic Oriental Studies." Toledano, a gaunt, hatchet-faced man wearing a multi-colored, knit yarmulke, nodded to Klug and briskly advanced to the lectern, setting down a worn and bulging leather briefcase. Placing elbows and forearms on the slant of the lectern, he leaned forward and began speaking, "How much do you know about Arab mentality, behavior, motivation, personality? I submit not as much as you think. For instructional purposes I should like to call this lecture, 'The Hidden Arab', the one beneath and behind the Arab commonly seen daily on our streets and byways." Without further ado, Toledano launched into his subject, offering insights into Arab psychology and behavior. An Arab tendency to follow a strong leader, the *"rais"*, he associated with the strong patriarchal structure of the Arab family, where the ultimate authority is the father, whose word within his domain, the home, was law. Early domestic conditioning smoothly translates into the political realm, resulting in a "natural despotism", the only political hierachy possible for the Arab. Because power and authority are so intertwined in the Arab mind, there was very little occasion for reason. All authority proceeded from the top, thus the military injuction to aim first at the officers in an Arab attacking force. Because once the directing authority is eliminated, the rank and file quickly become disoriented and demoralized, surrendering *en masse*. "And why does the Arab exhibit this tendency to fall apart in adversity, this overwhelming lack of personal resourcefulness in crisis, large or small?" Raising his hand in a gesture of foreboding, Toledano answered his question, "Because of the influence of the mother, who performs virtually every task for the male child, from guiding the stream of his water into the proper place, to carrying him in her arms to spare him the necessity of walking on his own two legs." Thus was a dependency upon family succor instilled into the Arab child from the earliest infancy, a dependency never outgrown. Upon sexual maturation this deep-seated dependency, along with family and societal pressures, forces the Arab male to seek a mate. Conditioned by years of infantile gratification, he is unable to contain his appetite. This pattern of early marriage promotes the high birth rate of the Arab. With marriage occuring in the prime sexual years of both mates, excessive child production was inevitable. The "average Arab female of the species" had a good thirty years of fertility ahead of her. The cycle came full circle, when the young wife supplanting the mother, becomes the husband's maid as well as his vessel of sexual gratification. The conventions of Arab culture lock in its participants, both male and female, into juvenile, demeaning, and primitive roles, preventing the development of normal, mature, adult personality.

Visibly sweating, Toledano stepped in front of the lectern and wiped his brow. Despite the heat, he was attired befitting his dignity, in dark suit, white shirt and tie. After a futher pause to drain a glass of ice water, he returned to his subject, "Now some of you may be thinking to yourselves — and that is good, we want you to think — 'Of what use is this to us as soldiers?' I will tell you. Because the Arab mind is unaccustomed to rational thought, for the reasons already established, military strategy is beyond its capacity. Why do you think there have been no memorable Arab military leaders in modern history?"

"Because they kill them before they can make a name for themselves!," someone shouted from the back of the room.

"Ah, very good," said Toledano smiling, "I see we have a joker among us. Sure they kill them, but thanks to you boys we help them kill them. So let us give credit where it is due — thank you, kind sir, that was a good point — to our own superior strategy and capabilities. As an example let us consider their tactics — always small-scale, raids, one-man suicide assaults. Militarily they are anarchists, bombthrowers, unable to function in an organized, large-scale manner. Their record with land forces is dismal, *humiliating*! Two dimensions are difficult enough for them without compounding the problem with that of the sky above. Such levels of coordination can only be hypothetical, whenever they attempt to put them into practice they must fail. From the logistical to the technological, in modern, mechanized warfare they are incompetent, incoherent . . ."

"This character is too much!," exclaimed Basil. Amon, seated alongside, shrugged his shoulders. Ignoring the remark, the professor forged on, "Most of you have experienced occupation duty. You may have been trained to grab the offending Arab by his hair. Not because it is a good handhold, it is not, the hair often being short and greasy. A good grip of the back of the collar is better. The reason you grab them by the hair is because that humiliates them. One good humiliation is worth a thousand blows. An Arab humiliated is an Arab destroyed. The Arab male's sense of manhood suffers permanent damage from humiliation, whereas the use of physical force is counterproductive, only making the typical Arab offender more sullen, more defiant.

198

Being a product of a primitive society, he may use the occasion of a beating to show off his disdain for pain. But a well executed ceremony of humiliation, performed in full view of the womenfolk of his village, or if that is impractical, his friends and neighbors, will often frustrate the offender to tears. Research has shown that more drastic measures of humiliation are necessary for the older, more hardened terrorist. Some commanders employ dragging in the town square for these miscreants. Additional methods I leave to your imagination. For the Arab, a product of a masculine preferential society, to be reduced to shame in front of his womenfolk, is a fate often worse than death itself. It is really one of the better forms of counter-terrorism.

"So gentlemen, don't be fooled by the sound of the word. Psychology may sound sissified, but in truth it is a very powerful force . . . perhaps more powerful than bullets. As an illustration, let us imagine you have a locked door. You want to enter. Do you smash the door to pieces? That is the way of brute force, very effective, but then you have no door, a door you may want. No, you place a key in the lock and presto, you are inside. You have gained entry and yet still preserve the door. Psychology is that key . . . " Toledano hesitated, from the front rows necks craned toward the sound of the disturbance behind them. Basil had risen from his chair and was noisily shuffling past knees and boots towards the aisle. Turning to his right, he saw Klug get up and proceed down the other side of the room. A lieutenant rising to assist Klug was waved back. Outside, the high-pitched voice of Professor Toledano could be heard through the open doors. Basil waited for Klug to draw within spitting distance before asking, "Say Klug, you got a cigarette?" He knew Klug knew he did not smoke. For a moment Klug stood stock-still, lips pursed, face reddening. Then with a snort like that from a small animal, he turned and walked back into the building.

199

They were still talking about his "walk-out" at dinner. From the sound of it, he had more support than he would have imagined. His mates — the lawyers, teachers, bureaucrats and businessmen making up a large proportion of the populace of a capital city were not so bad after all. Amon had told him the unit was relatively liberal. Relative that is, to some of the other units, the ones from places like Askelon and Afula, or the border towns and settlements. Units from those regions had a heavy representation of settlers and Sephardim. The former's motivation was obvious — they wanted land. Sephardic attitudes were less easily related. The combination of traditional conservatism and new-found patriotism was not a formula for tolerance.

Of course, being "liberal" did not imply softness on Arabs. Liberals were far too cautious for that. Like snakes coiled about a tree, they were on all sides of an issue at once. A vague word in any language, it was even vaguer in reference to politics. In the present context, liberal probably suggested a more sophisticated appreciation of reality. As applied to that afternoon, it meant that an influential minority was sympathetic to his demonstration — that is if it correctly grasped the act's intent, because standing alone it was open to ambiguous interpretation.

"I thought he wanted to go to the bathroom. And when Dr. Klug returned so quickly after following him out . . . ," said one, a lawyer when not soldiering.

"Klug never said a word. Now if that was me, an ordinary guy, he would have been all over me."

"Actually, you missed the best part. After you left he started in on Islam."

"That's what bothered me," said Basil, "his subtlety."

"In my opinion," declared the lawyer, "the impact of your demonstration miscarried. If you found the speaker's words objectionable, you should have said so at the proper time."

"You're not suggesting I should have taken you by the

hand?," replied Basil. "I led, you could have followed. Don't blame me now for not insulting your intelligence. And now if you'll excuse me, I really have to go to the bathroom."

He didn't have to go to the bathroom, he was being ironic. It was as appropriate a way as any to end a futile discussion.

18

"Hey Basil, you awake?" It was impossible not to be once the importuning voice in the lower bunk sounded its nightly call of reverie.

"Yeah, I'm awake," answered Basil resignedly from his perch overhead.

"I thought so. I just wanted to tell you that was a good thing you did today."

"Yeah, yeah, what's the catch?"

"No, I'm serious . . . Say, wasn't that you I saw giving the girls the old two-eye after dinner?"

"One thing I like about you, Amon, you're not disingenuous in the least."

"Yeah, and I have your best interest at heart at all times. Did you see anything that ah . . . took your breath away?"

"No, my imagination isn't as powerful as yours."

"Yeah, I read you. Those uniforms do put a strain on the imagination. Maybe you'd like to see something where you don't have to use your imagination."

"Finally, the inevitable, followed by the inevitable 'no'."

"OK lad, have it your way. You'll be sorry someday

I'm sure . . . You hot up there? Where's that desert breeze tonight?"

"How should I know? Why don't you try sleeping, you might enjoy it?"

"You ask that of me? A man with my problems? Foolish boy . . . Say Basil, did you ever have a woman wrap her legs around your neck and squeeze? I'll bet you didn't. That's this woman I was telling you about . . . "

"Now it can be told . . . "

"As I was saying, she gets me in this scissors lock and cradles the back of my head in her tender hands. God, I could go for some of that now. I feel that smooth, cool butt on my chest. It is slightly clammy, much moisture has gone down the road, her cup overfloweth . . . "

"Hold it, you're mixing your metaphors again."

"Metaphors? What are metaphors compared to love? You should have a girl like her . . . To recapitulate, she opens her thighs, you feel their inner velvet against your cheeks, you are dying for a piece of this pie . . . and she knows it."

"OK, OK, I'll do it. But just go to sleep will you?"

"Aha! I knew you'd come around eventually. Primchek, you won't regret this. In fact, I expect you'll be thanking me some day . . . Tomorrow we strike at dusk. In the meantime, try and get some sleep."

The next afternoon the temperature was 109 — in the shade. Amon took it as a good omen, it was ideal "showering weather". About an hour before the usual dismissal time, they slipped away from the firing range and returned to the barracks. Timing was essential. According to Amon's calculations the shower windows began spewing steam about eight to ten minutes after the girls came in from the field. That meant they probably started showering about five minutes after entering the barracks. Therefore, they should allow for that lead time before making for the fence. Basil insisted upon being the first up, reasoning that as a volunteer it was only fair he be first. Boots were exchanged for light, rubber-soled sneakers to make standing on the back less punishing. Basil, who had forty pounds on Amon, suggested they practice the necessary acrobatics before starting out. After running through the procedure three times, they agreed there was little more they could do in preparation.

He found himself caught up in the spirit of the exercise, his earlier indifference replaced by a kind of suppressed excitement. Actually, he conceded, it was an alluring proposition, like treasure hunting. Certainly, for the both of them, no more precious treasure awaited discovery in Wadi Jamil.

The camp commissary being near the women's barracks, they made it their jumping-off point. Seated in the commissary's cafe, they had a clear view of the barracks' starboard side. Amon patted his empty cardboard box, meanwhile keeping an eye out for the quarry. Despite the scheme's comic aspect, both were somewhat nervous. "Didn't I tell you this would be exciting?," said Amon, "I'll bet you're even more nervous than I am."

"Yeah, this is a great sport. They should make you entertainment director for this desert Devil's Island."

"Listen, why do you think the Army sent those girls here? They could have left them in the Galilee where the duty is a hell of a sight better. They're here for one reason — morale. Of course, we can't all have one, the ratio is too skewed. But that's the way the Army works, it figures illusion is better than no illusion at all. Hope, it gives us hope. We'll tolerate this hell-hole better that way . . ." Amon fell silent. The girls were beginning to file into the barracks.

They spent the five minute lead time watching the barracks for any change in routine that might alert them to a different pattern. Seeing nothing unusual, Amon gave the order to move out. "Remember," he enjoined, "walk like you own the place and keep talking until we hit the corner of the fence. Then follow me . . ."

The approach went as planned, Basil gesturing and speaking animatedly, while Amon, the sham box under an arm, nodded and gestured with his free hand. No one — the few men and one woman they passed on the walkway — gave them a second look. From the shower room windows came puffs of steam. It was indeed a good day for showering.

Amon slipped through the gap in the fence. Basil followed, forcing himself through the constricted space. Amon was already in position under the window calculated to give the best angle for viewing the shower room's interior. Mounting Amon's back, he slowly raised himself to the level of the open window's sill, a too rapid movement of the head and it might have been all over. He could hear their chatter, the discordant female voices mixing with the bass drone of the showers reminding him of a disagreeable piece of modern music. From the volume he judged the room well populated. However, he was there to see, not hear.

She was about three meters away, eyes closed, head tilted back, her chest receiving a shower's stream. Miniature rivulets of water ran down over her navel and groin, channelling into the intensely black bush. Her darkly tanned skin, wildly accented by white breasts and loins, glistened from the moisture. He felt his crotch heave. "Let's go! It's my turn!" whispered Amon hoarsely from below. To be rushed at such a time was more than annoying, it was maddening. He wanted to yell "Quiet!" but his face was at window level. Looking down momentarily he caught sight of Amon's head. He could have kicked it . . .

It all happened very quickly. He had been seen, it was too late to duck. A face, masked in rage, was screaming at him, setting off a chain reaction of shrieking, fleeing figures. Suddenly he was on the ground. Getting up, he saw Amon wriggle through the gap in the fence and run. He tried to follow, but leaving was harder than entering. His shirt torn, he did not look back but ran as fast as he could after his cohort. He wanted to overtake him, jump him from behind, drag him down into the dust. But Amon had too much of a start, it was all he could do to follow him into the barracks. "Hey schmuck!," he cried between gasps, "Next time you decide to take off like that, how about warning me? I could be lying back there with a broken back, you wouldn't know."

"Sorry, but it's every man for himself when you're caught. How the hell did you let them see you anyway?"

"Blame yourself, animal, they heard *you*. You had to start making noises . . ."

"You're the animal, fathead, a clumsy animal. If I had been up there this would never have happened . . .By the way, did you see anything?"

"We can talk about that later. Right now let's clean up and get over to the mess. I don't want to give that bitch who raised the hue and cry any grounds for suspicion. Did you see that bunch looking at us running over here?"

"Yeah, so what? They probably took us for a couple of gung-ho commandos having our evening race."

They entered the mess a minute apart. If anyone wondered where they had been for the past couple of hours, they had the sense not to ask. Between forkfuls of food Basil snuck glances at the girls, hoping to fit face to body. For their part, the girls did not seem noticeably upset by the incident, eating and conversing with the usual vivacity, apparently none the worse for exposure. But then they could have been dissimulating, hoping thereby to lure the offender into a trap, it was too soon after the fact to be seen approaching too closely. He had ten more days in which to claim her. Meanwhile, neither would be going anyplace.

She was standing with a troop of girls near the end of the opposite serving line. Ringlets of black hair lay wet against her face and neck, corroborating the brief image he had of her. He studied her movements and mannerisms as

205

she moved through the line, then to her table. "She's here," he whispered to Amon.

"Where? Point her out."

"Third from the left, sitting with her back to us . . .I'll have to catch her outside. Wait with me until she comes out, it will look better that way."

They waited opposite the mess hall's back door, the exit people used after depositing their trays at a galley window where Arab scullions collected them for washing. She came out with two other girls. He waited until he could read her name tag before stepping in front of her and announcing in an authoritative tone, "Private Aboulafia, Headquarters would like to see you." He was telling the truth, Headquarters *would* like to see her. As expected, they were too intimidated to question the demand. "You can tell your friends not to worry. I don't think it's anything serious."

Introducing himself, he apologized for the pretext, saying it was necessary to avoid an awkward situation. Put simply, he wished to make her acquaintance. Confessing to being flattered by the attraction, she willingly accompanied him to the camp theater for the evening's feature film. After the show they walked to her barracks, agreeing to meet the following evening.

Rachel Aboulafia was a Sephardi of Moroccan parentage from Tel Aviv. Her immediate ambition was to become a medical technician, "not a nurse but in administration" she hastened to explain. "Medical records" was the area of her interest. Attached to a medical unit, she was receiving valuable experience in the profession. Her detachment had been assigned to Wadi Jamil for a few weeks training under desert conditions. The heat didn't bother her, she was a "beach person"— as her dark tan manifested. He mentioned his involvement with the Eilat International project, pointing out that as a beach denizen she might be able to suggest a few refinements. She was impressed, but as one of the many

206

blissfully unaware of his recent celebrity, she had little to relate to. Of course, the issue for him was her architecture, not his.

19

Even preparations for war took a holiday, and in Wadi Jamil the Shabbos was holy. That was the day the camp swimming pool took on the appearance of a giant, open can of live sardines. A prohibition against mixed bathing had men and women using the pool at different times. Officially, the rule was in consideration of Israel's powerful Orthodox element. But practically the problem was placing fifty to a hundred bikinied, nubile females, in with a force of perhaps two to three thousand pent-up, reservist males. The military abhorred a scandal. So it did what armies usually did in similar circumstances, it compromised — no mixed bathing on military reservations while leaving the matter discretionary for military personnel in areas under civilian control. For those who found swimming in the camp pool too restrictive, there were buses to take them to Eilat. Basil had gone there the week before with Amon wanting to study the lay of the beach for the purpose of drawing up the sketches promised Portnoy. Thus, it wasn't a total loss when in the few hours allotted, they failed to meet a couple of tourist beauties.

Today's Shabbos held better prospects. He had persuaded the sergeant in charge of the motor pool to let him use a jeep, purportedly to take in the rock formations of the surrounding wilderness. A timely gratuity was offered and accepted. In order not to arouse envy, or worse, scandal, Rachel was to discretely await him near the camp entrance. The outing had been described as an opportunity to explore the desert's geological attractions. They could "sunbathe" on one of the rock formations. He had never sunbathed in his life. The word conjured up rows of chaises with sickly people taking the sun on the grounds of some mountain sanitarium. The suggestion was a concession to hypocrisy.

The jeep was ready when he arrived carrying four water filled canteens and a bound roll of blankets slung over his back. The pass from the motor pool sergeant would get him through the gate. At two minutes to the hour he drove out of the motor pool, turned to his right and made for the appointed spot, stopping only long enough for her to get on board. After briefly halting at the gatehouse, they headed into the monotonous horizon of desert, their destination a large outcropping of gneiss rock known locally as the "seven old ladies". On the way they exchanged small talk about the weather, the army, her family (she was the oldest of seven), the desert, and rocks (she had no knowledge of geology). She had become more relaxed and spontaneous in his presence. They had already exchanged addresses and she knew his tour of duty would be over in two days. He had also given her his telephone number at work and suggested they get together on her next leave, yet similar averments of mutuality had evaporated before. Perhaps it was her youthful naiveté, but she appeared to believe him. Nineteen seemed too young to have been through the mill. There was even a possibility she was a virgin. It would be a first, he had always come somewhere down the line on the scorecards of his women. Bodies like hers did not long remain intact without some fairly rigorous chaperoning, and universal conscription was not conducive to the maintenance of traditional authority. The state's interest in sex went only as far as the regulation of marriage and children. Virginity was a concern left to the rabbis, mullahs, popes, and other assorted male authoritarians who still insisted upon treating sex as a religious rather than a medical problem. She would do what she felt like doing, that was the way women did things. If she wanted him she would please him. It was as simple as that.

"Look! There they are! They do look like old ladies, old Arab ladies." Excited by the discovery, Rachel, moved forward for a better look at the rock formation coming into view. The sun, now directly overhead, sparkled in the granite particles of the gneiss rock. He stopped the jeep and reached behind for one of the large desert canteens. Uncapping it, he gallantly offered it to his companion. After drinking she handed it back, a trickle of water dribbling from the corner of her mouth. He felt his member quicken. He could have taken her there, through pith helmet, khakis and boots, but instead took a long draught of the cooling water.

"You were thirsty."

"It's hot."

He parked below a pair of megaliths by the formation's margin, attracted to the spot by a large, flat outcropping. Before unrolling the blankets over the sun-heated rock he searched the surface for signs of vermin or vipers. Even vermin knew not to go out in the midday sun but he had to make sure. Rachel called his attention to a small accumulation of government issue tins and the charcoaled remnants of a fire, artifacts that could have been last year's or last month's, there was no way of knowing. In the not too distant past wandering Bedouin made camp here. Now it was the army's, reserved for its exclusive and absolute use. Rachel's modest discovery stimulated further exploration of the rock's secrets. A path led through a narrow defile which opened onto a cul-de-sac, the base of the larger group of megaliths. Now they towered above, blocking their advance. He caught her as she turned, driving her body against the vertical wall of rock. She made a perfunctory gesture of resistance, raising, then dropping her hands. Grabbing her wrist, he alternately pulled and lead her through the defile, back to the blankets. Needing no prompting, she nimbly divested herself of the formless, khaki cocoon. The white patches of her breasts and loins gave the chestnut body an animal savagery, like a bongo or okapi. There was no swimsuit. She had not gone into the desert with him to bake in the sun. Drawing her into him, he sank onto the blankets with her, ravishing her breasts, indulging in the ravenous impossibility of swallowing them. Upending her, he lifted the untanned portion of her buttocks to eye level, burying his face in the confluent flesh. He had been starving for intimacy. Like most starvelings, having it, he could not get enough.

The sun had fallen behind the tops of the two mega-liths, the interposition casting a welcome shade. But another problem had arisen — a sudden onset of flies, hundreds of the buzzing obscenities, crawling on his face, over his balls. Like most wild creatures, they possessed an unerring sense of smell. Now they were demanding their due, attracted by the humors produced by the two bodies in the process of their reciprocal flailing. To the civilized, their presence was an intolerable distraction. The decision to terminate was regrettable but the future belonged to white-sheeted beds in fly-free hotel rooms, nature in the raw was definitely an ambiguous proposition. Still, days like this were unique. "You know," he said, standing by while she dutifully rolled and tied the blankets, "what we did here deserves to be engraved in stone. We made history." Ignoring the remark, she threw the blanket roll into the jeep, saying, "We better be going."

Amon reacted with awe and admiration to the story of his friend's success. One of them had broken through the khaki curtain, covering himself with glory. When told they would be meeting in Tel Aviv on her next leave, he said he felt "like a father".

20

It was the morning of the last day of camp. He was sitting in the camp's processing center, waiting. Outside, buses stood by to carry them back to Jerusalem. They were waiting for their files, which were in the process of being validated with a record of the month's training in the specific military categories qualified (armor-infantry, gunnery, night combat and march, ordnance, etc.). The training had sharpened their coordination. Waging war would come easier for them now, all "offense was defense" hypocrisy aside. The strategy was total war, a process the rag-tag Palestinians were ill-equiped to resist and Arab states too weak to oppose. The Israeli Defense Forces moved swiftly, relentlessly, prodigiously. It was the only way. Israel was not America, a protracted war was beyond its means. America was inexhaustible, its wars far-flung and imperial. Israel's wars were those of a nation in transition. Fortunately, its enemies were even less capable of waging protracted war. Two weeks of war and they were stretched to the limit, frantically petitioning the UN for a truce. The Vietnamese fought thirty-five years against three world powers until victory. Heaven help Israel against such a foe.

He first noticed her huddling with an officer in a corner of the room. Periodically, one or both would turn and look in his direction, as if confirming his identity. He returned the looks. In the circumstances that seemed the normal reaction, there was no retreating now. It was the woman from the shower room, the one who screamed out the alarm. She had the same look of blood in her eye, only now better focused. It was obvious he was the topic of discussion. What was she after — the right to spit in his face? She would swear it was him, the face, the moustache. Few Israelis had moustaches, many already resembled Arabs

211

too closely. He speculated on their next move. Would they inform Klug? What could he do? The officer appeared to be temporizing, caught between the woman's harangue and his own better judgment. Apparently, she was discovering the transition from accusation to prosecution was less than automatic. Minutes passed, they were waiting for someone or something. Basil recognized him immediately when he entered the room. It was Rabbi Boren, one of the camp's military rabbis. He had addressed the men at orientation, urging them to attend Shabbos services. He had seen Basil's name on the roster of incoming reservists and sought him out after the orientation period. They had briefly discussed his design for the Third Temple. Rabbi Boren fancied himself an archeologist, it was a national passion.

The officer and the woman briefed the rabbi, then, struggling not to appear obvious, they pointed him out. He waved, making sure to catch the good rabbi's eye. Bowing his head in response, the rabbi turned to his appellants and eyed the woman scornfully. A short, one-sided colloquy ensued, whereupon Rabbi Boren strode indignantly from the room. A moment later his accuser took the same route, but not before throwing a last, bitter, hateful look in his direction. He conceded her the satisfaction. It was still very much a man's world.

At home, anxious to see how work on the clinic had progressed, he quickly changed into civilian clothes. In his absence he had entrusted its supervision to Ulrich Fesser. He was uncomfortable delegating authority, believing the many complex decisions connected with a building's construction were the natural province of the design architect. However, except for Bustanji's stonework which was self-directed, most of the final touches had been stayed pending his return. Before leaving he checked his mail. There was no letter from Portnoy.

Bustanji was working on the scaffold when he pulled

up. Seeing the stonework of the facade in place was a cause for satisfaction. More than a fantasy image, it constituted substance, something he could stake a reputation on. "Hey Arab!," he yelled to the seemingly oblivious Bustanji, "I go away for a month and here you're still not done. What do you think I'm paying you for?" Ignoring the remarks, Bustanji bent over a pile of stone, hoisted a large slab, then rested it precariously on a length of scaffold pipe. "Hark! The hero returneth from the wars only to fall victim to a tragic accident at his beloved medical clinic."

He knew Bustanji was joking but watched him closely nevertheless. The stone was intimidating enough without being in the hands of a hostile Arab. "Accidents like that don't happen in Israel, the mob would tear you apart. Or are you proposing to emulate one of your crazy suicide bombers?"

"Why not? It's better than waiting to die from one of your bombs," said Bustanji, climbing down from the scaffold and shaking Basil's hand. "One Yahoodi, one Arab, in that proportion, and before you know it we would have won the war."

"This is a fine 'how do you do'. I come home and rush to get over here and all you talk about is killing each other . . ."

"And where were *you* this last month — at a prayer retreat? Did they teach you any new techniques for killing Arabs . . . if it's not revealing any precious military secrets?"

"Nothing new. If the club doesn't work, use the gun . . . Look, if you're trying to make me feel guilty you're not succeeding, because I'm not."

"You're a liar. You're as guilty as the rest. I can see it in your eyes. But like most 'good Jews', you're too stubborn and cowardly to admit it. By the way, the old man, Fesser, he's not a bad fellow."

"We can't all be bad."

"A gentleman. He was a refugee from fascism . . . or

maybe you knew that."

"No, but I knew he was of the old school."

"We had a long discussion one afternoon. The *Roosiya* came by too."

"You met Olga? What did you think of her?"

"I can never forgive the Russians for dumping their Jews on us. They should have sent them to America where they belong . . . 'What did I think of her?' Charming, obviously an exception, she speaks Arabic with a Russian accent. I gave her the grand tour. I would venture to say she was impressed . . ."

Bustanji pointed out his progress during Basil's absence, predicting that the job would be completed in four to five weeks. By then, he remarked parenthetically, he would have saved enough money to take a vacation in Lebanon. (He joked, no one vacationed in Lebanon anymore.) The major stonework was completed except for the installation of the courtyard columns. The plan called for columns of Italian marble inlaid with tesserae in varied patterns. On order for months, the front office had recently received a notice of shipment from the Italian manufacturer. Bustanji had his brother and another stonemason help with the larger stones and scaffolding. He paid them the "going rate" — which was whatever he got. He had insisted on a two tiered formula for wages, a declared rate and an undeclared bonus or "gratuity". The purpose was to avoid some of the taxation imposed upon Arab workers by the government, a taxation naturally resented. Israeli employers benefitted also. The less tax the Arabs paid, the less they had to be paid — and less was what they got.

After thanking Ulrich Fesser for assuming his responsibilities, he reported to Olga, walking into her office as she was emptying her ashtray. She greeted him warmly, remarking on his newly acquired tan, an incident of desert life. He noticed the office had been cleaned as well as articles rearranged. A wooden grid held the blueprints and drawings previously stacked higgledy-piggledy in corners. Except for the small brass ashtray and a small collection of papers, the desk was clear. Olga had something to tell him. In the month that he had been gone, she had received inquiries on his availability to design private residences from four different sources. This kind of thing was the bread and butter of a beginning architect, she said. Moreover, she knew for a fact two of the callers were very rich. Handing him the memorandums of the calls, she suggested he contact them as soon as convenient.

The clinic, he asked, what did she think of the clinic? She thought it splendid, she said. But she had liked it from the beginning, from the first sketches. Seeing it *in situ* was another dimension, the ultimate dimension for an architectural idea. There was no doubt in her mind but that it would be listed in future Jerusalem guide books. Leaving the subject, she remarked upon his appearance, that he looked tired, that perhaps he should go home and rest, it was already past two. "In fact," she declared, "*I* am your commanding officer now, and I am ordering you to go home."

As he was walking out he remembered he had something to ask her, " . . . . what did you think of my man, as-Sayyed Khalil Bustanji?" He used the Arabic for "mister".

"Oh yes . . . a fascinating man. Obviously one worthy of respect . . . . as are many of the Palestinians. Or don't you agree?"

"Of course."

He slept until his father came home from the bakery. During dinner he started to relate some of his experiences but Lev Primchek seemed more interested in discussing the Portnoy deal, wanting him to get right on it. He reported going over to the clinic twice to moniter progress. As a first effort it was commendable, but a multi-million dollar commission it was not.

Later Basil telephoned the Jerusalem Hilton. Portnoy

was out of the country but was expected back on the weekend. He assumed Portnoy's negotiations with the government had been successful, operators like Portnoy usually got what they wanted, give or take a few million. It was time to begin working up the designs.

The conception of the beach houses was simple — two story, whitewashed, stuccoed structures with half of the second story devoted to an open terrace. Slatted wooden awnings could be rolled up and down over metal tracks. Large European-style shuttered windows faced the water. To provide architectural relief, roof heights were staggered. The casino was more elaborate, with an entrance eight meters high, carved oak doors, deeply inset window openings, and dome roof, its design inspired by the Al-Bazzali mosque of Cairo. Stores, laundries, and restaurants conformed to the beach units. Planned as supporting elements, they were set back amidst groves of acacia and eucalyptus.

The proposed solution to the security problem took the form of a five meter high wall composed of large, quarried stone blocks. Stretching from one end of the beach village to the other and forming a protective arc, it was wide enough to accomodate a roadway along its top. Situated at appropriate intervals were portcullised entrance gates. While no Great Wall of China, the wall had the potential of being a touristic attraction in its own right. Set against shifting sands and swaying palms, it evoked a Roman ruin or a scene from *Beau Geste*.

21

The memo on his desk said to "call Rachel after 7:00 p.m., she will be waiting". The peculiar printed script was Olga's. Like many new immigrants she learned Hebrew in the army where writing was a lessor priority than speaking and reading. There was time enough later for such refinements as handwriting. For the army's purposes, being able to sign one's name was enough.

Rachel took the call at the camp telephone center. She had been waiting since 6:30 — in case he called early. Was he going to see her again? He assured her that he was, in fact, the sooner the better. He spoke under constraint, his father sitting within earshot in the adjoining room. She spared him further embarassment by doing most of the talking, describing in exaggerated detail the suffering she was experiencing because of their separation. She had reached a point where she wanted to leave the army and go home but her commander persuaded her to compromise by accepting a five day leave. Did he still want to meet her in Tel Aviv?

He was way ahead of her, he had already made the necessary inquiries. She should meet him at the Hotel Excelsior, he would be there Thursday morning. The country's distances favored them, Tel Aviv was just down the road. "Until Thursday," she said. Her voice had lost its tentative quality and taken on a lusty confidence. He hung up the receiver and sat by his father.

"A girlfriend?"

"I think that's a reasonable assumption."

"I couldn't help hearing, she's from Tel Aviv. Where did you meet her?"

"In a shower . . . no, actually at Wadi Jamil. She's doing her military obligation."

"A young one, eh? What is she?"

"Moroccan. She's the oldest of seven brothers and sisters."

"Enjoy yourself. You've got what every old man would like to have."

"What, a young girl?"

"No, youth."

Miriam's letters contained plans and suggestions for the European rendezvous. She chose England because of its many associations, and also because he had never been there. October, she wrote, was an ideal time. The summer crush of Americans abroad would be over, and except for the English, they would have the country to themselves. The plan called for renting a car in London then wending their way through the countryside, their itinerary determined by guide book and personal momentum. He imagined bedding down with her on the bed and breakfast circuit, the small body underneath a fluffy, paisley quilt in a quaint English bed. The idea was appealingly romantic, even exciting. Belatedly, from five thousand miles, he was beginning to realize certain things. But he wasn't going to England, he was sure she would understand. A short answer was preferable to a long explanation that could only bore or hurt her.

Herbert Portnoy telephoned Shabbos morning. He had arrived the night before and was anxious to see the drawings for the Eilat International project. Basil went right over. He found Portnoy without his usual entourage, looking absurdly lonely in the vastness of the prodigal hotel suite. He asked about the family — "Michelle, Elaine, the girls". "Fine, fine, they're all fine," Portnoy matter-of-factly replied while taking the folder of sketches from Basil's hands. Removing the drawings, he juxtaposed them on the dining room table, made two circumambulations, then looked up exclaiming, "Great! We won't change anything. They're just what I had in mind. But let me ask you . . . this wall here. Do we really need that?"

"Well, you wanted something to stop terrorists. We can always throw down concertina wire and the concrete barriers they put around the White House. That's hardly conducive to the atmosphere you want to create for a resort."

"Yeah, but this thing is going to run into the millions. Quarried stone blocks! That's a little much. What's wrong with poured concrete?"

If you don't know, then by all means make a wall of poured concrete." He didn't mean to sound testy. He had dealt with enough clients to know how often arguments cropped up, how so many had to be persuaded against doing a job on the cheap. "You have to realize, Herb," he continued, "this is the Holy Land. That concrete you see out there, that's in spite of people like me. I can probably design you a barrier at one-one hundredth the cost, face it in brick. It's your decision. The anti-terrorist barrier was your idea."

"It was? OK, but what about all this peace talk? This wall could be the biggest white elephant in Israel if the PLO finally goes for peace."

"Only six weeks ago your family was afraid to walk in the street for fear of terrorism. Now that there's been a lull and talk of peace is in the air again you think the problem's gone away. I'm not the prime minister and even if I were I'm not sure I would be in any better position to answer your concern. Let me put it this way — when I see it I'll believe it. Until then you're going to need some sort of security. Troops, police dressed in white linen, beach guards, I don't care what you call them. This thing is a lot bigger than the PLO. One threat, or worse, one bomb, from one crazy faction, and you can forget about making money . . . I don't know, maybe that's not a concern, the wall was designed to address that problem. Those two-ton blocks are more psychological than physical necessities."

"I guess I was looking too close at the bottom line. We'll go for the wall as is. Sorry to doubt you, if anybody should know about these things it's you. Hell, what do I know? I'm just a rube from Florida."

Portnoy was confident the consortium would approve the project. The drawings would work to resolve any lingering doubts about feasibility. Some of the Americans had been searching for a good investment situation in Israel. Asked about the status of his negotiations with the Israeli government, Portnoy responded, "Oh that. That's all been taken care of."

The occasion, declared Portnoy, called for a toast. Ringing room service, he ordered drinks brought up. While they were waiting, Portnoy asked about business, his father's business, whether he had a girlfriend. It was small talk, filling the time. Americans were a chatty people and except for places like elevators and toilets, conversation was the norm. Often the subject was personal but superficially personal so not to give offense. Americans liked to think they took a personal interest in others. Whether they were sincere was immaterial, it was primarily a function of human relations. He treated Portnoy's questions with a polite tolerance, it was impossible not to. "Yes," he said, he had met a "very nice girl" during his recent stint with the reserves. Realizing he had said too much, he followed with a quick qualification, "But you know how these things are, they come and go." Portnoy's reaction was a knowing nod.

When the drinks came Portnoy raised his glass in a toast to the "project and its architect". He expected the loose ends to be wrapped up in the coming week. Getting up from his chair, he apologized for having to be short, but he needed more rest to recoup from the constant jetting about. Seeing Basil to the door, Portnoy reiterated his satisfaction with the designs, suggesting that he "sit tight" for the present. He would be in touch as soon as capital commitments were firm.

He left the meeting with a sense of quiet jubilation. Back at home his father was less restrained. The occasion, he declared, called for a celebration. He knew just the place, an Arabic restaurant located on a small square in the Old City. Seated at linen covered tables with only the blue sky overhead, they could dine on appetizers and the specialty of the house, stuffed vegetables. The restaurant was patronized by a mixed clientele of Israelis and Arabs, mutual hunger enforcing a truce between them.

22

Arriving in Tel Aviv Thursday morning he went directly to the hotel. He asked for a room in back, away from the noise of the street. After checking the room's amenities, he removed his clothes and laid on the bed, too anxious to read, even a newspaper. Finally, to escape the nervousness of waiting, he removed the coverlet and got under the sheet.

He was awakened by a light tapping on the unlocked door. Rachel entered, shutting the door behind her. She was facing him, back against the door, her dark, kohl-rimmed eyes reviewing the situation. From her shoulders she let fall an oversize jacket. Underneath she wore a buttoned dress, underneath that, nothing. She stood, as if awaiting a signal, her naked body idealized by the room's half-light. He lifted the sheet. In a moment she was against him.

It was hunger that finally forced them from the room and on the town. After a dinner of steak and fries they strolled the commercial area, looking in shop windows when not looking at each other. The hotel's entertainment guide advertised a klezmer band at a nearby club. He found it hard to believe she had never heard klezmer music. She found it hard to believe he had never heard of some of the new groups, like "The Pooks" and "Charnel House", they were "international". Wasn't klezmer "old European ghetto music?" Two hours of klezmer modified her opinions somewhat, but she still held out for the newer music, saying that he should begin to get with it. "Yeah, *bookra*," he replied, using the Arabic term for "tomorrow".

She came by early the next morning, so early he wished he had given her the room key the night before. There was something sanguine, even bouncy, about her mood. She had told her parents about him — but only that she had met him at camp and that he was presently in the city on business. They wished to meet him. Would he come home with her for Shabbos dinner? Her parents were expecting him. In the circumstances there was only one possible answer, "Sure," he muttered, "why not?"

It was a brave soul who drove an automobile on the Shabbos in some areas of Israel. Jews had their own contingents of stone-throwers, roving bands of Orthodox zealots prepared to mete summary punishment to blasphemers of the holy day. Her neighborhood was free of such intolerance she said, as she directed him through the intricacies of Tel Aviv's Moroccan quarter, her people believed in "live and let live".

The quarter resembled an Arab town, its randomly parked vehicles and street litter suggesting a condition of permanent disorder. Indeed, the inhabitants themsleves resembled Arabs, perhaps itself sufficient reason for the collective segregation. Officially there were no ghettos in Israel, only "quarters". "Ghetto" was a word Israelis were understandably sensitive about applying to themselves. If anyone had a ghetto mentality it was the Arabs, insisting upon resisting the right of Jews to live anywhere and everywhere in Eretz Israel. With such an attitude they created their own ghettos.

Home for the Aboulafias was a three story fortress-like structure perched on a corner. Its applied cement surface was pocked with holes and cracks, laying bare the underlying blockstones. The family occupied a second floor apartment, five rooms and a bath. Adequate for a family of four, it groaned under the burden of nine. The dining room had been converted into a bedroom. The family took their meals in the living room, the kitchen being hardly big enough to cook in. The Aboulafias were fortunate, living space was in short supply in Israel. It was better than living in some village in the boondocks near a border shared with Arabs, the dumping grounds for many new immigrants. Now he knew where the poor disappeared to at night. If there was one advantage wealth enjoyed, it was in not having to endure cheek-by-jowl existence with others of the race.

Despite the built-in inadequacies, the apartment evidenced the effect of a deliberate cleanliness. Reflecting its tidy, if transient, orderliness, were the children. Each was impressively sanitized and attired, boys' hair combed, girls' in ties. Mother Aboulafia, a tired-looking woman somewhere in her thirties, arrayed her brood for introduction, oldest first. It was no use his trying to remember all the names, there were too many. The younger ones stared at him ingenuously, as only children can. Was he the first their sister had brought home? As if reading his thought, the mother pointedly remarked that meeting a friend of their sister's was a new experience. She apologized for the absence of her husband, he was at his office, a ship was arriving from France in the morning. Rachel had described her father as the owner of an independent trucking business, adding that he often worked long hours. Now she emerged from the kitchen carrying a tray holding three glasses of chilled orange juice. Mother Aboulafia again apologized for the delay, but her husband was expected any minute, as soon as he arrived they could begin serving. She hoped their guest liked "Moroccan-Israeli food".

Dinner began with a soup of lamb and vegetables. He thought he detected cumin and turmeric in the soup's medley of condiments, both were commonly used in Moroccan cookery. Chicken and vegetables were also *au Morocain*, baked in a terra cotta roaster. Conversation was minimal. The family took eating seriously, efficiently skeletonizing the four chicken offering. Afterwards, the female family members cleared the table of its dishes and trapping, then folded its legs and placed it against a wall. The host, Nagi Aboulafia, showed Basil to one of the room's two stuffed chairs. Seating himself in the other, he spoke of the problem that had occupied his attention for much of the day. A container of machinery from Marseilles was arriving in the morning. His trucks had to be waiting at the port, the machinery was part of a rush order. A businessman had to be responsive to his customers' demands or he wouldn't remain in business very long, competition being what it was.

They were trying to get him to talk, about himself and his enterprise. The obvious they already knew — that he was an Ashkenazi from Jerusalem, had won some kind of national architectural prize, and was rich, the best evidence of that his new model metallic-blue automobile. The question was how rich? Their probing was oblique, almost lawyer-like. Would his business be bringing him to Tel Aviv often? Was his father an architect also? How long had he been practicing? The route was circuitous and prudent. It had to be, their daughter's future, indeed, the whole family's, was involved. Only so many questions could be asked at one time.

It was coffee time. The rich brown of the brew being poured into the white demitasse cups reminded him of her coloration, the dark and light of the cuirass-like torso. Seeing mother and daughter together allowed him to make some superficial comparisons beyond the obvious relationship the tinted image in the framed wedding photograph proved, the relationship time and seven children were working to deny. He was struck by the transformation, or rather deformation, between then and now, the formerly handsome figure of the mother dissolved into a waxen lump, one body given up for another, nature giving and taking. Motherhood was often synonymous with sacrifice, yet, in Rachel, life's cyclical cruelty found justification. The hypnotic dugs and authoritative rump were the cycle's highest extension.

It wasn't until after eight that they were able to break away. On the way back traffic seemed heavy, but not being a resident of Tel Aviv he really had nothing to compare it with. He noticed two troop lorries passing in the opposite direction, going north. The army was always going somewhere in Israel. With the Yom Kipper war came an increase in vigilance, especially on weekends. Arriving at the Excelsior, he turned the car over to the hotel garage attendant, a young Arab. Inside the lobby the desk clerk was motioning to him, "Sir, have you heard? A general alert has been called."

"No," said Basil, "I don't know anything about it."

"Yessir, it was announced shortly after seven o'clock. All reservists have been ordered to report to their units."

"Is that so? Thank you for the news item but my wife and I have had a hard day. We're very tired. May I ask that we not be disturbed?"

Patriotism had its limits. His icy rebuke made it plain those limits had been exceeded. The desk clerk uttered a compliant "yessir" and went about his business. In contrast, Rachel reacted with confusion and surprise at her companion's attitude. Confronting him in front of the lifts, she whispered nervously, "It's an alert. You're not going to ignore it, are you?"

"My dear Rachel, I don't know about you, but *I* am going to our room. Only last week you went on about leaving the army. Now, after a few days of freedom, you're ready to put the bridle on again."

"But . . . what if there's an attack?"

"What if there is? Do you think *you*, or I, will make any difference? They can throw us into the sea for all I care."

"You're not serious?," she shot back incredulously.

"What's the matter? I thought you liked the water. Hey, *you're* not serious? I thought only Arabs still believed in those fantasies." He stepped inside the lift, his hand holding its door. "Well," he said, "what will it be . . . me, or duty and country?"

If she was still confused, and there was no doubt she was, she must have decided to damn it to hell, because in an instant she was in the lift, clutching his hand, going up. It was another example of women's superior judgment when presented with a practical alternative.

It was nearly check-out time ,when he finally roused himself from bed. He had twice told the maid to "come back later". He remembered sending Rachel home in a cab around three AM, part of the game he was obliged to play in their "home and away" series. At this stage of courtship appearances were still important, he wasn't ready to claim her yet.

The newspapers in the lobby carried banner headlines — "COUP IN SYRIA . . . SYRIAN REGIME FALLS". He bought two, scanning the lead paragraphs for more information, ". . . heavy fighting said to rage in capital . . . armored units involved on both sides . . . heavy loss of life reported . . . news blackout . . . Cabinet orders military alert."

So the Syrians should run hell-bent toward Israel because they have a new *rais*? The government's calling of the alert was cynical, an attack would have been utterly improbable. Nevertheless, the coup itself was extraordinary, the deposed *rais* had ruled the country with an iron hand for the longest time. Evidently, rust had set in somewhere. The news was encouraging, an affirmation that bad things also came to an end. Yet, given the record of Arab government, there was little cause for optimism, the new regime was unlikely to be much of an improvement.

At the check-out desk he inquired whether there had been any new developments. He was told the alert had been called off but the army and air force were maintaining a state of "high preparedness". That left him out, the air eagles could keep eyes peeled for Syrian rats. Syrian eagles no longer dared, they got shot down much too often.

The road to Jerusalem was heavy with military traffic, troop convoys going north and west carrying reservists back to their home bases. Being out of town had probably spared him a miserable night of waiting at the reserve depot. He began thinking about how best to invoke the alibi — whether to say he found out about the alert too late, or whether he should tell the truth, down to the juiciest details? Would they be sympathetic, or would they take him for a crazy man? They might send him to a psychiatrist, but the psychiatrist was sure to send him back certified sane. He was amusing himself with confrontational fantasies, allowing his imagination to run wild. But one absence did not a deserter make. The army had more important priorities than disciplining him.

During his absence both his reserve unit and Amon had telephoned, but were told only that his whereabouts were unknown. Mark Lerner had also called wanting to know what they knew about the situation in Syria. That was like Mark. He probably wanted to present the Senator an intelligence memorandum garnered from his own "informed sources" inside Israel. He would refer Mark to the Senate Intelligence Committee, they had the most up-to-date weather reports. It was useless to return the call, he only knew what he read in the papers.

More news came in later. Fighting continued in and around Damascus with the rebels still in control. The Fifth and Third Army Corps had gone over to the rebel side and

Radio Damascus was broadcasting martial music in the name of the "National Patriotic Revolutionary Council". A curfew was in effect and all troops except forward forces were confined to barracks. From all accounts, the Syrians were in no position to do anything.

A discussion on the events of the week-end was already in progress when he arrived at the office. Everyone had an opinion to express, everyone that is, except Olga. He had never seen her participate in any of the office discussions. Indeed, she seemed to exhibit a studied indifference to her subordinates' political wranglings, sitting them out in her office. The news that morning focused on speculation surrounding the coup's alleged leader. Described in the press as a "suspected Marxist" and as being from the "pro-Soviet faction"of the Syrian army, his ascendance was characterized as a move "sharply to the left". Analysts were cautiously pessimistic, predicting the developments had dashed any hopes for peace, at least for the foreseeable future.

"This thing has KGB written all over it," declared Shmooel Glazer. "They've finally got one of their own in power. All the others have faced toward the West in one way or another. I think there's a tremendous potential for mischief here. I'm afraid we're going to continue being the pawns in an East-West struggle."

"I agree we are pawns," said Ulrich Fesser, "but how many times have we blamed the Russians for not controlling the Syrians? Which Syria do we want — one out of control or one under control?"

"Neither!," responded Ben-Judah with characteristic forcefulness. "We're dealing with Arabs here and no matter how much the Russians try they'll never be able to change that. Look at Afghanistan. They take their Moslems on sufferance just as we do. Internally they have their own problems with them, that's a fact. They are outbreeding the Great Russians three to one and showing no sign of letting up. Thrity years of investment in the Arab world and what have they to show for it? Nothing but the miserable Syrians, the rest sent them packing. And tomorrow the Syrians would do the same if they had any assurance they could get as generous a sponsor somewhere else.

"As for this coup leader — he's a goddamn Christian Orthodox! And I have that on good authority. Now how long do you think Moslems, I don't care what kind, Sunni, Alawite, Shiite or Druze, how long do you think they'll put up with a Christian at the helm? They'll slit his goddamn throat!"

"I wouldn't rely on that, Eliezar," said Basil, "the Orthodox don't like us. And 'that's a fact'."

"So they don't? Jew-hating is what makes them accept-able to the Moslems. But in his case that's not going to be enough, this Christian's life isn't worth a lead crucifix. You can forget about Russian influence, they'll soon be back in Arab doghouse, saddled with the same Moslems who deem them anathema. The Russians have the short end of the stick, in over their heads with the Americans and fighting a losing battle with the Moslems. They're hopeless."

Basil glanced at Olga. She was seated at her desk blowing smoke at the ceiling, a benign expression on her face. She had to be listening. He flicked the back of his hand at Ben-Judah and walked to his desk. The world only had room for one pope at a time.

He left the office before lunch and drove to the clinic. One of the electricians said Bustanji had gone for lunch to the restaurant around the corner. He found him sitting there with his brother Aziz eating a kind of hot cheese soufflé *en croute* with syrup. Rising from his chair, Bustanji gestured for him to join them, pointing to an empty chair at the table. Basil had never seen him like this — he actually looked as if he were glad to see him . . . or was he celebrating?

"I take it you approve of what happened over the weekend," said Basil.

"You mean the so-called 'coup'? Your people actually took that seriously. What part of the dike were you sent to plug?"

"I really don't know. I was in Tel Aviv and missed the alert completely."

"Good for you. Keep it up and someday you might become respectable. Listen, we've already eaten, but stay here and be our guest. Don't say no because we have a proposition for you."

The Bustanjis owned a piece of property near their home. Their father had used it for his truck and quarrying equipment. Presently it was being rented out as a garage. But with a modest investment of resources it could be converted into an architect's studio. However, there were complications, "minor, but still complications." They could not sell him the property. Too much Arab land had fallen into Jewish hands that way. "Let them steal it like they did our father's quarry!," interjected Bustanji bitterly. Although unable to put up any money for the conversion, they offered their labor gratis. In sum, they would be glad to lease the property provided he finance the conversion, his costs to be applied against future rent. If that was agreeable there was one more condition — as an earnest of good faith and upon ordinary principles, the "architect lessee" must hire his brother as a draftsman. "We are not asking for anything unusual," explained Bustanji. "You are an employer. Aziz is unemployed and needs a job . . . And he is a good drafts-man, take my word for it."

During the negotiation Bustanji did the talking while Aziz remained silent. Although two years older than his brother, Aziz gave the impression of being the younger of the two. In addition to being smaller physically, a birth defect had left one leg shorter than the other, giving him a permanent gimp. In spite of a special elevated black shoe, he walked with a pathetic, rocking asymmetry. Unlike his brother, whose eyes tended to flare menacingly, Aziz's maintained a calm placidity, reflecting the personality behind them. One of those souls whose existence was becoming ever rarer, he seemed a straggler from a gentler age.

After eating, Basil spoke of his meeting with Portnoy and the residential design inquiries received. He would need an assistant, someone to supervise construction, as soon as the Eilat International project was announced. If Bustanji wanted it, the job was his. "What!," exclaimed Bustanji mockingly, "shall we become rich together?"

Olga was beckoning to him from her office. Except for a brief colloquy the day he got back from training — when she sent him home to bed — they had not spoken. He regretted the omission, but in the past two weeks events had more or less climaxed for him. Entering her office, he noticed a newspaper lying on her desk. "Hello!," he said, "What do you think of the situation in Syria?"

"If you believe the newspapers you would think we Russians wanted to take over the world."

"Well don't you? Millions of capitalists can't be wrong."

"But they are. Russia is a world of her own. We have over ninety language groups in our country. A scholar could study from the cradle to the grave and still not be able to converse with half of them. She has one-sixth the world's land mass, what does she need more for? Let them keep their wealth. Can one pick up Venice and carry it away? Russia has never looted. Who possesses the Elgin marbles? Where is the gold of the Incas? Look at me," Olga got up and came round her desk, sitting on it, dangling her black-booted legs, "I leave a socialist country to a capitalist one and still I work for the government. So who is capitalist and who is communist?," she asked, leaning forward for emphasis, putting her face close to his, her progressive loss of weight revealing its sensual triangularity. Outfitted in a forest green sweater and skirt, she was poster-perfect as a model of a young *Komsomol* pioneer. The most outrageous desires were running through his head, the kind one entertained but rarely practiced. What was he waiting for? She had given him an abundance of signals. "Olga, how are you at receiving compliments?"

"That depends on who gives them. Why? Are you contemplating giving me one?"

"I'd like to. You know, you keep this up and someone's going to grab you right off the street."

"What makes you think someone has not already done so?"

It was unintentional but his remark had been tasteless. "I don't know, have they?," he answered lamely, embarrassed by his own ineptitude. Olga slid off the desk and walked back to her chair. "Excuse me," she said, "I have much work to do." She was dismissing him.

By Tuesday morning the question of who was in control in Syria had been resolved, the victorious rebels lifting the news blackout and dusk to dawn curfew. A statement was issued justifying the seizure of power as an emergency necessary ". . . to foil imperialist and Zionist plots set into motion against the Motherland by the confusion and treachery flowing from a leadership vacuum at the highest level." The statement, the usual collection of complaints against Zionism, imperialism, and corruption, was notable for what it did not say, specifically, the disposition of the former *rais*. In response to reporters' inquiries, a rebel spokesman would only say that he had died "naturally". In his last years a progressive enfeeblement had forced the *rais* to relinquish much of his rule to ambitious proxies. Trips to Moscow, both secret and announced, billed as "consultative conferences", were actually ill-disguised resorts to Soviet medical arts. The grave diagnoses of the doctors, inherently subversive of the despot's power, remained state secrets, power being incompatible with feebleness in the Oriental mind. Although the theory of a natural death had few adherents, no one was demanding an autopsy. Revolutions were no more finicky about their facts than about the rights of those foolish enough to question them.

In the meantime, the coup remained a puzzle with missing pieces. Based upon the studied conclusions of Mossad and other Free World intelligence services, the coup had been carried out by young, disgruntled, junior officers concerned over the country's political inertia and lack of direction. Modeled on the Nasserite pattern, it replaced the nominal civilian ruling hiearchy with one drawn almost exclusively from the ranks of the military. Major Salim Nafsi, the Syrian army's research and development chief, was identified as the coup leader. Nafsi, holder of a doctorate in physics from Moscow University, was reported to have had some "Western exposure", having served as military attache at the Syrian embassy in London some ten years previously. While there was as yet no hard evidence of his political leanings, in view of his background it was thought he would tilt strongly to the Soviets. On the other hand, as a Christian he was open to challenge by the junta's Moslem members. His present position of leadership was believed to be temporary pending resolution of a struggle for power among his Moslem confederates.

23

Of all the powers invested in government, those classed as discretionary have to be among the most vexatious. Instead of specific and literal laws an appellant can readily cite, the vague and slippery notion of "public policy" provides the source for much of authority's exercise. Permits for new construction on Arab owned land are not easily obtained from the occupiers. Applicants might wait years for a decision only to be finally denied. The process was a discouraging one, as no doubt it was intended to be. Yet, in his case, there were grounds for optimism. The prestige of the Authority as well as his own not inconsiderable reputation was in his favor. In the course of his duties he frequently made application to the Bureau of Buildings and Construction, becoming familiar with many of its personnel. Wishing to begin construction before the winter's rains, he requested the matter be expedited.

"You know this is Arab property?," demanded the scowling clerk, studying the application before him.

"Yes I know but . . ."

"Well we can't approve it. That's been our policy."

"Wait, you know I'm going to be leasing the structure, that fact is included in the specifications."

"We're sorry, Mr. Primchek. It has nothing to do with you, policy is policy."

Not to be put off, he clamly explained his plans for the property, its restricted use, and the fact that it was located in a quaint part of the city, a section comporting with his personal architectural specialty, "I understand the reason for the policy, in fact I support it," he declared. "However, I believe that in this case it is misapplied. It *is* Arab property, no question about that. But who's going to be building on it, using it, and probably end up owning it? . . . I mean what are we about in this country? . . . Please, do me a favor . . . go back and explain it to Yitzhak, or would you rather I tell him myself? If at all possible, I'd like to avoid an appeal on this."

"No . . .," said the clerk, now much less certain of his position, "that won't be necessary. "I'll tell him."

Re-emerging five minutes later, the clerk's relieved expression inkled the result. "Yitzhak said OK. If you don't get the permit in ten days give us a call."

234

The appointments with his new clientele went well, resulting in at least a pair of commissions. One client, a member of Israel's high-tech entrepreneurial class, and heavily involved with the military establishment, regularly dropped names of cabinet members and generals in conversation. In addition to connections with establishment higher-ups, he enjoyed a reputation as a liberal on labor issues. His shops hired both Israeli and Arab, mostly women, to perform the detailed and demanding work of computer manufacture. His incentive plan was one of the more successful in that the workers actually worked harder. The form of his future mansion he left to the architect, specifying only that it contain the grandest master bedroom and bath in all Israel, incorporating the latest in push-button computer gadgetry. Money was no object. It was build and let the chips fall where they may.

More than two weeks had elapsed since the coup, yet news from Syria still rated front page copy. The day before the Syrians had anounced the expulsion of the Nazi Alois Brunner and two compatriots, flown out on a Lufthansa jet to the Federal Republic of Germany. Demands for extradition of suspected Nazi war criminals had previously been ignored by Syrian governments. World opinion was overwhelmingly favorable, the belief that Nazis deserved no refuge was almost universal. Nevertheless, the summary action drew criticism, some citing the apparent absence of due process as one more example of lawlessness, holding that between the public hangings and expulsions nothing had changed. One commentator termed the expulsion of the Nazis "a cheap publicity stunt", a transparent attempt by the regime to score points in Europe and the United States. The statement of the Syrian government, attributed to Salim Nafsi, was characteristically terse — "We do not want any Nazis in our country, German or otherwise." So it was with a mixture of shock and surprise that he reacted to the article on an inside page of *Ha'aretz* that Olga was holding up to

his face. "Mordechai Levy Associates Chosen as Project
Architect for Eilat Development" read the headline. For a
moment there was a lag in impact, a gap between seeing
and believing, then it registered.

> "Mordechai Levy Associates today con-
> firmed its appointment as project archi-
> tect for the Eilat International project,
> the beach resort and vacation develop-
> ment planned for the Eilat area. Moshe
> Shechtler, Minister of Tourism, yester-
> day announced the successful conclusion
> of negotiations between the Government
> of Israel and a consortium of interna-
> tional investors headed by Mr. Herbert
> Portnoy, the Miami, Florida developer
> and suburban town planner and builder.
> The project, touted as Israel's answer to
> the Riviera, will stretch for nearly two
> kilometers, combining primitive beach
> living with modern facilities. In addi-
> tion to reflecting traditional architectural
> motifs, the project's whitewashed stucco
> buildings, designed to government spec-
> ifications, will respect the area's unique
> and fragile environment. The project's
> total cost is estimated to be in excess of
> 100 million dollars . . . Shechtler pre-
> dicted the development would attract
> thousands of American and European
> tourists, thereby making a significant
> contribution to the country's balance of
> payments . . . The largest architectural
> firm in Israel, Mordechai Levy Associ-
> ates has many national and international
> accomplishments to its credit, a fact said
> to have weighed heavily in the firm's
> selection . . ."

An architectural drawing of a beach house accompanied the article. Except for the elimination of the functional wooden beams and some decorative devices, the design was indistinguishable from his own. Olga was staring at him, a gravely angry look on her face, he was conscious of his face and ears being very warm. *"Amerikanski,"* she huffed disgustedly, "they lie." "Yeah . . . so they do," his voice trailing off as he thought of the people he had informed about the project — his father, Bustanji, Rachel, Miriam. His father would be tremendously disappointed. With Bustanji it was different. Having offered him the position of project supervisor, he now felt foolish, very foolish. "I don't understand it," he muttered, "he said he was very satisfied . . . Maybe they thought I was too inexperienced . . ."

"You were not too inexperienced when he needed to pick your brains," exclaimed Olga indignantly. "What are you going to do?"

"What can I do? Form is in the public domain. I don't have a patent on the past, no one does. In this business everyone copies from everyone else. We might have had a contract . . . but if that's all then I have nothing. Imagine . . . me against the government, Mordechai Levy Associates, and Portnoy Properties."

Olga's expectation of stern action notwithstanding, there was little he could do. His chances were dim for prevailing in a court of law. As a locus for a suit Miami was out — meeting Portnoy on his home grounds was too much of a handicap. Even dimmer was the possibility of obtaining justice in Israel, Mordechai Levy Associates and the government were too formidable a combination. Suing the extablishment was a lost cause. They would roast him in the press, he had seen enough slanted news articles to realize how easy it was to portray someone in a mean and negative light. The sensible course was to contact Portnoy and demand a clarification.

237

But convincing Olga was another matter. She remained adamant in her condemnation, refusing to attribute anything but the worst of intentions to Portnoy and Mordechai Levy. Sometimes it required a crisis to reveal unsuspected elements of a person's character. Only now did he realize her sense of moral outrage, her militancy. She spoke as one prepared to storm barricades, denouncing the act as "grossly unprofessional . . . larcenous . . . contemptible." There was no doubt in his mind that if Portnoy had been in the room, she would have duly nailed him to the wall. She wanted her pound of flesh boiled in the villain's blood.

He picked up Olga's telephone and dialed the Hilton. Portnoy had checked out, calls were being referred to his Miami office. He decided to try later from home, it was only three in the morning in Miami. "You are wasting your time," said Olga, "this man will avoid talking to you."

That evening he tried three times, at hour intervals. The initial response was an unvarying "Who's calling please?" After indentifying himself he would be told, "Mr. Portnoy is not in. Would you care to leave a message?" During the third attempt he heard his father holler, "Forget the sonofabitch!" Still, he left his telephone numbers. It would put the responsibility for returning the call on Portnoy. But that was the sum of it. He did not expect a call from Portnoy, ever.

Two days later it was Bustanji who was waving a newspaper at him. Shouting, "HE'S WIPING THEM OUT! SALIM *AINI!* HE'S WIPING THEM OUT!," he held up an Arabic newspaper and pointed to a particularly grisly photograph of several bodies hanging from a common gibbet. The Syrian practice was to leave the dead hanging until sunset when the bodies were given over to the families for burial. It was a busy time for the hangman, the junta condemning to death dozens of the former regime's officials and police, sparing neither high nor low. After a brief glance Basil handed the newspaper back, saying, "I've already seen this, a couple of our papers printed it. Apparently this stuff turns you on."

"Sure it turns me on, *full blast*. If you read Arabic you might be turned on too . . . Shall I read you some of their crimes?"

"No, spare me, I have a pretty good idea. From all reports hanging was too good for them. They probably deserved to be boiled in oil."

"Now you're talking sense . . .," Bustanji hesitated, "Something's bothering you, what is it?"

Deferring the bad news was pointless, Bustanji read him too well. Relating the details, he described the attempt to get through to Portnoy via telephone and his own bafflement at the sudden turn of events. "I'm sorry," he said ruefully, "I hope you weren't relying on it . . ."

"*Me?*," exclaimed Bustanji, "I should rely on the promise of an American capitalist? For 350 years they have lied, why should they stop for you? At first when you said 'bad news', I thought it was the building permit . . . No, I wasn't relying on it or you. The Falestinian has learned to be modest in his outlook. Who knows? Tomorrow another war or pogrom and we join the others in the camps or grave. Between the two there is not much difference.

"But you, what have you lost? A promise? Promises are made and broken every day. Wait, after we build your studio you will have plenty of business . . ."

Although the words were meant as consolation their implication was obvious — he should be an Arab, then he might have something to complain about. Actually, the reminder of his privileged status was in itself a kind of consolation.

Were it not for a letter received from Miriam two days later he might have consigned the incident to the memorial of bitter lessons. Inside was a copy of one of his sketches for the Eilat project. As her letter explained, one of the firm's draftsmen had seen the collection of sketches and recognized the back-to-back graphic design of the letters BP, the one he used to sign all his work. Presuming he and Shames were cooperating on the project, the draftsman showed Miriam the sketches. Why, asked Miriam in the letter, hadn't he told her about the reconciliation with Shames, and when and how had it happened?

He reached Miriam at the office. After a prelude of pleasantries she correctly guessed the reason for his call — the sketches.

A few minutes of discussion was all he needed to confirm that the long arm of Shames was behind the conspiracy. "I should have known," he said, "I was a fool not to have thought of it."

"You mean Portnoy never told you Shames was an investor?," she asked.

"Obviously not or I wouldn't be asking you about it. But that's all immaterial now, whether the omission was deliberate or unconscious I should have known he would be an investor, it was his kind of thing." Now that he knew, there was no point in discussing it further, it was beating a dead horse. He switched the conversation to other topics — her parents, her latest opera, his plans for an office. He told her he was sorry about the aborted trip to England, but between his job, attending to recently acquired commissions and building the office, there was no way he could leave. She understood, agreeing that it was important he stay and take care of business. Nevertheless, she wanted him to know he could count on her, ". . . I mean it, don't hesitate to give me a call if you think I can be of help."

"No, please," he pleaded, "don't say anything. I'd rather he not know I know. I'd like to deny him the satisfaction."

24

There had been a step-up of raids on suspected terror-ist targets in Lebanon. Carried out by squadrons of three or four jets, the strikes were of the "surgical" category, directed against structures identified by military intelligence as terror-ist concentrations. Although the increased frequency of the raids was publicly attributed to a rise in terrorist incidents, it was privately conceded that the motivation was "strategic" — testing the resolve of the new Syrian leadership. A plan by the General Staff to send a large squadron of jets over Damascus to rain down a storm of sonic booms over the city, was scotched at the cabinet level as premature and of dubious psychological benefit. Despite this example of cau-tion, there was a general feeling of frustration at the reac-tion, or lack of one, of the Syrians. It was as if they refused to acknowledge the messages being sent them. It was hard to explain, but this did not prevent his colleagues from trying.

"The regime is exhibiting withdrawal symptoms, a phase common to all new governments. Governing is not easy — especially a country as backward and ethnically diverse as Syria. I suspect this Nafsi fellow will have his hands full for a long time . . . and that may be to the good. If Syria abandons its pretension of being the champion of the Palestinians and as I say, withdraws inward, we may yet see peace in our lifetime."

"With such optimism you should join those fools in the Foreign Ministry."

"Why not? With you around someone has to be optimistic."

"Peace . . . yes, a beautiful concept. But how many whippings must we give these Syrian dogs before they learn? Now they lick their wounds, but tomorrow they come back snapping and yapping at our heels. It's time we took a page from history, American history, and do a General Sherman on them, burn and pillage from Aleppo to Damascus. That will give us peace . . . for a hundred years!"

He was tired of hearing history stood on its head. He heard the same wild claims at reserve meetings, on the radio, read them in the papers. The Arab menace, the Syrian menace, the terrorist menace, a chorus of a thousand voices in maddening harmony. He told Orlit he was going out to check his jobs. It had been weeks since his last participation in one of their morning coffee debates. They were accustomed to him sitting at his desk and drinking his coffee at a distance. They probably thought he wasn't interested, politics and current events weren't for everybody. So when he left they kept right on, hardly turning their heads.

There were seven men on the job — Khalil Bustanji, his brother Aziz, and five others he had never seen before. Bustanji had lost no time in beginning work on the office. He said he wanted to move fast, before some bureaucrat got wind of what they were doing and decided a mistake had been made in granting the building permit. Recent acts of resistance had made things hot again and the government was cracking down anywhere and everywhere. "If they need a scapegoat they don't have far to look, here we are!" Bustanji ordered the men to break for lunch and handed Basil an eggplant sandwich, pieces of fried eggplant rolled up in the floppy Arabic bread. He pointed him out to the five Arab workers, telling them in Arabic, Aziz translating, that he was to be the tenant, "Do a good job because he is a very particular Jew. But remember, he will only be a tenant, the property is ours. Someday soon, God willing, we will be in a position to demand our rents on all our property." "So what do you think," asked Khalil, turning to Aziz and speaking in English, "shall we make an exception of this Yahoodi or should we evict him with the rest?"

"Let him stay," said Aziz, "he is a good fellow. But he must pay his rent."

His talk at the monthly luncheon of the Jerusalem chapter of the Association of Israeli Architects had been billed as "The Past as the Measure of the Future, the Unbroken Link". Many in the audience were curious, professionally curious, to hear his views, winning the Third Temple competition had made him more notorious than noted. A group from Mordechai Levy Associates was there, having driven in from Tel Aviv that morning. He wondered how much they knew, if anything. The presence of some of the firm's architects presented him with an informal opportunity to advise them of his "interest" in the Eilat project. Mordechai Levy could then ignore him or turn the matter over to an attorney for disposition. They might offer a nominal sum. Should he refuse it, they could say they were sorry but were not obliged to give him anything. Either way he would be humiliating himself. It would be more effective to wait for the project to be completed, then reveal the conspiracy. For his purposes, the best forum would be a professional one, perhaps an article in an architectural digest.

There was clatter of polite applause at the conclusion of his remarks, as if confirming an opinion generally held among his fellows that his was truly a voice in the wilderness, one not to be taken seriously. In the question and answer session the issues raised in his talk were ignored to focus on the political–economic problems posed by the Temple's extravagant design. Judging from the pedestrian manner in which the meeting dissolved, the overall response bordered on a patronizing indifference. As members and guests left the room, two of the Association's officers stayed behind to offer obligatory congratulations. Thanking him for "sharing" his ideas "so eloquently", they informed him that a visitor from France had asked to meet him.

243

Bernard Gluckmann was an architect from Strasbourg. An architectural preservationist, he represented Patromoine Architectural, a fledgling organization dedicated to the defense and preservation of significant architectural monuments and environments throughout the world. Jerusalem had been designated as "critical". On his third trip to the city in four years, he hoped to enlist support for a plan to resist further encroachments upon the city's architectural character. Finding it difficult to stimulate much interest in the proposition, he was almost prepared to consider his mission a failure. Not being fluent in Hebrew, he had asked one of the architects present to summarize the talk. Encouraged by what he had heard and believing they shared a common concern, he wanted to discuss the matter further. He was, he said, soliciting him to become a member of Patrimoine Architectural and join in the effort to preserve not only Jerusalem, but great architecture everywhere.

Basil took the Frenchman to view the medical clinic, the only, and thus best, example of his work in Jerusalem. When they arrived nurserymen were in the process of landscaping the courtyard while painters and tilesetters worked in the rooms. After seeing the clinic they went to a cafe where Gluckmann elaborated on the objects and purposes of his organization. Founded in France, the preservation movement had in the space of less than six years spread to almost every major capital of the industrialized world, establishing chapters in Western Europe, the Americas, Australia and Japan. United Nations recognition was in the offing, a development which would contribute to legitmizing their cause in the Eastern Bloc. However, it was the Third World which was most in peril of being seduced by the rationalization of modern architecture. Hundreds of quarters and thousands of structures were in various states of neglect and decay, threatened with destruction to make way for larger, more efficient, modern units. Given Jerusalem's immense symbolic importance to both East and West, a successful campaign here would act as an "open sesame" for entry to the East — other governments would feel constrained to emulate the Israeli example. It was the Third World whose culture was under the greatest pressure from modernism, whose economies were least able to resist the political and economic dominion of the West. In Gluckmann's view the East was under siege, threatened by an insidious neo-colonialism, perhaps one more pernicious than the naked military colonialism of the past. Western clothing, mores, music, machines, and now architecture, were overwhelming the East, imbuing its masses with a massive cultural inferiority complex. What was needed was reassurance from the West that the cultures and arts of the East were worth saving. Organizations like Partimoine Architectural stood ready to provide the artistic, architectural, and scientific assistance necessary to allow countries to move into the future without burying the past. But efforts would prove vain unless trends could be arrested, in Europe as well as the East. Both regions were under attack by a "brave new world". "Winning the battle of Jerusalem could turn the tide."

Gluckmann was a zealot, convinced of the rightness of his cause, fervent in its expression. In Basil he had a sympathetic but pragmatic ear. He had held his peace, listening intently while the Frenchman expounded his case for a more perfect world. Now it was time to respond, to advise the visitor of certain realities, realities a stranger might not be in a position to know, "Monsieur, I agree that something must be done, but I am not sure this is the place to do it. I must warn you that a Third World status as applied to Israel is one of the realities my countrymen prefer to ignore. In spite of our geography we like to think our destiny is with the West. My point is that this is a political problem. If it were only economic, a mere problem of real estate value, I believe it would be tractable. But with political realities what they are, there is a great stimulation to build. The policy is settlement, and the settlers are our shock troops and missionaries in carrying out the policy. Even if we could save Jerusalem — and that's a dubious proposition now — it would be a Pyrrhic victory, the process would be shifted somewhere else. Monsieur, we are at war with the East, physically and spiritually. This makes us even more defiant. We're proving we can do anything with the land, it's ours to use or abuse as we please. Forgive me . . . but people like you and me . . . we're fighting a rear guard action. We're up against a hubris, only a catastrophe can bring it down. Sadly, the whole world is going that way."

"What about the UN?," asked Gluckmann, "When it accredits us, don't you think that will help?"

"The UN can go to hell, we don't need them."

"I understand your position, perhaps better than you think. There are problems, major problems. But they are not insurmountable. If I didn't believe that I would not be here today speaking with you. I respect your prudence and sagacity, I can only tell you that I am optimistic. You can help our cause, Mr. Primchek. Become a member of our organization, sign this petition to the premier and Knesset." Gluckmann unfolded a blue-backed paper on the table, between the empty demitasse cups. The petition called on the Government of Israel to submit future plans for development of the city and its surrounding area to the UN, where they would be reviewed by an international panel of architects. Of the eight names already subscribing to the petition only two — academics from the University of Haifa — were known to Basil. There were no Arab signatories. Obviously, Gluckmann was aware of at least one reality. "This is internationalism by another route," said Basil, "they'll never agree to it."

"Indeed they may not," replied Gluckmann, "but it never hurts to ask. It is one more pressure, at some point they must make a decision. You see, we understand politics too."

"Alright, I'll sign . . . for whatever it's worth."

246

25

The day before he left for Greece with Rachel there were widespread demonstrations on the West Bank. The Arabs were protesting the "get tough" policy instituted by the government in response to the recent upsurge in terrorism. Implementation of the policy involved nocturnal arrests, collective punishments, and for suspected troublemakers, deportation. With curfews, punitive school closings, confiscatory taxation, and other incidents of occupation, it didn't require a vulcanologist to predict that at some point there would be a blowup. What first began as an uprising in one or two refugee camps had spread to the towns and cities. Merchants closed shop while school children took to the streets shouting slogans, burning tires, and hurling volleys of stones at police and soldiers. Although commanders were said to be under orders to refrain from using deadly force, as often happened in confrontations between occupier and occupied, there were shootings. The government tally of three dead and eight wounded differed from the seven killed and thirty-five wounded figure of the victims. But that was to be expected, the actual toll was almost always higher than that announced by the authorities. In keeping with prior practice, Jerusalem stood firm, accusing PLO and Islamic fundamentalist groups of causing the disturbances. The accusations were for external consumption, Israelis had long grown inured to the periodic manifestations. Public opinion polls showed a solid majority for the government's policies in the territories. A substantial percentage demanded even harsher measures.

The manifestations had occurred at an inopportune time. Sentiment in Greece was overwhelmingly pro-Palestinian, a sentiment quickly made evident by the look of unspoken contempt from the passport officer at the airport, flicking their passports back after a cursory examination. The incident unnerved him. Israelis had been killed in Greece, they had to be careful. The airport itself could be infiltrated by a terrorist apparatus, incoming Israelis monitored, and hit teams alerted to their presence. As a male and female travelling together they aroused suspicion, it was the kind of cover Mossad or any intelligence agency might employ, disguising agents as ordinary tourists. They would avoid the large hotels, the ones patronized by tourists. But the police checked all passports and terrorist groups could have infiltrated them too. He cautioned Rachel to speak English, to use Hebrew only when they were alone. He tried to conceal his nervousness, yet each time she lapsed into Hebrew he would whisper, "English". Her English was poor, but in the circumstances anything was better than Hebrew.

Scanning the crowds, he searched for faces that might be Palestinian. It was useless, the resemblance was not coincidental. The Philistines were said to have been Greek in origin. Greeks had been settling in Palestine for a long time, perhaps for as long as Jews. Peoples as well as cultures underwent cross-fertilization. People often remarked that he looked Lebanese or Circassian. And Rachel, with her sun-darkened skin and Sephardic features, came even closer to the Arab physical type. For once the shared physical traits worked to his advantage.

After seeing the Acropolis, he had a better appreciation of the phrase, "The Glory that *was* Greece". Somewhere in the sprawl and pollution of modern Athens lay the answer to the riddle of what had gone wrong. The four days allotted to the trip was too short a time to see much more of Greece than a few mainland sites and Hydra. He promised that on their next trip they would follow the tourists through the Aegean where she could satisfy her curiosity by visiting some of the topless beaches. He had wanted her to pose nude on the steps of the Parthenon, a modern Aspasia.

He would have taken the photographs early in the morning before the Acropolis opened for business, a small gratuity paid to one of the guards would have gained entry. The black and white prints would have been perfect against the austere white walls of the new office. However, she would have none of it, her conventional nature recoiling at the idea. Although prepared to bare her boobs at any topless beach, "That was different," she said. He didn't try to persuade her, she was too stubborn for that. She turned him on, that was enough.

The rude reception of the passport officer had proved to be an exception, the rest of their stay in Greece was all to the good. Nonetheless, he was careful to continue speaking English, telling Rachel she needed more practice in the language spoken by a quarter of the world's population. Meanwhile, back in Israel the manifestations had ended, the Arabs had buried their dead, and conditions had returned to normal.

As he pulled up to the nearly completed office he was met at his car by Bustanji, "Don't get out," he said. One of his men had lost a comrade in a car explosion near Nablus two days before and was overwrought, at times weeping and crying for vengence. The police said the four men in the car were killed by their own bomb but no one was buying that version, settlers or Israeli Intelligence were believed responsible. Because of the intense feelings Bustanji feared a confrontation. His cohorts might consider the presence of a Jew on the job a provocation, there was no telling how they would react. He did not want to be put in the position of defending a Jew from the wrath of his comrades, they had a right to their rage and cries for blood. Bustanji got into the car and directed Basil to park in front of his house where they would be out of sight. "While you were gone there have been developments," he said. "During the disturbances Salim Nafsi issued a call for Falestinians to join the Syrian army and serve in their own units."

"You're not thinking of going are you?," asked Basil, shaken at the idea of losing his chief man.

"I find it difficult to refuse. 'The Syrian Mother awaits the reunion with her orphaned children' was the way he put it. I wept when I heard those words. It has been a long time since a leader referred to us with such respect. Were it not for my mother and sister I would go today. However, I am still considering it. I support what's taking place there — the people being issued arms, the settling of accounts with the tyrant's agents. There is a new seriousness, at long last a prospect of justice."

"Khalil, I never asked you . . . but your religion, it's Sunni Moslem isn't it?"

My religion is your religion, Yahoodi, *this!*" Bustanji clenched his fist, showing a large bicep under the sleeve of his shirt.

"Yeah," muttered Basil, pausing respectfully, "but if I were you I'd think long and hard before such a move . . . it's rather final. You could find yourself hung up on religious differences there."

"What religious differences? There has been a revolution, a man's religion is now irrelevant. It is a crime to assert it."

"I shouldn't say anything. I have a selfish interest in keeping you here."

"Listen," said Bustanji, pulling a folded piece of paper from his pocket and handing it to Basil, "there's going to be a demonstration in Fujnine, it's on the road to Bethlehem. A large contingent of your people are leaving here tomorrow morning, they think the army may demolish the family home of one of the detained protestors. You say you are for peace? Let's see how much."

"What's he charged with?," asked Basil.

"Does it matter? Hurling Molotov cocktails. What of it?"

"Are you going to be there?"

250

"I do not beg before my oppressor," replied Bustanji coldly.

"Then why should I go?"

"Because *you* are the oppressor," answered Bustanji. "If that isn't reason enough, the boy's father has eight other children."

"Who asked him to have them? . . . No, I'm not interested, I can't get involved with this stuff, it's a bottomless pit."

"Suit yourself," said Bustanji, getting out of the car, "I thought you might want an opportunity to ease your conscience."

That evening he fiddled at the piano, but visions of the "house vigil" scheduled for the morning kept reappearing in his thoughts. The destruction of the house was a distinct possibility, the government did it all the time to the homes of suspects. A party of soldiers would arrive at a residence, order its occupants out, then bring the house crashing down with either a bulldozer or a few well-placed charges. Destruction usually preceded conviction, which for all practical purposes, was irrelevant to the process. Nor was it necessary for the accused to own the dwelling, the structure need only be a residence of the accused or belong to his family. Undoubtedly the practice worked hardship, but the ends justified the means. It forced rebels to contemplate the consequences of acts against the occupying authority, literally bringing home the consequences of rebellion. Often a home was a Palestinian family's only real possession. Without it the prospect was bleak, a refugee camp or emigration, reconstruction was forbidden.

The regulations providing for the destruction of houses and other collective punishments were applied against His Majesty's Palestinian mandatory subjects during the rebellion against making "Palestine as Jewish as England was English". Such laws had served the Empire well in its four hundred years of wars against the wogs of the world. In

251

emulating its former patron, Israel was in good company. Jews were the equals of Englishmen, a principle Jewish rebels had taken pains to impress upon the English enemy in the War of Independence. The laws and their penalties were sanctioned by time, practice, and lineage. Above all, they were effective.

He removed the flyer from his inside coat pocket. The sponsoring organization was "Israelis for Peace and Reconciliation", one of the many small groups opposing government policies, especially its expansionist program for the territories. Composed of the usual assortment of do-gooders and idealists, the groups had met with a singular lack of success in the narrow welter of Israeli politics. Sometimes referred to as the "disloyal opposition", the groups were strictly marginal to the political process. For some reason the IPR had chosen the present cause for a renewed attempt at convincing the state of the error of its ways. The flyer proclaimed a twelve hour, dawn to dusk vigil outside of the Silwan family home in Fujnine, the vigil to continue until the authorities publicly announced that the house would not be destroyed. Calling upon "all persons of good will and fairness" to join in demonstrating against "the Draconian measures in force against Arab resistance to an unjust and repressive occupation", the flyer demanded the "application of due process of law to both friend and foe."

He was an architect, not a doctor. As such he was under no inherent obligation to preserve the existence of dwellings. The old, the decrepit, the superannuated, were torn down every day. The house threatened with destruction was not part of any irreplaceable Palestinian heritage, the loss of which he as an architect or member of Patrimoine Architectural was duty-bound to act to prevent. Fujnine, like most West Bank villages, was architecturally unexceptional. From an architectural standpoint, the entire village could be leveled and forgotten. Indeed, in the recent past, hundreds of Palestinian villages had been wiped from the face of the earth, destroyed to make way for kibbutzim, military reservations, new towns, or whatever the state in its infinite wisdom deemed. He recalled a *New York Times* review of a film about a Gaza refugee camp. The reviewer had closed her review by calling the depiction of the destruction of Palestinian homes "cheap shots". He hadn't seen the movie. It may have been as reviewed, a too self-conscious portrayal of one people victimized by another. Yet he remembered wondering at the mentality that would permit one to employ such a cliché, seemingly unconscious of the irony, against such a pathetic practice.

He left the house and drove downtown to the Authority. Inside the office he went directly to the stationery cabinet and took out three of the Authority's long forms. With its raised dark blue letterhead on parchment paper, the form was properly impressive. Next, he rang up one of the two numbers listed on the IPR flyer. A female voice answered. Identifying himself, he said he would like to join the vigil, could he have the address of the house and the full name of its owner? "The owner is Mohammed Silwan, Mr. Primchek. And the address is just Fujnine. It's a very small place, everyone knows everybody else there. You won't have any trouble finding it, we'll be standing in front of the house. We appreciate your participation, Mr. Primchek. If you know anyone else that would like to help, please inform them too. The more people witnessing the less likely the government is to move against the Silwans, they don't like publicity. By the way, my name is Beatrix Brunwasser. You won't be able to miss me, I'll be the one with the stringy red hair."

After promising his contact he would be there in the morning, he placed a sheet of the paper in a typewriter and decreed his "ORDER",

"BY AUTHORITY VESTED IN ME
AS AN OFFICER OF THE GREATER
JERUSALEM REBIRTH AND

253

REDEVELOPMENT AUTHORITY, I HEREBY DECLARE THE STRUC-TURE KNOWN AS THE MOHAMMED SILWAN RESIDENCE, OF FUJNINE, OCCUPIED TERRI-TORIES, SAMARIA, TO HAVE ENDURING HISTORICAL VALUE. WHEREFORE, IT SHALL BE EXEMPT FROM DEMOLITION, DESTRUCTION, OR REMOVAL; AND ANY AND ALL ORDERS TO THE CONTRARY, FROM WHAT-SOEVER OFFICE OR AUTHORITY, ARE HEREWITH SUPERCEDED AND DECLARED NULL AND VOID."

The style was exactly what he was seeking — offi-cious, final, peremptory. He made a copy to send to Mark. It fit his description of the law as "ninety percent gas and the rest shit". The ingenuity of the caper amused him. In one stroke he was bearding authority and showing Bustanji that here was a man, a real "Yahoodi".

In his glee he had forgotten to sign and seal the orders. The Authority's seal was kept by Olga in the top drawer of her desk, he had seen her use it on papers. He hoped it wasn't locked, he didn't want to have to force it open. Happily, the drawer was unlocked, the seal in its usual place. After signing and dating the papers, he impressed each with the seal on the bottom left-hand corner. Now they were official.

The village of Fujnine was a cluster of twenty to thirty houses. Alone, none possessed any particular architectural importance. Yet as a whole, they were preferable to the prefabricated sterility of Israeli developments. And of course there was the human element, people lived in such villages, they were not just *mise en scenes* for Orientalist painters and

254

aesthetes. He saw the protestors, about thirty, standing in front of a two story, flat-roofed structure. She was speaking with a group of Arab women, apparently villagers. Seeing him, she broke away and ran toward him, waving excitedly, "Mr. Primchek, I'm so glad you could make it. I recognized you from your picture in the paper, I'm Beatrix Brunwasser."

She did indeed have "stringy red" hair. Intensely red, it shot out from the oval face like stylized thunderbolts, making her look like a motif from the *Weiner Werkstaette* or an Art Deco frieze. Her face had a classic Jewish beauty, reminding him of the curiously calm faces of the women in some of the equally classic Holocaust photographs showing German stormtroopers herding Jews to eventual death and destruction. Her dress was simple — a down jacket over a simple cottony dress with high-topped hiking shoes. Taking him by the arm, she introduced him to the other protestors, many of whom also knew of him. Most were students, although a smattering of housewives and elderly were represented. A couple of Arabs were also present, perhaps to give the group balance. It was his first introduction to the "Movement". For their part, they were excited to have him. He was a catch, a big fish from the legitimate world of business and commerce. Although most Movement organizations had pretensions to recruiting members from this class, from the nature of things it was not disposed to penetration. Mainstream individuals stayed with the mainstream parties, the organizations best reflecting their mainstream interests. Meanwhile, the mother of the accused along with some of the village women present, were occupied with seeing that the vigilant did not want for food and drink. Stacked loaves of Arabic bread, a bowl filled with the local green olives, and tea, were set out on a table in the kitchen. Like most of the village's men, the head of the house, Mohammed Silwan, was at work. Of necessity, the exigencies of survival precluded their participation in the

255

politics of vigils.

Looking for some spicy copy, a newspaper reporter asked why he was there. He replied circumspectly, taking care not to show his hand, "Oh it seems to me a cause all of us can support, if only for the humanitarian aspect, not to mention the many others." If the statement was not as sensational as the reporter might have wished, it seemed to satisfy the protestors gathered around him, who, nodding their heads in encouraging agreement, were glad to have such a sober spokesman as ally. It was a welcome contrast to their own rather shrill pronouncements.

A continuous changing of the guard was taking place, with people coming and going throughout the morning. At least a score of vigilants would be standing outside the house at all times. The vigil had a military aspect of its own. It had to, the enemy attacked without warning. Nevertheless, he was becoming impatient, he had not planned waiting all day for some subaltern in Jerusalem to make a decision. He considered leaving the order with Beatrix, but it was his idea and responsibility, he couldn't expect her to carry it off with his authority. He had volunteered, made a commitment, there was no backing out. Still, the vigil could last for days, weeks. The government had a huge advantage, it could disrupt the lives of scores of people for months, they were crazy if they thought they could change history by saving one Arab's house. As much as he sympathized with their cause, the business of vigilance was not for him, at some point he had to leave, he had a job to do. Catching Beatrix alone he expressed his misgivings, "I don't want you to think I'm running out on you, but I'm going to have to leave for work soon. My original impression was that the army was going to show up this morning, that's what brought me here. You know they like to play games . . . Is there some reason you think they're coming this morning, or whenever?"

"Keep this to yourself, Mr. Primchek, but we have

friends. They told us to expect the troops today. Of course, as you say, the government changes its mind, the officer class is a bunch of bastards. All I can tell you now is that our intelligence has proved reliable in the past. I can understand your apprehension, making revolution is not for the faint-hearted . . . Excuse me, I didn't mean to imply . . . We appreciate your help, Mr. Primchek. I wish we had more time to talk, maybe some other time. Right now we're ready to put our bodies on the line against the troops and bulldozers when they come. This government has to understand that for every action there is a reaction. We're not going to stand by and let them tear down the house of fraternity we've built with our Arab brothers and sisters, we're going to maintain it, strengthen it. As a progressive architect you should think about building with us. The time to stop fascism is now, Mr. Primchek, right here, today, Fujnine, the West Bank. Sure, I agree, it's an inconvenience. But it's nothing compared to what will happen if the fascists take power!"

She was earnest, ardent, impassioned, idealistic, she was also very appealing. His idealist side admired her pluck even as his rational side was attributing her behavior to youthful rebellion. At sixteen years she was a prodigy for the revolution. In this game you started young, she said, there wasn't time to arrive at the truth by stages. Events were moving too fast, making all bourgeois values irrelevant and passé. She was taking off from school but no revolution ever came without sacrifice. "Where would Cuba be today if Fidel Castro or Che Guevara had put their careers before their duty to the people?" The answer was self-evident, career goals were on the lower end of priority, her goals were the goals of the IPR — "peace, reconciliation between the Israeli and Arabic peoples, self-determination for the Palestinian people inside and outside of Israel, and revolution."

"That's a tall order," he said.

"Revolutions are made by people with tall visions, Mr.

Primchek."

There was no use arguing, nothing was going to change her mind. She would have to learn from the crucible of defeat the daunting odds prevailing against the realization of youthful illusions. The chance of any one of her goals happening was extremely remote. But all of them? That was pure fantasy, revolutionary fantasy.

By complaining he had made it worse for himself. Talking with her made him feel guilty about leaving. Before, he could have faded away, his reputation and self-esteem intact. He was hooked, there was no way he could walk out now. While wondering how he got himself into such predicaments, one of the protestors came running down the road shouting, "They're coming! They're coming! They've brought a bulldozer with them!"

They drove up in three jeeps, simultaneously halting and dismounting as if by the numbers, suggesting the maneuver was the product of long practice. The truck hauling the bulldozer had stopped on the road outside the village. He counted eleven men in all, led by a lieutenant and a non-commissioned officer. Armed with long wooden sticks, they formed up before the house, Around the house, like a human chain, stood the vigilants, their arms interlocked, waiting. Reading from a paper, the lieutenant proclaimed his authority declaring, " . . . the house of Mohammed Silwan is accused of harboring terrorists. Under the laws of the state of Israel it is subject to administrative demolition. I hereby order you all to disperse!" As if by design, his words were accompanied by the voluminous start-up roar of the bulldozer from its place on the road above the village. Facing directly ahead, the vigilants held their ground. "Don't be fools!" cried the lieutenant, "You are Jews. Do not force us to use force against you!"

He had been standing between the protestors and the troops. Now he stepped forward, confronting the lieutenant, a young Sephardi, "Fortunately, Lieutenant," he said, hand-

258

ing the order to the officer, "that won't be necessary. This house has been determined to possess national importance and is protected from destruction by decree of a ministerial agency of the state of Israel. The order I just gave you supercedes your orders." The lieutenant, clearly perplexed, called his aide over to look at the document. "And who are you, sir?," demanded the lieutenant, after seeing that his underling had no more notion than he of the document's effect. "Basil Primchek, state architect for Jerusalem Rebirth and Redevelopment Authority. That is my signature on the order. I'm sorry that you and your men had to make a wasted trip here, but at least there is a happy ending — we caught you in time to prevent the commission of an illegal act."

He was holding his ground, staring down the younger, smaller man, deliberately intimidating him, exploiting — rightly as it turned out — his size and Ashkenazi heritage against the Oriental, the effect of which was enhanced by the Bogart military type raincoat he had on. Before such ostensible authority the officer had no choice. Retreating to his jeep, he spoke over a mobile telephone. After a brief exchange he reported back to Basil, "My commander has ordered us to return to base in order to examine your order. We are sorry if we have caused you any inconvenience."

The troops departed but the bulldozer remained. He tried to tell them the troops would be back but they weren't listening. They were too occupied with hanging on his shoulders and pulling on his arms, caught up in the primitive rite of pressing the flesh. One Arab woman had grabbed his hand and was kissing it furiously. They were thanking him in the way they knew best — spontaneously. Beatrix Brunwasser had hold of his other hand. There was no mistaking the look in her eyes.

Finally, their enthusiasm spent, he was able to speak, "Today we had a victory of the spirit — the spirit of each of you united in resistance to an atrocious policy. Unfor-

259

tunately, that victory is only temporary. The troops will be back. I'm sorry, but I don't think I can be of much help when that happens." The two Arab IPR activists translated his words for the villagers. He was unaccustomed to uttering encouraging words about discouraging events. It was really oratory he objected to, the art of speaking too much to too many. At some point in the dim orgins of the race, oratory and incantation had become one, mankind still hadn't separated them. Oratory was like architecture, potentially too devastating a power to be left in the wrong hands or wrong mouths. His sense of responsibility was too strong to permit the raising of false hopes. That would have been unconscionable.

He was leaving on a personal high note, a far cry from the pedestrian departure he had contemplated only a short time before. Beatrix walked with him to his car, listening quietly as he explained the idea behind his action, " . . . the house will be destroyed, my little ruse probably only made them more determined. Yet one has to start somewhere. Your group can get some publicity out of it and more people will be made aware of the cruelty of these policies. That's about all one can hope for now."

"What do you think they'll do to you?," she asked.

"Oh they'll be looking for blood at the Ministry when this gets back to them, but cooler heads will probably prevail. They can only hurt themselves by making an issue of this. I'm not worried." Getting in his car he wished her luck saying, "Call me if you think I can be of use some other time . . . that is if you don't think I've outworn my usefulness." He turned the car about on the narrow road and headed toward the city. He looked in his rearview mirror. She was standing in the middle of the road, waving.

When he arrived at the Authority he saw Olga motioning, holding a telephone to her ear. As he entered her office she gestured to a chair. "Yes, yes," she said, "I'll have a talk with him . . . Naturally . . . But as yet I have heard nothing from him. I am not going to be responsible for the private acts of an employee of the Authority . . . Yes, he does his job, superbly I might add . . . No, I had no advance knowledge of this thing, do you think I am his confessor? . . . What do I intend to do? Frankly nothing until I have talked with him. He has an independent mind and if he wants to support the IPR that is his business, we do not inquire into the political attitudes of our people. How long do you think I would last if I involved myself in these matters? As director I am responsible for the quality of my staff's work, nothing more, we do not operate a nursery here . . . Yes, of course I will tell him . . . Yes, good-bye." She had spoken firmly, in a conversational tone. The small radio in her office was on, she did not want the others to hear, they would find out soon enough. "Well?," she said when she hung up, "I hear you have been doing a little politicking. That is the second call I have received this morning."

"Yes, the Silwan aff . . ." She cut him off, "No, don't tell me the cause, I do not want to be your interrogator. All I am bound to determine is whether you acted in the name of the Authority in serving a paper with our letterhead and seal upon the soldiers, nothing else."

"Yes," he said.

"Good. And what, may I ask, did you intend to accomplish by this procedure?"

"I have a modest objective — some publicity. Someone has to oppose these things."

"Yes, you are right, and someone does. The IPR has opposed hundreds of 'these things' and has not prevented a one. What makes you think you will do any better? Of course, it is too soon to judge whether you have been successful in the publicity area, but you have certainly upset a lot of people in the Ministry. I expect I shall be on the telephone for much of the day with them. They are frustrated, they can't believe this . . ."

"You mean the notorious laureate of the Third

Temple?"

"Exactly. They are unable to reconcile the two acts. They want to believe maybe you are eccentric. I suggested Bertrand Russell to Zuckerman, he was the first to telephone, both the army and police had called him. But he was too dense to make the association. In any case, they are confused. I will try to see that they stay that way. But tomorrow, I don't know, they may recover their wits. Listen," said Olga, leaning forward in her chair, "you cannot help them. They must learn to help themselves. The siege of Leningrad — could they have endured what we did against the Germans through a Russian winter, when a crust of bread was all we had, when we had it? Of course I do not speak for myself, I was not born. But suffering? We Russians can teach the world the meaning of the word. It is a pity, but this people is not ready for resistance, it is too compromised by comfort. They will lose their existence piecemeal, hoping and praying from compromise to compromise." The telephone rang and Olga lifted the receiver, "Olga Shalansky . . . Yes, Mr. Minister, I am aware of it. Excuse me one moment . . ." Olga put her hand over the mouthpiece, "This is a small country, word travels quickly. Go, I will take care of it . . . I'm sorry, Mr. Minister, go ahead . . . Perhaps the incident may be overblown. He is a man, he has his own ideas of right and wrong . . . Yes, yes, I will tell him . . ."

The next day he decided to try to visit the job again. He was hesitant about going back after his reception of two days before, but hoped enough time had passed for the Arab to have gotten his grief under control. When he walked through the entrance six Arabs were there to greet him, offering their hands in congratulation. "A giant-killer!," exclaimed Bustanji proudly, "Unarmed save for a worthless piece of paper, he faced the enemy and won the day. You were right about this Yahoodi, Aziz. You always were a good judge of character."

They knew about Fujnine, now they wanted to know what had happened subsequent, what the reaction of the establishment had been. "The predictable complaints," said Basil, "or so Olga told me. She was the one on the receiving end, I've had nothing yet personally. Anyway, I did what I could, which in the circumstances wasn't enough. They'll still raze the house."

"So they will, and a thousand more like it," said Bustanji, "But this time they were stopped, and by one of their own. The act will stick in their throats. Don't underestimate yourself, you did well. You honor us and yourself."

The office was strangely quiet when he entered. Fesser and Glazer were busying themselves at their desks, heads bowed. Orlit's response to his "good morning" was curt, furtive, as if she were concealing something. There was nothing furtive however about Ben-Judah's look. As seen through the coke-bottle lens of his glasses, it was direct and accusatory. Shrugging it off, he went to his desk and sat down, the reaction was not unexpected. He had interrupted a session of kangaroo court in which he had been charged and found guilty — *in abstentia* of course. With Ben-Judah as judge the verdict was a foregone conclusion. The others, nominally opposed to his inanities, would agree with him. On this issue they'd have to, the action had been "inappropriate, unprofessional". He had brought the Authority into disrepute, reflecting upon all. Ben-Judah rose from his chair. He watched the stern-faced, Levitical figure approach. So did the others, the confrontation had been long in the making. Rivalries gave drama to life, everyone liked a good fight. "You surprised me, Primchek," said Ben-Judah, now standing in front of Basil's desk, "I didn't know you were such an Arab-lover."

"Really? You know, Eliezar, if you weren't such a fucking racist you might be one too."

The retort was more a challenge than an answer, the kind that called for a "Yeah?" or some such monosyllabic inanity. Ben-Judah gave better than that, "Alright, Prim-chek," he warned, thrusting an ominous finger in the air, "you'll remember this day." Turning, Ben-Judah strode angrily back to his desk, fists rigid at his sides. Choosing neutrality, the others lowered their eyes, alliances with such evenly matched adversaries were dubious, if not dangerous, propositions. Not so Olga, seated at her desk across the room. Head up, she was looking directly at him, a smug sneer on her pink-cheeked face.

26

"Avram Chabrot called me today. He heard from Omlert at the Ministry that you were involved in some demonstration with the IPR. How come I have to hear this from somebody else?" Lev Primchek was upset over getting the news second-hand through a telephone call from a friend. Was it true? What was going on, and why the secrets between them he wanted to know?

" 'Secrets'? I don't have any secrets," said Basil. "You should ask the press that question, they're the ones who think it's a secret, they haven't printed a word about it. If it were such a big deal you should have been able to read about it in the paper. Although it's sure to be featured in the next issue of the party organ. It comes out tomorrow. If you want I'll get you a copy. But I can tell you right now how they'll treat it — 'Hundreds Protect Arab Home from Effect of Nazi Laws'. You can read how we brought the govern-ment to its knees by putting to flight a battalion of troops and police sent to raze a falsely designated terrorist safe-house. At the end of the article there may be a note stating that after going to press, army sappers arrived and blew the house to bits. So that's it, big victory. Any other 'secrets' you'd like to know?"

"How long have you been connected with these people?"

"No secret, we just met the other day . . . Who have you been talking with anyway, the Shin Beth?"

"No, just Avram. He told me the whole story, how you served the troops with a phony order from the Authority. Who put you up to that?"

"It came to me in a dream. Or don't you think that as an architect I'm entitled to an occasional inspiration?"

"This isn't architecture, sonny boy, this is politics. And at times it can get pretty nasty. Unless you have some very powerful friends, you do not want to get involved. You get in trouble with these people and not even your father can help you. It's nice to be sympathetic to a poor Arab family, but what happens after? You get a reputation as a subversive, they go gunning for you, anybody with a grudge can finger you . . . And they'll get you. They'll chop you in pieces and throw you to the ravens, you haven't friends in government to protect you. The first thing you know, you're going to lose your job. What does Olga say about this?"

"If I told you she was sympathetic, would you believe me? She took the heat for me from the Ministry. But essentially she agrees with you, she doesn't think it was worth it."

"See? I told you. She's a Russian, she knows how they operate. You don't cross the government and get away with it. They mark you. It's simple now, everything on one printout, your whole record at the touch of a button. Bureaucrats and police come and go but your record is forever, no matter the party in power. I told you to listen to that girl, she has savvy, she didn't get where she is without it. If you don't want to tell me, your father, tell her. You need someone who can rein you in. Those years in America, they were too easy, you were a student, it's not your fault. You lack experience. You got a taste of it with that bullshitter, Portnoy. People use you if you're too easy. So keep your guard up, protect yourself. Life is a disease with the worst germs people. You're always at risk, you've got to be careful, that is if you want to survive . . . You never answered my question — how long have you been flirting with the IPR?"

"I wasn't misleading you when I said I just met them the other day, the day of the demonstration. I saw one of their flyers and showed up with the order. By the way, it wasn't phony. I signed it."

"Is there a girl somewhere in this?"

"What makes you say that?"

"These left groups aren't above using sex for recruiting. Not only governments use sex as a snare."

"You think I'm a sucker for sex?"

"You wouldn't be the first."

At his reserve meeting two days later no one mentioned the incident. The omission was not evidence of any deficiency in military intelligence, the transgression was probably duly noted in the normal course of business. It was just that human rights protests were outside the military's present orbit of interest. Anti-war resistance was the big concern now. Since the war in Lebanon such activity had shown a marked increase, and many resisters were either serving or had served jail terms, in some instances, repeated. A government, particularly a democratic government, had to be selective in its prosecutions, it shouldn't be all over the map stamping out dissent. Human rights were marginal to society's functioning. Unless the abuses were pervasive and prolonged, life went merrily on.

One of the items of training that night was an introduction to the newly improved fleshette ordnance from

266

America, designed for use against human wave attacks. Slightly different in operation and effect than the terrifying cluster bombs, the shells spewed lethal clouds of tiny, whirling steel arrows against an advancing enemy force. A review of the item was particularly apropos in view of the news that Syria and Iran had earlier signed a treaty of mutual defense. Indeed, the pact was all anyone could talk about ever since it came over the four o'clock news. In addition to the usual provisions wherein each state pledged itself to aid the other in event of attack, the Syrians undertook the quartering of thousands of Iranian recruits (no one knew how many) on Syrian soil, to be trained by Syrian army instructors. There was no reason, declared Nafsi, why Iran should not be able to field one of the finest land forces in the world, and in a relatively short span of time. Moreover, Syria, as a fraternal ally, stood ready to lend her "Islamic brothers" blood and treasure in the "sacred struggle against imperialism and its minions". Given Syria's Soviet connection, the declaration sent shock waves through Jerusalem and moderate Arab capitals. A high-level Israeli diplomatic and military delegation was already on its way to Washington to discuss this new threat to peace. While the Syrians tended to speak in "code", the Iranians made no effort to evidence a similar sensibility. The "liberation of Jerusalem" was openly declared a priority of the "Islamic nation".

The pact, the first major diplomatic initiative of the new Syrian regime, provoked the usual spate of speculation. Many predicted Syria's demise, swallowed by the larger, more fanatic, Shiite nation. The allegorical talked of "spider courtship" and "Trojan horse". Others saw the pact as evidence of Syria's isolation and desperation, it would never work they said. Despite the depreciation and pessimism of the pundits, the Israeli Defense Force — upon whose strength and integrity the nation's very existence depended — prepared for the worst. The lessons of '73 would never be forgotten.

27

It was one of the infrequent times when he preceded everyone else to the office. His colleagues, still gun-shy from the exchange with Ben-Judah, must have been inhibited by his presence, because it was some time before they got to talking. Argument was stimulating but it could also get out of hand. And when it led to personal insults and attacks it was no longer argument but conflict. Nevertheless, feelings and attitudes had a way of eventually coming to the surface, and it was the rare organization absent some form of internal strife. They talked — the subject was on everyone's mind — but they were prudent, prudent not to exceed the limits imposed by the conflict or to provoke either antagonist. As usual, he listened passively from his side of the room. Although the line separating them was an imaginary one, the others were as conscious of its existence as if he had marked it with his own urine. The situation was akin to the dog whose patient disposition is habitually taken for granted. Until one day, for whatever reason, it reacts by snarling and baring large white fangs. Thereafter, things can never be quite the same.

"Christian, Marxist, fundamentalist, Russian, terrorist" — they were searching for shorthand adjectives to describe the events, broad labels to encompass what they thought was happening. What that was, none of them knew any more than he, but language has a tendency to summarize and categorize in order to make things logical and comprehensible. Words forestalled doubt, justified, satisfied; truth and authority were one. The Christians finessed it best — "In the beginning was the Word and the Word was with God and the Word was God". To make it conclusive there were good and bad words. "Israeli, American, Jewish, Free World, West", were good. "Syrian, Russian, Arab, Marxism, communism", were bad.

Before going home he stopped at the new office. The painting and plastering completed, it was ready for occupancy. A circular stairway led to an upper loft, a living space with bath, while a section of the former garage was retained to house his car. The three arched front windows had been fitted with louvered blinds. The interior was simple, elegant, and practical, as befits an architect's studio. He had wanted wood underfoot. Bustanji located an old cabinet maker who had trained under a Scottish carpenter during the Mandate. The laying of the fir flooring and the curved staircase were his work.

Bustanji was by himself, broom in hand, sweeping up the debris of construction. "The rent begins tomorrow," he said, sitting down in one of the leather and wood director's chairs and surveying the final product, "Ah for the life of the landlord, to live off the fat of the land . . . your fat. So don't fail, we have a stake in you.

"By the way, I see you have sent a crack team of bagmen to America. How much will you get this time?"

"Whatever it takes and more. They have a stake in us and don't want to see us fail."

"Very good," said Bustanji, "you understand relationships . . . but fail you will." Spreading open an Arabic newspaper he pointed to a fuzzy photograph of a man in fatigues and a black-bearded figure in white turban and black gown. It was a photo of Salim Nafsi and Habibollah Ali Fahunzi, the commander of the forces of Iran, taken in Damascus at the signing of the Syrian-Iranian pact. Habibollah Ali Fahunzi — the Iranian Alexander, young, devoutly loyal to the goals of the Islamic revolution, distinguished for his victorious offensives against the Iraqi enemy. The pair stood behind a table, their arms around each other's shoulders. Flanking Nafsi were his Syrian comrades-in-arms, all similarly fatigue-clad. On their left stood the bearded, black-robed Iranians, equally undifferentiated. To the uninformed eye the juxtaposition presented a curious amalgam of the military and religious, the robes of the Iranians giving an impression of dignified piety. However, each black gown clothed a revolutionary Islamic fighter sworn to undo the humiliation of Islam by the Great Powers, foremost among them, the "Great Satan", the United States of America. It was a natural alliance between complementary fanaticisms — Syria, the heart of the Arab awakening and the champion of the unredeemed hopes of the Arab people; and Iran, heir to the art and glory of Persia and now the self-annointed bearer of revolutionary Islam athwart the banners of Ali, son-in-law of the Prophet and patron saint of Shiite Islam, the Islam of the poor, the persecuted, the despised. The potential was earth-shattering, volcanic.

"They look like they're fond of each other," remarked Basil. Ignoring the comment, Bustanji refolded the newspaper and inserted it in his back pocket. "You're finished, Yahoodi," he declared, getting to his feet.

"And there goes your religious freedom," answered Basil.

"Who needs religious freedom?," said Bustanji.

He drove Bustanji the short distance to his house. A young girl attired in a uniform of white blouse and navy shirt, of the type favored by Arab schoolgirls, was standing on its stoop waving when they pulled up. The sight of her long black hair and Madonna-like face caused him to linger for a longer look. Her lips were moving but all he heard was *"ya akhi"* (O brother), the rest was unintelligible. Before going inside Bustanji turned momentarily in his direction, eyes glaring. He felt like an intruder, eavesdropping upon a private moment. Attempting to cover for his curiosity, he waved weakly, then drove off.

He thought about what he had seen, recalling how she had taken her brother's elbow, opening the door. He envied the gesture, the solicitude in her voice and face. Perhaps it was the bearing, or the elegant carriage, but she intrigued him. It was an idea, one he was reluctant to admit, even to himself.

28

The caller did not identify himself but simply said he wanted "to convey a message" — the Arab working in his office must go and be replaced with a Jew or no one. His first impulse was to suspect Ben-Judah, but of his colleagues only Olga knew of the arrangement with the Bustanjis. As required by law, he had registered Aziz with the Labor Ministry. Any number of clerks handling the registration could have noted the Arabic name. In that case pursuing a line of suspicion was futile, the possibilities were endless.

While the policy of hiring Jews only had been a principle since the early days of Zionist settlement in Palestine, it had never enjoyed complete acceptance by Jewish employers. Periodically, zealots would attempt to revive the rule but such efforts were doomed to failure, the laws of economics were superior to concepts of racial or national exclusivism — Arabs worked cheaper and harder. Nevertheless, he was taking the threat seriously, there had been too many unexplained killings lately, "itinerant" Arab workers found slain. The problem was in informing Bustanji of the threat without creating the impression he was pressuring his brother to quit. He did not, even falsely, wish to be held responsible for Aziz's departure.

They met for lunch at the restaurant near the medical clinic. Bustanji began the conversation by discussing Nafsi's recent trip to Moscow. Coming so soon upon the treaty with Iran, the visit was interpreted by Damascus watchers as solid evidence of Nafsi's consolidation of power. Early analyses of his Iranian connection were now believed to have been "premature". The latest authoritative opinion held that Nafsi had adroitly enhanced his power base by hitching himself to the fundamentalist cause, neutralizing in the process any fundamentalist opposition at home and in Syria's sphere of influence, Lebanon. The visit to Moscow was another diplomatic, if not strategic, success. Received in the manner of a returning hero, he was toasted at a state dinner and given a high-ranking military sendoff, headed by Marshall Simeon Rodzinsky. The developments were giving the Americans fits. Similar consternation was being evidenced by Mossad and its voices in the Israeli press. The man whose obituary they had prewritten was apparently settled in for the winter, and who knew for how long thereafter? The analysts had learned a lesson said Bustanji. Henceforth, they would by playing Syria by ear.

Not wishing to cast a pall over the meal, he delayed telling Bustanji of the call until they were finished. Bustanji's calm reaction came as something of a surprise. It was nothing new he said, Palestinians were accustomed to threats, they were an incident of weakness. He would inform his brother, but didn't think his response would be any different — and he himself was not flinching. The real question, he suggested, was the tenant's resolve. In that regard he trusted the investment in leasehold improvements would prove persuasive. "Incidentally," he added, "my mother asked me to invite you for dinner. Which do you prefer — *mansaf* or *maloobi*?"

They left the restaurant together, stopping outside to take in the sun's rays, now coming through what had been an overcast sky. He knew it was considered forward for strangers, even acquaintances, to ask Arabs about their families, especially the womenfolk. But it seemed a proper time to broach the subject, he was only being curious. "Say, Khalil, how old is your sister?" In the context the question was unexceptional, even relevant. Thus, he was unprepared for the vehemence of Bustanji's response, "Never mind about my sister," he exclaimed, eyes flashing. "You take our country, our lives . . . now you want our *honor*? Before that, this!" Bustanji jerked an index finger across his neck. In the context, it was no idle threat.

Two days later Aziz Bustanji reported that an Albert Haddad had stopped at the office. He had heard about the "Jewish architect" from one of his brother's crew. As Haddad was leaving for Kuwait in a few days, he asked to be contacted as soon as possible.

Albert Haddad was a Palestinian from Ramallah who had gone to Arabia in the early 60s and established a string of appliance stores and automobile dealerships. Like many an immigrant Levantine, he left with the notion of returning, hopefully with a fortune. As luck would have it, he returned the owner of a commercial empire, the name Haddad known throughout the Gulf. Hugely successful, his motto was "If it exists, I can get it for you." The medium for that success had been oil, creating a general prosperity and endowing millions of formerly sand-poor souls with the wherewithal to purchase the "basic necessities" of modern existence. Providing the refrigerators, washers, watches, TVs, Toyotas, and Mercedes was Albert Haddad, merchant extraordinaire, friend and purveyor to kings and princes and a leading member of the Palestinian expatriate bourgeoisie, better known outside than inside his country.

Haddad wanted a classic villa, a structure that would reflect his standing while satisfying a debt to his native land. Although recognizing that the political situation was unsettled, he owed it to his countrymen to make a statement affirming the right to live upon their land. As a businessman, he was aware of how helpful politics could be in fostering a commercial climate — he owed his own success

273

to the freewheeling practices of the Gulf states, states where bribes and baksheesh were the normal and expected incidents of business. He had deferred building his villa, waiting until the politicians produced a solution. But after twenty years, he realized that those who wait for politicians wait in vain. The tendency was to temporize, to protect the *status quo*. The Arabs he said, needed a strong man, a man who was above politics. He was not a communist he insisted, but the best example he could think of was Fidel Castro. However, there was no hope of a strong leader emerging, Israel and the United States would combine to defeat him like they did Gamal Abdel Nasser. What did he think of the Syrians? He admired the efforts of the new leadership to build up the country but thought they were relying too much upon socialistic methods. Arabs were too individualistic to ever take to socialism, "buying and selling was in the blood, the language, the religion". The dependency on Russia was regrettable, but with America giving Israel all that it asked, the Syrians had no alternative. The alliance with the Iranians was a good move however. It would assure a strong moral tone and put the Syrians in a better position to extract concessions from Israel.

At appropriate intervals Aziz would replenish the thick Arabic coffee, pouring it into the small cups from a brass vessel. The Arab custom of doing business over cups of coffee or tea was more than an empty ritual. It enabled buyer and seller to know each other better prior to striking a deal. In that regard Haddad's conversation was exemplary, dealing mainly with business and politics, and alluding only generally to the proposed villa. When building a house a man should be prudent, he said, the character of its builder was more important than its wood and stone. The rule was bound to be applied more rigorously between Arab and Jew, ostensible adversaries. "I heard good things about you," said Haddad, "how you supplied the men with food and drink while they worked on your office here. And how you intervened to save a Palestinian's house from destruction . . ."

"Only temporarily," interrupted Basil, "the house was subsequently demolished."

"Ah, there, see?" said Haddad, "You are modest too. A modest man is an honest man. But listen, I will be frank with you. One reason I am here is because as an Israeli you should have less of a hassle with government restrictions on Arab building or obtaining supplies . . . Am I right?"

"Perhaps . . . but things are done differently here than in Saudi Arabia or Oman. Sometimes no amount of money can override ideological considerations. Aren't there a couple settlements near you? If I'm right, the Torah and Land is strong there."

"Yes, but the settlements are a kilometer distant and are relatively autonomous. We have had no trouble from them . . . at least not yet."

Ground-breaking for Villa Haddad was set for the spring, following the rainy season. He was to be both architect and contractor for the project, an arrangement that would considerably augment his fee. That much was agreed over a midday lunch at the comparatively modest Haddad family home in Ramallah. The villa was to be built upon a hill overlooking an olive grove, a grove that had been in the family for generations. They still pressed its oil, giving the surplus to friends at Easter. Haddad claimed to have seen hundreds of palaces and villas in his travels through the region. He pretty much knew what he wanted in a house, down to the meter-thick walls, oak double doors, and drip watering system for the garden. As Haddad described aspects of the future house, his wife, a slender woman dressed in a tawny silk robe, sat by his side, listening without comment. Mansura Haddad had her own career as an ornithologist, one of the few in the Arab world.

Bustanji had bought a freshly slaughtered kid for the *mansaf*. The meat was cooked in yogurt, which was then ladled over a bed of rice and brought to the table on a large salver. A supplementary hotpot of the yogurt sauce sat on a trivet nearby. During the meal he snuck furtive glances at Bustanji's sister, Sumaiya. The viewing tended to be desultory, because directly opposite sat Bustanji, going on about Nafsi's latest speech, the one in which he served notice that Syria was off-limits to perpetrators of "unauthorized acts of resistance". The factions were too many, out of control, and subject to manipulation by the enemy, he had declared. The result was a resistance hopelessly compromised, at the mercy of "agents provocateurs, spies and bandits". Syria was undertaking a program of "preventive action". Suspects (including virtually the whole of the Western news corps), were being rounded up and expelled. Reentry was possible only after SPSF review (the Syrian Peoples Security Force, the police state apparatus established by the regime to replace the one purged).

Bustanji's enthusiasm was making him an apologist for the regime. There had indeed been a recent upsurge in terrorism, both in Europe and Israel; and Palestinians as usual had gotten the worse of it, the Palestinian cause taking a few more knocks. The growing volume of war talk and the American Secretary of Defense's visit to Jerusalem were likely to have been much more persuasive in influencing the Syrians, argued Basil. Syria was reverting to its old policy of reining in the Palestinians whenever it suited its purpose.

"Let them join the Falestinian units in the Syrian army if they think they are so brave," was Bustanji's answer.

"They're not that brave . . ." or dumb, the last two words he discreetly left unsaid.

Following dessert, the women attended to the kitchen and the men the salon where Bustanji revealed they were considering sending his mother and sister out of the country. They had a cousin living in Des Moines, Iowa, who, some years back, had visited them with his wife. At the time

276

they had suggested their sister come live with them and attend school in America. They had continued to keep in touch, occasionally receiving a card or letter. Sumaiya was approaching college age and while they wanted her close to home, the political situation foreclosed attendance at one of the West Bank universities, the Israelis were constantly shutting them down for months at a time upon the slightest pretext. He had forbidden her to engage in political demonstrations, but once she was away from home and in a university setting she was likely to be caught up in the struggle. It was no use telling her she would be no good after stopping an Israeli bullet, she would take the risk with the rest. They could afford to send her abroad — and their mother too, she would have to accompany her. He realized the value of studying in an environment free of "national humiliation", but he was concerned about the effect American culture, "the strongest in the world", would have upon her. The picture he received of American women from TV and advertising was discouraging, he did not want to see her transformed into a "painted tramp with some stinking French hairdo", they had their father's memory to consider. Yet, one of these days he would have to decide, preferably before events forced the issue. He had heard that Iowa had more pigs than people, thus it couldn't be too bad a place.

Upon arriving home, Basil continued the discussion with his father. The Syrians, maintained Primchek père, were only exporting blame. There wasn't the slightest pretense about regulating terrorism in Lebanon, where Syria had long exercised a shadowy, often pernicious, influence among that country's numerous and quarrelling factions. Indeed, the prediction was that those "expelled" from Syria would merely transfer operations to Lebanon, allowing Syria to have its cake and eat it too. Yes, he said, the threats *were* having an effect, the Syrians were exhibiting a justifiable nervousness. Nafsi was only following the Soviet example — Lenin made peace with the Kaiser and Stalin with Hitler.

National survival always came before alleged revolutionary considerations. Nafsi had inherited a third-world country, even God almighty would be hard-pressed in his situation. As time passed Nafsi would see his position as hopeless, Israeli and American power was too formidable a combination to oppose. Being a scientist, he would be more likely to see the light than your typical Arab tinhorn despot. There was even a possibility he might surprise everyone by undertaking a comprehensive peace, that is, if the Iranians allowed it. To attack Syria now would only drive Nafsi into a corner and cut off his options. By refraining from attacking, Israel was taking a chance — but what other choice did it have if it truly wanted peace?

29

He heard his father calling, he was wanted on the telephone. "Who is it?," he asked. "I don't know," said his father handing him the receiver, "maybe a client."

"Primchek speaking."

"Mr. Primchek," asked the voice on the line, "do you know who I am?"

"No, who the hell are you?"

"Rabbi Khak, Mr. Primchek, Rabbi Benjamin Khak. I'd like to talk to you, Mr. Primchek, I'd say it was urgent. Can we meet at your office, your *private* office?"

"Yes. What time?"

"Thank you, Mr. Primchek. I knew you were a reasonable man. I'll see you there tomorrow at ten. Goodbye."

"That was short. Who the 'hell' was it?," asked his father, mocking him.

"Rabbi Khak."

"Rabbi Khak?"

Rabbi Benjamin Khak, the politico-religious leader of Torah and Land, reputed to be the most aggressive of the settler groups, infamous for its practice of creating *faits accomplis* through squatting on lands still officially off-limits to settlement. Khak preached blood-and-guts Judaism, infusing his homilies with references to Amalek (the Amalekites, ancient precursors of Arabs), and Israel's divine mission of conquest and empire. Whatever might be said of the Khakites, they were not hypocrites, they practiced what he preached. When not successful in gaining their objectives by menace or organized tantrum, they were perfectly capable of going further. It was an open secret that Torah and Land was implicated in a series of bombings and killings of Arabs in Israel and the territories, actions the press dubbed Terror II to distinguish them from an earlier episode of Jewish terror. Khakite gangs were at their most lawless in Gaza, where allied with followers of Yahoshoah Aharoni, they terrorized and cowed Arabs living in the teeming shanty-towns and camps of the "strip", assuming a role akin to Pinkerton agents over the area's Arab day-labor. Given the unspoken mutuality of interest between government and settler, the occasional spasms of official censure were really exercises in hypocrisy and connivance.

He despised the settlers for their swaggering arrogance and pistol-packing pugnacity. But more than that, he despised them for their medieval ideology, their special brand of rabbinical rubbish. Armed with Bible and gun, they represented the worst in Jewish chauvanism. Compared to the Khakites, Ha'itzer Bnai Azadoi Beshallim was an association of Sunday school teachers. Like many nations, Israel was an amalgam of expediency, of dissonant and irreconcilable elements hastily compressed together. Jewishness, or as it was sometimes mystically entitled, "peoplehood", was not of itself sufficient to subordinate differences to a common

279

weal. Because of the peculiar nature of the Jewish state, the religious and the secular were constrained to coexist. Were it not for the unifying forces of Amelek and American patronage, the present historic phase of Jewish sovereignty might have broken down into a parody of its victimized neighbor, Lebanon, now synonymous with misery and savage, internecine strife.

His father was for compromise, which meant giving Khak what he wanted. Considering the alternatives, it was a cheap price to pay, because Aziz Bustanji could get other employment. In fact, he could have a job at the bakery. Not as a baker, but as a manager. Someone trustworthy was needed to check the day's receipts, keep the books, there was a raft of administrative duties he could perform. He would be paid well, at least the equal of his current remuneration, perhaps more, anything to make the move less galling. His father would talk to him, help persuade him of the wisdom of the move. There was the possibility of adding another manager at the Maale Adumim store in a few years, business was that good. In the meantime they best be politic, Khak had to be appeased, it was no good having him on one's back, he had allies in and out of government. In a year or so the matter would be forgotten and then he could rehire Aziz if he wanted. Perhaps the international situation might be better then too, with the settlers suffering a loss of power. There was no telling his own influence then, he was the winner of the Third Temple competition and the government — his father had friends in the Labor party — might throw some contracts his way. It was not beyond the realm of possibility, that was the way things were done in Israel with its revolving door governments. The country was like a family, grudges had a finite duration, usually short.

Lev Primchek was throwing out optimistic scenarios, attempting to make compromise more palatable. It was a father's duty to preserve his son and Lev Primchek had always been faithful to that duty. Because his involvement was incidental, his willingness to sacrifice — which was, after all, the essence of compromise — came easy. The others, including his son, proceeded from more complex motives. As a rule, principles were always more resistant to compromise.

It was 9:20 when he drove into the office's garage. Aziz was inside at the drawing board. Informed of the meeting with Khak, he got up, put on his jacket, and said he would return in a couple hours. He watched Aziz limp out the door, turn, and go up the street. It was morality that determined his responsibility, the obligation of the fit to those who, cheated by fate, nature's God or accident, were less fit. Aziz would expect it of him, the handicapped had a right to the expectation. It was too basic a right to require explanation, only a pig would deny it.

Rabbi Khak was late, about half an hour late. After a preliminary handshake, he pulled a chair up to the desk. Physically, Khak was the image of his photographs and TV appearances, his most singular characteristic a snarl. He had only to open his mouth and his face would break into one, the thin upper lip curling one-sidedly as he spoke. A black, close-cropped beard and angled, flaring brows added to an impression of evil. He wasted no time in coming to the point. "My apologies for this imposition, Mr. Primchek, but sometimes a personal intervention is unavoidable. I understand that some time ago you received friendly advice concerning an Arab working in this office. That is correct is it not?"

Basil nodded, resisting an urge to answer sarcasm with sarcasm. "Yes, unfortunate," continued Khak, " 'procrastination is the thief of time.' Allow me to explain our position, Mr. Primchek. Israel is the only territory we Jews lay claim to, yet in that same territory we provide a home for millions of Arabs. Moreover, consciously or unconsciously, we are encouraging the anomaly by providing this unwanted element

281

with permanent and well-paying jobs. Obviously, it is a situation boding serious consequences for the Jewish state. Whether from misplaced generosity, stupidity, inertia, or outside pressure, we cultivate cancer in our midst. We cannot be both Jew and Arab and survive. We must return to the tenets of the pioneers before we are drowned in a folly of our own making. They understood that only a strict policy of Jewish exclusivity would be effective in colonizing the land. They were hard, we are soft. Disregarding this policy has meant more and more Arabs, unemployment, terrorism, drugs for our youth. This must stop. Torah and Land has a solution, a practical solution, a first step to the problem. Restrict the Arabs to day labor, to jobs which are either unfit for Jews or unappealing to them. The remainder, the positions the control of which determines who shall rule and who shall be ruled, must be Jewish and Jewish alone. I am here to inform you that the position now held by your Arab falls in the latter category. I trust I need not remind you of the unemployment situation in this country, the fact that tens of thousands of fully qualified Jews languish without work largely because the market favors the Arab, a competition the Arab is bound to win because he willingly works cheaper. But don't think you are alone, some of Israel's largest employers allowed themselves to be swayed by such false economies. After we explained the error of their ways they mended them, without exception. I repeat . . . *without exception."* Khak reached into his jacket and drew out a folded piece of paper. "We want to cooperate with you, Mr. Primchek, to make the transition to patriotic professionalism painless for you. I have here a list of six Jews from this area with a brief resume of their qualifications. Surely, one from this list will be a suitable replacement for your Arab. Indeed, if by some remote possibility this list proves inadequate for your purposes, then by all means, let us hear from you. We have been very busy with this campaign and sometimes our people have not always gotten their facts

282

correct. So please, let us cooperate. I appeal to your patriotism, that which was so ably demonstrated in your beautiful plan for Israel's Third Temple." Khak left his seat to go over to the wall and admire a framed copy of the Temple drawing. "Wonderful, wonderful," he crooned, "let us pray this holy edifice be reborn at the earliest time consistent with the will of the Almighty and our own good works.

"You will forgive me if I have overstayed my time. Rabbis sometimes speak too much, yet we mean well. By contrast, I am embarrassed by your silence. Forgive me if I interpret it as assent. Now I must be going, my driver is waiting." Khak tarried at the open door, there was one more thing, "You are a gentleman and a scholar, Mr. Primchek. I expect this matter to be speedily resolved at that level, that is why I insisted I should talk to you personally. Doubtlessly you were under a misapprehension about our motives. I hesitate to depart on an unpleasant note, but I am constrained to remind you that we do have enforcement procedures. I pray it will not be necessary to activate them, that would truly be regrettable."

A retainer held open the back door of a Mercedes sedan, then followed the rabbi into the car. Khak was in enemy territory now, on Amelek's turf. A shot from a pistol, a toss of a grenade, even a well-thrown rock could take him out. Rabbi Khak was brave, but like most brave men he knew when to be prudent.

Thoughts racked his brain as Khak's car disappeared from view. He should have said something, simulated an agreement. But then how does one respond to a *diktat?* The slightest negative would have been interpreted as resistance. Remaining ambiguous would keep them guessing, buy time. The means of persuasion — would it be applied against him, a Jew with one Arab employee? They were making an example of him, zealots thrived on examples. He knew they could be ruthless, they had brought out their biggest gun with the rabbi. What was next — a beating, a bombing?

283

The front windows were vulnerable, but a sober appreciation of reality rather than any special prescience had prompted him to install wooden shutters. There were other measures, all requiring time. If he was serious about mounting a defense, there was little to waste.

He left a note for Aziz, then telephoned Amon Amitai. Amon was in the electrical business and had contacts. He met Amon in Independence Park. Explaining the situation, he made it clear that he was "seeking help, not advice". "Bogorodov, Viktor Bogorodov," said Amon. "He's an electronics expert, the government and politicians use him. He also runs a security agency, leases bodyguards to millionaires and industrialists here and in Europe. At least that's his cover. With his skills I assume he's into other areas, secret stuff, import-export, arms. You know the type, shadowy, they never open the closet door too wide. Anyway, he's your man . . . Tell him I referred you."

"Thanks," said Basil, "now I want you to do me a favor . . . locate an Uzi for me. Can you do that?"

"Sure, they're around . . . for a price." Amon paused, adopting a pleading tone, "Listen, why don't you avoid all this? Do what your father suggested and save yourself the grief. I know you don't want my advice, but I'd back out. You're a marked man. If you're wrong about them bluffing, you could be in for it."

"Yeah, I know."

His existence was being turned upside down. A few miscreants and an appropriate environment and one's back was to the wall. He had seen it coming. In fact, he could have predicted it but was too slow in getting out of the way. At this stage it didn't help to blame himself, he needed all the support he could muster, especially his own. Everyone had a breaking point, like vegetables in a pressure cooker, most people quickly turned into a mushy pliancy. He hoped he was of sterner stuff. He abhorred the idea of capitulation but the prospect of resistance daunted him, the process had hardly begun and he was already very nervous.

Later that afternoon he stopped back at the office. Aziz appeared even more serious than usual — or was he projecting? He summarized what Khak had said, then, as delicately as possible, described his father's offer of a position at the bakery, adding redundantly, "Of course it's your decision."

"Thank you, my friend," replied Aziz with his characteristic deference, "and thanks to your kind father for whose consideration I am grateful. However, my brother and I have discussed the issue at length. The rabbi's visit has really changed nothing. To bow to their demands can only further injure our cause. This is our land, my crime is working it. Indeed, it is a crime for us to be here. Concede them this and next they shall demand we quit our home. No. Let them throw us out, but do not expect us to go like scared lambs.

"We appreciate your concern, but we have lived under the sword for so long that when they threaten us with it — even in the hands of these fanatics — it does not frighten us. We realize your investment in the property, but we cannot be responsible for these developments. They are political, a product of the nature of the Jewish state. At any time the full force of injustice can fall upon us. This is our fate and until we are freed from it, we are its prisoners . . . Forgive me, but the decision is not mine, but yours."

If he needed an example to stiffen his spine he had it. While he hadn't taken Aziz for a pushover, he was somewhat surprised by his adamancy. Between him and his brother Khalil the difference was one of emphasis — Aziz spoke softer. He informed Aziz of his plans to use the living quarters of the office. To involve his father in the hide and seek of defense against a speculative attack would be an imposition as well as an embarrassment. He would tell his father of the rabbi's threat in the subjunctive, one of those aleatory possibilities incident to life in Israel. His life becoming more complicated, he needed an extra residence, a

285

retreat. Rachel had applied for a position at Hadassah and Sha'are Zedek hospitals and was scheduled to be discharged from the army in February, now only weeks away. It was a good excuse.

He secured an appointment with Viktor Bogorodov for the following morning. Initially Bogorodov had said he was too busy to accept new clients, but at the mention of Amon's name, reversed himself. Bogorodov's offices occupied the second and third floors of a small, unmarked building on Naftali Street, which in Jerusalem, is somewhat off the beaten path. Cramming both floors was electronic gear of stupefying variety. A mantle of dust covered much of the stock, heightening an impression of claustrophobia. Stocky, bald, with a thick Russian accent, Bogorodov looked to be about fifty. Informal and plain-speaking, he was occupied with soldering wire connections on one of his gizmos. "Yes," he said, it's alright if you don't want to tell me who threatens you. I could be a sympathizer, or even one of them . . . then your goose would really be cooked. Terror is terror, whether from the left or right, it kills and maims with equal impartiality . . . However, you'll have to trust me . . . at least to the point of examining your house and office. And if you have a car . . . that increases your exposure terribly. But inquire of Amitai about my reputation, at least I've never been accused of duplicity. Oh I've lost a few during my career. But not here in Israel, only abroad where I wasn't there to hold their hands. So they got careless and *boom*, over in a flash. Carelessness. You know what causes it? Every day that passes without an attempt against them. After a while they lose the fear. Fear! The instinct preserving the lives of hunted animals. Imperious, dominating, omnipresent fear, friend Primchek, always the fear of death it must be with you. The enemy is patient, he waits, a false step, a wrong move, an opportunity presented. You are only one man, a bodyguard would give you two more eyes and hands. But you don't want a bodyguard now,

286

you think you don't need one . . . yet. You may think you are not important enough for a bodyguard. At first it is embarrassing, you are self-conscious with him about. Don't think I am trying to sell you on the idea. It is you who decides if the threat warrants the extra expense. Of course, you have not yet been attacked. They want to bend you to their will, not harm you. That is how I interpret your story. A matter of forcing you to do something you don't want to do or punishing you for something you have already done. It sounds as if it is political, that you have ideological enemies. Too bad, and you seem such a pleasant lad. A promising career, a great architect, you should have *enemies*? Bogorodov interrupted his monologue to perform a particularly sensitive maneuver with the soldering iron. "Yes, a pity you should have enemies," he resumed, wiping his hand on his apron. "But such shenanigans keep me in business. And in a country like this where the enemy sits on one's back fence, business is perpetual. Most of my clients are older, successful men, politicians, industrialists. Wealth and position have made them targets of all sorts of groups, not only Arabs. You, you are too young and handsome to die. The others, well they have lived their lives, you've only begun to live yours and they may want to kill you. A pity. Isn't this a dog-eat-dog world? You've convinced me, let's go and see if we can do something about keeping you alive." Bogorodov removed his apron, grabbed a light jacket, and slammed the heavy metal door behind them.

After an examination of the neighborhood, street, and the building's exterior and interior, Bogorodov prescribed certain precautions. The front and back doors were the most likely points of entry and should be tied into an alarm system. That was simple, a mere mechanical fix. The rest involved the human factor and required studied vigilance and deception. Number one, his car had to be secured. Driving it to and from work set up an obvious behavioral pattern. Bogorodov advised using it only for special occasions unless, of course, he was prepared to hire a chauffeur. However, a chauffeur could only provide limited protection. The car still had to emerge from a garage onto a narrow street, where it was vulnerable to an assault from a passing car or motorcycle. To get around the city he should begin to rely on a mix of taxis, public transportation, and footwork. Entering and exiting by the back door avoided the street, it was there that he was most likely to be watched. It followed that he should keep his eyes open for anything unusual on the street — a beggar, an old lady, a truck, with or without markings. Some terrorists were enamored of disguises, they appealed to a sense of drama. Others, less imaginative, might hire a poor wretch to do their surveillance, perhaps some inoffensive Arab, the type that would normally elicit one's sympathy. Here Bogorodov emphasized his words — "Trust no one not known to you." The space in front of the building was the place for a car bomb. Bogorodov pointed down the street to where an assassin could be sitting in a car with a detonator in hand waiting for him to emerge, "From that vantage a getaway is easy. A bomb is surer than a bullet, it usually kills cleanly and leaves no traces. For the professional, the bomb is the preferred method of operation."

Inside Bogorodov advised applying chickenwire against the windows to prevent the entry of grenades or firebombs. He should sleep in the least exposed area of the house, out of the line of gunfire from an accessible window. A fire extinguisher should always be handy in the event of incendiary material such as a phosphorus grenade. Entrances were subject to booby-trapping so special precautions had to be taken when opening doors, Bogorodov had a special pole for this procedure. Of course, even with all possible precautions there was no guarantee. Outside of secreting oneself in an impregnable fortress, there really was no infallible protection. "If someone wants to kill you badly enough they will do it. The best you can do is make if difficult, hopefully, too difficult." However, most terrorism was not that single-minded so the ordinary citizen had a fighting chance. In the final analysis, it was a game of wits, the victim against the terrorists. The game begins with the terrorist having an advantage, but if counter-measures are taken the advantage can be reduced to a stalemate.

Bogordov's analysis had reassured him. No longer nervous, he was now cooly assessing possible scenarios for an assassination attempt. Bogorodov was right — it was difficult to kill someone who, forewarned, undertook measures to frustrate the objective. While some, fatalistically, might abandon themselves to their doom, that was not his way. If one must die it should not be like a dog, shot down by homicidal scum for some vile cause or price. The scenarios he was concocting in his mind may have been farfetched, but it was best to prepare for the worst. Death was too final an event not to oppose with all one's might.

30

The announcer interrupted the musical offering to report the latest location of the hijacked Pan-American jumbo jet. Cairo airport had granted the 747 permission to land for refueling only. Larnaka and Rhodes had previously denied the plane permission to land, claiming their runways were too small to accommodate the big jet. The hijackers were thought to have boarded in Cairo, but other reports spoke of Athens. Both airports had been accused in the past of lax security provisions. While the nationality of the terrorists was described as "unknown", they were reported to speak English with an Arabic accent. Shortly after the plane

289

was commandeered over the Mediterranean, the Sixth Fleet had sent up some of its jets, then recalled them when the hijackers threatened to blow up the plane. As much as the Americans loved the phrase, "You can run but you can't hide," it just was not true. Terrorists, like phantoms, had been running and hiding for years with impunity, in the process bedeviling the American psyche. Whether against the phantoms of terrorism, or the phantoms of Marxist-Leninism, Americans ached for combat. Their gargantuan military establishment was employed at every opportunity to show, like a garland of garlic, their talismanic flag.

The first fatality was announced when the hijacking was into its ninth hour. Who, why, or how the person was killed was unclear. Shortly thereafter, the plane made contact with Damascus airport. Speaking in the name of the "Palestine National Salvation Front", the terrorists demanded the right to land. There was speculation the hijackers were putting Syrian solidarity with the Palestinian cause to the test. While Basil sympathized with the jet's passengers, he was relieved that the plane was an American carrier. Had it been an El-Al plane there would have been hell to pay, a reprisal at least, perhaps a war. Elements in the establishment had been pushing for a confrontation with the Syrians for months. He did not want to be a sacrifice to that policy. He hoped the passenger killed had not been a Jew.

The aerial drama was still unfolding when he waved good-bye to Olga and walked down the stairs out the door, stopping to look up and down the street for anything suspicious. As advised, he had altered his daily arrival and departure times. He had described the changes to Olga in terms of a new "fitness schedule", getting in shape for some possible summer hiking in the Italian Alps. Olga naively suggested they run together in the park. She didn't want to call attention to herself by running in the streets of Jerusalem, she might cause a riot. She knew nothing of his predicament nor was he about to tell her, she would insist on helping him. In view of her rivalry with Ben-Judah, it was better to keep her involvement minimal. Ben-Judah had been too quiet lately — suspiciously quiet.

He was about to pass Bustanji's house when he saw Sumaiya Bustanji open the door and wave, crying, *Mar* (Mr.) Primchek, wait!" Did she have some news on the hijacking? She reemerged a moment later holding a small purse suspended from a red cord. The purse was embroidered in the Palestinian style, the stylized floral pattern of reds and greens contrasting with the purse's natural cotton body. "Excuse me," she said shyly, "but I made this purse for you to give to your mother."

"That's very kind of you, Sumaiya, but unfortunately my mother is deceased."

For a moment she appeared at a loss for words, her embarrassment compounded by the unexpected, "Oh, I'm sorry . . . I didn't know."

"That's alright, how would you?"

"Then I want you to have it," she said. "Will you take it please?" She placed the purse in his hand, and before he was able to make his thanks, excused herself for a second time and ran back to the house, turning at the door to wave good-bye, leaving him holding the purse. It was a nice gesture, indeed, a brave one, the presentation had probably involved no small amount of courage. Like most Arab girls, she shied from too direct a look. Looking into a strange man's eyes, or worse, returning his gaze, was not permitted. Among the devices of the well-bred Arab maiden there was no place for coquetry. He looked up at the house and waved — in case she was watching — before moving aside, out of the way of an approaching car.

He tucked the purse in a pocket of his jacket. He had no idea whether her brothers knew of the gesture, but if they didn't they weren't learning it from him. Entering the office, he heard the voice of the news announcer, Aziz had his radio tuned to the same station. "I've been hearing that guy all day," he said, "anything new happen in the last half-hour?"

"They landed in *ash-Sham,*" replied Aziz, using the Arabic term for Damascus.

"Have they released any passengers?"

"None. They say they are negotiating. For what I don't know."

"Maybe they want amnesty. What do you think the Syrians will do now that they've 'outlawed' terrorism on their territory?"

"I don't know. They say there are some dead. It may be a provocation." Aziz went over to the radio and turned it off. "Palestine National Salvation Front," he exclaimed disdainfully, "they are going to save us by making a few more Americans nervous?"

Later that evening Amon Amitai telephoned. The baby had been prematurely delivered. They should get together and celebrate.

In Athens, where the plane landed after leaving Damascus, some passengers were too shaken to comment. Others spoke of an ordeal of terror involving the execution of two passengers with negotiations dragging through the night between the terrorists and the Syrians. There was a rumor that Nafsi himself had been at the airport to take part in the negotiations. However, none of that could have prepared the passengers of "Pan-Am Flight 1054" for the hijacking's grisly outcome. Shortly before daybreak the terrorists had filed out of the plane flashing victory signs. Approximately one hour later the four men and one woman terrorist were seen being led, hands bound, toward the plane, it appeared as if a novel extradition process was about to take place. Only when the five were stood against a nearby wall was it realized what was actually in store for them. They were shot down by a squad of Syrian soldiers within clear sight of the plane's passengers, their former captives. Not until the bodies were thrown into a truck and driven away was clearance granted for the plane to take off. The bodies of the other hijack victims, the two slain passengers, were turned over to the Red Cross. The Syrians described one, an "Aristotle Diamond", as "an American of Greek ancestry". The United States State Department, although deploring the summary manner of the executions, nevertheless welcomed the Syrian government's demonstrated intention to punish perpetrators of international terrorism. "The terrorists," said State, "reaped their own whirlwind. While the Government of the United States was not yet convinced of the present Syrian regime's commitment to peace in the region, its swift prosecution, albeit flawed, of the guilty parties, was a substantive step toward reestablishing its *bona fides* as a responsible member of the community of nations."

Public opinion in Israel was less generous. Where Syria was involved Israel conceded nothing. The basic assumption was that the terrorists would have gone free had a Jew been slain. The killing of a Greek-American allowed Nafsi to throw a sop to the Greek tourist industry, under siege for years from sporadic acts of terrorism. Furthermore, the executions would have been unthinkable were it not for Israel's stern campaign against terrorism, a campaign it instituted and which the Americans had joined comparatively late. The executions were proof of the campaign's effectiveness — countries harboring terrorists were compelled to clean house or else find themselves on the receiving end of vicarious punishment from the military arms of terrorized nations. On an even more primitive level, the executions were credited with exposing the cowardly nature of terrorist regimes and their leaders. Major Nafsi's constituency was Syria, not Palestine. Thus, he was only continuing, even more brazenly than in the past, Syria's pattern of slaughtering Palestinians whenever expedient. It was an amoral policy, but when did Marxists ever have morals?

He would have expected the executions to weaken

293

Syrian influence. Actually, they had an opposite effect. The action, seen as forceful and decisive, was interpreted as an expression of power. Bustanji's attitude was fairly typical, "Would it be better for the Americans to bomb Syria?" he asked. The Arab masses knew a non-issue when they saw it, he said.

Three days later Beatrix Brunwasser telephoned. The news of the executions had been very upsetting. What did he think? She was not against capital punishment but it had no application to political offenses, and airplane hijackings clearly belonged in that category. Such actions had the support of the masses, to punish those carrying out their will was a serious political error. "Furthermore," she said, "it was very unmanly to kill the woman commando. She should have been given a lesser sentence. Does it make sense that Laila Khaled was a hero while she got executed for her effort? Believe me, this is very confusing to the masses."

"You're not suggesting she wasn't equally responsible?"

"That's *exactly* what I'm suggesting. Everyone knows the position of women in Arab society. It's worse than in Israeli society. They're second class citizens, third class actually. She was acting under the orders of men. That was clear from the testimony of the passengers. *Men* killed the passengers. To hold her responsible for their actions is to create a double oppression!"

She had a point he said, but events didn't always follow a predictable logic. As for Laila Khaled, a lot of sand had passed through the glass since then, the rules had changed. Perhaps if they had not killed the Greek, "What did Nafsi say? . . . 'We have a treaty with Greece.' "

"Sure they have a treaty with Greece — to protect its tourism. Syria doesn't get any tourists from the West. To sacrifice their revolutionary potential for the benefit of a bunch of Greek comprador capitalist hoteliers and innkeepers is crazy."

"You don't think having the support of Greece — at

294

least moral support — is important to Syria?"

"Pardon me, Mr. Primchek, but support from social democrats? . . . Don't make me laugh."

"I don't think I could if I tried. But seriously, what if I told you my information indicates the executions were a non-event in the Arab World?"

"Who have you been talking to anyway?"

"The masses, Beatrix, the masses."

She said they should talk in person sometime, the telephone was not a proper medium for carrying on a political discussion. They agreed to keep in touch, she could always be reached at the IPR office or at home.

31

The thumping he heard wasn't a dream, it was coming from the front door. His first reaction was to reach for the Uzi and throw off the safety. The pounding was louder now, more rhythmical, he heard the word "fire" in Arabic. Donning pants and shoes and brandishing the Uzi, he bolted down to the ground floor. "Who is it?" he hollered. "Your house is on fire" came a voice from outside. Disarming the alarm and opening the door with Bogorodov's device, he saw an agitated figure pointing at the building's front, the fire's light illuminating an oily, moustached face. "Someone started a fire on your store . . ." the man's eyes widened, he had caught sight of the Uzi. "No! Don't shoot!," he pleaded, the fingers of his hands spread in a gesture of innocence. "I was driving by when I saw the fire . . . Look, there's my taxi!" Reaching out and grabbing the man by the shirt, Basil pulled him inside. Then, lifting an extinguisher from its place on the wall and pushing the man in front of him, he squirted foam over the blaze, quickly extinguishing the flames. Apologizing for his rough treatment, he invited the man inside where he atoned for his behavior by presenting the confused volunteer with two bills of large denomination. It was a "reward" for stopping. He took the driver's name and cab number but asked him not to report the incident, it was a "private affair", he said. Alerting the police might interfere with his own investigation. In the circumstances, the driver was only too willing to comply.

He had set his alarm clock to ring before sunrise, he wanted to try and remove the effects of the fire before the street awakened. After sweeping up the jagged green shards of glass, he scrubbed the blackened portion of the stone facade. Although a stain remained, the effort was successful in removing the more obvious evidence of fire. When Aziz arrived, he informed him of what had happened and warned against admitting strangers.

He ate dinner hurriedly that night, skipping dessert and after-dinner conversation with his father. He was anxious to get back to the office. He felt a sense of relief when he turned the corner and the building's illuminated facade came into view. Its stone walls and pitched tile roof gave an impression of security. Indeed, it was one of the more secure structures on the street. Nevertheless, its capacity to resist destruction was limited.

When he picked up the telephone he expected to hear Baruch Lapidus on the other end of the line. The industrialist had been calling almost daily wanting to make sure that when construction began again, his villa would have priority. But the voice was Mark's, "Your father gave me your number. You didn't tell me you had a new office. What happened to the government job?"

"I still have it, but I got some private jobs lately and decided to open an office. But what have you got . . .

insomnia?"

"So it's three in the morning, let me worry about that. I wanted to talk to you — number one, how are you doing?"

"I'll live I think."

"Whaddya mean, you 'think'? Didn't you get a girl yet?"

"Ages ago, I thought I told you. But that's the least of my problems. Haven't you been reading the papers lately?"

"Yeah, what the hell is going on over there? Is the right going to take over, or is all this confusion one of the results of the Syrian-Iranian axis?"

"I don't know. Probably a mixture of both. What do the great panjandrums in Washington say? That's the key."

"That's why I'm calling, our intelligence is only as good as the source. We're making that trip I told you about. We'll be over in late March or early April, the plans haven't been finalized yet. You'll be there won't you?"

"Sure, where am I going? Just give me advance notice so I can keep the dates open."

"You *better* keep them open because guess who's coming with us?"

"You make it sound so threatening . . . OK, I give, who?"

"Alison Cleveland. How's that grab you?"

"I never would have guessed. What's her interest?"

"She's a free-lance correspondent now. She'll be covering our trip. She said she was looking forward to seeing you again."

"Yeah? I wonder what for? She got the only two balls I had."

"That was last year. Time heals all wounds — even imaginary ones. Keep your options open, she could be one of them . . . "

Mark was talking but the words weren't registering, he was absorbed by the prospect of seeing her again, thinking

297

of what he would say when they met, whether to be ingratiating or flippant and cavalier? He wondered what had changed with her to justify the new leaf. He would serve her now as he did then — as a convenient pot of information. But this time his opinions were not for attribution, they had caused him . . . "Hey! Basil! you still there?" Mark's alert jarred his reverie, bringing him back to earth. They would be flying in from Rome. The senator planned an audience with the Pope and was considering an inspection of Sixth Fleet headquarters in Naples. Although he was up for reelection, he would be asking Israeli politicians some hard questions. The country's drift was a cause for concern, frank discussions were anticipated. At the same time, the senator wanted to elicit Israel's "special needs". If Israel needed help she would have it. The trip was being billed as the senator's most crucial mission ever. These were critical times concluded Mark gravely. More than democracy was at stake. War, peace, and the fate of a generation were involved.

32

Living in the Arab quarter, he was accustomed to hearing sounds of awakening, the car horns, the shouts of vegetable hucksters. But this morning the noise was different. Persistent and insistent, it demanded one's attention. Unlatching a shutter, he looked in the direction of the tumult. A police car and small crowd blocked the way, drivers were blowing their horns and backing up. A woman's voice keened, *"Ya waili! Ya waili!"* He dressed

rapidly, then ran out. "Aziz Bustanji! Aziz Bustanji!," someone cried. Pushing and pulling people aside, he bulled
through the crowd to find a policeman standing over a body.
Nearby lay a long, wooden-handled meat knife, its blade
tinged red. "Get back!," ordered the policeman. "Wait!,"
cried Basil, "He works for me!" Stooping down, he turned
the body over and saw the eyes' blank stare, the bloodless,
morbidly gray face. The policeman's "He's dead" was redundant. He let go of the body and stood up, there was blood
on his hands. A twinge of weakness ran down his scrotum
through his legs. Unsteady, he reeled from nausea and dread
— the dread of facing Bustanji whose rage and grief would
surely be cosmic. Someone else would break the news to
him, it was not his place to do so. The faces in the crowd
— some he knew to see, but that was all. They probably
knew him though, "the Yahoodi". They would inform his
mother, perhaps someone was telling her now. He didn't
want to be there when she came down. He wished the
ambulance would hurry and get there. She might not be
home, perhaps she was shopping. He asked the policeman
how long the ambulance took and got a perfunctory reply.
Looking down at the body, he saw that a pool of blood had
formed in a small depression in the ancient sidewalk. It was
drying, maroon in the morning sun. He swore at the slowness of the ambulance. Finally, he heard the siren and saw
the ambulance coming the wrong way up the one way
street. After a brief discussion with the police, the ambulance attendants wrapped the body in a sheet, placed it on a
stretcher, and slid it into the back of the ambulance. Then
turning around, the ambulance sped off, siren screaming. He
was reminded of a film he had seen on the siege of Beirut,
showing ambulance drivers picking up, like so many sacks of
shit, shattered bodies off the street after a bombing raid.
The body gone, the police ordered all those with knowledge
of the crime to report to the police station to make a
statement. Next of kin could reclaim the body from the

morgue. "Everyone else should go home or to their work. You, sir," said the policeman to Basil, "you will please come with us."

The investigative process was remarkably similar to a scene from an American detective film of the forties. Taken into a high-ceilinged room on the second floor of police headquarters, he was introduced to Inspector Gol Lautman, the person who would be heading the investigation. He was offered a cigarette and when he declined, a glass of water, his hosts seemed to be going out of their way to make it easy on him. Lautman, a fairly personable fellow, apologized for the inconvenience, qualifying the apology with a reference to the crime's seriousness. Short and heavy jowled, with large, bleary eyes, Lautman could have been the inspiration for the fictitious Bulldog Drummond, so much did he embody that breed's singular and homely qualities. When speaking his lower lip protruded, exposing pinkish flesh. Lautman's assistant, a younger man Basil knew only as Kogan, was armed with a large, yellow pad of the type favored by lawyers, upon which he scribbled sporadic notation. Other than note-taking, Kogan's contribution to the post-mortem was minimal. His main function seemed to be to act as a reinforcer of the opinions of his superior. This he did by steadily nodding to Lautman's points, sometimes before they were made.

After listening attentively to Basil's narrative of events, Lautman referred to a series of recent incidents involving inter-Arab struggle over the issue of Arabs working for Jews. They were classed, he said, as political crimes, which, next to motiveless crimes, were the most difficult of solution. Because Arab society tended to be a subculture in Israel and the territories, both victim and perpetrator tended to be anonymous. This type of crime was related to the struggle between Jewish nationalism and Arab nationalism, now in a state of heightened conflict "with each other and with themselves". For the police, these developments compounded an already complicated situation. If at times the police could not produce results as speedily as one might expect, Lautman wanted his unfortunate guest to know the reasons why. "The story you have told us, Mr. Primchek, while plausible, is, I am afraid, merely a theory based upon coincidence. Allow me to explain. One, you say it began with telephone calls ordering you to dismiss the deceased. Two, you were visited by Rabbi Khak who *asked* you to replace the deceased with a person from a list of Jews, a list which you say you possess. Three, a Molotov cocktail of some unknown flammable material was thrown against your office residence some nights ago. And now today, the murder of the deceased. Ahh yes . . . the Rabbi mentioned the possibility of enforcement were his request ignored. As I said it is a plausible chain of events. To you, the victim so to speak, it makes very good sense, practical sense. If I were the public prosecutor I would say it suggests a motive . . . *suggests* a motive. Because the motive here is shared by at least two opposing movements. Did any of the callers or the Rabbi make a specific threat against life or limb of the deceased? . . . No? If they had, perhaps a murderous intent could be attributed to them, but without more I am afraid we cannot do that. In fact, based on what you have told us, and the evidence collected in a killing like this, a meat knife — which, by the way, is primarily a weapon employed by Arab criminals — I would be exceeding my authority were I to arrest the Rabbi for questioning. And as you know, in matters such as these we must be very careful because we, the police, are between the hammer and anvil. Imagine the furor we would cause were we to request the Rabbi report for questioning — a request I am not at all certain he would honor. His people would demonstrate against us, there would be a debate in the Knesset, the public order would be called into question, more I need not tell you. Let us not get into that can of worms — that is if we were to proceed only on what you have told us. The question is not one of disbelief, Mr. Primchek, I want that clearly understood between us. You are indeed a reputable person, a sincere person. But we must have more than sincerity to crack this case. Consider that approximately two hours have passed since the commission of the crime. How great it would be if every crime could be solved in two hours, in a day, in a *month*! That would indeed make our work a pleasure. But the real world of police work is usually quite different. A major percentage of cases are solved only after many hundreds of man hours of dogged investigation by teams of officers following the slightest lead, regardless how minor they might appear at first.

"Yes . . . I would not want to tell you how to build a building, Mr. Primchek. You are a highly trained technician of international reputation. That is your business. So this is our business, the business of crime. It is a paradox, but we police must be able to read the criminal mind, to think like one, in some cases even act like one. In war, a good general tries to predict where the enemy will attack. So — forgive me if this is elementary to you — we must be trained in psychology, sociology, anthropology, medicine, uh . . . the martial arts, all the disciplines that fall under the heading of criminology. If that seems like a waste, all this investment to deal with so corrupt a problem, my answer is that that is life. Man is a combination of good and evil, when evil predominates we have the criminal. It is human nature . . . Excuse me, you know these things. So all I am asking you now is to exercise a little patience, understanding I am sure you have. Just a little patience, to give us time to develop this case because — and I say this as one with twenty-seven years of experience in these things — the cases that appear to be simple usually turn out to be more complex than expected. Deceptively simple, yes, deceptively simple . . ."

He declined Lautman's offer of a ride, instead hailing a cab outside the station. There would be questions, people would want to know what the police said. He would have to face them, all of them, including of course, the Bustanjis. Thinking about what to say was useless. Words would be worthless, or worse, obnoxious pretense. To be sacrificed in a fight among Jews was a cruel irony of fate, they had suffered enough at the hands of that race. "It should have been him" they would say, a legitimate reaction when the guilty survived the innocent.

People were still milling about when the taxi dropped him in front of the office. Pointing to the bloodstains, they shook their heads in despair and disbelief. As he stood watching, unsure of what to do or say, three men approached. The trio's leader, a small man with a thin moustache, introduced himself. "Sir," he said, speaking in English, "I am Bashir Jalajil, proprietor of Jalajil Dry Goods and Linens. My friends, Faris Aoun and Butros Khail, are also businessmen in the neighborhood. We understand Aziz Bustanji was employed by you in your office here."

"Yes, that's right."

"It is a terrible crime. Have the police any suspects?"

"I just came from a long talk with them at headquarters. They said it was still too early . . .," he hesitated, as if too much talk might tip off the murderers, "so I just gave them my suspicions."

"And what are they if I may ask?," said Jalajil.

"The Torah and Land."

"In this neighborhood? But we have no quarrel . . ." Stopping in mid-sentence, Jalajil glanced at his companions, then ended the conversation with a hasty "I thank you for your time, sir. We can only hope that those guilty of this crime will be brought to justice."

The afternoon was spent making himself available — to friends of the Bustanjis, neighbors, reporters from a couple of the smaller radical weeklies. His father came over to discuss the situation, urging him to come home. An IPR member stopped to offer the organization's support and deliver a written message from Beatrix Brunwasser, a message consisting of one word — SOLIDARITY. Apparently, the IPR did have good intelligence, in both camps.

It was dark by the time he left to walk the short distance to the Bustanji house. He walked slowly, like an old man, taking deliberate, small steps. Rounding the corner he saw the house's lighted windows, people standing on the two-sided stoop. Their presence was encouraging, he had fears of being alone. As he approached he saw they were adolescents, students from Sumaiya Bustanji's school. Inside it was standing room only. He saw Bustanji at the far end of the parlor holding an oversized white handkerchief. An older man was standing by his side, he recognized him from that day at the slave market. Another man was trying to steer Bustanji toward a chair. Resisting the attempt, Bustanji continued standing, cursing in a hoarse voice the Jews, the Arabs, the Americans, and God in heaven respectively. Surrounded by a wall of grief and rage, his indifference to consolation was a judgment upon its impertinence. Farid and Jasim, two workers from Bustanji's crew, greeted Basil silently, shaking his hand. Aziz's body lay on a makeshift bier covered with a white on white embroidery. The eyes were closed now but the face still bore the pallor of death, the Arab world having resisted the art of the embalmer. Death had drawn the skin over the cheekbones, pulling back the lips, hinting at a final grimace of pain. Light from a floorlamp profiled the prominently lobed brow and high-bridged nose, recalling images of plaster death masks. In front of the bier, two black-clad old ladies made the sign of the cross. He was next. Aziz's mother and sister were seated on a small divan. Clutching his fingers, the mother thanked him for coming. He saw Sumaiya's lips move then contort with the face in a fresh burst of anguish. He felt a sudden, uncontrollable surge of emotion and his eyes well with tears, the warm moisture spilling onto his cheeks. He pressed a folded handkerchief to his eyes and moved on.

He found himself in the kitchen, the room where the

overflow from the parlor had congregated. An old man spoke to him in Arabic, then, realizing his mistake, switched to Hebrew. An old-timer, he had grown up in the thirties. The Bustanjis he declared, were "*shuhada*", martyrs. The British hanged their grandfather, he had fought "Wingate and the Jews" in the "great Palestinian revolt". Aziz, he said, was as much a part of that tradition as if killed by a British bullet or hung by a British rope. "England brought us the Jews, trained them to take over our country, and when they bit her hand turned them over to an even crueler master, the Americans. The Americans killed Aziz. They give the Jews billions to kill us. Their Congress votes anything for Israel — cluster bombs, the best and fastest airplanes. Do you know this Senator Maudlin? . . . He is an assassin! An assassin! I would kill him with my own hands if I had the chance. Tell me," demanded the old man, abruptly changing the subject, "what do you think of Salim Nafsi?"

Basil hesitated, he had not expected to be drawn into a political discussion, a "wrong" answer could be compromising. The old man's militancy had attracted an audience of young, Hebrew-speaking Arabs. He hoped they knew his relationship to the Bustanjis, one *shaheed* was enough. "I think he's good for Syria," he said.

"What is good for Syria is good for Palestine," replied the old man.

"Is that said as a Palestinian or a Syrian?"

"Both! When the next century begins there will be no difference, the curtain will have rung down on imperialism, its creations vanished like crusader kingdoms."

"Do the Americans know about this? It might be the chance they've been waiting for to beat their swords into plowshares." It was a flippant reply. Indeed, how was one to answer such fancies? Wish masqueraded as thought in Arab political thinking, it was impossible to take seriously. The old man's assertions were but another variation on the old refrain — the perennial Arab wish for Israel to go away. The hundred to two hundred years that used to be predicted for the process had been telescoped into ten to twenty. Perhaps with all the talk of an imminent end to life on earth, they wanted a few years to enjoy the dream.

Sensing the impasse, the old man brought the conversation to its inconclusive end, sounding a passive "we'll see". The opening shot heard round the room had fallen to earth with a thud. If the audience of young Arabs had expected an adversarial battle royal between Arab and Jew, they were disappointed. Tired of oracular pronouncements and indeterminate prophecies, they wanted finite answers, the kind Salim Nafsi gave.

There was a trailing off of sound from the parlor. The muezzin, Abdel Malik Al-Amyuni, had arrived and begun reading from the Quran, commencing with the plaintive Sura Yusuf, the Quranic retelling of the story of Joseph and his brothers. Of course, the story had only a minimal relation to the present. Like all religion, it was pure coincidence. However, there was nothing coincidental about the emotion in the voice of the muezzin. Timeless and universal, it was a lament on the never-ending tragedy of the human condition. That the words were recited in a religious context was merely one more coincidence. The separation between the sacred and profane had been an artificial one from the beginning.

The wail of the muezzin was relentless, dominating the senses. He saw Bustanji start for the door. Hesitating momentarily, he followed, making his way through the crowded parlor. Outside, Bustanji was leaning against an adjoining dwelling. "I know what you're thinking," he said, "but don't worry, no one's blaming you. This time you're innocent. I'm leaving tomorrow. If I come back, it will be for one purpose only — to kill. My mother and sister will take care of themselves. Their needs are simple, they will survive. With him went my last illusion." Bustanji strode back into the house. He walked quickly down the street, the choked wail of Abdel Malik al-Amyuni growing fainter in his ears.

When he arrived for the funeral in the morning there was a jeep full of soldiers parked in front of the house. The funeral was off they said, "*Mamnu*" (forbidden). The Jerusalem' military command had information indicating PLO and communist agitators were planning to use the occasion for a demonstration. The army was acting to forestall a serious threat to public order. With Passover and Easter only weeks away the terrorists were trying to create a climate of fear, Jerusalem would not be permitted to become an arena for terrorist outrage and intimidation. The funeral had been "rescheduled" for eight that night, the mourners limited to a total of twelve, inclusive of family members. A military escort would accompany the mourners to the cemetary to supervise the enforcement of the order.

Bustanji was gone, having departed before dawn. The others were in no position to resist. The exigencies of death effectively narrowed the alternatives to one — compliance. The dead being beyond punishment, the attempt to restrict funerals was an insult to the living, denying them one of the last outlets remaining. As a policy it was more contemptuous than dangerous, even despots conceded people the right to mourn the dead.

It wasn't quite noon when he walked into Olga's office and sat down. He told her what happened, recounting the story of the killing, from beginning to end. The depth of her reaction was unexpected, "Forgive me," she said between reaching for a tissue and blowing her nose, "I am touched. We Russians are an emotional people. The death of your Aziz is the bitter fruit of an evil tree. I fear its poison is spreading . . . Khalil, his brother, where is he?"

"Gone. He didn't say where, but I'm sure it's Syria. He said he wasn't coming back . . . except to *kill*."

"Can you blame him?," she asked.

307

The major dailies gave the slaying cursory mention on inside pages, reporting that the matter was under investigation but that the police as yet had no suspects. No motive was suggested. By contrast, the *Call*, the weekly organ of the IPR, gave the murder full coverage, including the fact that the victim was slain while walking to his employment, "the Jerusalem studio of Architect Basil Primchek." The article challenged the police to apprehend those responsible and demanded the government control the settlers before their outrages "provoked a civil war."

Amon Amitai and Viktor Bogorodov telephoned to express regret and concern. Assuming his suspicions were correct, he could relax, said Bogorodov. They had made their point, "They were too smart to go around killing Jews." His colleagues, save of course Ben-Judah, offered perfunctory condolences. Ulrich Fesser elaborated on his by sidling up to him and confiding that he was against such tactics, that "the end did not justify the means". He hadn't heard from Rachel but that was understandable, she didn't read the newspapers. Eventually she would find out, but it probably wouldn't make any difference, she wasn't the type to be overly concerned about others, least of all Arabs.

Following the tragic events a rash of tire slashings and car window breakage hit the neighborhood. Molotov cocktails, three this time, were thrown against storefronts and houses. Although damage was negligible, people were nervous and angry. A delegation from the neighborhood went to the mayor's office to demand extra police protection. The police, they were told, were doing all that was possible, no police force in the world could provide its citizenry with "absolute protection". After a three day lull came "the night of the bombs", one of which blew out the front windows of Faris Aoun's falafel palace. Shortly thereafter, Aoun got a call promising the attacks would continue until "the traitor Primchek left the neighborhood." According to Aoun, the caller claimed to represent *"Kaas Yisroel"*, a group no one had ever heard of before. Apparently, breaking him was not enough. They were also out to ruin him.

It seemed an appropriate time to renew contact with Inspector Lautman, there was a possibility the police had evidence relating the acts of vandalism and terror to the killing. The inspector was cautiously optimistic. Yes, they were working on the case, "doggedly". But they still had nothing to show for their efforts. He was reluctant to hazard a prediction, but "any day now" the case might be solved, all they needed was a break. In the meantime he prescribed patience, "as hard as that may be for you."

"I don't understand it," said Basil, "with all the acts against automobiles, the firebombs, the bomb blasts, there has to be a gang involved. I can't see why the police can't apprehend at least one of them during their rampages."

"I'm in homicide, Mr. Primchek, so those things are out of my department. But look at it this way — if we could have gotten them we would have. It's not as simple as you think. This is a big city, people going in and out at all times of the day and night . . . plus some of these characters are young, they don't have a criminal record, the member- ship lists of these organizations are secret. So where do we begin? I know you wouldn't advocate a dragnet. I can sympathize with your concern, but don't forget, we've got to respect the rules, we just can't go out and arrest every- body. Again, Mr. Primchek, a little patience, we'll get them eventually, I'm sure of it."

33

The return address of the envelope read "Metri Eide, Advocate, Jaboor Building — Suite 26, Ramallah, West Bank via Israel." Inside was a one paragraph letter typewritten on legal stationery —

> Dear Mr. Primchek:
> I have been retained by an association of Jerusalem property owners and businessmen to represent them in the matter of acts of violence and threats against their homes and property. It has been represented to me that the aforesaid violence and threats are related to your use of the premises known as 161 Amir Farhan Street, as an office and/or residence. A meeting to discuss your occupation of said premises and its potential to the peace and welfare of my clients as well as the surrounding community will be held on Wednesday evening, March 1, at 8:00 p.m. at the Jalajil Dry Goods and Linen Store, located at 14 Salah ed-Din Street. Your attendance at said meeting is urgently requested.
> I remain, sir, yours faithfully,
> Metri Eide, Advocate

He tossed the letter onto the table. He was disposed to ignore it, the organizers of the party couldn't be so silly as to expect him to attend his own lynching. "Occupation of said premises?" — their lawyer must have confused him with the Israeli government. They never were much good at distinctions he told himself, that was one reason for their present predicament. The blandishments of "His Majesty", the "100 year diplomacy of the PLO", and the rotten carrots of Israeli peace proposals kept them in a state of perpetual indecision. But his case was different, they could decide it in minutes — over coffee. He imagined them in the makeshift kangaroo court, deliberating self-importantly, one of them standing and proclaiming, "Brothers! The Jew, the Jew is the cause of our troubles." A chorus of assent and it would be unanimous — the Jew should go. Peace, meaning business as usual, would again reign. Disgusted, he reread the letter, searching for a flaw or weakness in its bland fabric. A second opinion was in order, an unbiased one. That eliminated his father.

At the Brunwasser residence Beatrix picked up the line. She was glad to hear from him but hoped it wasn't more bad news. He read her the letter from the lawyer. What did she think, should he go to the meeting? "You'd be handing them a victory on a platter if you don't," she said. "That's exactly what they want so they can dismiss you and say you don't care about the community. It's a crude scapegoat operation with the Torah and Land using the merchant Palestinians to punish you for standing with the masses, they want to show progressive Jews the futility of allying with them. But they're bound to fail because the merchant bourgeoisie isn't the masses, it's nothing but a decadent and craven economic element kept alive by the distortions of the occupation. Because it exists with the consent of the authorities, it naturally seeks to avoid incurring their displeasure. And of course the authorities exploit this fear, cynically using this rotten class as a control device. But getting back to you, you're going to have to actively oppose them. It's your responsibility now."

"I thought you'd say that," he replied, a note of resignation in his response. "You know I'm not disputing anything you've said, but I have to question what my chances would be were I to attend the meeting. It's got to be stacked

311

against me."

"Sure it will be stacked against you, they're not going to call in the Bustanjis for support. Of course, now that Aziz is dead they'll hypocritically invoke his memory. But where were they when he was alive and defying the terrorists? They didn't give a fig for him then and they don't now, that's *our* cause. As for chances — did you ask Aziz Bustanji what chance he had in opposing the Khakites by continuing to work for you? If you did, I'll bet I know what he told you. What chance did the thousands of other Palestinians have who fell fighting the British Empire and the Jewish Yishuv in the thirties? For that matter, what chance did the driver of the truck have, when he drove into the US marine compound in Beirut and detonated himself and three hundred marines? I can go on you know."

Yes, he said, he realized that. But he got the point, a struggle was built on the accumulation of thousands of acts of resistance, some great and some, like his, quite minor. In the context, winning or losing was irrelevant. It was a process and like it or not, he was now a part of it. Of course, Beatrix was a believer, faithful to the vision of a better world, an eventuality for which she entertained not the slightest doubt.

When he arrived at Jalajil's store, three of his presumed opponents were conversing outside. He greeted them with a "Good evening, *sadati.*" One, a pin-striped individual with a briefcase under arm, threw down a cigarette he had been smoking and extended a hand, *"Mar* Primchek I presume," said the man, using the Hebrew for "mister", "I'm Metri Eide, glad you could make it." Eide portrayed himself in a humanitarian light, disclaiming any interest in the outcome of the evening's deliberations, "I am here tonight only as a peacemaker, sir, wishing only to help my clients and friends here, resolve an unfortunate situation." Eide made a point of telling Basil he was a Melkite Christian, and though relations with the Israeli government were not always what they

312

should be, he had many Jewish friends in and out of the legal profession. Being a Christian, said Eide, was to be from a tradition of minority status, "Even when the Greeks ruled us they treated us as a minority, so we are used to living under masters of many faiths. They come and go, and yet here we are, the survivors. And, I dare say, we shall survive the present Judaic era." Of course, he said, being a minority implied a heightened sensitivity to the rights of others, if only because one is outnumbered. "So one must compromise . . . But that is life is it not?" Basil nodded in apparent agreement without comment. The advocate's words were a trifle too artful.

The others were arriving now. It was after eight, but it was a rare Arab meeting that ever began on time. He recognized some of the men as they entered the store to take their seats on the wooden folding chairs set up for the purpose. There was Naji Sumsum, the king of the mother of pearl and olivewood tourist trade; Kamal Shibli, restaurateur; Naif al-Hazzam, operator of a car rental and guide agency; Abdullah Atallah, the owner of al-Aqsa Hotel and Pension (he remembered the place well because years before he spent a night there with an English tourist, which was probably as close to England as he ever got); and Faris Aoun, the plantiff allegedly most aggrieved.

After calling the meeting to order, the host, Bashir Jalajil, had each man stand and give his name and business. Metri Eide then gave a short resume of the problem and the issues raised (essentially a restatement of his letter), stating that "our Israeli compatriot" would have the right to answer.

The plaintiffs' case was simplicity itself — strife was bad for business and with Easter and Passover approaching, doubly bad. "Why," exclaimed one of the plaintiffs, "even the Israelis recognized this by unleashing the war that won them Jerusalem in early June, midway between Easter and summer, our two biggest tourist seasons." Bashir Jalajil summed it up when he stated that "the tourists are our bread and butter. If we lose them we may as well prepare for emigration, because we are nothing without tourism . . . And tourists do not travel thousands of miles to come to a battleground." As evidence, Jalajil asserted that over 85% of his business was directly or indirectly connected with tourism.

It was Basil's turn to speak. Taking a cue from the plaintiffs, he couched his answer in equally simple terms — avoiding such irrelevancies as legal right and Arab-Jewish friendship — in an effort to appeal to the primary interest of the hardheaded businessmen. "It was a criminal element that demanded I dismiss Aziz Bustanji from my employ. When I did not, they killed him. If their object was what they claimed it to be, that should have settled the matter. But then, with typical insincerity, they make an additional demand, that I leave also. The next demand could be for some of *you* to leave. What assurance do you have that even if I did vacate, that would be the end of it?"

"I can answer that," exclaimed Bashir Jalajil. "We have assurances from the sources involved that your removal from the neighborhood shall lay this matter to rest completely, finally, and forever. You have my word on that."

An argument had broken out among the plaintiffs. A group had gathered around Abdullah Atallah and was vehemently remonstrating with him, in their anger and excitement reverting to the Arabic vernacular. Apparently, Atallah had set himself apart from the majority. Why, Basil couldn't tell, even a translator would have been hard pressed to make sense of the sonic tumult. Although the men were shouting at each other, it was a typical Arab donnybrook among friends. In a few minutes the fury would subside and friendship resume unimpaired. At this point Metri Eide intervened to remind the disputants that a "guest" was present. Speaking in English "for the benefit of our friend," he confessed to feeling no small measure of pain because of the dispute, "a pain I am sure all here share. Indeed, what is this rancor if it is not its manifestation? Each of us is a fair man, a just man—or we prefer to think ourselves such. But sometimes there comes an issue that changes our nature, our disposition to good, and forces us to be unfair. I believe the issue before us tonight to be just such an issue. Here is a man . . . who I am sure in the goodness of his heart has tried to do the decent thing, and as God is his witness he may indeed be so judged. Yet we, His children, in the short duration of our existence on earth, cannot wait for our vindication on that day of judgment when all will be set right. We can only try to do our best, hoping that when the Lord above judges our conduct, He will be merciful.

"Tonight there are two rights represented in this room. Which should prevail? I believe that the maintenance of peace must be paramount. If peace can be restored . . . as our brother Bashir assures us, then I say that the rights of Mr. Princhek must give way before that objective. There has already been one tragedy from this dispute and God help us if we permit another."

He had ten days to vacate. They were sorry they said, but it was the occupation, it was responsible for this cruel dilemma. They hoped he would show understanding, they meant him no ill will. As he prepared to leave, he was approached by Metri Eide asking for a final word, "Forgive me for speaking out as I did, but it is a foolish lawyer who thinks he can be neutral. It was rough justice, but considering my clients' greater exposure to harm, I believe it was the right decision under the circumstances. You really haven't lost anything yet, so I suggest you quit now while you're still ahead . . ." Eide wished Basil good-bye, rejoining the circle of satisfied clients waiting to congratulate him.

Two days later Rachel arrived for the weekend. Discharged from the army only a few days before, she was scheduled to begin work the following Monday as a medical records clerk at Hadassah Hospital. He gave her a summary of developments since their last meeting, careful not to

315

burden her with the issue's complexities — she would only absorb so much. She was vaguely sympathetic until he offered to rent her the office. "No thank you!," she snapped, taking the offer seriously, "I should live with these *Arabushim*? Give me the nurses' dormitory, at least it's not crawling with Arabs. Why you chose this place when you could have a downtown office with the other architects, I'll never know. You must have been mad to live among them, they hate us. No matter how good you treat them, in the end they turn on you."

It was the first time she had raised her voice to him. Her use of the term "Arabushim" disturbed him, as if what she thought reflected upon him or his taste in women. He thought of telling her she would pass for an Arab anywhere were it not for the Star of David she wore around her Moroccan neck. But they were alone and nobody's feelings had been hurt, least of all an Arab's. Her attitude was too representative to be cause for more than passing embarrassment. So she didn't like Arabs, who did? The remark was only a blow to pride, his intellectual pride. Standing up, he walked over to where she sat, legs up, on a leather-padded chair. Taking hold of the bottom of her T-shirt, he jerked it over her head and arms, uncovering the olive breasts. Placing his hand over one, he began squeezing, watching her face for a sign of the pain he knew she felt but refused to acknowledge, increasing the pressure until the dusky nipple, with its delicate network of veins, bulged through his fingers. Only when her eyes filled with tears did he relent. He told her he wanted to see if she had feelings. Yes, she said, wiping her eyes with her fingers, she had feelings, "and pride too."

The telephone was ringing. Rachel leapt out of bed and ran down the stairs crying, "I'll get it!" She liked answering his telephone. It was a kind of territorial imperative, like treemarking. His bedside clock showed 8:40. He wondered who would be calling so early on a Saturday. "Mr. Jalajil," answered Rachel from below.

As she came up the stairs he noticed her breasts, one was black and blue, while the other had blood bruises about the nipple. "Wait a minute," he said, "let me see those things. Animal attack?," he asked with mock seriousness. She gave a slight nod, modesty apparently preventing a more affirmative response. Yet her posture — the expanded and puffed-out chest — suggested pride. She was proud of her wounds. Like brands burnt into an animal's hide, they were a sign of ownership, that he claimed her for his exclusive use and pleasure.

Jalajil was calling from his store he said. With him were two young Palestinian doctors looking for office space in the city. "They could relieve you of a big responsibility," said Jalajil. "They seem very interested and look to me to be two very substantial individuals. If they like the place I am sure they would have no objection to signing a lease, with you or Mrs. Bustanji. They want to see it . . . Would it be alright if they came over right now?"

Jalajil was pushing it. Only two days into the "grace period" and he was already applying pressure. Suppressing his resentment, Basil responded civilly, "I appreciate your thinking of me, Mr. Jalajil, but I'm really not prepared to receive anyone now. As a matter of fact, I'll be occupied through this weekend. If you don't mind, I'd like time to think the matter over, I really haven't had a chance to examine the alternatives."

"Alright, sir, as you prefer." Jalajil said good-bye and hung up. Arabs were a nervous race, especially the Christian ones. When he came back upstairs Rachel was sprawled on the bed waiting. "Was it a client?," she asked.

"No," he said, pressing against her, "it was one of the Arabs. He had a couple doctors who want to rent the place."

"You're going to rent it to them, aren't you?" He didn't answer, nor did she press the point — he was entering her again.

34

A week had passed since the notice to vacate. The neighborhood had been quiet in the interim, no bombings or Molotov cocktails disturbing its peace. It was either a coincidence or an "arrangement". At the Authority that morning there was a message waiting for him from Dr. Mansura Haddad in Ramallah. The message said "urgent", a word that had been wearing on him of late. Words like urgent had a limited currency, excessive use debased their meaning. However, unlike Baruch Lapidus, who sometimes telephoned three or four times a week leaving "urgent" messages to call back, this was her first.

He reached her at her aviary. She had been anxiously awaiting his call she said. "Something terrible has happened — this morning the workers found the three ancient olive trees, the ones that were to be the focus of our garden, cut down." Her husband was in Bahrein and because she couldn't telephone him from Ramallah she was considering leaving for Amman that afternoon. He responded by reassuring her, telling her that it was premature at this stage to involve her husband, suggesting she stay put until he arrived and got a first-hand look at the damage. She agreed to wait for him, adding, "I can't imagine why anyone would do a thing like this."

In spite of the fact that Thursday was a school day, he immediately telephoned Beatrix Brunwasser, hoping to catch her at home. Beatrix was not home said a woman answering the telephone, "May I ask who's calling?" He assumed the voice belonged to her mother, it had an unmistakable upper-class confidence and precision, "Basil Primchek, the architect."

"Oh yes, Mr. Primchek, Beatrix has spoken of you often. She's in school now, but I expect her home about half past one. May I give her a message?"

"Would you please have her call me when she gets home? It's uh," he almost said "urgent," "important."

Four hours was too long a time to wait. After being routed through various school offices, he ended up speaking with one of the student advisors, " . . . we do not like to disturb our students during school hours unless a genuine emergency exists," explained an officious voice. "Pardon me, madam," he said, applying some pressure of his own, "we have an archeological dig planned for this afternoon in Judea and Beatrix happens to have information important to the health and security of the participants. Can we avoid an argument? I wouldn't want to come over there and make a scene. I really must talk to her." The threat worked, an exception would be made, "but only this once."

With Beatrix finally on the line, he quickly explained the situation, asking if she would accompany him. "How long will it take you to get over here?," said Beatrix.

"About fifteen minutes. Why, can you get off now?"

"You just be out front, I'll be there."

They went directly to the Haddad residence in Ramallah, picked up Mansura Haddad, and drove the two kilometers to the site. When they arrived they found the trees lying where felled, the gray-green leaves still vigorous, as if unaware of their recent amputation. The contorted and muscular trunks of the olive trees had been cleanly cut, a few minutes of chainsaw action undoing centuries of growth. The three Arab workers preparing the site for excavation confirmed that the trees had been cut the evening before, after they had left the job. A witness, a local shepherd, saw two men in a small pickup truck drive onto the site and cut down the trees. "Where is the shepherd now?," asked Basil. One of the Arabs pointed to a line of hills some three hundred meters distant, "He is with his flock in the valley beyond those hills." Leaving a depressed Mansura Haddad sitting gloomily on one of the fallen trunks, Basil and Beatrix set off to find the shepherd.

The summit of a hill gave them a broad view of the valley. It was the time of year when the Judean landscape, uncharacteristically prodigal, put forth multitudes of flowers, the bounty of lupines, buttercups, cyclamen, Solomon's slipper, and violets making for a naturalist's nosegay and a grazer's delight. However, the section of ground they stood on was bare of vegetation. Sheep droppings, their dark chocolate glossiness evidence of recent passage, littered the dusty soil.

They located the sheep on the opposite side of the valley, clustered under a small grove of trees. The shepherd, a boy of about fifteen, they found sitting against the base of an olive tree snacking on bread and *zaatar* (Arabic thyme). When he first saw them he took them for hikers. A lot came through these hills he said, especially now in the "season of flowers". Beatrix explained that they were with the workers preparing to build a house on the other side of the hill, then questioned him about the men who cut the trees. There were two he said, he didn't get a good look at them but he remembered the color of the truck, it was sand. Could he tell whether they were Jews or Arabs? *"Mush Yahood, hummi Arab,"* he replied in the local Palestinian dialect, "They weren't Jews, they were Arabs." They spoke Arabic and he heard one call the other "Ahmed". He was sorry, he thought they had been empowered by the owner of the land to cut the trees. If he had known their purpose was evil, he would have taken the plate number of the truck and tried to get a look at them, it was still light out. Basil handed him a bill equivalent to approximately fifty dollars US and asked him — with Beatrix translating — to keep an eye out for anything suspicious because they would soon begin laying the stone for the foundation and walls, and there could be further acts of vandalism. The boy stared at the bill in his hand, then back to his benefactor's face before breaking into a paean of gratitude for the unexpected beneficence, swearing to "watch night and day for

320

you kind people, by God!"

"Well," he remarked as they walked away, "I'll be calling Jalajil when we get back. I don't want to be like those stupid governments who take a no negotiation with terrorism position, this thing has caused enough grief. People, trees, stones . . . they'll strike at anything connected with me. To go on with this thing would be selfish. What am I trying to prove . . . or for that matter, what have I got to prove? So I'll be losing an office. I can get another, downtown. It won't have a bed and bath but that's the least of my problems . . ." He was thinking out loud, confiding in her. Her silence said she agreed, or what amounted to its equivalent — she had no counter argument. It was only when Mansura Haddad and the fallen olive trees came into view that he realized they were holding hands.

Back at his father's house there was the inevitable lecture to endure. His experiment had been admirable but premature, the country was not ready for Arab-Jewish amity, ". . .let others establish such beachheads, like the do-gooders and leftists. They are prepared to fail, you are not." He had to pick up his career, that meant staying away from political issues. It was a bitter, even tragic lesson, but as the old saw said — "before jumping, test the water". It was his bad luck to get caught "in a cross-fire between the far right and farther right." Politics in Israel was like playing the stock market, when you went one way, it went the other.

"*Roma* calling *Gerusalemme*! *Roma* calling *Gerusalemme*! Are you there, *Gerusalemme*? *Are you there?*"

"*Siamo qua*, Roma. *Siamo qua*. Marc Antonio, *we are here.*"

"Eh, *amico*, how did you know it was me?"

"A humble premonition I'm sure."

"Hey listen, we had that audience with the Pope today!"

"Did you kiss his ring?"

"You know we Jews don't go around kissing rings of Christian potentates."

"Yeah, that's right, ass-kissing is more our speed."

"I'll ignore that . . . but the Chief did, bent right down and grabbed his hand. Hell, I thought he was going to swallow his finger the way he went at it."

"Well, you know what the Goyim say, render unto Caesar . . ."

"Speaking of Goyim, she's with us and *looking good*. I ought to know, I sat right behind her on the way over. Don't tell her this — but you know how these girls leave their blouses unbuttoned? Well, when I stood up to leave my seat I looked right down in there . . ."

"Did you see anything?"

"Did I see anything? I felt like Moshe on Mt. Pisgah! I got up from that seat so many times they thought I was Jack-in-the-box. She never took notice though, just kept reading. She's got a stack of books with her, most of them on the modern history of the Middle East, books like *The Arab Awakening* and stuff by Lilienthal and Chomsky, all of it written from a pro-Arab bias."

"She probably wants to find out if there's life after Jewry. You should have thrown in a Torah for balance. But that's the way she operates, she's a crammer. Fifteen minutes of reading and she's an expert. I'll tell you one thing, if she read about this area for the rest of her life, she still wouldn't be prepared for the experience."

They were departing Naples tomorrow on an Air Force plane, said Mark. The schedule called for a ceremony at the airport. After that they would head directly to their hotel, the King David. The Senator liked to take it easy the first night of arrival so Mark had set up a little dinner at the King David, clearing it beforehand with the hotel's French chef. It was to be a relatively intimate affair, only the Senator and close members of the staff would be there. Basil was advised to attend, Alison Cleveland was also coming.

The following day the American Embassy was throwing a reception for the Senator and there would be a trip to Yad Vashem, the Holocaust Memorial, by now obligatory for the official visitor. The other parts of the itinerary could be reviewed when they met, he was open to suggestions. The fullblown tour of the country once contemplated was not possible, only three days could be allotted to the present trip, most of which would be spent in the Jerusalem area where the Senator would meet with various Israeli big-wigs. A side trip to the Negev to inspect some of Israel's air force bases was a must. The Senator wanted to be able to confirm that American support of Israeli defense preparedness was money well spent.

35

The US Air Force jet landed punctually at 2:15 PM and taxied onto an area secured by a ring of military vehicles and Uzi-armed commandos, access by pass only. Israelis had a passion for security, particularly as it affected their political leaders, the country's closest equivalent to crown jewels. The opening of the plane's door was the signal for an Israeli military band to strike up the *Star Spangled Banner*. Moments later Senator Maudlin appeared waving, then quickly stiffened into a proud salute. A platoon of troops marched smartly into position as a color guard stepped forward carrying both countries' flags. They went well with each other — the red, white and blue of the Stars and Stripes, and the simple blue and white of the Star of David. In horsey terms, the flags represented the flashy nag of the New World and the old gray mare of the Old. The USA, desperate to extend the American Century for a few more decades, but increasingly running into the problem of diminishing returns; and Israel, the Rip Van Winkle of nations, which like old Rip, had overslept and awakened too late into an unaccepting and unacceptable world. Nevertheless, there they were, the superpower and the minipower, living embodiments of the Judeo-Christian tradition, the ethical and moral glory of the West, on a hot and baking tarmac beneath a shiny aluminum fuselage glinting fiercely under an implacable Palestinian sun.

People were pouring from the plane now, called to the colors by the sound of their national anthem. Worthington T. Carter he recognized instantly. He saw Mark duck his head at the door and emerge squinting into the light followed by three Secret Service types. Then no one. A feeling of disappointment crept over him — she wasn't on the plane. It was only after the other passengers had formed up on the tarmac and the band began playing *Hatikvah* that she appeared. He suspected it was the actress in her, unable to resist a chance to upstage a senator. She hesitated, but only momentarily, before descending in step with the music's solemnity. She was wearing a khaki safari suit, its open jacket exposing a white satin blouse underneath. A squarish, long-billed desert cap perched on blond curls completed the outfit. Finding a small patch of shade under a wing, she joined the American delegation. The final strains of *Hatikvah* having been played out, Israel's Minister of Defense stepped to the microphones to deliver his welcoming speech, a speech focusing on a "historic relationship between two nations, unprecedented in history . . . the United States and Israel side by side . . . an eternal friendship sanctioned by common ideals and destiny . . ."

Now it was the guest nation's turn. Clad in an elegant Palm Beach type suit and striving not to appear affected by the heat, Senator Maudlin responded with hopes of peace and threats of war, "In the name of the American people we pledge with you a determination to peace, democracy and freedom . . . We come to this outpost of freedom in an unfree part of the world to affirm, indeed, if any affirmation is necessary, this nation's in-de-feasible right to existence . . . let those both to the right and left of freedom's spectrum know of our resolve . . ." It was warmed-over John Kennedy, the finest cold war rhetoric. Basil saw Alison, eyes hidden behind dark, designer glasses, searching the crowd of spectators. He struggled forward into the first row, bumping a couple young girls aside with a perfunctory "sorry". She saw him now. Waving, she ignored the reproving stare of a woman next to her. Experiencing that old feeling, he flashed her the victory sign.

Inside the terminal, Mark introduced Basil around as "my man in Israel". He renewed acquaintances with Worthington T. Carter, now Maudlin's right hand. Maudlin had need of one — shaking hands with him was like squeezing a rotten fish. He saw Alison standing at a snack bar having a soft drink, observing the goings-on behind her designer sunglasses. He was becoming anxious, the reunion with Mark and company had gone on too long, he was afraid she would leave without their having a chance to talk. Before he could excuse himself, Mark pointed to Alison and whispered, "I think there's someone over there who wants to see you . . ."

"I was beginning to think I didn't *have* a friend in Israel," she exclaimed, thrusting out a hand, "How are you, Basil?" He apologized for not coming over sooner, declaring that the "snub was purely unintentional." She *was* looking good — lushly wholesome would be a more apt expression. He gulped down the saliva in his mouth, it was a bad time to be seen drooling. "Alison," he began, "I'd say you were looking good, but by now you must be tired of hearing it . . . but is that a double chin there, or are you just 'heavy-set'?"

"Well, I see you haven't lost your wit — or your

memory. I know, it's frightful isn't it? We were two days in Rome and I kind of pigged out on pasta and zabaglione. But if you must know, it was the excitement of seeing you again . . . I couldn't help myself."

"No, but somebody sure helped you. But anyway, I kind of like it, it makes you look even more earthy."

"Then I've come to the right place, you Middle Easterners like your women substantial don't you?" He didn't answer, he was looking at Alison's cap. "Alison, I don't like to be critical on such short reacquaintance . . ."

"No?," she interrupted, "You're doing a very good job of it." Ignoring her protest he continued, ". . . but where'd you get that outfit — at a *Wehrmacht* Army-Navy store? That headgear . . . it makes you look like a refugee from Rommel's *Afrika Korps*. It may be bad for fashion, but you are now in the world's largest Jewish ghetto and people around here are sensitive to such things. My advice is to stow it until you leave. You'll alienate less people that way."

"Thank you," she replied, "your advice has always been appreciated."

"Yeah, I'm sure . . ."

"OK you two, break it up before I call in the UN, we're on a peace mission here!" It was Mark, they were ready to leave the airport and Alison was going with them. "Let me take her, I've got air-conditioning," said Basil, adding in the same vein, "Who wants her anyway?"

"Who wants her?," howled Mark comically, "Who *wants* her? The PLO and just about everyone else, that's all!"

In the car she explained the reason for her job switch. She had tired of the Channel 13 interview show. Although New York was a great place and the pay was good, both the program's format and the city were too confining for her. So she pitched the show and went with Cabletown News, the TV and broadcast syndicate run by Bill Baker, the maverick media millionaire. She had gotten her wish for excitement — she had only been at the job for six weeks and already she had been to Nicaragua and an island off the coast of British Columbia, where she reported on the struggle of the Haida Indians to resist the destruction of their tribal forest lands at the hands of "Canadian-American lumber barons". When she heard about the Maudlin junket to Israel, she called the Senator's office, got transferred to Mark, and now here she was. "You didn't think you were going to get rid of me that easily, did you?

"So what have you been up to since we last saw each other?" She wanted the whole story, "unedited". She had been thrilled to read about his winning the architectural competition in the *New York Times*. "Alright," said Basil, "you asked for it." He told her about Eilat International and the discovery of evidence implicating Shames in the killing of the deal, his taking an office in the Arab part of Jerusalem and that action's tragic consequences. "The straw that broke this camel's back was the bum's rush treatment I got from these 'Christian' Arabs. Cutting the olive trees convinced me I should 'cut and run' too. I rented the place and now I'm back with my father, who in retrospect, I never should have left, Aziz Bustanji would be alive today."

"I guess no occupation's a picnic. If you think I can be of help, please let me know. And I'm not just saying this . . . I want to help in any way I can."

He appreciated the offer but said she could help him best by helping herself. "Find some other place to be a reporter. Chile, Mexico, South Africa, Uganda, the Philipines . . . anyplace is better than this place. You're not the type to take orders. You step out of line on this issue and they'll ruin you."

"Thanks, but I'm a big girl now," said Alison, running her hands self-consciously over her hips, "sometimes I think too big. I think I can handle it." They were at the King David now, the Senator and his staff were getting out of their cars in front of the hotel. He saw Worthington T. Carter barking orders to two soldiers whose duties appar-

327

ently also included baggage handling. "Well, I guess this is where I get off," said Alison, opening the door and stepping onto the sidewalk. "You're coming to dinner tonight, aren't you?"

"You going to be there?"

"Of course."

"Then I'm coming."

By the usual standards of Congressional junkets it *was* an intimate affair. There were nine in all, Alison the only female. True, they wanted her for themselves. But to have placed her in the company of the two women staffers on board this junket, would have been, to say the least, socially embarrassing. It was generally assumed that Maudlin hired the women as a concession to his wife, a former beauty queen whose alleged beauty had long since gone the way of all flesh. In any event, Maudlin was one of the few American politicians who did not always include his wife among his baggage, which considering the vulgarity of American political life, was an act either of great political courage, or simple hygiene. Of course, leaving the Missus behind may have been just another public relations gimmick, symbolic of the sacrificial seriousness of the mission. However, credit for selecting the evening's dinner guests rightly belonged to Mark. An informed host was expected to know who to seat next to whom and indeed, who to exclude altogether. Yet in a situation involving a lady, especially one as ravishing as Alison, it was standard procedure to defer seating arrangements to the final judgment of the "Chief".

Following a two drink session in the hotel bar where the dinner party had rendezvoused, the Senator stood behind the dinner table, about to make perhaps what would be his most important decision that day, "Young lady," he declared, speaking to Alison and pointing to the chair on his left, "I want you to sit right here . . . a combination of age and beauty the likes of which this world has rarely seen." Senator

Maudlin smiled his best smile. The rest had refreshed him, he felt good, having Alison by his side would make him feel even better. Worthington T. Carter did not have to be told where to sit — he sat at the "Boss's" right hand. Mark and Basil sat next to each other, Basil directly across from Alison. The other staffers sat where they belonged, on the ends.

Everyone agreed that the *noisettes de veau* and turbot *au diable* prepared by the King David's French chef were first-rate. Even the *mystere* and *profiteroles* were up to snuff, the ice cream being made on the premises. Conversation during the meal had been low-key and restrained, the diners occupied with the ordinary mechanics of eating. But with dinner done, and only coffee and cordials to occupy one's attention, it was controversy's turn. Alison Cleveland started the ball rolling by asking the Senator that if the Palestinian issue was the only thing holding up the peace process, and thus threatening Israeli security, wouldn't it be "more humane and cheaper" for the United States to pick up the tab for Palestinian statehood, thereby relieving both itself and Israel of the enormous human and material expenses connected with military security, "and if necessary, just pay Israel off too?" The Senator reacted by shaking his head in mock amazement at the questioner's audacity before declaring with a little smile, "Alison, you know I shouldn't answer that . . . By way of preface let me say that the young have a way — and I've seen this countless times in the classroom — of reducing the complexity of an issue to the point where they boil off its very essence. And as long as the practice is confined to the classroom it tends to be harmless. But you start positing these things in the political arena and people's expectations are raised — they want to know why such an obviously simple solution can't be implemented . . . Unfortunately, in human affairs, the simple way is not always the better way. Now let me explain what I mean by that . . . The Palestinians, I'm referring to those living on the West

Bank and Gaza, how many are they?"

"About two million," answered Alison. "And increasing daily," volunteered Mark.

"Do you know? . . . well, no you don't, because it's been one of our better kept secrets, but a few years ago I and some of my colleagues made a proposal to the State Department. In effect, we said this Palestinian issue has been bugging us too long, let's liquidate it. 'Well,' they said, 'how do you propose to do that?' Our answer was that we should bring the Palestinians to the United States . . . Now I know what you're thinking, but this was no forced march like the Russians did to the Germans in Eastern Europe, or the Greek-Turkish population exchanges after World War I. No, this was planned as a strictly voluntary program, an offer to those Palestinians *will-ing*, of United States citizenship, fair compensation for their land and businesses, and transport to the United States. Now there are already thousands of Palestinians in the United States. New York, San Francisco, Chicago, Detroit, they all possess sizable communities. They're in business, the professions; they've had no problem integrating into the mainstream; they're good, average citizens. If they ever had any terrorist impulses — except for one notable exception — coming to America resulted in leaving them behind. But what did the State Department tell us after making the appropriate inquiries? They refused it! That is, their 'leaders' refused. The same PLO and the other cock-eyed, radical, terrorist elements said, 'No, you can't buy our honor or our country, what's ours is ours. Go jump in the sea!' " The Senator paused, letting his point sink home. "Now I challenge you — go to any one of these camps, ask one of these poor devils whether he'd like to go to the United States . . . why he'd give his *right tittie* — excuse me young lady — for the chance!

"So let's not be diverted by a little superficial suffering, the result of the Arabs not getting all that they wanted. Regardless of what these people say, the United States is not responsible for all the world's problems, it can only solve a select few. For us, for this region, that means the maintenance of a continuous, uninterrupted supply of oil, and stopping communism. And if anybody here thinks the threat from communism, or radical change — and I include the Islamic fundamentalists in the equation — is nothing to worry about, then I say look eastward to Major Nafsi and his Iranian hordes, waiting, *wait-ing* for us to drop our guard . . . You say there's a 'Palestinian problem'? Listen, these characters couldn't care less about the 'Pal-lest-tin-ni-an prob-blem'! The Palestinians are only a means to an end for these people, either a Marxist or Moslem end . . . My friends, this is war, and *Godammit*, we better have the good sense to know whose side to be on, because if we lose, you can kiss civ-vil-li-za-tion good-*bye* — and that includes those *noisettes de veau* and *profiteroles* we had tonight!"

Maudlin's methodic and pompous delivery was a provocation in itself. Like a walking, talking man-o'-war, his presence acted to influence a country's policy, insuring its consistency with America's interests. Basil wished Bustanji were there to answer the florid-faced American. It was strictly wishful thinking because in real life things like that never happened. If anyone was going to prick this marauder's balloon, it was going to have to be someone safe, an "inside man". "Senator," he began, "from what you've just said, I get the impression the Palestinian problem is something to be sacrificed on the altar of America's long-range interests. For years now, the Palestinians have asked two things: one, an end of the occupation; and two, an independent state of their own. None of this would threaten Israel's security." He felt Mark's shoe against his. Ignoring the pedal pressure, he pressed on, "I don't know anything about your 'American plan', but why punish the Palestinian people for an alleged obduracy of their leaders, an obduracy I am not at all convinced was unjustified? It almost seems that the United States is the one against a solution, projecting its opposition onto the Arabs, who, most of us at this table would probably agree, are really not all that bad. Those lop-sided UN votes are telling us something, Senator. End the occupation and ease up on the gamesmanship. The next time around more than Arabs could get hurt."

They were watching Maudlin now, waiting to see how he would deal with this challenge from one, whose argument, whatever its weaknesses, at least carried the ring of authenticity. The Senator however, was in no hurry to reply. Eyeing his adversary, and placing his hands on the table, he leaned back, inhaling deeply, "Mark, you didn't tell me your friend was a peacenik . . . So, brother Primchek, it's a projection problem is it? Well I'm *glad* you said that, because I'm going to prove how really phony this issue of occupation is right now . . . Mark, do you have those stats handy?"

"No sir, they're up in the room."

"Well, how about bringing them down, I want to show our peacenik friend here a thing or two." During the wait for Mark, the Senator talked about similarities between the two allies, the United States and Israel, " . . . We're like family, it's the things we have in common that hold us together. Why, we even staged a revolt against the same mother country. By the way, what two countries are involved in the longest continuous struggle for national liberation in history — save Israel's of course? . . . Anyone . . . I'm waiting for an answer . . ."

"Well," said Basil, "I've heard it said God sent the English to punish the Irish . . ."

"Very good, brother Primchek, *very* good!," exclaimed Maudlin appreciatively.

" . . . and the Jews to punish the Arabs."

At that point Mark returned carrying a large, black, tab-marked loose-leaf binder. "I think this is the part you want, Chief," said Mark, opening the binder and setting it in front of the Senator.

"What's that," quipped Basil, "the Senate Bible?"

"The next best thing, smart guy," retorted Maudlin, pulling his reading glasses down on his nose to eye his cheeky antagonist.

"Oh yes, here it is," said Maudlin, "West Bank population '1967, 164,000; 1982, 747,000. These are the latest figures we have. By the way, they're from the *UN*. What's that — about a five hundred percent increase? Infant mortality — 'during period 1967 to 1982 infant mortality in West Bank and Gaza reduced by more than fifty percent.' Infant mortality in West Bank in 1982 25.6 per 1000 live births, compared to Jordan 68; Egypt 80; *Syr-ri-a* 61; and our friends, the Saudis, 112 . . . Must be that sand." Mark's "Or the oil in their crankcases" remark drew a look of senatorial disapproval — there was a lady present.

"Next, life expectancy — in 1967 estimated 48 years on West Bank, in early 1980's estimated 62 years. 'Conclusion: during the period of Israeli *ad-min-is-tra-tion*, the Palestinian population . . . rapid growth, improved economic and health conditions . . . markedly reduced infant and child mortality . . . increased life expentancy.' Now Mr. Primchek, sir . . . does *that* sound like gen-o-cide, op-pres-sion, dis-crim-in-a-tion, racial or religious? This is the most benign occupation in history! If nothing else, these figures prove that. I think the young lady here can perhaps appreciate their significance better than the rest of us. And yes, 'Employment . . . Conclusion: Palestinian women *in* Israel, West Bank, Gaza are better off . . . *better off*, than women in Arab countries. *Is-ra-el* has opened up *new* job opportunities for women . . .' "

The table was all smiles as the Senator laid down his glasses. Alison was smiling too, whether at Maudlin's antics or his own supposed discomfiture at being squelched was unclear. From across the table, Maudlin, chin in hand, fixed him with a placidly triumphant look. "Has anyone noticed how quiet it's suddenly become?," remarked Worthington T.

Carter, rising from his chair grinning, exposing a piano's octave of ivory teeth.

"Wait a minute!," cried Basil.

"Hey man," exclaimed Carter, "ain't you had enough? You're just running on will power now. Give us a break, eh? The Senator's got to take care of business." Ignoring both the speaker and his remarks, Basil addressed himself directly to Maudlin, "Senator, have you ever visited an Arab refugee camp?"

"I don't think so . . . They don't vote do they?," cracked Maudlin, turning towards Alison and arching his brows. This time, however, she was not amused.

"Well," declared Basil, "I'm throwing down a challenge to you and your staff — it's about time you saw one up close, flies, sewage and all. Of course, I expect it will be a little different than your usual embassy cocktail party . . ."

"See Mark, he's my appointment man," said Maudlin, gathering up the black binder and making his exit with Carter and another staffer. "If he can fit it in our schedule, fine . . . Excuse us, please . . ."

The morning would be the best time for the visit, said Mark, they were scheduled to have lunch with the Defense Minister and General Staff. Although he didn't believe the idea particularly dangerous, he was requesting additional security. "Anything can set those Arabs off. Even Jimmy Carter had a bad experience with them." It was best to abide by the Boy Scout maxim and "be prepared". If it were not for Dick Saybaw, the Arab-American real estate investor, he would be inclined to redline the idea. As the Senator pointed out, "Palestinians don't vote". But with Saybaw on "some bullshit mission to provide Palestinians with jobs", they had to come up with some gimmick for him too. "Good," said Alison, "we'll get pictures of the Senator and Saybaw handing out quarters to the outstretched hands of the camp dwellers. It should play big on Wall Street and Beverly Hills." "Hey," exclaimed Mark, "since when did *you* become anti-Semitic?" "I think she's been hanging out with the wrong crowd," said Basil, "but don't worry, Mark, you can be our gum man. We'll let you pass out the Chiclets." Mark was not amused.

Allison suggested that they go some place where they could "talk". Mark declined to join them, it was almost nine and he still had to set up the morrow's event, notify the press, and do all the other little things essential to a well-run junket. In that case, said Alison, she wanted to go to her room and "freshen up". She asked Basil if he could come back in about an hour and pick her up. He used the time to go home and telephone Rachel. She'd love to go to Fagan's she said, but she had to be in by twelve. "That's alright," said Basil, "you can meet a friend who's travelling with the Maudlin party."

"Going out again?," called his father from the salon.

"We're just going to have a couple of drinks with this woman reporter friend who's here covering the Maudlin visit."

"How did the dinner go?"

"Same old shit, Maudlin hasn't changed a whit."

"That's not what I meant. I hope you stayed on the man's good side."

"Good side? I don't think he has one."

Rachel was waiting in the lobby of the nurse's quarters when he arrived. She was wearing her black and white jump suit, the one with the midriff cut-out. A dark-brown, belted leather jacket covered bare shoulders and arms. "We're very fetching tonight," he remarked as they walked to the car. She thrived on notice and approval, it made her feel appreciated, that she was doing the right thing by him. Appearance was important, especially at Fagan's, now Jerusalem's number one watering spot for the late-night crowd. There beauty was always skin deep. Inside the car he untied the jacket and slid a hand between her cleavage, feeling the smooth, slightly tacky skin, kneading willing breasts. He was tempted, as he always was, by the wide mouth and satiny brown skin. Resisting his impulses, he started the car and headed for the King David.

If there was a problem of protocol between the two women, it was settled by Rachel's preoccupation of the car's front seat. He was unsure how much importance people ascribed to such things, but in the parlance of show business it might be characterized as "taking a back seat to a virtual unknown". Rationalizing to himself, he deemed it an "experiment in human relations". He thought the introduction went well enough, a little handshake between two strangers. Alison's reaction was predictably blasé, she was too much the trouper to react otherwise. She held a box wrapped in brown paper under one arm. "That's not a bomb you've got there is it, Alison?," he asked, trying to make conversation. "I think someone has a guilty conscience" was all she said.

Inside Fagan's the table with the moustachioed young man and the two sultry women drew an uncommon amount of attention from other patrons. People openly stared. A trio of girls at a nearby table stared and whispered at the same time, trying to decide whether the man with the two starlets was an actor or director. In any case, he had to be somebody big, a celebrity, his companions were evidence of that. Stars from Israel's fledgling international film industry helped make Fagan's what it was — the place to be seen in Jerusalem. Alison was still wearing her safari suit (for all he knew she may have owned a half dozen), except that the blouse she wore at dinner was gone. There was nothing but skin under it now, he had guessed that much when he met her in the lobby of the hotel. Under Fagan's artful, indirect lighting, his suspicion was confirmed. Meanwhile, Rachel, spotting a table holding a couple of her co-workers from the hospital, begged to be excused. He and Alison watched her stalk away, head high and chest out, in that characteristic strut affected by women conscious of their sexual worth. Her departure acted as a signal for Alison to unleash a series of questions — how long had he known Rachel, how serious was he about her, was their relationship an exclusive one, how could she walk away and leave him like that, wasn't she jealous? "I know I would be, you're the kind of cad that requires a twenty-four hour watch. This may sound catty but I really don't think she's for you, you don't seem to have all that much in common . . . But then she may satisfy your basic urges, which for most men seems quite enough."

Perhaps, suggested Basil, he could address her points best with a story, "I had a friend in college once, a Kurd, a fine mix of the gentleman and savage. One day I think I may have questioned his taste in women, it tended to the indiscriminate. His answer to me was, 'If you can't eat meat, eat bread.' "

"You know, that remark reveals a lot about you. I really wonder what you would do without all your little male maxims to get you through the day."

"Ah, but the bread is very good!," he exclaimed, drawing close to her face for emphasis. Seconds passed as she stared intently into his eyes, as if searching them for some unknown quality. Then, glancing at the table where Rachel sat chatting animatedly with friends — a man in an Israeli Air Force uniform had joined the group — she reached under her chair and produced the wrapped package. Holding it between her hands, she appeared to be in doubt as to what to do with it. "Well," he said, "I guess it's not a bomb. You'd make a terrible bomber. You're too indecisive."

"I know," she said, "I'm also having a hard time saying this . . . but at our age we're not full-blown perfect. I may have been immature . . ."

"Is this some kind of apology?"

"You can take it as that."

"Except that I prefer mine in writing. Otherwise they're not effective."

"You haven't changed, have you?"

337

"Pardon me, but I believe the question is have *you* changed?"

"Touché. Alright, what do you want me to do?"

"You heard me."

"God! You Middle Easterners! How much different are you than any bloody sheikh? You all want your women on their knees, palms up. Here, take this!," she exclaimed, thrusting the package across the table, "I hope you like it."

The package was light but sturdy, while the wrapping paper with its raised, ruled lines, and elegant texture hinted at Italian origins. He was right — the sticker on the package's end read, "DA FILIPPO — ROMA, FIRENZE". "Well," he remarked, carefully unwrapping the layers of paper, "we already know what it's not . . ." As soon as he saw the tan leather studded with protuberances he knew — it was an ostrich briefcase. Opening it, he ran his fingers over the plump and vital skin, the elegantly crafted ostrich and suede interior with its slits, slots, and recesses. "Touché yourself," he said, putting his nose inside the case and inhaling the intoxicating leather fragrance. Taking a voyeur's pleasure in watching him make love to the object she had brought him, Alison sat back in her chair, her gifting judgment vindicated.

She also had a story to tell him, it went with the briefcase. While walking in Rome, she came upon a little leather shop. Like him, she was also intoxicated by the smell of leather. When she saw the ostrich, she had to get it for him. The little, gray-haired shopkeeper gave her a 20 per cent *"sconto"* and told her that of all the women who had ever been in his shop, she was the most beautiful. He begged her to let him kiss her.

"And did you?"

"I couldn't refuse, he was such a nice man. I really didn't know what I was letting myself in for. I don't know how he did it, but he must have had four hands. In fact, if it weren't for my clothes, I think I would have been raped.

I'm not complaining, he was very passionate. When I think about it, I'm sorry I didn't take them off. He probably would still be hanging onto me now."

He could have had her, there, that night. But it was too late, he had outsmarted himself. He saw Rachel get up and bid goodbye to her friends. She was all agog when she came back to the table, the man in the uniform she had been talking with was none other than Major Raffi Golani, one of Israel's top aces, with nine kills and three probables to his credit. Golani's current assignment, she reported, was military sales, he had an office in the Defense Ministry. He was playing a key role in the promotion of the *Dybbuk*, the Israeli armament industry's contribution to the international commerce of fighter planes. He had just returned from Guatemala where he had helped establish a training progrm for the Guatemalan military. Her friend was a friend of a friend of his.

Although Alison appeared to be mildly amused, he found the conversation embarrassingly boring. Hoping to derail the obsessive monomania with the great Golani, he interrupted to tell her that Alison was from New York, "Yes, New York is number one on Rachel's must-see itinerary," he said. The effort proved in vain as she quickly returned to the subject of Golani, stating that, "Raffi told us about some of your fabulous restaurants, they make this place look like an ordinary café. He's eaten at many of them." At the limit of his tether, he stood up and announced that it was getting late, that they better be leaving. "Is that *yours*?," asked Rachel, seeing the briefcase for the first time.

"Yes, Alison picked it up in Rome for me."

"It's beautiful."

He dropped Alison at the King David, telling her he would see her at breakfast in the morning. In contrast to her volubility at Fagan's, Rachel's mood in the car was somber and taciturn. Beyond advising him she was tired and wished

339

to go directly to her quarters, she said little.

Alison was to ride with Senator Maudlin and Worthington Carter, the Senator insisted upon it. His rationalization was that it would help her in her "future political career" to be able to say she "rode with Maudlin" in Jerusalem. "Stay the way you are, nev-ver, nev-ver change," he crooned, parodying the song, "because if you ever reach thirty, young lady, I would hate to have to run against you, *hate* to! You are not only out-*rage*ously beautiful, but you are damn devilishly clever. And that combination in a woman today is ab-so-lute-ly unbeatable, *unbeatable!*"

"Listen to him," said Mark to Basil as they stood waiting for the soldiers to organize the convoy, "the fucker's sweet on her. He wants her at his side so he can press those thighs of hers."

"The question is," said Basil, "is he pressing anything else?"

"I don't think so . . . If he is, she's too good an actress to show it. I take it nothing happened last night between you and her."

"Nothing. We just talked, I didn't even get a kiss goodnight." The information was misleading but the drama had too many actors to be handing out adolescent progress reports.

"OK peoples, take to your cars, we're ready," ordered the captain in charge of the security detail, six jeeploads of troops under the command of two officers. The government was taking no chances with this senator. He had defended Israel in too many forums against too many adversaries on too many occasions to subject to risk. Some Israelis, not without a trace of chutzpah, referred to him as a "national treasure". In the United States Senate, that greatest of all deliberative bodies, there were scads of "Israel firsters". But in reputation and devotion, Maudlin towered above them all. He was, for Israel, a *primus inter pares*, a first among equals.

340

Their destination was Jeisheh, a hotbed of Palestinian radicalism, a refugee camp of 8,000 plus souls, young and old, but mostly young, packed into a sweaty, stinking, dusty warren of stone, tin, tar paper and canvas shacks. Privately, there was a "Is this trip necessary?" attitude among the Senator's staff — who wanted to see all those miserable people? But Dick Saybaw and his pleasantly pretty, blue-eyed "Irish-Polish-German-English-American" wife were all for it. "People needed to see how the Palestinian refugees lived," declared Mrs. Saybaw in her earnest, low-keyed manner, "so they could sympathize with their plight." Alison had spoken up for it too. And when Alison announced herself for something you could almost be certain that the Senator would be right behind her, trying to sound as if he had been for the idea from the start. So it was settled, they were going to Jeisheh and damn the torpedoes. Or as the Senator exclaimed in his colorfully vernacular style, "Goddamn the torpedoes!"

The sun was shining warmly but the temperature outside was still pleasantly cool, April was a fine month to be in Jerusalem. In fact, it was the absolute best time of the year in the Holy Land, with the winter rains ending, giving rise to green hills and moist valleys, insuring ample nourishment for men and beasts. God must have realized that too, because he picked the time for His Son to die and the children of Israel to flee from Pharoah into the wilderness, thus inspiring the holidays of Easter and Passover. It made good sense, because logically, God was the Holy Land's first tourist.

Today they were taking the high road to Jeisheh, the new one built for the settlers, the road that bypassed Jeisheh by a comfortable margin — many cubits more than a stone's throw. How well he remembered that first stone. In his ignorance he had taken the old road. He knew better now, everybody knew better. The merest concentration of Arabs — especially the young — and you had a mob, a stone-throwing, riotous mob, the kind requiring the services of police and soldiers. Of course, sometimes people were hurt, some fatally. But that was the price of disobedience to the law. They knew that — especially the young — they had no excuse.

Seen from the road the camp was as he remembered, a panorama of deliberate decrepitude, like shantytowns everywhere, composed of the available and expedient. Emerging from the car, he ran into a wall of stench, the unmistakable miasma of human sewage, of the "raw" variety. They had parked near the camp's drainage pipe, drainage being gravity flow. Others were holding their noses and making little cutesy "Pe-yoos!, Phews!" and "Whews!" Mark was inspired to utter a vulgar "Who shat?" Of course, people didn't like it but flies did, literally thriving on the brown mounds of offal. He saw Maudlin waving a hand in front of his face — flies liked the smell of after-shave too. Alison diligently began photographing, taking shots of the sewer drain and a couple with the Senator in the foreground. He had a harassed expression on his face, one that said, "Let's get the hell out of this place!" Unfortunately, there was no retreating now, Alison was leading the way, photographing some of the shabby little tykes crowding around the camp entrance and staring at the unfamiliar strangers and soldiers. Israeli and American television crews were also in place filming Maudlin's entrance into Jeisheh.

The first hint something was awry was the sudden appearance of two Arab youths holding a "MAUDLIN, ZIONIST STOOGE!" banner between them. Breaking ranks, Dick Saybaw ran forward to confront the youths in his best Amerarabic, "*Aib! Aib! Sobbi! Nahnu ashab!*" (Shame! Shame! Boy! We are friends!) "Speak English!," the Arabs yelled back. Then came the deluge — from alleyways, doors, and seemingly from out of nowhere they poured, young, old, women, children, hundreds filling the modest "plaza", chanting at the top of their lungs, "MAWD-LEEN!

MAWD-LEEN! MAWD-LEEN! MAWD-LEEN! . . ." The chant was not that triumphant litany of convention or caucus music to a politician's ears, but a derisive and humiliating jeer relentless in its contemptuous repetition. Maudlin, Worthington Carter, and the two army officers were in a huddle, it looked like they were going to call a withdrawal. Mark was eyeing Basil with pursed lips and shaking his head. The officer was motioning for them to go back now, the troops had surrounded Maudlin and were escorting him back to the cars. Maudlin's face was a humiliated red, he had probably never experienced such hostility, even Republicans possessed more civility. Alison continued to take pictures of the chanting and fist-shaking mob until the Israeli lieutenant grabbed her arm and ran her back to the Senator's car. And none too soon because just then the first volley of stones came raining down. A furious Worthington T. Carter accosted Basil, yelling, "You commie son-of-a-bitch! You set this up!" There was no time for recriminations as Worthington, crying out in pain, was hit by a large stone. They were both running now, back to the protection of the cars. A last effort by Dick Saybaw to placate the crowd drew another shower of stones. Holding his head in his hands, he was hustled back into his car by a distraught Mrs. Saybaw.

Then it happened — the knee-jerk reaction of power challenged by counter-power — the soldiers had raised their guns. In an instant Basil was out of the car and hollering "*Lo lirot! Lo lirot!*" (Don't shoot! Don't shoot!) Almost simultaneously, a red-faced Senator Maudlin burst from his limousine, running and screaming, "Don't shoot! You fools! . . . *Don't shoot!*" The shouted imperatives confused the troops, staying them and their commander from the commission of a massacre. Worthington had followed directly upon his chief's heels, shielding him with his own body from the mob's lethal and sub-lethal missiles as they ran back to the safety of their car. A pair of Secret Service agents had collared the Israeli captain and were ordering him to form a protective perimeter around the cars. The efforts were successful because not a shot was fired — not even in the air — to cover the retreat. But then the mob, seeing victory, realized it was pushing its luck, and so shied from an all-out challenge.

On the trip back no one was talking — neither Mark, another staffer, nor the driver. Mark dismissed Basil's one attempt at appeasement with a summary, "I don't want to talk about it!" An ambulance was waiting when they pulled up in front of the King David. Medics placed a protesting Dick Saybaw in a wheelchair and wheeled him into the ambulance where an obviously upset Mrs. Saybaw joined him for the ride to the hospital. His bald head bloodied but unbowed, Saybaw made a jaunty thumbs-up sign while being transferred to a stretcher. The major damage from the "Palestinian grenades" appeared to be inanimate. Most of the cars had shattered or broken windows and badly marred and dented bodies. Some of the party were occupied with inspecting the damage, while others threw dirty looks Basil's way and muttered ominously. He saw Alison looking at him, a sympathetic expression on her face. He was about to approach her when a Secret Service man confronted him, saying, "Mr. Primchek, do you mind if we ask you a few questions?"

"Yes, I do!," he snapped. "Go back to Jeisheh and ask them! To imply that I had a hand in it is insane. I only live here, that's all." Except for Alison, a sea of hostile faces surrounded him. Even Mark, his friend, still shaking his head in shock and incomprehension, was no help. "I'm sorry," he said, turning to Mark, "You can give the Senator my apologies. It's obvious my presence has become an embarrassment." Walking away, he wanted to look back, but couldn't.

Olga was surprised to see him before the completion of the Maudlin visit. "What's this?," she asked, checking her

344

watch, "It's only eleven o'clock. Did they give you a break for lunch?" He pulled a chair up to her desk and reported what had happened. She took it all as a joke, a joke on the *"Amerikanski"*. "So the *Amerikanski* Arab millionaire took a direct hit, did he? Wonderful! Let them get a taste of the receiving end for once. Oh I wish I had been there!" She wouldn't worry about it she said, let them think what they will. They had reason to be paranoid, conspiracy was a way of life for them. "But the CIA should have warned them not to visit a refugee camp, particularly Jeisheh, that 'tiger cage'. " Olga stood up and grabbed her jacket from a coatrack. "Come on," she said, "let me take you to lunch. You must be hungry after all that excitement." He wasn't, but he accompanied her anyway, she spoke his language.

The afternoon news made no mention of the Jeisheh incident. Neither did newspaper late editions. Their front pages were given over to the Senator's visit to Yad Vashem, a photograph of the Senator laying a wreath to the victims of the Holocaust was prominently displayed. The morning's fiasco had apparently not stayed them from their appointed rounds.

His father was also surprised to see him. He had expected him to be with Mark and the Senator. "Even dogs get a break," said Basil, avoiding the certain displeasure of full disclosure. The evening TV news protected the secret, completely suppressing the incident. Typically, its lead-off item was the Yad Vashem wreath-laying ceremony. He pointed out Mark and Alison Cleveland to his father, the TV camera unable to resist a close-up of the tow-headed, safari-suited, lustrous-lipped Alison, her sculpted nose carrying the over-sized designer sunglasses. His father was impressed, exclaiming, "That's your friend? The one who gave you the briefcase? No wonder you didn't want to come home."

36

It was a blast, a big one, shaking windows and rattling cups. He saw Ben Judah rush to the windows, open one and stick his head out. The others, gathering behind him, were eager to know what he saw. " . . . a tremendous black cloud rising to the sky, in the direction of Independence Park. The bomb must have been huge! . . . I'm going over there, they're going to need help!" Olga had come out of her office and was trying to see over the shoulders of Shmooel Glazer and Ulrich Fesser. "Oh my," she said nervously, "I hope it wasn't a bomb." For about a half-minute there was an eerie quiet, as if the city and all its myriad motions had shut down. Then, all of a sudden, from all points of the compass, sirens began screaming and whooping. He picked up his telephone and dialed the police. But apparently he wasn't the only one so inspired — the line was busy. Ulrich Fesser turned on a radio and tuned in the twenty-four hour news station, " . . . in central Jerusalem. All drivers are requested to avoid the city center. We repeat: there has been a bombing in the city center. All vehicles are urged to avoid the area in order to permit the entry of lifesaving and firefighting equipment. We repeat: there has been . . ." Glazer announced he was going too, " . . . they may need all the hands they can get, there may be digging to do." He looked over to Basil for a sign of reinforcement. "Go ahead," said Basil, "but the streets will be sealed off. I doubt whether you'll get within a kilometer of the blast. They'll only be letting essential personnel and equipment through." Basil was right said Olga, exercising her prerogative as director to arbitrate, "Our job is to stay and remain calm unless instructed to do otherwise. For that I believe our best source of information will be the radio."

They continued at their posts as advised, listening to

the news. The announcer promised more momentarily, they were expecting another report from their reporter on the scene. Initial reports had spoken of serious casualties, survivors taken to various hospitals and medical centers, a sapper team from the Israeli army at the scene supervising excavation of possible survivors. Meanwhile, people were advised to remain calm, everything that could be done was being done.

Finally, the report they were waiting for came over the airwaves — "There has been a serious terrorist attack at the intersection of Ben Yehuda and Ha Malakh George streets with great loss of life. The motorcade of United States Senator Michael Francis Maudlin was apparently the target of the attack. According to a police reconstruction of events, a Mogen David ambulance loaded with an estimated 500 kilos of explosive was driven directly into the side of the motorcade and detonated as the motorcade was proceeding down Ben Yehuda street, resulting in a huge explosion and fireball. Preliminary estimates of casualties are high, up to 100 killed and wounded, many still buried under the rubble of buildings collapsed by the explosion. While the fires caused by the force of the explosion are no longer blazing, police and army search teams on the scene say it will be hours before a final casualty toll can be determined. An emergency has been declared and all citizens are urged to avoid the city center, as the presence of unauthorized persons may interfere with ongoing rescue attempts. We repeat: the motorcade of Senator Michael Francis Maudlin has been the target of a terrorist suicide bombing in city center, initial reports of casualties are high . . ."

Except for the interminable voice from the radio, the room was silent. Everyone seemed too stunned or engrossed for comment. He saw Olga standing in the doorway of her office. She was looking directly at him, her face expressionless. "The Americans aren't going to like this," said Fesser breaking the silence, "this could mean war." "Against whom?," queried Glazer. The sound of footsteps coming up the stairs interrupted the post-mortem. Three casually dressed, grim-faced individuals appeared. Identifying themselves as Shin Beth agents, they motioned to Basil to come with them. Interposing herself between the agents and Basil, Olga demanded the reason for the arrest. "We have our orders, Madam, we have our orders," was all that their leader, a short, stocky Sephardi, would say. The other two agents pulled Basil's arms behind his back and snapped a pair of handcuffs on his wrists. He went quietly, telling Olga not to worry, they had nothing on him. On another occasion he might have been embarrassed, but now his thoughts were of Alison, hoping against hope she hadn't accompanied Maudlin. He wanted to kick himself for not telephoning her the night before, but now maybe the agents would do that for him, "but not in the nuts, not in the nuts," he thought. In the car, he asked where they were going. "Moscobiyya" came the terse reply, a place known as the, interrogation center for those suspected of political offenses, so-called by the Arabs because of its location in Jerusalem's Russian Compound. On the way he saw ambulances going to and fro, sirens screaming and lights flashing. At the entrance to a blocked-off street, their car was stopped then waved on at the words "Shin Beth". Inside the Moscobiyya he was led down a stairs to the basement, then through a dimly-lit corridor lined with cells filled with shouting, cursing Arabs. An overpowering stench of male body odor and human wastes hung in the air, trapped by an oppressive lack of ventilation. Finding an unoccupied cell, the Shin Beth men placed him inside and removed the plastic handcuffs, then slammed the cell's barred door shut. They laughed when he asked how long he could expect to be there. "Until we build your Third Temple," said one, setting off another round of derisive laughter. Their laughter mixing with the curses of the Arabs, the three agents disappeared down the corridor.

The cell was bare except for a metal "sanitary bucket," its interior flecked with a skim of dried excrement. He noticed that the former "hole" for the deposit of wastes had been cemented up. The bucket was an "improvement", a reminder to the Arabs of their "origins". Their cursing was contagious; he began cursing too, silently — fate, his jailers, the cell, the "suicidal bastard" who got him there. He was pacing now, around the two by three meter cell, nothing to sit on but a cold cement floor. Thinking to use the bucket as a stool, he upended it with his foot. He considered placing his handkerchief over the bucket's bottom to protect himself from the filth, but he only had one handerkerchief, and there was no telling how long he would be there. The handkerchief might be needed for other sanitary purposes, he didn't want to have to blow his nose through the fingers, Arab style, God knew how many dried encrustments of snot and sputum were already on the cell's walls and floor. He spotted some Latin characters on the back wall. "Shaiban Harb was here 2-11-86," it read in the meager light. A joker in the pack. The rest of the graffiti was in Arabic. He wondered what the squiggly lines said, the slogans they proclaimed. Finally, realizing he was going to be there for some time, he relented and sat on the bucket. It's bottom, he decided, was reasonably clean.

Hours had passed since he was arrested and jailed, he hoped they hadn't forgotten him. During that time they had brought in dozens of Arabs, packing them five and ten to a cell. He felt comparatively privileged in having a cell and bucket all to himself, like being in a private hospital room rather than an anonymous ward. Although he suspected his jailers were playing psychological games with him, his accommodations reflected his first-class status. As a Jew, even a disloyal one, he was entitled to be treated with dignity. Otherwise, what indeed was the purpose of a Jewish state?

His privileged isolation ended abruptly when a jailer

crying "Company!" opened the door of his cell just long enough to allow two guards to push a disheveled Arab youth inside. The youth's hairless face was puffed and bruised and streaked with tears. It was obvious he had been beaten. He stood facing the corner of the cell, trying to conceal the source of his embarrassment — the crotch of his pants was soaked through, he had wet his pants. Apparently it was his first experience with the process of arrest and interrogation, thus his mortification was understandable. Basil attempted to put the youth at ease, offering him the bucket to sit on and getting him to talk.

His name was Ghazi Khanqan and he was from Jeisheh. He had been in custody since six the previous evening when troops and border police raided the camp, arresting over two hundred. He apologized for his wet pants and showed Basil his wrists, red and raw from the plastic handcuffs that had held his hands behind his back until a few minutes before. He had spent the night in a cell with over twenty others, taking turns lying on the floor because of the crush of bodies. In the morning he was taken into a room and forced to squat for hours. When he couldn't hold it any longer, he relieved himself in his pants. His interrogators beat him for wetting himself, calling him a baby, threatening to call in a woman soldier to put a diaper on him. But it didn't matter he said, " . . . they beat you if you piss your pants and they beat you if you don't." They wanted to know who was behind the demonstration against Maudlin at the camp. He didn't know, there was a demonstration and he participated. *"Wallah!,"* that was the truth he declared. But they wouldn't believe him and kept hitting him in the face and stomach when he answered he didn't know. Even if he had known he wouldn't have told them. They would have beaten him anyway, it made no difference to them.

Basil told the lad not to worry, that the worst was over and that he probably would be released soon. Events were overtaking the authorities, the bombing was the concern now. Being in custody when the bombing occurred ruled him out · as a suspect. The boy's face brightened at the mention of a "bombing". They all heard the explosion but couldn't tell if it was a bomb or what. "Do you know what happened?," he asked expectantly.

"The last news I heard — which was about half past eleven — was that a Mogen David ambulance carrying an estimated 500 kilos of explosives had driven into the motorcade of Senator Maudlin and exploded, causing heavy casualties."

"Allahu Akbar!," cried the boy, leaping to his feet, fists clenched, "I hope it took him! I hope it took him! *ALLAHU AKBAR!*"

Another hour went by. Watching the guards take more Arabs away, he began to despair of being released that day. He did not look forward to spending the night, horses slept standing up. "Hey Raful!," he called to a guard whose face was now familiar, "When does my turn come? You make me wait much longer and I'll demand to call my lawyer."

"We're sorry, sir, for any inconvenience, sir," responded the guard with a commensurate sarcasm, "Shall I get you a pillow, sir?" His mind leapt to American prison movies with their scenes of convicts banging metal water cups on cell bars. Metal against metal, the bucket was certain to create a din. Someone would come running, perhaps a flying squad of club-wielding brutes. Gas was another possibility, they were not averse to using it outside or inside. But now he had another consideration — his new cellmate. The lad had suffered enough. To subject him to another round of punishment for an act with such a flimsy chance of success would be irresponsible. Finally, there was the bucket itself. He did not want to touch it — it was missing a handle.

Somebody upstairs must have been psychic because when the next batch of detainees arrived, he exchanged places with them. Bidding good-bye to his young Arab

351

friend, he went with the jailers. Emerging from the basement's clinging stench he saw that the building's fluorescent lights were on, while police and soldiers moved about purposefully. He was escorted into a large corner office where a trim, bespectacled man sat behind a wide, steel desk, poring over a sheaf of papers. The man was Asher Solomon, deputy director of Shin Beth, Israel's internal security bureau. Dismissing the guards with an abrupt "Have him sit down," Solomon, deliberately ignoring Basil's presence, began reading out loud, "Primchek, Basil, age 29, university education United States, former Shames scholar, sergeant, reserve unit Judean command, employed as staff architect Jerusalem Rebirth and Renaissance Authority, superior Olga Shalansky, grand prize winner Third Temple competition sponsored by Ha'itzer Bnai Azadoi Beshallim. Father, Lev Primchek, mother deceased, marital status, single . . ." Solomon raised his eyes and removed his glasses, rubbing the lenses between a handkerchief. "Any of that you'd care to take exception to, Mr. Primchek?"

"No," replied Basil, "you've obviously been doing your homework."

"Yes," said Solomon, "we pride ourselves on our accuracy. But the activity here tonight is more than homework . . . Israel lost one of its staunchest friends today . . ."

"Then he's dead?"

"Yes . . . I suppose you might not know. Sorry about that, but we're running a little behind. It took us somewhat longer than anticipated to get to you. I trust your stay in our 'hotel' was not too unpleasant."

"Oh no, charming. A definite 12th century flavor . . . and odor too."

"Good. It's been a long hard day for us, Mr. Primchek. Nothing like this has ever happened before. You prepare for it theoretically, for the possibility. You take all the practical precautions against it . . . but still it happens.

"I will come to the point with you, Mr. Primchek . . .

352

What would you say if I told you we have evidence that implicates you in the attack on Senator Maudlin?"

"Apart from the appropriate vulgar response, I'd say you were putting me on."

"Then you deny it?"

"Absolutely."

Solomon brought the finger tips of his hands together, studying for a long moment the face of the man before him. "Alright. I'm authorizing your release. There isn't enough evidence to hold you. The fact you backed out of an obligation to accompany the Maudlin party today merely raises an inference . . . and under the law an inference is insufficient for conviction. However, yesterday's events raise another inference. Our information is that visiting Jeisheh was your idea . . . Is that correct?"

"Yes," replied Basil impatiently, "that's an inference upon an inference . . ."

"I see you are familiar with some principles of law . . . But I won't belabor the point other than to say that the dossier holds more inferences. Sorry to say, the picture is not one of a man looking out for the welfare of his country . . . You know, the nation hesitates before the question of disloyalty, unwilling to believe Jews would be so dastardly as to betray other Jews. But actually Jews are no different than anybody else, every nation has its share of the disloyal. As police, our job is not to explain disloyalty, but to interdict its practice. I'm sure you've heard it said that if you are not for us, then you are against us. You might think that over. You've got a good support system going for you, your father and Director Shalansky have been calling here all day. These people obviously think a great deal of you, don't let them down. The nation thinks a great deal of you . . don't let us down." Basil made no response. "That's all," announced Solomon, "you may go now."

There was a lavatory in the hallway outside Solomon's office. Stripping to the waist, he soaped up face, arms, and torso, finishing with a splashing rinse, ignoring the quizzical stares of other lavatory users. From there he went to the telephones and called the King David Hotel, asking to be connected with Alison Cleveland. Holding his breath, he listened to the repetitious rings. "I'm sorry, sir," reported the voice of the operator, "but the party does not answer;." He hesitated, unsure of how to put the question, "Operator . . . Miss Cleveland, have you any information on her condition or whether she was a casualty in the bombing?"

"We are referring all inquiries concerning the casualties among the Senator's party to the American Consulate. They have the latest figures on the tragedy." He put the receiver back on hook to clear the line and tried the Consulate — the line was busy. Running out of the police station, he headed for the Consulate, not much more than a stone's throw distant. The barriers blocking the streets had been removed, but soldiers were still patrolling the area. Seeing him running, two soldiers pulled alongside in their jeep and ordered him to halt, letting him go with a "Good luck" when he explained the reason for his haste. At the gate of the Consulate he was stopped by a US marine guard. Finally, a staffer emerged to escort him into the building. Inside, a small group was gathered around the casualty list, tacked up on the Consulate bulletin board. Listed first under "DEAD" was "Michael Francis Maudlin", followed by the two women staffers, then "Worthington T. Carter, Senatorial Aide". After Carter there were no surnames beginning with c, but then the list was not in alphabetical order. Apparently names had been added as they were received from reporting institutions — the morgue and various hospitals. He double-checked the list of dead, running his eyes up and down the column of names. The heading over the list said "Latest Figures — 6:30 PM". Reading the injured column, he found Mark's name, it was fifth on the list — "Mark Philip Lerner, Senatorial Aide — Moses Montefiore Hospital". He checked the list of injured once more, making doubly sure Alison was not on it. The dread he harbored lifted, somehow she had survived unscathed. Bombing injuries could be terribly traumatic, crushing and mutilating limbs, he didn't want to think about it. He asked the Consulate receptionist to call him a cab, he wanted to go to Moses Montefiore Hospital straightaway.

"Superficial wounds" reported the duty nurse when he inquired about Mark at the nurses' desk, "He was very lucky."

Mark was sitting up in bed, sipping a drink from a plastic cup. A gauze bandage covered the left side of his face, another was wrapped around his left hand. "Mark Philip Lerner, Purple Heart," intoned Basil as he approached the bed.

"Basil!" exclaimed Mark setting down his drink, "your father called. He said you were arrested by the Shin Beth."

"Yeah, I just graduated with a degree in penology from one of their leading dungeons. It's too bad you weren't there to room with me, I know you would have enjoyed the view — three walls, and a 'sanitary bucket'. And that fragrance, eau de *shit*! Fifty fucking buckets loaded with the stuff. Weren't you the one who used to tell me you can judge a society by its jails? Well Mr. Israel booster, this one stinks! I should have brought you a piece of that stench, it was thick enough to cut with a knife. If that's an exaggeration, you'll have to excuse me, I'm just indignant. I'll get over it when I shower and have these clothes I'm wearing boiled. By the way, which one of you bastards fingered me to the police?"

"Easy will ya?," said Mark nervously, indicating the old man sleeping in the other bed in the semi-private room. "He's dead," said Basil, "shall I call the nurse to prove it?"

"Listen," said Mark, now almost whispering, "*thirty-five* people died. We were wiped out, we lost sixteen, I was one of the few lucky ones. So when they came to me and started asking questions, what was I supposed to do, clam up? They were bound to find out you went with us to the camp, I didn't tell them anything that wasn't common knowledge. You were at Jeisheh. It was your suggestion we go there. You would have told them the same thing, you would have had to. I thought they would just question you. I had no idea they would throw you in the slammer."

"Yeah, I guess you wouldn't . . . Forget it, I'm out now. So what's going to happen now?"

"The President is sending Air Force One to pick up the Senator's remains. There's going to be a full state funeral . . ."

"Remains?," exclaimed Basil, "Has he got any?"

"Yeah, there were a few. Lemme tell ya, that was some bomb, the end of the world! This war business is bullshit."

"Is he in pieces or is he flat like the characters in those roadrunner cartoons? Come to think of it he's got to be flat. That bomb had to make him pass all his gas."

"Hey, are you nuts? They can hear you out in the hallway!" Mark grabbed the on-off control for the TV and switched it on.

"Aren't you afraid you'll wake Lazarus here?," asked Basil, pointing to the still soundly sleeping old man.

"The hell with Lazarus! I'm concerned with you and your big mouth."

"What's the matter? He's going out in style. They'll bury him in Arlington with his widow and children saluting at graveside. Tell me, will there be one of those riderless white horses with the stirrups reversed in the procession?"

"How should I know? Who do you think I am, Cecil B. DeMille?"

"No, just Maudlin's logical successor, that's all. If you were thirty-five you could finish out his term."

"Thirty," corrected Mark, "thirty-five is for the presidency."

"That's even better, you can pass for thirty easily. What's three years? Women subtract ten from their ages regularly without batting an eye. Yes, Mark lad, with Carter gone wit de massa to dat big cabin in de sky the way is clear . . ."

"Hey look, Basil," exclaimed an exasperated Mark, "Carter was a nice guy . . . I don't know your problem, I'm really sorry about the jail thing, but will you do me a favor? . . . Promise me you won't talk like this to the press — Israeli or American. They have absolutely no sense of humor. And that goes for Alison too."

"What happened to her? She wasn't on the casualty list so I assumed she was one of the lucky ones. I called the hotel, she wasn't there."

"Thank *God* she didn't go with us this morning," said Mark with relief. "She called me and said she had a stomach ache. I don't know where she is now."

He telephoned his father and Olga from the hospital, letting them know he was out and thanking them for their calls to the Shin Beth. "What are friends for?" said Olga, "I'm sure you would do the same for me." At home, his first act was to drop his clothes in a pile and get into the shower. While the hot water removed all physical traces of the experience, his father related how Olga had alerted him, and then how he had called some of his friends in government. The Shin Beth he called every half hour. They didn't like it, but it put them on notice they would be held accountable. His advocate, Sheminovsky, had advised that tack. In Sheminovsky's opinion, it would have been a waste of time and effort to pursue the usual legal remedies. In such emergencies the police had *carte blanche*. "He asked me if you were guilty. I wanted to say 'no', but all I could say was that 'I didn't think so'. Which was embarrassing for me as your father, that I don't even know what my own son is doing." This time, he emphasized, he was serious. He wanted him to stay away from anything smacking of politics — "and that goes for politicians or their friends." The day's events had demonstrated how far he had gone in pushing his luck. The fiasco at Jeisheh was a blessing in disguise, "Yes,

357

a blessing in disguise," he repeated.

It was nearly eleven when Alison finally returned his calls. "I just got in," she said, "isn't it terrible?" She had been out all day with her crew getting pictures of the destruction and havoc. The footage would be shown on American TV that evening. Furthermore, she had just come back from a meeting at Cabletown's Jerusalem studio — they were showing their footage of the Maudlin party's visit to Jeisheh Camp. Worthington Carter had called her the day before and asked her not to release it to the network. He said it was a special request from the "Boss". She had agreed, but reluctantly. Apparently, the other networks agreed to kill it too, because none of them ran it. But now that Maudlin was dead, she saw no reason for suppression. Actually, she said, seeing the footage would help people understand the context in which the bombing took place — "the symbolism of attacking a United States senator. Unfortunately, this time more than stones were employed." So Cabletown was running it tonight with some of her stills. It would be a scoop of sorts, her first, she said proudly.

She had planned to interview Mark at Moses Montefiore Hospital but ran out of time. Basil remarked that her stomach ache had saved her life. It wasn't a stomach ache she said, "I didn't like the way they were talking about you after the Jeisheh thing. It was very offensive." It was then she decided to go her own way. "Then that trip to Jeisheh saved both our lives," said Basil. "I know," she replied, "isn't it romantic?"

The expression encouraged a thought his mind had been nurturing while they spoke — the idea of going over to the King David and ravishing her. She would be exhausted and in no condition to resist. Women's resistance was among the first of war's casualties. Whether it was stress, anxiety, relief at survival, or a factor in the female biological inheritance, something pushed women to put themselves at men's disposal during that time. There was every possibility that the next embrace might be the last.

It was a mad idea, one of a succession he had about her. Dismissing it, he continued the conversation, telling her about his arrest and incarceration at the hands of the Shin Beth. She couldn't understand it, "you didn't do anything," she complained. "This is the Middle East," he said, "you don't have to do anything. Democracy, if I may use that term, is very superficial here . . ."

She would have liked to come over and interview him about the jail conditions, but she was exhausted and was leaving on another assignment in the morning. "Keep in touch," she said. Then, adding a touch of her own, admonished "Listen!" There was a long, chirping, squeaking sound. "What was that," he exclaimed ominously, "the Shin Beth?"

"No, you fool, a kiss!"

37

The nation, flags at half-staff, was in mourning. Israel had lost a great friend in the senator from New York. Yet, lest the world forget, the majority of casualties had been Israeli. Overnight, the numbers of dead had to be revised upward. Two more, one a three year old girl, had died in hospital. And now, in the aftermath of the bombing's turmoil and confusion, someone realized that two Mogen David ambulance medics were missing. One of the missing, a Shimon Tabro, was identified by pathologists from his fingerprints — there was that much of him left. The body of the other ambulance attendant was thought to have been "carbonized" along with the ambulance's terrorist hijacker, or indeed, hijackers. The force of the blast made it impossible to determine with any certainty the actual sequence of events. But police and army explosive experts speculated the terrorists had killed the two attendants in the process of hijacking the ambulance, then took their lifeless bodies with them on the fateful suicide mission against the Senator.

Opinion varied on the type of explosives used. Press accounts gave the usual abbreviated nomenclature for the complex chemical makeup of suspected explosives, plastic and otherwise, said to originate in Czechoslovakian and Bulgarian laboratories. Initial attempts to assign responsibility for the act were placed on hold to allow popular enthusiasm in the Arab world to run its course. Hard as it was for Americans to imagine, millions saw in Maudlin's end a sign of just and condign punishment. Demonstrations in celebration of the event took place throughout the West Bank and Gaza and in Arab urban centers, from Benghazi to Baalbek. It was as if an archangel had vanquished the Devil, causing the people, down to the smallest schoolchild, to erupt in joy. Syrian television showed a large demonstration in the center of Damascus, another at the University. If the Syrians were concerned about retaliation, it was not evident in the faces of the demonstrators as they fairly danced over an effigy of the hated "Mawdleen". Nafsi made a statement, widely quoted, that while the Syrian government had not changed its policy of opposing terrorism, the "execution" of Senator Maudlin had nothing to do with terrorism, but was an act of legitimate self-defense taken by the Islamic people against a "savage and criminal representative of American ruling circles", guilty of supporting "savage assaults" upon Islam, and threatening its peoples with atomic destruction. Arab reaction was replicated in Iran where Habibollah Ali Fahunzi, in a militant speech to thousands of chanting revolutionary guards in Martyrs Square in Teheran, pledged his nation to come to the support of Syria in the event of an attack from the "Great Satan or its rabid dog, Israel."

In the United States, senator after senator rose in the Senate chamber to eulogize their fallen colleague. The mood was solemn, serious, as Washington's most powerful men paid tribute to the memory of Michael Francis Maudlin, a liberal domestically and a giant in the field of foreign affairs and intelligence. The grief expressed was measured, befitting the Senate's dignity and tradition. They were being watched these men, by a nation and history. It was an occasion where sycophancy and hypocrisy competed in the choice of the right phrase, the most memorable expression, to describe their friend and colleague, "Mike" Maudlin, a "man's man", a man of wit, probity, integrity, and yes, charisma. He could have been president said some, he had that kind of charisma, the smile, the charm, that "special sense of destiny". He "was an American," said one senator laconically, "an American through and through." "A towering figure" said another, "a great servant of the Republic." "A genial son of the Celts of County Cork," alliterated a fellow Irish-American. They were good words, memorable words, words worthy of a great man's demise. But it was Senator Bruce "Buck" Brainard, the young and dynamic first-term senator from Idaho, who set the tone for the tributes to follow. Brainard's speech, coming as it did near the end of the senatorial encomiums, was the kind that stanched tears and brought blood to the temples. It was a fighting speech, the kind "Mike" Maudlin would have made had fate spared him and taken another. "America has had it with Arabs," declared Brainard. "The only two senators to die by violent means this century were killed by Arabs. That tells us something, my friends. Arabs don't like us, they *don't like America*. Lest some of you out there succumb to a false concern, I say to you that this is not racism, this is recognition!" America had but one course, thundered Brainard, that of justice. "The obligation vouchsafed Americans by Mike

Maudlin is a simple and solemn one, and that is that Mike Maudlin shall not have died in vain, but to keep this great country and its citizenry free. And free we shall remain, so help us God!" When Buck Brainard sat down, everyone knew retaliation was a foregone conclusion. The only question was against whom and what.

Despite the arrest and interrogation of thousands of Arabs, and thousands of house-to-house searches, a solution to the attack was no closer. The police dragnet turned up no hidden cache of explosives, no sophisticated laboratory set up by Comintern agents in some secret, Old City cellar. Yet for the government of Israel, the failure was mitigated by other, more compelling considerations.

In the days following the attack, much was made of the "burden of retaliation". Some said the burden was Israel's. However, in leaks to the press ascribed to "high government sources", this course was questioned. A raid by Israel for and on behalf of the United States would lend credence to the perennial charge that Israel was little more than a regional gendarme for the Americans, a charge Israel wished to live down. All the available evidence pointed to the conclusion that the terrorists originated from outside Israeli administered territory. The attack was directed against a symbol of American power, a United States senator. Therefore, concluded the sources, the responsibility for retaliation was American, not Israeli. The fact that for some time Israel had desired an increase in American military involvement in the area went unmentioned. For that purpose, the attack on Senator Maudlin was a blessing in disguise.

Miriam's telephone call reflected the tension and war fever in the United States, or at least in New York City. Having just finished reading his letter, she had to call him. "Too bad it's true," she said, "it would make a good novel." She asked if he had heard about the "Sense of the Senate" resolution. Passed by acclamation that afternoon, it put the Senate on record for retaliation against those responsible for

362

the Maudlin attack. The intent was to send a message to terrorists everywhere that an attack upon an elected American representative anywhere was an attack upon the American people, and that retaliation would be swift, sure, and overwhelming. The vote was unanimous. No one wanted to be seen as soft on terrorism, especially when one of their own colleagues was involved. There were reports elements of the Sixth Fleet had left port and were moving toward the Syrian coast. The media was talking up an attack on Syria again, Mindell's dispatches from Jerusalem full of warnings about the "Marxist-mullah threat" posed by Syria and Iran to the moderate Arab regimes, especially Jordan; how Syria was preparing for war by building anti-tank defenses on the Damascus plain and bomb shelters through-out the country. She hoped he wasn't in any danger.

"From whom," he asked, "Americans, Israelis, or ter-rorists?" She could stop worrying he said, the only way the Americans would bomb Jerusalem was by mistake. "Pity the poor Lebanese or Syrian mother putting her children to bed," they had a billion times more chance of getting hit with an American bomb than he had. He was joking of course, but the irony of his remarks was clear.

The Maudlin affair had been the catalyst for a great deal of activity in the office lately, reported Miriam. A big fund-raiser for Israel was in the process of being organized and the "big chiefs had held a powwow in Shames' office." Shames was also occupied with soliciting contributions for a memorial to Maudlin, "something more than the usual 1200 tree forest." Rabbis had been going in and out of his office all week like "bees in a hive, gathering pollen while the sun shines." Miriam was not one to mix her metaphors.

After hanging up he dialed Rachel at the medical cen-ter. It was late — twenty after eleven — but tomorrow was Friday and it had been a long while since their last session, two weeks of while. Her telephone manner was pleasant enough — until she realized who it was. "Do you know what time it is?," she demanded indignantly, reminding him she got up at 5:30. "Yeah, I know what time it is," he answered, "night time." He was reminding her that tomorrow was Friday, they had some lost time to make up. She told him to call her then, she was too tired to think. "Alright," he said, "I hope you'll be feeling better." Ignoring the remark, she said goodby and hung up.

She seemed testy to him lately, almost cocky, no longer the diffident girl he remembered from Wadi Jamil. Perhaps it was her job. The past few days had been stressful, with victims of the bombing arriving at the hospital dead and disfigured. He was kidding himself, the bloom was off the rose. It had been eight months since they met and whatever expectations she brought with her had dimmed, casualties of time and familiarity. Once he took her home for dinner and introduced her to his father. Other than the usual conventional remarks exchanged upon first acquaintance, the two hardly spoke. After dinner, sitting in the parlor, she was uncomfortable, out of place. Now, out of the army and working, she had a new peer group, perhaps new admirers among Hadassah's countless doctors and interns. No longer dependent on him for emotional sustenance, he might be just a penis to her, something that filled her and thrilled her on weekends in rented rooms. He tried not to let such thoughts affect his attitude. In the past her good points always kept him from dwelling on their social disparities. The thought of being with her again and squeezing the marvelously smooth brown flesh consoled and excited him, putting aside doubt.

The following morning he spent going from job to job, checking their progress. His crew was still laying stone for the Haddad villa, large stones, requiring pulleys to lift them in place. There had been no further incidents since the olive trees were cut down. Nevertheless, the nearby presence of the Torah and Land settlers was a constant source of anxiety. At any time, for whatever reason, he might run afoul of Rabbi Khak and his goons. His foreman reassured him, reporting that the settlers had lately been keeping to themselves, not venturing into Arab territory. The garden courtyard now had five new olive saplings. Barring war, continued vandalism, or sheer human viciousness, in another two hundred years the saplings might be fitting successors to the destroyed ancients. Yet with deforestation, overpopulation, and runaway industrialization continuing unabated, their actuarial possibilities appeared grim.

Olga was standing over her desk examining blueprints when he walked in, sat down, and suddenly blurted, "That dinner you promised, I've been waiting for it patiently. Any day next week is alright by me."

"So someone is hungry?," she said, drawing out a pair of tickets from the top drawer of her desk and holding them up for his inspection. "If you promise to stay that way until next Tuesday, we can go to the Philharmonic. I was going to go with my friend Nadezhda Ikrova . . ."

"Wait," he protested, "don't let me upset your plans."

"Never mind, you've already upset them. Nadezhda won't mind either. She will be glad to hear her replacement will be a man. I will cook dinner and after we can go to the symphony."

He regretted waiting as long as he had. He conceded that he might have been a little intimidated by Olga, there was a mystique about her, a power, an electro-magnetism. In that respect she resembled Alison — expect for one important difference: Alison's power was always on, brilliant, like a Broadway marquee; Olga's was like an avalanche, irresistible once set in motion. He hadn't expected her to be so forthcoming so quickly. The instant social success lifted his spirits, he was already looking ahead to a long and torrid romance. Although the possibility loomed somewhere in the future, he imagined they might emigrate together, to some place where they might never see a rabbi and the struggle for existence was not defined by a fascist reality. They could form a partnership. She had the kind of free spirit that would be open to the idea.

Rachel, said her roommate, had left no message. When he couldn't get a satisfactory answer concerning her whereabouts, he went to the Medical Center to check for himself. Trying the office of medical records, he found its door locked, "Closed for Shabbos" said a passing nurse. At the emergency room they referred him to Obstetrics, saying the administration sometimes assigned new technicians to temporary duty there. At Obstetrics they knew of a Dr. Roman Aboulafia, but a Rachel they had never heard of. At that he decided to call it quits, he wasn't about to search the whole building. Back at home, he called the al-Aqsa to cancel his room reservation, reminding the clerk to be sure to bill him if the room wasn't rented. "Don't worry, Mr. Primchek," said the voice on the line, "we'll rent your room. Thank you for your courtesy in notifying us." It was his old "friend", Abdullah Atallah, the al-Aqsa's owner.

On Sunday night he watched "Newsline", the American television news show beamed live by satellite to Israel. The topic was the Maudlin bombing and the possibility of an American retaliatory strike. Newsline's moderator began by citing the polls — a military strike against the terrorists enjoyed the overwhelming support of the American people. People were frustrated he claimed, they were demanding something be done. After all, he reasoned, they had the costliest and "most muscular military establishment in the world, perhaps it was time we gave our military athletes a run for the money we spend on them." Elbert Wilton, the conservative pundit, a Newsline regular, opined that it was bad enough people were prevented from traveling to Europe and "over or through" the Middle East, but when "the nation's duly elected representatives couldn't or wouldn't visit these areas because of a legitimate concern for their lives", it was an obstruction of the workings of Congress and an attack on the democratic process. Were this state of affairs to continue unabated, the executive branch of government could end up absorbing Congress's advise and consent role. "Such a situation would be a novel one for the Republic and could lead to the unthinkable — the modification of our tried and true system by a relatively small collection of political gangsters, loosely united by an insane and fanatic hatred of the United States and Israel." In any case concluded Wilton, the American people were not disposed "to stand idly by while seeing their elected representatives blown up on television."

Following the free-wheeling discussion of the pros and cons of an American military strike, the American under-Secretary of State for the Middle East, L. Patterson Keys, joined the group. He was not at liberty to discuss specific evidence, said Keys. However, the United States had reason to believe that "a certain Middle Eastern terrorist nation may have been involved." The expectation of reasonable disclosure had to be weighed against the need to protect intelligence sources. "In military matters, leaks, from whatever source, could spell death for American servicemen." That was why the United States "had to be prepared to act alone." Keys characterized as a "canard" the charge that the United States' special relationship with Israel was the major factor behind Middle-Eastern terrorism, stating that " . . . it would exist independently of that regardless. The terrorism that is directed against us is primarily a phenomenon of disgruntled elements seeking to blame the United States for all the world's ills, when the real culprits are the Marxists and totalitarians who flout their peoples' demand for liberty."

When Amon Amitai called, he was practicing at the piano, preparing for his coming encounter with Olga. Amon had some news for him, "Guess who was in Yossi's shop last Friday? . . . A hint — she was a certain Air Force officer."

"Jane Fonda," said Basil with mock seriousness.

"Rachel! The beauteous Rachel. I'm told Raffi Golani bought her a lovely silver bracelet . . ."

'Is that all?," he exclaimed, his cavalier reaction masking his anger, "I could have bought her a gold."

"Maybe it was those dress blues. I thought you were meeting her Friday. What happened?"

"I got shot down. Raffi can add me to his kill total along with those stupid Syrians. They say he never misses. Now that he's on the ground, let's see if he knows what hole to put it in."

"Be optimistic, he may still be groping . . . But seriously, an Aboulafia doesn't come along every day. You'll go some before she'll be replaced."

"She's probably irreplaceable. But one has to be philosophical about these things, I gave her a chance and she took it. Amen and farewell."

Resuming his place at the piano, he pounded the keyboard in a reasonably recognizable facsimile of the opening bars of Chopin's Revolutionary Etude, *forte con espressivo*.

38

He paused to exchange glances with Olga, their eyes saying silent "good mornings" through the glass of her office. She was standing in front of her desk, resplendent in a form-fitting suit of maroon velvet and polished black muskateer boots, her favorites, the ones she wore with her darker garb. The boots provided an elegantly martial effect, reminiscent of the uniform of a czarist cavalry officer. Olga's eyes followed him as he walked to his desk, the expression on her face sternly serious. He had seen that expression before, it was one characteristically her own. He thought he understood what it meant.

At two he heard Olga tell Orlit she was leaving for the day. He assumed she would be occupied with domestic chores that afternoon, shopping, preparing the meal she had promised him. Four hours later, when she met him at the door to her apartment, she appeared to still be working. Wearing a large apron, she greeted him cordially, holding his hand as she led him up the curving stone stairs to the building's upper, residential level. Inside, he was struck by the number of oriental rugs — on the floor, hanging on walls, draped over ottomans, fashioned into pillows — their colorful designs framed by the ambient white of the apartment's walls and drapes. Antique, inlaid mother-of-pearl tables and cabinets made up the wooden furniture. The dining table, a small two-person affair, covered with a red and indigo linen, was set with hand-blown, clear crystal goblets. A pair of large, hexagonal dinner plates were decorated with Arabic Kufic lettering. Overall, the effect was quite stimulating, like a visual aperitif. He had never expected Olga to be so wonderfully domestic, Russians weren't supposed to be like that. He regretted not having brought flowers.

She invited him to examine the two bedrooms in the rear of the apartment. The smaller of the two had a corner devoted to exercise equipment. There was a contraption for toning the abdominal muscles, and a combination rowing and bicycle machine. She had bought them from an *"Ameri-kanski"* who was leaving Israel to return to America, they were part of the conditioning program she had established for herself. As proof of its efficacy, she extended her upper arm, inviting him to feel it. *"Formidable,"* he exclaimed, using the French. For a woman, the arm was remarkably solid. "I am waiting for a man to take advantage of a woman's weakness . . . but so far I wait in vain," she joked, as they walked back to the kitchen. She apologized for being behind schedule, dinner would be ready in a few minutes. In the meantime, she offered him a beer poured into a frosted glass. He sat down on the divan and stretched his legs out, suppressing an impulse to remove his shoes. He didn't want her thinking he was "taking advantage" of her hospitality — at least before dinner.

Dinner was tastefully simple — roast milkfed lamb, the tiny creature garnished with sprigs of mint, served with green beans and salad. Olga sliced off a back leg and the section of breast containing the chops, heaping them on his plate. This was no rack of lamb, conveniently pre-cut for a diner's easy access. Eating an entire lamb breast took time, it was not a cut to give up its treasure to a few motions of knife and fork, such as a slab of beef or filet of fish. Lamb breast was the kind of thing one consumed methodically, a rib at a time, extracting with teeth and lips the nutty flavored meat from bones and joints. Don't worry she said, they could take their seats in the hall after the Beethoven overture. But by the time dessert (a *crème de caramel* of appropriately light consistency) was served, and the dark little cups of thick coffee (that invariably ended an Arab meal) were drunk, an evening with the Philharmonic had lost much of its attraction. The problem was distance. After a bout with food and drink, to suddenly forego a meal's afterglow by a compulsive and wrenching flight to a concert hall, required a deliberate act of will, one clearly beyond his present disposition. He was content to remain where he was, the prospect of being jammed into less than a square meter of space, in the midst of a thousand other mortals, however "spiritual" the entertainment, a bit incongruous given the present intimacy. Olga agreed, suggesting that next time they begin their evening a couple hours earlier. Beethoven and Tschaikovsky would not miss them.

Perhaps she read it in his eyes, or noticed the way he slumped in his chair while sipping the coffee. But he had drunk most of the wine and eaten most of the food, so she told him to go and lie down while she cleaned up. He sat on the divan and took off his shoes . . . "Lie down", meant lie down.

There is a time when one awakes from sleep, when the inhibitions and tensions governing waking behavior are subverted by more primitive responses. It was to this feeling of primal impulse he surrendered when he awoke in the magic darkness of the unfamiliar but congenial surroundings. Rising from the divan and relying on the thick concrete floor not to betray him, he moved softly toward the light from her bedroom where seated cross-legged at a vanity, she worked a file across her fingers, a billowy-sleeved, sheer peignoir offering a risqué view of the flesh underneath. She had seen him, he saw her eyes shift to his reflection in the vanity mirror, undressing in the doorway. She waited, watching until he finished, then rising, she threw off the peignoir and stood facing him, palms on hips, her sturdy Russian legs spread defiantly, as if daring a taking. Surprised by the sudden revelation, he paused before the puffy-nippled breasts and flamboyant torso, the creamy glaze of skin, the months of imagery and fantasy finally confronted by the flesh. It was an exquisite moment, a mystical moment, like virginity, a moment unique in time. As such it deserved to be preserved, or failing that, milked of its awe and excitment.

It happened very quickly, Olga flicking off the lamp, her hand catching his member, pushing him onto the bed. She was on top of him, her kness on his chest, he felt the coolness of her wet hair and tongue on his loins, she was holding onto his organ, squeezing, pushing down on its base, her mouth ravishing its head while her rump, in wild syncopation, bumped against his face. He tried grabbing her thighs, her waist, to anchor her in position, to restrain the fury of her movement. He wanted to cry "stop", to plead for an easing of the pressure but his eyes shut tightly and he was sitting up, his hands gripping her ankles, experiencing the orgasm's surge, the spasms following each other in excruciating succession under the relentless suction. Finally, she stopped, but only after he had let go her ankles and fallen gasping back onto the bed.

He felt his forehead. Still hot and damp, it was as if he had "blacked out". Olga was beside him, her arm under his head. The breast she pressed to his lips he took avidly, burying his eyes in the soft tissue, suckling dreamily, then voraciously as she rubbed his restored member against her vulva, wedging him between its lips. He was on top of her now, hands spreading her cheeks, fingers probing the spongy lips ringing his member. A sudden flux of wetness made him drop precipitously upon the bunlike vulva, pressing it against his lips, while her pelvis writhed and arched against his face. She was speaking now, "*Moi bik! Moi vilikolepni Russki bik!*", holding his ears, pulling him up to her, "*Vzhboltay menya! Vzhboltay menya!*" The language was Russian but in the context translation was superfluous, the tense was imperative. He came up catching her under the knees, tilting her upwards, pinning her arms over her head. Using the upthrust loins as a fulcrum, he began a desperate run to climax, thrusting hard and deep, banging against her womb. She was crying, tossing her head from side to side, "*Bog! Bog! Bog!*" He felt her cul-de-sac open, his organ wringed and pulled, her pubes pressing against its hilt. He put his mouth over hers, sucking out the breath, seeking her ether, her elan — he was coming, his body crumpling on top of her.

The light was on, he was being shaken. She was afraid he might fall into a deep sleep and there would be no waking him. It was almost two she said, he had to go. She couln't have him seen leaving the apartment in the morning, it would be an "insult" to her neighbors. He did as he was told, sitting up on the side of the bed while she helped him with his clothes, buttoning his shirt, putting on his socks, bending over and tying his shoes, exposing for the first time, her backside. "Next time," he remarked, his hands massaging the well-knit back, "there should be some light on the subject." "If you like," she replied, getting up off her knees and putting on her chemise. The stairwell she left in darkness as she escorted him down to the street, bidding him an unceremonious good-bye.

Walking to his car, he reflected on the experience. It was a painful way to end an evening, but he had to respect her reasons for making him leave. It was, after all, the Holy Land, still a monument to atavism. Yet, he was leaving with a good feeling, the feeling of being well-used. Oddly enough, the logical choice for immigration was Russia. She would go with him, he was sure of it. Although not a communist, they would take her back, the Russians made a big thing of welcoming back immigrants to Israel, their "prodigal sons" returning to the forgiving bosom of the Motherland.

He had never thought of Russia before, it would have been madness. Returning to his roots, his ancestral homeland, the great Slavic hinterland — that was crap. Yet with Olga it all made sense. Admittedly, architecture was dismal in Russia. Like most nations, her glory was behind her. But they were keen on preservation and that meant there would be a place for him. It was something to think about.

39

There was a line at the counter when he walked into Flom's News Emporium. Flom's had Jerusalem's best selection of foreign press and periodicals. A hand-printed sign taped to the magazine rack read, "JUST ARRIVED — DIE KUGEL — A FLOM'S EXCLUSIVE. Maudlin Blast Survivor Granted Exclusive Interview with Syrian Strongman Nafsi." A stack of the English language edition of *Die Kugel*, a left-leaning magazine of the muck-raking tendency, published in Hamburg, sat on the floor below. He let a woman reach in front of him before reaching down and taking two copies. Pointing to the dwindling pile of magazines, he asked the clerk whether it was all they had. "No, we have another three bundles in the back," said the clerk, "They quadrupled our usual consignment. These Germans aren't so dumb, they know how to exploit Jews."

Waiting in line, he opened the magazine to the interview. "Die Kugel Exclusive!" blared the top of the page bordered in red, "SYRIA'S NAFSI GIVES FIRST INTERVIEW SINCE SEIZING POWER." A photograph showing Alison standing in front of the Old City's Lion Gate occupied half the page. Projecting outward and shading her blue-toned eyes was the bill of the questionable cap, the one suspiciously similar to those worn by Rommel and men in the Afrika campaign. In addition to demonstrating a talent for self-promotion, Alison's behavior evidenced a strong streak of defiance, she was no respecter of taboos — Jewish or otherwise. He paid his shekels at the counter and went directly to a nearby café where, finding a table among the early morning coffee addicts, he sat down for a leisurely read.

"Damascus, a city under seige. Sandbags piled ten feet high surrounding the sides of my hotel, the Semiramis, where I and other hotel guests were roused twice during the night in mock air raid drills. I had come to Damascus to await my contact for an interview with Salim Nafsi. Then, punctually at 8:00 AM, the third day of my stay in Syria, I was picked up at the hotel entrance by a black Mercedes sedan. I sat in the back seat between two fatigue-clad Syrian army officers armed with Kalashnikov assault rifles. Inside the car I was blindfolded, then driven to a secret location. Upon arrival the blindfold was removed and I was ushered into a large, second-story, reception-type room. Seated behind a long banquet table were Dr. Salim Nafsi, the head of Syria's revolutionary government, and a quartet of his comrades, identified to me as Khaled Abdel-Kader al-Khatab, Minister of State Planning; Omar Baladyan, Minister of Interior; Abdel-Karim al-Khalu, Minister of Resources and Development; and Shafiq al-As, Chief of Staff Armed Forces, all attired in the same, identical olive green military fatigues. An interpreter, apparently a civilian, the only other female in the room, sat behind the two junta members on Dr. Nafsi's left. Another man, a soldier, operated a tape recorder and kept the Council (the Revolution's highest governing body) members and myself supplied with glasses of iced lemonade during the course of the interview.

"The interview itself was subject to two conditions, one: no photographs, and two: any editing of the interview had to be approved by my hosts, the Syrian Information Bureau. However, mindful of present tensions, we decided to print the interview in its entirety, avoiding a possible delay or dispute over editing. Dr. Nafsi speaks excellent English with a pronounced English accent, evidently the result of four years in London where he served as military attaché. Prior to the commencement of the interview, Dr. Nafsi announced that it was the Council's decision that he answer all questions, or as he put it, 'This revolution shall speak with one voice and that voice shall be mine.' What follows is the interview with Salim Nafsi, complete, uncut and unedited, including as well, your correspondent's pauses, blips, and inept phrasing."

The nod to modesty at the end of the introduction, calculated to ingratiate herself with the reader, was the kind of thing she would think of, as was placing the title "Dr." before Nafsi's name, a device to enhance authority. Or did she, in her power-hungry way, really believe it? She could forget the characters from Channel 13, the New York-Los Angeles media bums and princesses she stroked for entertaining tidbits to feed the famehunger of her anonymous and star-worshipping audience. She was on the mountaintop now, not on Central Park Pond. Real power was exercised here — the power of war, peace, life, death, it couldn't fail to impress her. Had she approached the Syrians or had they approached her? She didn't say, but the result was an arrangement felicitous for both, giving each a platform to the world. He read quickly, through the first part of the interview, the part that touched on the mechanics of the coup, the alliance with Iran, Syria's relations with other Arab countries and other internal events. Some of her questions got measured responses. Others, like the perennial American concern over the spread of Marxism and Soviet influence, undisguised contempt. Dismissing the Marxist label, Nafsi denounced it as nothing more than imperialist-Zionist propaganda, " . . . the same cry that once served the Hitlerite fascists in the thirties has been taken up by the America-Zionist axis."

For her part, Alison seemed convinced of the merits of her hosts' positions, becoming more sympathetic as the interview progressed, posing questions in the manner of a defense attorney out to exonerate a client.

"Q. Dr. Nafsi, yesterday I visited the Torture Museum, the museum set up after the Revolution as a monument to the cruelty of the past. I saw some gruesome instruments on display there and read the museum's dedication decree — 'to those who suffered to end suffering', the pledge to the Syrian people that never again would they have to live in fear of torture. Yet, your critics charge you with operating a police state, a quote, 'vast totalitarian dungeon where justice is meted out at the end of a noose or the barrel of a gun' . . . That's a question, sir.

A. The Revolution has kept its pledge, the practice of

torture in Syria has been liquidated. As to the final part of your question — those who combine with our enemies, to destroy the Revolution and wipe out its achievements, can expect to be dealt with pitilessly. The Revolution will never apologize for defending itself.

Q. Recently the United States government claimed it has 'hard evidence' that Syria, or factions under its control, was behind the killing of Senator Maudlin and members of his staff. What is your response to that?

A. Syria has rejected these charges in the appropriate forums. It exercises no control over the many popular resistance groups struggling for national liberation in the region. Although we have already spoken on the issue, we repeat: the liquidation of the American senator was a legitimate act of self-defense, and as such, sanctioned by the UN Charter and international law.

He skipped over the few remaining questions, he had found the one he had been looking for, the question basic to all the others, the crux. Alison had characteristically reserved it for the interview's end. For once Nafsi was not niggardly with words.

"Q. Dr. Nafsi, for years Syria has been perhaps the leading frontline state against Israel, has fought many wars with that country, and has generally championed the cause of the Palestinian people. My question is this — whether Syria is prepared to make peace with Israel, and if so, what would be its conditions for such a peace?

A. To answer your question I must invoke history. However, I will be merciful and restrict myself to the modern era, the world subsequent to 1914. It was a time when many, including those of Syrian nationality, foresaw a future of liberation. However, there were those with other plans for the region, imperial plans. Like vultures they waited patiently for the conclusion of the war, then descended upon a starving and weak Syria to pick its bones. France, inspired by memories of crusaders and divide and rule policies, separated its share into two parts, Syria and Lebanon. Later, in a particularly mean and base maneuver, parcelled yet another part to Turkey. English designs were even more reprehensible. For it was England which seized Syrian Palestine with the blessings of its creature, the so-called League of Nations, converted it into a base of empire, inviting hundreds of thousands of Zionist Jews from Europe to colonize it, making the Palestinians outcasts in their own land so that one of Israel's leaders could later state, 'Where are the Palestinians? I don't see them.' Well, we see them. They are our orphaned children, as much a part of Syrian motherland as refugees from the *Julan*. And so now we have Israel, a state that pretends to speak for all the world's Jews. And what has it brought us for the sacrifice forced upon us? Woe, a century of it, suffering, underdevelopment, terror. When we asked peace, Israel and its patron, the United States, answered with war, massacre, and continued schemes of hegemony.

"Yes, Syria is for peace, but peace based upon compliance with UN resolutions, the restoration to Palestinians of their land and homes — throughout *all* of Palestine, a final and definite end to Israel's relationship with American imperialism. Those are the conditions, the *minimum* conditions for peace."

Alison's little epilogue following the interview — describing the serving of sweets and coffee, the Syrians asking questions about life in America — did not make him feel any better about the prospects for peace. Left, right, center, Christian, Shiite, Sunnite — none of that really mattered. It was the 100 year war the Arabs had predicted, a reprise of the 12th century. Although he interpreted the summation as an expression of journalistic hyperbole, a nice, upbeat, ominous note to end on, it was certain not to endear her to the powers-that-be, "One left Damascus impressed with the will of this small and backward country to face the future with a calm and heroic stoicism. Along the way the

378

country's revolutionary leadership will probably have to indulge in some active pushing and pulling, but such "persuasion" is what revolution is all about — the dislocations and changes in the economic rules of the game that make revolutionary change so painful, and to the ordinary foreign observer so incomprehensible. Islam is on the move and Salim Nafsi and friends, including of course, revolutionary Iran, are riding its dark horse, determined to restore Islam to it former pre-eminence in the region. With the US and Israel standing firmly in the way a major collision appears unavoidable. As this correspondent sees it, the question at this late hour is whether US policy makers have the sense to understand that in this part of the world, the times they are indeed changing, and that two thousand pound bombs are no answer to an old idea whose time has come anew."

He wrote the words "ENCORE! ENCORE!" on a small scrap of paper, then clipped it to the copy of *Die Kugel* he had bought for her. She wasn't in her office when he arrived, so he placed it on her desk. Since their night together she had been keeping him at a discreet distance, discussing projects with him in a tone of austere professionalism. A sort of tacit no-man's land had been established between them. While he accepted the necessity of maintaining appearances, he still would have liked to hear an encouraging word. Yet he had to be careful to avoid giving the impression he thought her a sexual bauble to rub everytime he got the urge. He decided the best course was patience, to give her the space she obviously required.

A few minutes later he heard Olga's boots sounding their characteristic eighth note staccato run up the cement stairs. Before entering her office she uttered a perfunctory good morning to the staff, conspicuously avoiding a look in Ben-Judah's direction. Basil saw her pick up the magazine. She had seen the note on its corner and was looking at him, her lips hinting at a smile. Sitting down, she opened the magazine and began reading.

379

He was surprised to be receiving a call from Beatrix Brunwasser so early in the morning. She explained she was calling from school. Apologizing for the gap in their communications, she said she had a "confession" to make to him. But right now she was calling to alert him to the Nafsi interview in *Die Kugel*, had he seen it? "You have?," she exclaimed with surprise, "Wasn't it great?" She had read it that morning at IPR headquarters. She wanted to know about the interviewer, she had seen her on television, the "American correspondent that accompanied Maudlin on his final mission for American imperialism, you must know her . . ." He started to ask her how she knew that but was cut off, "Let's have dinner together tonight, alright?" They agreed to meet at a Palestinian restaurant near IPR headquarters.

He waited until the office emptied for lunch, then walked into Olga's office. "What did you think of Nafsi's interview?," he asked. "Yes," answered Olga, holding up the magazine with the attached note, "me too, but where?" It was a difficult situation she said, they could not continue meeting at her apartment, she did not want a reputation as one "who entertained men". Their "peculiar situation" demanded discretion. She trusted he would continue to act with circumspection, those in the office "must never suspect". Jerusalem was a conservative place and they were both too well-known. It was unfortunate, but the Judaic and Arabic cultures possessed a repressive heritage, both being rigidly anti-woman and disapproving of anything "outside of the traditional arrangement". There would have to be a sacrifice.

He responded by suggesting a series of possible trysts — a drive to the Galilee, Tel-Aviv, Acre, Beersheba, weekends. They mustn't forget weekends, he said, they came once a week. She hesitated before the string of possibilities, finally agreeing to take them "under advisement". "By the way," said Basil, "you never answered my question. What did you think of the interview?"

"Oh yes . . . this Alison Cleveland, did you know she was going to interview Salim Nafsi?"

"I had no idea, she never mentioned it. It was probably a secret, she indicates that in her forward — if you can believe it."

"Why do you think the Syrians chose her as their vehicle?"

"I don't know, maybe they're getting smart."

Beatrix was seated at a table by the restaurant's front window. "Mr. Primchek!," she cried, getting up and rushing to greet him, "I'm so glad to see you again. I've been wanting to talk with you." She apologized again for the long time between communications. She had postponed contacting him because of the incident involving Senator Maudlin at Jeisheh camp, believing he might have blamed her for what happened. "Why should I blame you," he asked, "were you one of the stonethrowers?"

"No, but I helped organize the demonstration against him," she replied proudly. "It was supposed to have been non-violent, we're not out there to get people killed you know." He was curious as to how she knew the Maudlin party had decided upon a visit to a camp, specifically Jeisheh camp. "You remember I told you we had good intelligence, Mr. Primchek? Well, you're one reason why. You were the source for that information. The day we drove to Ramallah . . . you mentioned then that you had a friend working on Maudlin's staff and that you were thinking about suggesting they visit a refugee camp while in Israel. So I put two and two together — Jeisheh is the camp closest to Jerusalem — and told our operatives in Jeisheh to keep a watch out for Maudlin, and that if he dared show up, to be ready with an appropriate welcome. So the welcoming committee got a bit rambunctious. We had no control over that, the masses were justifiably angry at the man's audacity.

He thought he was going to make a nice, leisurely visit to one of his Third World zoos. Well, we let him know we didn't want any of his corn . . ."

"You know," he interrupted, "that's exactly what Nafsi said about the bombing."

"You're damn right!," she exclaimed defiantly, "I'll go with Salim any day." She had gone over to the offense, abandoning her earlier apologetic manner for a style more in keeping with the championing of the cause of her assumed wards, the despised Palestinians. Now she wanted to know about Alison Cleveland, how "a woman with such obvious progressive sympathies" managed to infiltrate the Maudlin press contingent. He decided to tell her his side of the two day ill-fated visit, from airport reception to stinking jail cell, ending his narrative with an allusion to the fact that the demonstration had probably saved his life, ". . . Alison Cleveland's for sure. Were it not for that 'stomach ache', she would have been sitting right next to Maudlin that morning. On the other hand, I don't think you'll ever know how close those demonstrators came to getting shot. That was really another stroke of luck."

Beatrix, who had been listening intently to his description of events, now spoke up, "You know," she said pensively, "this must be the first time I ever saved anyone's life . . . You don't feel obligated to me, do you?"

"No more obligated than I would be to the driver of a car going in the opposite direction passing without a collision. Although I must say it was a good idea, I'll give you credit for that. I'll never forget that non-plussed look on Maudlin's face — when your boys came out carrying that banner, 'Maudlin, Zionist Stooge'. I'm glad he lived long enough to experience that. Although I'm sure he died unrepentant. These scoundrels are like that, evil to the core."

Beatrix appeared preoccupied during dinner. Besides being uncharacteristically non-verbal, she picked at her food, employing her utensils as nervous playthings. Finally, with some diffidence, she broached a question to him, "Mr. Primchek . . . you don't have to answer this if you think it too personal — but did you ever consider the possibility of taking a mistress?"

"Sure. So what does that make me in your book?"

"That's not why I asked. How do you feel about me . . . I mean as a mistress? Naturally you would have to find me attractive."

"My dear Beatrix, if it is any consolation, I find you not only attractive, but appealing. But will you cut out this 'Mr. Primchek' stuff? I believe I should insist upon that. By the way, this isn't your adolescent insecurity speaking is it?"

"No, I haven't time for such things. Actually I was just wondering."

40

He left the work crew at the Lapidus house sitting around a radio, too engrossed in the latest battle reports to give him much more than the barest notice. He was driving to Ramallah to do a check there also, of the Haddad villa. The reports on the American raid against terrorist base camps in Lebanon had been coming in all morning. The fighting was apparently over, the main issue now being damage assessment. It was too early for an official tally of dead and wounded, but from all reports the Americans had not come off well. The US command's only comment relative to casualties was a terse "heavy". By contrast, Radio Damascus was much more forthcoming, repeatedly announcing the latest count of "martyrs", victims of the American bombing and subsequent helicopter-borne ranger assault. Some of the participating brigades were named — "the Imam Musa as-Sadr, Kanafani, Izzedin al-Qassam". The last-mentioned perked up his ears, that was Khalil Bustanji's unit. His mother had received a letter from him informing her he had joined the al-Qassam brigade, an all-Palestinian unit of volunteers attached to the Syrian Army. He was very possibly involved in the day's fighting, he hoped Bustanji had been given adequate training. More than zeal was required when doing battle with the Americans.

Not making much sense of the Arabic, he switched to an Israeli station. It was in the process of giving the latest tally of American dead and wounded, "recently announced over Radio Damascus". With reports still coming in from the field, there were now 304 dead and 82 wounded, the small proportion of wounded to dead attributed to the fighting's savagery. The Americans had launched their assault shortly before dawn on Friday, the Moslem sabbath.

When he pulled up before the uncompleted shell of the Haddad villa, he found his foreman, Jasim Harb, sitting outside with the rest, the inevitable radio tuned to Damascus. "General Narciso Sonoma, the commander of the Americans' anti-terrorism Omega Force, the Syrians have his corpse!," announced Jasim excitedly. "And over three hundred others! They dropped from their helicopters into a valley of death, a hell of fire and pain. Not one walked away. We have won a great victory!" Although the others were less expansively verbal, the bright expressions on their faces said it all. One Arab was violently flicking the beads up and down the string of his *masbaha*, the so-called "worry beads" carried by Arab men. Others were exclaiming as they listened the man of the hour's name, *"Ya Salim! Ya habibi Salim!"*

Jasim was translating for him now, "the American pilots dropped their bombs in the dark of night . . . while we picked up the mangled bodies of the dead and dying . . .

more came, like a plague of locusts darkening the sky . . . murder in their hearts . . . the knights of Islam were ready, slaying the enemy . . . sending their souls to a bottomless hell . . ." Although the language was excessive, it spoke the truth. The Nafsi regime had demonstrated its mettle against the world's greatest terrorist force — the combined land, sea and air forces of the United States of America. The Arabs he saw in the streets and coffeehouses later that day, it wasn't his imagination, they *were* standing a little taller, a little prouder. The victory of Arab arms had given a tremendous boost to morale. If the Americans had thought that with one swift, punitive raid they would — to use Nafsi's expression — liquidate "terrorism", they were all wet.

That evening, on Jordanian television, he watched a Syrian newstape featuring a pretty, green-fatigued, English-speaking girl soldier, lead the viewer on a Cook's tour of the area outside Baalbek where most of the fighting took place. First to be shown were scenes of the shattered and bloody bodies of those killed in their homes by the Americans' pre-dawn "smart bombs", followed by the main battlefield, the artichoke field where most of the attacking helicopters had disgorged their troops, now covered with burnt-out helicopter fuselages and row upon row of bagged American bodies waiting delivery to the Red Cross. Syria was waiving the right to demand reparations, said the narrator. By returning the invaders' bodies, it hoped to deprive the Americans of an excuse for another raid, or a series of raids. "Syria did not want a war with America, but if attacked it would resist," she declared redundantly. A Syrian army officer exhibited some of the weaponry used in the raid by the Americans — shotguns, grenade launchers, rockets for blasting through stone walls, German MPS 9 millimeter machine guns; Belgian NATO arms, one with a 700 round per minute rate of fire, another having a 900. The officer was asked how Syria's weaponry stacked up against that of the invaders. "Obviously ours are better," he replied, "no amount of weapons can defeat a people united."

There was a brief shot of Syrian doctors operating upon an American soldier who, the viewer was told, later died from his injuries. A visit to a hospital ward showed the more seriously injured invaders, minus some of the limbs, faces and hands they had taken for granted the day before. There were close-ups of some of their faces — bleary-eyed skinheads, the vacancy of their expressions testimony to the shock and trauma they had experienced. "What were they doing *here*," asked the personable guide, "these boys from the farms and forests of America, sent thousands of miles to kill and be killed for the cause of American billionaires and international Zionism?"

The report was an amazing production, smacking of a professionalism and sophistication that a year ago he would have thought impossible for any Arab regime. Now, nothing the Syrians might do would surprise him. They were indeed "getting smart".

On Saturday there was the usual emergency session of the UN Security Council passing the usual resolution with the usual veto by the United States. However, Italy, France, and even England, its Laborite government claiming an "independent foreign policy", abstained. The days of Korea when the US could drag the UN into wars against barefoot people were over. Since then, most of its European allies had learned to be skeptical. The prevailing opinion was that the Americans were "a bit crazy".

In Israel there was bewilderment over the fact that the Americans had suffered yet another Lebanese debacle. One commentator compared the situation to a child who wakes up one day to the realization that its father can't beat every other father. "Israel has come of age" declared another, stating that the history of the Gentiles is "ambivalent in regard to Jewish survival." "A second declaration of independence, emulating the spirit and courage of the first made in spite of a hostile world, was an imperative for the Jewish

386

people," said a third.

The statement of *Newsline's* guest, retired general and onetime CIA chief, Clayton Sumpter, that all counter-terrorist operations were gambles, drew an outraged response from the program's regulars. "I for one am sick of this military fatalism. Whose idea was the bombing?," demanded an infuriated Frank Crabbe, Capitol correspondent for ABS. "That let the cat out of the bag and gave the Syrians the time they needed to aggregate their forces . . . Poor planning, poor training, poor strategy. Poor! Poor! Piss-poor!" It was a vulgarism, but if anybody could get away with it, Frank Crabbe could. A former captain in military intelligence, he knew the corridors of the Pentagon like the back of his hand, it was his beat. Elbert Wilton was quick to announce, in his elegantly subtle manner, his "selective association with the words of our brother, Franklin." The Commander-in-Chief had gotten bad advice, there was no way declared Wilton, wagging a finger at the camera, "*no way*, a military force, albeit an admittedly elite force, could have gone in there and come out without taking horrendous casualties." As authority for the proposition, Wilton quoted the "respected Israeli military analyst, Lumi Fisch", to the effect that the Israeli army would have never attempted such an operation without a force of regimental strength. "And that implies a campaign that takes on the dimensions of full scale war, where the various military arms are able to coordinate with each other, and where you are in depth. Not like here, where if you couldn't catch a helicopter out, chances were you'd wait an eternity for another."

The weekend journalism was only a warm-up. On Monday morning Americans awakened to a replay of the disaster. Televison newshawks camped in parlors catching the tear-jerking reactions of gold star moms and dads to the sad tidings. "How do you feel about your son?," they were asked. "They been wanting a go at them Shitites for a long time," blurted a brother of a deceased proudly. The President was shown in a two-way TV hookup making a special call of bereavement to General Narciso Sonoma's aged mother, an Alzheimer's disease patient in a Tucson, Arizona nursing home. It was unclear from the brief exchange whether the wrinkle-faced old lady understood the import of the call, it was reported she suffered the additional handicap of not speaking English.

In Congress those who had been outspoken advocates of retaliation regretted their original zeal. The resourceful among them went back to their statements and speeches, plucking little snippets of cautionary phrases, such as "these countries represent a danger", and "the lives of our men are infinitely precious", to show that they knew all along there was a possibility the operation could go haywire. The few congressmen talking "investigation" were warned by senior colleagues, such a course could only be of comfort to America's enemies. In times like these, Americans stood together, behind their president and the flag.

In the confusion of voices, Al Abel's column in Tuesday's *Times*, entitled "Who Goofed?", was a call to reason. Presidential speech writer, friend of kings and prime ministers, resident conservative wit, Abel's credentials were well known. Abel stood for a strong America, a strong Israel. The backbiting had gone on long enough, the time for blame was over, for in truth wrote Abel, "the answer is that all of us goofed. We goofed when we said we couldn't afford to support Israel in the style she had become accustomed to, and which we knew in our heart to be the minimum necessary for her security. We goofed when we complained about the costs of Israel's fighter and rocket program, a program we knew would help make her militarily and economically self-sufficient. We goofed when we sold billions of dollars of modern weaponry to Israel's enemies, thus increasing her insecurity at a time when we most needed her to protect our security . . ." No one in the Jewish community could or would have said it as well as Al

Abel. He had courage, the courage of a conservative, a man very much in the American tradition. People quoted Al Abel's column, big people, important people, people in government. So when after a series of "We goofed(s)" that some enthusiasts compared to Luther's Ninety-Five Theses, Abel concluded that the United States was a naval and air power, not a land power; that it was time we recognized that "Israel was the greatest land dike against the Marxist and Muslim tide that we could ever hope to have in the region"; that Israel was a greater bargain for America than a hundred nuclear powered and armed aircraft carriers; millions concurred. The article was reprinted and distributed in the millions, from every synagogue in the country, the pen at the service of the sword.

41

The recent infusion of US funds and military credits were designed for the specific purpose of "increasing military cooperation" between the two allies. The object was to restore the Israeli army to the readiness existing prior to a series of damaging budget cuts, cuts that had particularly affected the reserve training program. Training sessions that had been reduced to a monthly or bi-monthly frequency were being put back on a weekly timetable. Doctor Klug made the announcement at the Thursday night reserve meeting. Actually, claimed Klug, the "revival" had been in the works for some time, bureaucratic inertia having delayed its implementation. The recent set-back suffered by the Americans had finally convinced them to get moving. Naturally, the Americans wanted something for their money, with dispensation went obligation. They were talking war by late summer. The Americans were holding their presidential elections this year and neither party wanted to be considered soft on terrorism. "In fact," said Klug, "the marching orders might be on the Defense Minister's desk right now. This time you can expect an occupation, a long one. So don't be surprised if the government extends the normal thirty day duty to forty-five, maybe sixty days . . ."

The assembled reservists received Klug's preview of coming events in sullen silence, it was not something they wanted to hear. Klug had a penchant for speaking ominously of war or the threat of war. Repeating the latest rumors and using the credibility his platform gave him, he seemed to take a sadistic delight in playing upon the legitimate fear of his audience. However, as a reserve captain his knowledge of future military plans was no greater than any other private citizen. Like a lot of people, he was just good at reading newspapers. And when it came to beating the drums of war the Israeli press deferred to no one. The following Monday the morning papers reprinted an article by David Mindell from the *Times'* Sunday edition. Entitled, "Um Shintyan, the Death of a Village", Israeli newspapers gave it headline treatment, "Shiite Survivors Tell of Syrian Horror", and "Nafsi Allies Level Village with Syrian Guns" blared two of the more sensational.

> "In the annals of villages condemned to be wiped from the face of the earth for resistance to tyranny, another name has been joined to those of Lidice, Our-a-dour, Pestano — Um Shintyan, a village situated in a pleasant valley in the Lebanon, once home to 230 souls. Earlier this month, in a savagely methodical two day artillery barrage, Lebanese Druse from elements loyal to Syria's

Marxist dictator, Major Salim Nafsi, armed with Soviet-supplied T-72 tanks from Syrian Army stockpiles, shelled Um Shintyan into a state of total and complete delapidation. During those two days, an estimated 5,000 rounds of 125 mm caliber ammunition struck the village's formerly picturesque rock and cement houses, reducing them to so many rockpiles. An inspection . . ."

Repelled by the article's exaggerated style he read quickly, making his own reduction of the various assertions: a dispute had arisen between Palestinian and Shiite factions. A Palestinian patrol had been ambushed. In reprisal, the Shiite faction was itself ambushed and two of its members were thrown from a Syrian army helicopter to splat against the roofs of the village. Then, for further emphasis, the village was shelled into rubble. The end. A sad story, Lebanon was full of them. But with only six villagers, including the "fighters", reported to have been killed, as a typical Lebanese day's work it was hardly worth mention. And it would not have been were it not for the fact that it was one more shot in a stepped-up propaganda war against the Syrians. Since when were Americans concerned about the lives of Lebanese Shiite villagers?

Angered, he dropped the newspaper in a nearby trash-can. It was one ism after another, terrorism, Arabism, Marxism, fundamentalism, all the official fixations. Why couldn't they be like him and be content with ordinary fixations? He was meeting Olga that evening at the al-Aqsa Hotel — they would not be talking politics.

There was a message at the office to "telephone Bernard Gluckmann, Strasbourg". Although he had been getting Patrimoine Architectural literature, he hadn't heard from Gluckmann since they met. He had a feeling Gluckmann would be asking something of him, something impossibly impractical. Haunted by his father's negative advice, he had no appetite for taking on yet another lost cause. So far his political peccadillos had gone unreported and his politics had proved immaterial to his clients, but a reputation as a political kook could change that quickly enough. He was beginning to make money, gain commissions. Putting that at risk with another exercise in futility made no sense. With that in mind, he picked up the telephone and dialed Gluckmann's number.

Gluckmann had called to request his intervention in a local matter. Investors were proposing the building of a modern, enclosed, shopping mall on property in the Old City. One of their arguments was that the present structures were "antiquated". The majority of the land for the project had already been acquired from the government or private parties. However, a key parcel was owned by the Armenian Patriarchate and it was as yet unsold. Gluckmann wanted him to study the proposal and prepare a critique, then meet with the Patriarch to present Patrimoine Architectural's arguments against the project.

It was a modest request, not the kind he could or would refuse. He told Gluckmann he was familiar with the proposal but expected it to pass easily. While there was some opposition to the plan, it mainly emanated from the Arab community, thus there was little chance of it being effective. Nevertheless, he agreed to look into the matter and try to get an audience with the Patriarch or a representative. He had no idea whether his intervention would have any effect. He had never dealt with a patriarch before.

42

Dear Basil,

I have decided that my mother and sister should leave Palestine as soon as conveniently possible and go live with our cousins in Iowa. It will be better for them there and Sumaiya can eventually enter the university. I have written our cousins to expect them. I trust you will give them the benefit of your experience and help them with the necessary papers and transfers of monies. I would appreciate your letting the house for rent to a reliable tenant.

Khalil Bustanji

The envelope, postmarked "Amman, the Hashemite Kingdom of Jordan", was addressed to the ill-fated office. There was no return address. He went over to the Bustanji house that night and showed them the letter. They had been waiting for him, reported Mother Bustanji, they had received a similar letter only two days before. Having considered the move for some time, they were prepared to leave as soon as the necessary documents could be obtained. The summer recess being in effect, there would be no interruption of Sumaiya's schooling. After a discussion of the steps to be taken, the inevitable coffee was served and they sat and talked — "visiting" they called it. It was not his first visit to the Bustanjis, mother and daughter. From time to time he would stop, checking on them, inquiring of their needs. The periodic visits were also an opportunity to be in the company of Sumaiya Bustanji, and now with just the three of them present, he was free to study, without fear of repercussion, the innocent face with its deep black eyes.

Tonight the topic of discussion was life in America. Her apprehensions were normal he said, exchanging the familiar for the strange had been cause for anxiety since the first man climbed over the summit of the first hill. Nevertheless, he warned, America was peopled with an inordinate proportion of demented souls and certain areas were definitely dangerous. The simplest advice he could give her was to never accept rides in automobiles driven by strangers, and to be in her own bed by eleven every night. It may have been a somewhat impudent thing to say to a young, well-bred Arab girl, but he knew her brother would have approved.

When he got home his father had a message for him — "Call Beatrix at the office. She said she'll be waiting." He wondered what was up, she had never called this late.

"Hello, Basil?," she said, picking up the receiver at the first ring.

"Beatrix, how did you know it was me?"

"I didn't. Can't you hear? I said 'Hello, Basil?', that's a question. Enough of philology, what are you doing tonight? I'd like to come over and see you . . . that is if you wouldn't mind."

"Of course I don't mind, but it's Shabbos. Doesn't that mean anything to you?"

"Yeah, it means I run over the first rabbi I see. I'll be over as soon as I lock up here. Goodbye."

She arrived five minutes later attired in a shining, silver body suit that in addition to naughtily showing off the slender body's girlish curves, relieved the imagination of virtually its entire burden. Appended to a thin gold strap draped over a shoulder was a small gold lamé purse. Sensing his amazement, she did a pirouette, self-consciously inquiring, "Am I gold or am I silver? . . . What's the matter, capitalist? Don't communists have the right to be sexy too?"

"It's not that," he said, it's those crazy Jews. They catch you dressed like that, Shabbos or no Shabbos, and they just might unzip you right on the spot." He pointed to the large zipper running up the front of her suit from pelvis to neck.

"Let them try it. What do you think I wear this thing for?" Beatrix opened the purse to reveal a leather-covered blackjack. "I pray for the day one of those Levitical perverts lays his grubby hands on this woman."

"Hey, where'd you get that?," asked Basil, brandishing the blackjack in front of her face.

"Never mind," she said, snatching the weapon back as Lev Primchek entered the room, a stunned expression on his face, seemingly incredulous at finding the Medusa-haired, blackjack-wielding, shining creature in his home. Basil made the introduction, amused at his father's discomfiture confronted by Beatrix's nippled breasts, brazenly visible under their thin silver covering. "How do you do, Mr. Primchek?," exclaimed Beatrix enthusiastically, giving his hand a vigorous shake, "It's always a pleasure meeting the father of the man." "Yes, how do you do," quickly replied Primchek père before retreating to the relative security of the parlor. Beatrix suggested they go someplace where they could talk, someplace where they wouldn't be disturbing his father. "Don't you have a room?," she asked.

"Sure, but it's a bedroom . . ."

"That's fine, let's go there then . . . By the way, how are you tonight?"

"I'm OK, why?"

"Oh, I just want to be sure you don't have a headache or something."

Once inside the room, she reached over and pushed the door shut. Before he could offer the room's single chair, she had kicked off her shoes and sat down hard on his bed, bouncing up and down as if making a test of its sturdiness. "Make yourself at home," he said, still unsure of the motive for the late-night visit. After the Omega Force attack, she had called and they had a long discussion. It seemed logical to follow with the latest in the chronology of events, "Did you read that rubbish on Um Shintyan? You know I know the guy who wrote that, he interviewed me once."

"Rubbish is right," she replied, "so let's not talk about it. As for David Mindell, we're wise to that bastard."

Beatrix ran the fingers of a hand across her forehead and through her hair, asking "May I use your shower?" Basil opened the bedroom door and pointed to the end of the hallway, telling her where to find the towels.

"Who is she?," whispered Lev Primchek, brow furrowed, "Is she planning to stay the night or what?"

"I really have no idea," said Basil, "but don't be put off by appearances. Underneath that flashy facade is really a very nice girl."

"You're telling *me*? I've got eyes too you know. So where's her family? Or did you just find her on the street one day?"

"I haven't met them, but I spoke with her mother over the telephone one day. Judging from the accent, they're definitely upper crust . . ."

"Wait a minute, she's not *Baron* Brunwasser's daughter is she?"

"Who's Baron Brunwasser?"

"You never heard of him? . . . He's a professor at the university, a specialist in laser technology, involved in all this defense research. You see his name all the time as a consultant to the Defense Ministry. If that's the case, you tell her *I* said she's welcome in this house any time. Did you ask her if she's eaten? There's soup and cheese in the refrigerator you know."

"She's not here because she's hungry, but I'll tell her what you said." Hearing the sound of the shower being shut off, he turned to go as his father admonished, "Remember, be a gentleman."

Toweling covered Beatrix's head and body when she returned, giving her the appearance of a slightly damp, Dervish youth. Sitting down on the bed, she unwound the towel wrapped round her head, patting the wet, red-orange tendrils of hair between it. He asked if there was anything he could get her, passing on his father's welcome along with the concern for her present state of hunger. She appreciated the sentiment but asked, "Is food the only thing old people think about? No wonder they grow fat. Did you ever compare the pictures taken of Mao during the thirties to those taken after the triumph of the revolution when food became plentiful? Talk about a capitalist roader. He went revolutionary first class, always on a woman or horse." It was unfair she said, the men of the Eighth Route Army had to go without either for the duration of the war.

Her model was Ho Chi Minh. Although he smoked, he realized it was a bad habit. Otherwise his conduct was exemplary, he lived humbly, eschewed the trappings and privileges of his position and slept on an ordinary woven mat. His whole life was a sacrifice for his people. "Why they cried for three days after he died," she claimed. That was love, "the love of man for man, not the bourgeois drivel that holds the highest good lies in human selfishness and what it achieves, diamonds, monopoly, power over others." As she reminisced about the revolution she had never known, her face seemed to take on a radiance — a shining light. He watched the large blue eyes fill with tears, then, when they could hold no more, release their contents, streaking the white face and adding to her general dampness. Until that moment he had tended to regard her passion for revolution and brotherhood as some kind of adolescent idealism, an eccentric phase, an expression of the "poor little rich girl" syndrome. Now there was no question about the phenomenon before him. She was a saint, as authentic as a Catherine of Siena or a Francis of Assisi or yes, a Ho Chi Minh. He considered himself rather hard-bitten, but her fervor had touched him too.

Beatrix removed the towel that had been wrapped around her torso and piled the bed's pillows against the headboard. "Well," she asked as she sank onto the bed, "am I better with or without clothes?" Like many of her questions, it was purely rhetorical. He was too preoccupied to answer anyway, studying the sylph-like, economical figure offering herself for his examination. With her yarmulke-shaped breasts and sleek shape, she resembled one of those German porcelain figurines of a young nude maiden, portrayed as only the Germans can, in a pose of innocent erotic abandon. "I hope you don't mind," she said, "but I feel sexy when I'm around you." She had taken to his bed like an old friend, as if there were an understanding of inevitability between them.

"Does your mother know where you are?" he asked, trying not to sound too stern.

"Oh yes, I told her," she replied matter-of-factly. "It was something that was going to happen sooner or later so it may as well happen with you, a person she considers 'responsible'. "

"What about your father, what does he think?"

"He's irrelevant. He does what my mother tells him. Any other objections you can think of?"

"One. What does Beatrix think?"

"I think I'm here to act as your mistress," she declared, raising herself to a sitting position, "or at least one of your mistresses. I hope you don't expect me to utter some drivel about love and devotion, I really thought your ego was stronger than that. Let's understand each other — I want a friendship based on mutual respect and recognition, freely entered into, between comrades . . . I would imagine you have a large libido, let us not complicate matters by injecting bourgeois norms and expectations. Personally, I'll be expecting but one thing from you, and that's desire, anything else is superfluous.

"Of course," she added reflectively, "it goes without saying that I wouldn't be here if I didn't like you."

"You've convinced me," said Basil, rising from his chair, "but then it goes without saying that I didn't need much convincing."

He remembered her slender arms reaching for him when he eased onto the bed, holding him, her body tensed against his, vibrating with excitement. How she climbed over him dropping kisses on his eyes and lips, straddling him with her legs, rubbing her body against his. He put an ear against her bosom where he thought her heart might be, listening to the excited beating while his fingers gripped her thighs and twiddled the moist loins. He was pulling her up but her inexperience told as she held on, not knowing to let go. Only minutes before she claimed to have read a spate of books on the subject. "Sex was a very simple proposition," she had declared, "you set up a duality — male, female — and apply friction . . . Romantic love was an over-elaborated hoax, a contradiction arising from the Christian confusion over love . . ."

She was still holding onto him when the morning sun entered the room dancing over their eyes. Ayesha was in the kitchen when they came out, standing ready to make them an omelette for breakfast. She was happy to meet his "sweetheart" she said, telling him to bring her for dinner soon. Beatrix spoke Arabic to Ayesha, asking her how long she had been working for the Primcheks and whether she thought she was "underpaid". Ayesha replied in Hebrew — with her employer present, it was the polite and loyal thing to do. *"Shawtra"* (clever), she remarked to Basil, referring to Beatrix. It was an Arabic word she used frequently, usually approvingly, to describe successful people. Sometimes the word carried a connotation of "devilishly clever," as when she would shake her head ruefully and say the Jews were *"shawtreen"*.

After breakfast he walked her to her car. She wore the same silver body suit she came in, declaring it "sheer conspicuous consumption" not to wear an outfit two or three days in succession. "I could wear this all week," she said, "but it's my Shabbos best." She was playing with the fingers of his left hand, pulling and pushing on them as one would the teats of a cow. As they walked, people on the street, his neighbors, looked at them, some dubiously. "Embarrassed?," she asked.

"No," he answered, perhaps too quickly, "what's there to be embarrassed about?"

"That's good, because those fools probably think I'm your whore. And that's exactly what I want them to think!"

"Wait a minute," he said, "I thought you wanted to be my mistress?"

"To you, my lover, I'm your mistress, your *compañera*. To them, the stupid busybodies, I'm your whore. Good for them! They'll have something to talk about now, somebody to talk about — *you* . . . Think you can stand up under the gossip, or will you use it as an excuse to dump me now that you've gone and ruined me?," she joked, getting into her car, her laughter emphasizing the remark's playful intent.

"I would never dump you, Beatrix," he said. Why he said it he wasn't sure, except that he thought the remark would be a negative enough expression of his feelings to endure any ridicule she might attach to it. But her eyes immediately bleared and she was kissing his hand and wetting it with tears simultaneously. She would come to him anytime, he only need call. She was "loyal" she affirmed, her eyes gazing up adoringly, "as all comrades must be."

43

He was met at the gate of the compound by a full-bearded ecclesiastic in black cassock. Speaking in English, the man introduced himself as "Brother Yeprem, secretary to his Excellency, Patriarch Kerkor. His Excellency was at prayer" reported Brother Yeprem as he led Basil through the

compound and into the building that was the living and
"working" quarters of the Armenian Patriarchate of Jerusalem, "but he is expecting you and will not be long."
Yeprem showed Basil into a long, gloomy, windowless room
illuminated by large beeswax candles set in footed brass
candelabra. Hanging on the room's walls were icons of every
imaginable size and composition. Some, of gold, framed
exquisite painted miniatures of the Christ. Others, decorated
with satiny tassels, were of silver, and contained effigies of
the Madonna and Child as well as various saints. The icons
were part of the Patriarchate's collection, many dating back
hundreds of years to Armenia itself. The room was the
Patriarch's "refugium", serving as a place of prayer and
contemplation for his Excellency. At times important visitors
were received in the room said Yeprem, pointing to a small
circle of chairs surrounding a silver and brass tray chased in
Arabesque, resting on platform legs. "You may sit here and
wait, his Excellency will be with you shortly."

The same elements that made the room so right for
veneration — the flickering candles, the fragrant if somewhat
cloying scent of burning incense — also made it suitable as a
chambre d'assignation. There had been rumors concerning the
Patriarchate, "orgiastic" rumors. Of course, no one had
come forward with any evidence to support the allegations.
Nevertheless, the rumors persisted, sex and scandal being
associated with celibate churchmen in people's minds, as if
they had always doubted that normal, ostensibly virile men,
would give up sex for something as vague and unknowable
as a diety. One didn't know what to believe, priests had
their passions too, a modern city, even one billed as "holy",
was perhaps an unfair place to test their powers of mortification. The Church had long since conceded the right of
the commercial sector to exploit the power of sex in the
marketplace. It would be an exceptional priest who never
saw an ad for lingerie, or a film showing a shot of a pair of
breasts, however fleeting. He studied the satiny pile of the

room's rug, its dark blues and reds predominating, amusing himself by speculating on the most likely staging area for sin. If the Vatican could have its "apartments", the Patriarchate could have its "refugium".

When he looked up he saw that the Patriarch, a stubby, sad-eyed man, had entered and was standing facing him, an elaborate silver and ebony shepherd's crook in hand. He stood up in place, unsure of the strictures of patriarchal protocol. As a Jew, he knew he wasn't expected to kiss the fellow's ring. Exhibiting that kind of servile ecumenism was hardly likely to influence a prelate in so grave a matter as peddling a prime piece of property. "Greetings, my son, may the peace of God be upon you," declared Patriarch Kerkor in deliberate bass tones. "Please," he said, indicating to one of the chairs positioned around the silver and brass tray. A black, tent-like headpiece covered the cleric's head and shoulders. Dangling above his waist, suspended from a chain around his neck, was a large, amethyst-studded, silver crucifix. "Many from your people visit us," said Kerkor, seating himself opposite Basil, "we welcome them as sincere friends and spiritual compatriots, we are all equal before the throne of God . . . And now I must thank you for the excellent presentation you have sent us detailing your organization's objections to the proposed use of the property. Indeed, it was so clear, that you must forgive me if I fail to burden you with questions concerning the points expressed, you are as excellent an advocate as you are an architect. I can assure you that, in our humble way, we shall give your statement every consideration. The sale of our property is something we have contemplated only after long and prayerful deliberation. Like yourselves, we Armenians are a people dispersed. Not so long ago we possessed a country, a poor country, yet nonetheless a country. Now we thank God for the little we have. Our existence here in Jerusalem is at the sufferance of God and the authorities. The Lord had been generous by providing us with this house, a truly magnificent mansion. Unfortunately, such magnificence requires upkeep, maintenance. As an architect you can readily appreciate the necessity and expense . . . The donations of the pilgrims and tourists who visi here do not even begin to meet our expense . . . " Kerkor concluded his litany of poverty by reiterating his assurance that if, after exhausting all other avenues, it is decided that the property must be sold, it shall only be "after long and prayerful consideration. We are in God's hands," he said, holding his palms upwards. Then, striking the floor thrice with his shepherd's crook, he ordered a bowing servant to bring them coffee. In Middle Eastern negotiations, if nothing else, one got coffee.

The meeting's final minutes were taken up by Patriarch Kerkor's expounding upon the historic similarities shared by the Armenian and Jewish peoples, "Did you know, my son, that the term 'genocide' was inspired by our own tragedy at the hands of the Moslems in the early years of the century? . . . Yes, 'Armenocide', one and one half millions expired in the massacres and marches. Next to the Holocaust it is the greatest slaughter in history . . ." It was another lost cause.

His father was late in arriving home that night. The frustration from his morning meeting with the Patriarch needed a release. Three and one-half percent was not a large figure in absolute terms, yet when measured against the multiple millions the Old City project promised to garner its investors, the interest was substantial. "Old City Enterprises" they called themselves, his father being one of about a score of investors who stood to gain from the project's completion. He had discovered the corporation papers in the Bureau of Lands and Construction while preparing the critique. Land deals were big business in Israel. People got rich from them, some virtually overnight. As usual, possessing good connections in government was a big help.

He heard the front door open, then shut. He waited until his father came into the kitchen, he wanted to see the expression on his face when he mentioned the three and one-half percent. "Trouble counting your money again?," he asked.

"No, one of the registers broke down and I couldn't get a repairman to come out. Computers! Better I should have kept the old manual registers."

"God," Basil exclaimed, "it must be hell to be rich, to have so much money one has to buy the latest in technological gimmickry, and invest in stews of corruption like 'Old City Enterprises'. "

Lev Primchek hesitated, he knew he was being set up for a fall. "How did you find out?," he asked.

"The angel Gabriel told me! Perhaps I shouldn't tell you this, but I doubt if it would matter." He handed his father a copy of the critique submitted to the Patriarch. "I met with the Patriarch today. If he's any indication, the only issue holding this thing up is greed — he wants more than you want to pay. So both of you are presently playing the waiting game . . ."

"Negotiation is the soul of business, my boy," said Primchek père, attempting to make light of the matter. "By the way, this Patrimoine Architectural, that's not something Baron Brunwasser's daughter got you into is it? It sounds like something she would have a hand in . . . "

"And an ass too!," exclaimed Basil indignantly, "I don't want to hear that pussy-whipped crap anymore! For your information, Partimoine Architectural is primarily an association for architects. I joined it after meeting one of its French organizers. Of course, like a lot of us, she's against the project, she's got good taste too. You know some of those buildings are *waqf* property, don't you?"

"So now you're a pious Muslim, are you? Well you ought to go to one of their countries . . . Do what you're doing here. Go ahead! Why they'd have your ass in a sling so fast you wouldn't know what hit you. You look at someone the wrong way there and you're dead. At least here you're free to talk, oppose the government, without having to fear someone's going to break down the door at three in the morning. Of course, such activity has its price — but you don't pay for it with your life. Beatrix . . . you can't expect to get away with what she does, she's just a kid. In a few years she'll be married and settled down and they'll have forgotten all about her. Other youngsters will be giving them fits then.

"Listen, I'm your father. Who do you think is going to get all this when I'm gone? When my father died I was lucky if he had a pair of shoes to leave me. Wake up. Leave saving the world to the Messiah, that's what He's for."

44

He sent off the Bustanji women on a British Overseas Airway jet, the lesser of available evils. El Al flew direct to New York, but like the flight, the connection with the oppressor was too direct, whereas the British were at least once removed. If, considering the country of destination — the United States — his respect for historical responsibility seemed an exercise in hypocrisy, it was. Nevertheless, people's sensibilities demanded it. He knew the Bustanjis would be more comfortable travelling with the British. They didn't say as much, but then they didn't have to.

The stop at London's Heathrow airport would allow them to say they had been in England, rather a questionable milestone except for the fact that the concept always reminded him of the English girl he had met and won in Jerusalem. He had noticed her sitting at an outdoor cafe near the Wailing Wall. She had come up from Eilat in tandem with her "mate", a girlfriend from her hometown of Leeds. Over-exposure to the hot Gulf sun had left them looking like a pair of cooked lobsters. Yet, to his eyes, the light blonde hair and white cottons gave them the appearance of angels, lovely pink angels. They had seen him looking at them and waved to him to join them. Margaret Ramsey — he remembered her name, the big, soft, white ass and floppy breasts roasted pink almost down to the nipples. She was soft and red and hot all over, and when he lay on top of her he sunk into her embrace like unto a bog. She had come to Israel "on holiday" to enjoy the sun and beaches and "have a good time", blissfully ignorant of England's relation to Palestine. To her, Palestine was a bit like Egypt, Englishmen had been there at one time or another. He was sure she had never heard of the Balfour Declaration, or even of the man it was named after, the Lord and Prime Minister. Even if she had, it wouldn't have meant the slightest to her. The evil done by her country lives after, yet there was no way to associate her with the remote and calculating men whose fiat condemned the region to a perpetuity of strife. Of that infamous history she knew nothing. She was an innocent abroad, taking her pleasure where and when she found it, leaving behind at least one memorial to her good works.

He switched on his car radio but was too late to catch the ten o'clock news. A commentary was playing — " . . . Major Nafsi's calling of the conference was another crude attempt to lay down the law to his Lebanese allies. Those not yet persuaded of the wisdom of capitulation to the Major can take note of the recent brutal assassinations of Joseph Kasrawan and Adil Deeb, leaders of . . ." Although the voice had a strong Russian brogue, it projected confidently. It was describing Nafsi's invitation to the various Lebanese factions to gather in Damascus for an attempt at unity. " . . . a preview of what lies in store for the Lebanon

406

should Syria's bloody regime ever establish itself in that unhappy land. In a two hour diatribe to the dragooned delegates, Nafsi decried 'the vipers at our breast' and 'the black collaborators of imperialism-Zionism', threatening his captive audience with a Syrian style damnation. These examples, my friends, are more than typical excesses of Arab rhetoric, they are distinct Nafsian code words for the moderate Arab governments, including for a starter, Jordan and Iraq. While Israel may have no present interest in a war between Iraq and Syria (what, after all, is the meaning of the strange alliance between Syria and Iran, an alliance of political opposites?), there can be no question that a Syrian grab for Jordan would trigger our immediate retaliation. Israel could not permit the establishment in Jordan of a hostile regime, and that means one allied with, or under the domination of either Syria or Iran. It would be well for Major Nafsi to realize that in Israel he is dealing with the spirit of a people reborn, a people whose defense forces have proven their strategic, technical, and yes, spiritual and moral superiority over the Arab enemy time and again. The Major may want to ponder the fact that this time the IDF may not just stand by and watch the Syrians turn tail and run. This time we may just pursue them to Damascus and beyond, in the process defanging the Syrian dog once and for all. Syrian people, Lebanese people, in all humanity I must ask you . . . who appointed this man to lead you in a 'holy war'? The answer is clear, the major's repeated trips to Moscow prove that. Perhaps an Israeli expedition into Lebanon this summer will give this Kremlin puppet's Lebanese thugs a needed lesson in civility. Indeed, if the Major is watching at that time, and we hope he will be, he may just decide that challenging Israel is definitely not his meat . . . This is Anton Wassilinsky, and that's my point of view."

He thought he recognized the voice — Anton Wassilinsky, the Russian *emigré* poet. Every so often one or two

of his poems "found their way" into a newspaper or magazine. The Russian *emigré* community was top-heavy with
poets and writers, Jews abused and misunderstood in their
native land. Indeed, it was said that disgruntled dancers and
musicians defected — mainly to the US and Europe —
while poets immigrated. It was as if they had all answered
the same ad, reading, "Wanted: Poet. Prefer anti-communist
but any Jew will do." Wassilinsky had respectable credentials
— he had done graduate work in Siberia under unusually
trying conditions. So when he finally landed in Israel people
celebrated, another son had come home, a famous and courageous son. He was a hero, people looked to him for
inspiration, a good word, demanded he receive the Nobel
Prize, vied for his allegiance. But Wassilinsky was coy, a
party affiliation and he would be just one more strident
advocate of this or that party line. No, Wassilinsky was a
pure soul, beholden to no man, a symbol of the triumph of
the Jewish spirit over Russian communist adversity. He
answered to a higher call, the sighs and moans of his
brethren in Russia yearning to be free. In attacking
Moscow's man in Damascus, he was acting on a grudge
formed in his mother's womb.

He let two weeks go by before moving into the Bustanji house. He made no attempt to rent the house, he had
intended all along to take it for his own. Khalil Bustanji had
asked that it be rented to a "reliable tenant" and so it had.
Who indeed was more reliable than himself? He arrived at a
rental figure by adding a twenty percent premium to
comparable rentals. A letter to his New York bank
instructed that a draft in the amount of three months rent be
sent to Iowa.

He heard the news of the killings from the radio — the
pair of "prominent Arab businessmen", one found strangled
in the back of his store, the other in a pool of blood in the
kitchen of his restaurant. Police, said the announcer, had no

leads in the murders of "Bashir Jalajil, 61, and Faris Aoun 47, both from leading Christian Arab families . . ." He wasn't glad to hear of the killings, but then he wasn't exactly sad either. Both men left the predictable number of widows and children, Aoun's youngest child was not yet six months old. Theft had been tentatively ruled out as a motive the broadcast said, nothing was missing from the persons or property of the two victims. Police were operating on the theory the killings involved an as yet unidentified band of Islamic fundamentalists bent on terrorizing Christians, and "by necessity, Jews also."

Later that afternoon he asked Olga whether she had heard about the killings. "Yes," she said unconcernedly. Then, with a look bordering on contempt, she asked, "Weren't they part of the group that forced you out of your office?"

"That's right," he replied, "the ringleaders."

Olga resumed studying the papers on her desk, "I wouldn't give it another thought," she said.

The following day on the way to their reserve meeting Amon Amitai broached the subject. He had heard it from a friend who worked in the medical examiner's office he said, "The one whose throat was cut — his skull was also fractured, by a blow from a blunt instrument. But the one that was strangled — his neck was wrung like a chicken's, the vertebra were actually *crushed*. The guy who killed him must have had the strength of an ape in his hands!"

There had been a perceptible change in the way people in the neighborhood treated him. When he walked into a store or café the merchants — especially the merchants — it seemed as if they couldn't do enough for him. They were smart, it didn't take them long to get the message, they could hear and see too. The two funerals had been staggered in time to allow the community to pay its last respects to both. Retribution had come. They hadn't expected it but arrogance seldom did, that was its nature. Where it came

409

from they didn't know, but they had their suspicions — well-founded ones. One thing they did know was that they didn't want to be next. So they did what most people did when faced with the threat of the unknown, they began propitiating the possible sources of danger, trying to "be nice", striving for rehabilitation. Their consciences were guilty, they knew they had stood by, or worse, gone along with the conspiracy to kowtow to the demands of the Jewish extremists. The others, the actual organizers of the capitulation, the ones who with their votes and conspiracies had sanctioned it — they had more than guilty consciences, they were traitors, traitors to the memory of a martyr, to their brothers, to themselves. They deserved to die.

Someone had given him the name, who, he didn't know, but it wasn't long before people in the quarter were addressing him as "Basil Bey", or as they were wont to say, "Bawzil Bey". The title was only an honorary one, but it was uttered out of genuine respect, a respect born from an appreciation that he and the retribution were connected, if only remotely. Some people avoided him, not wanting to get too close, he represented danger. Others were proud, proud of his presence in the community, proud of what had happened. They remembered Aziz Bustanji.

45

The divisions that had been poised on the northern border for the last week crossed over into Lebanon that morning. The government had been uncharacteristically candid about the twenty-two dead suffered in the ambush, this

410

time its purposes better served by a full and truthful accounting. There had been too many funerals of military personnel lately, all of them couldn't be accident victims, driving conditions were not *that* hazardous in Lebanon. The news photographs of the blanket-covered bodies lined up waiting for evacuation were emotionally captioned. "VENGEANCE!," one read simply. The funerals — the rabbis with their prayer books, the sobbing mothers and mates — played well on television. The time for retaliation had come. Only this was more than retaliation, this was war.

The orders were to report to his unit in the morning. The unit's mission was to function as a rear guard, protecting supply lines and preventing infiltration. It was dangerous, but appreciably less so than being at the front with the advancing regulars. He had told Olga he expected to be called up earlier this year — but for training, not war. He opted for a telephonic good-bye — he hated scenes — catching Olga as she was leaving for piano practice. "I hope you're not calling in regard to the invasion," she said, "it was only announced at five."

"Yeah, that's it," he said. "My unit leaves for Lebanon tomorrow . . ." He paused, waiting for her reaction.

"I expected something like this. But don't worry, we'll follow your instructions while you're gone, I'll make sure of that. You just remember to be careful and not do anything foolish. Do you hear?"

"Don't worry," he replied, "I'll be keeping a very low profile."

"Well, I'll say good-bye then. Good luck, Basil."

"Thanks. Good-bye, Olga." He waited until he heard the click of her telephone before hanging up. The farewell had been very low key, almost as if he were going on a hunting trip. Her manner left him feeling slightly let down, it was so accepting, so rational. In that respect, he told himself, they were alike. She was not one for scenes either.

He had one more call to make. "Do you want me to

come over?," she asked straight off. It was a hot night and the thought was unavoidable — it could be his last. At almost any other time he would have said "yes", but he knew what he was about to say would not go well with her, "You heard the news didn't you?"

"Of course I heard it," she replied. "Another war, the pay-off for the Americans. What did you expect, a peace offensive?"

"No, but I wanted to tell you . . . my unit has been called up. I have to leave tomorrow morning."

"You're not going?," she exclaimed, incredulous.

"I'm afraid I'll have to. But don't . . ."

"What do you mean, you 'have to'? You don't 'have to' at all! None of the comrades are going. Hundreds of others are resisting. You're no different."

"O but I am, Beatrix. I don't want to go to jail. But I promise you this — I won't fire my weapon. How's that?"

"Suppose you're fired at. What will you do then?"

"I'll surrender. The Arabs like Israeli prisoners. We make good hostages."

"Nafsi and the Iranians don't take hostages. You saw what they did to Omega Force."

"That's because the Amercians are gung-ho. Actually, we're just a bunch of cowards. Most of us will be looking for the nearest hole in the event of an attack"

"Well turn your guns on your officers then if you're such a coward! They're the ones who got you into this! They're the class criminals!"

She was shouting, there was no use reasoning with her. "You're becoming hysterical, I better say good-bye . . ."

"Hysterical, eh? Yes, say good-bye, you do that." She was speaking calmly now, deliberately, "Just remember, if you get yourself killed, I'm not mourning. And you better find someone else to push your wheelchair if you come back in pieces, because you're no hero, you're a *bum*!"

"Well OK, Beatrix, I'm sorry. Good-bye." He was

fortunate to have settled the matter over the telephone. Had she come over, it would have been very messy. She would have never let him go.

He left the house early the next morning under cover of darkness, not wanting his neighbors to see him in battle array. It was still dark when he arrived at Amon Amitai's apartment a half hour before the appointed time. Adjusting the seat, he lay back for some additional sleep.

He was awakened by the sound of Amon's knuckles rapping on the car window. Amon was also tired, but not from early rising. Claiming to have spent most of the night "in the saddle", he planned to catch up on his sleep on the bus ride to Lebanon. "See Lebanon and die," he declared before falling asleep almost immediately. Bernard and Yossi, the other car pool members, were too apprehensive to do much sleeping. Their concern was the Syrian Army, now hugely augmented by the best and latest the Russians had to offer, and, of course, the endless Iranian reserves. The invasion was too risky they said, the leadership should have stayed with the policy of working through local allies and mercenaries, to move into Lebanon in force was provocative and destabilizing. The government's warning to Syria not to intervene, threatening the usual "grave consequences", was a hollow one, it would take a general mobilization to counter a Syrian thrust, in the interim, Israeli troops in Lebanon could be cut off and overrun. Syria had the capability to move armor and men speedily and efficiently now, its all-weather maneuvers demonstrated that. The latest issue of *Paynes Military Digest* carried an article on the "revolution" effected in Syrian military capability subsequent to Nafsi's seizure of power. In fact, added Bernard ominously, Lumi Fisch had gone so far as to submit that only a "nuclear potential" would be adequate to compensate for the "overwhelming Moslem superiority in bodies." It was either that or "massive American aid", perhaps even "military coordination". As the car entered the military compound, the

413

discussion of future war ended, present duty supervening.

A line of trucks was waiting to take them to Lebanon, all available buses were taken. Of course it was a disappointment, the trucks' incessant rocking and hard bench seating, aggravated by the steady roar from the powerful truck engines, made sleeping nigh impossible. Conversation, when it did occur, consisted mostly of speculation on the duration of the stay in Lebanon. Most believed a long war was as unlikely as it was inconceivable, the incursions had developed a rationale of their own. Lebanon was Israel's Northwest Frontier, the terrorists the modern equivalent of the wild Pathan tribesmen perennially threatening Her Majesty's peace. Once a Hollywood warhorse, the theme inspired films celebrating duty, honor, country; films wherein as a reward for bravery, dashing captains were frequently assured the hand of the virginal daughter or niece of a commandant or governor. It was a simpler age then, permitting an uncritical acceptance of good and evil, an age when the relatively modern moral accretions of self-determination and racism weighed little, if at all, upon the popular conscience, an age when gentry danced the waltz and Englishmen literally left partners gasping on ballroom floors to ride off against a savage enemy. As the political and moral climate changed, the film industry adapted, in the beginning reluctantly, then ambiguously, eventually conceding the humanity of formerly unredeemed savages. You didn't have to be a John Ford or Michael Curtiz to realize that the hora would never take the place of the waltz, and that Israel's cosmopolitan and sometimes dwarfish stock would never be Englishmen. Indeed, could anyone imagine David Ben-Gurion on a horse, even a white horse? Or Menachem Begin on a pony?

The driver was working the truck's horn, they had just crossed over the border into Lebanon. Framed by the truck's caparison, he watched the dun-colored hills of the Galilee recede, becoming the dun-colored hills of Lebanon. "The Lebanon", the land that refused to be a nation, reverting to the rule of warlords and bandits. Nonetheless, he added it to his list of countries, seven now. Not many to be sure, but in the old days, the days prior to universal conscription, some never left the village. But here the distance involved was limited, merely a crossing of borders. No one wanted to go much farther, yet they were leaving it to the Syrians to "exercise restraint", a restraint their own government habitually and chronically ignored.

The convoy halted for lunch along a ridge overlooking one of the numerous Shiite villages in the area. The sun was at its highest, the time of day when people fled indoors to escape the summer's heat. Except for the cars huddled next to buildings and the television aerials projecting from roofs, it could have been ages ago, so little had the physical conditions of these villages changed. It was a peaceful view, not even the twittering of a bird disturbing the desolate silence of the undulating panorama.

Passing through some of the villages brought back memories, previous occupation duty, the months of patrolling Hebron, Bethlehem, and other West Bank towns and villages. There were the same sullen, blank faces, now standing in clusters by the side of the road. The children, the ever-present children, seemingly unmindful of the clouds of dust whirled up by the heavy tires as the trucks speeded through the villages. Convoys took the villages at a fast clip. One never knew when some military prodigy, perhaps a child of ten or twelve, might poke an RPG launcher out a window, and let fly a round with devastating consequences.

The first waves of troops had been charged with the duty of "sanitizing" villages near the road. Demolished houses were very much in evidence along the way, punishment for possessing weapons or suspicious persons. It was obvious each destroyed house could not have held an arms cache, there were too many. However, there was no shortage of suspects, busloads of bound and blindfolded Arabs passed them going south. This time, they said, there would be no single, large concentration camp for detainees, Ansar, a camp established by Israel during its '82 invasion, had created too many "administrative problems". The removal and isolation of dangerous and potentially dangerous individuals from the theater of operations, an activity of military intelligence, had been carried out with excessive zeal — the number of detainees quickly exceeding the camp's capacity. A situation developed where the most dedicated and hardened terrorist elements formed cells within the camp itself, the cells imposing their own rude justice and indoctrinating inmates with extremist ideology. Moreover, the sanitary situation was such that even camp guards sought out journalists to give vent to their disgust. Eventually, (when from a military perspective the camp could no longer be justified), it was deactivated. Jews, so it was said, were no good for the concentration camp business. The new plan was to establish a series of autonomous "field detention centers" where suspects could be processed quickly and efficiently, then segregated according to their level of dangerousness. Proponents of the plan were confident the revised procedures would eliminate the former defects, resulting in more humane conditions of detention.

He witnessed his first casualties on the third day. They were in the process of being loaded into helicopters for evacuation to Israel after treatment at a field hospital. A land mine had removed one man's foot, two others were badly shot up by automatic weapons' fire. After an initial period of relative quiescence, the incidence of guerrilla attacks had risen dramatically. Many were phantom in nature, like the remotely detonated roadside blasts that in combination with land mines, took such a high toll of men and nerves. It was another instance of oppression producing its nemesis — every invasion enhancing the level of resistance. The enemy was better armed, better trained, better motivated. The increased levels of terrorist competence prompting an order from on high that henceforth, reserve units were to carry out "anti-infiltration" and "search and destroy" patrols.

They were organized into eight-man squads and dropped off on the road at dusk. Each squad was responsible for three to four kilometers of roadway per night. The importance of keeping in contact with adjoining squads was strongly emphasized, there had been an accident in another sector where two squads opened fire on each other. But most shooting involved "pre-emptive fire", the practice of raking roadside areas with automatic weapons to discourage ambushes. Although indiscriminate and wasteful, it probably saved lives. Likely hiding places, such as ravines and orchards, provoked most of the fusillades. At other times, the movement of domestic animals, or even birds, touched off one-sided firefights.

He and Amon walked side by side lagging behind the others. When they reached the end of their allotted section of roadway, they were to turn around and go back. He still hadn't fired his gun. That way, he told Amon, he wouldn't have to clean it. In the unlikely event they should come under attack, he planned to hit the dirt and remain there until the all clear was given. There were "millions of Arabs", it made no sense to kill them, particularly on their own land.

It was almost dawn and his feet were tired from treading the hard asphalt. Suddenly the morning stillness was rent by the staccato reports of Uzis, followed by shouts of "Get down! Get down!" He and Amon almost collided getting prone under the slope of a hill. From above came a loud bawling sound, the cry of an animal in distress. "It's alright," yelled a voice down the road, "I think we got a cow." When they reached the creature, a big, brown calf, it was lying on its side, bawling pathetically, its gentle eyes glistening with shock and pain, rib cage shuddering as its mouth slowly opened and closed instinctively seeking air for its now useless lungs. "Give me that fucking gun!," cried

417

Basil to Israel Ozenk, the one responsible. Snatching the Uzi from Ozenk's hand and ordering the others to stand back, he placed a well-aimed shot into the back of the calf's head. "What an executioner!," exclaimed Amon, "I didn't think you had it in you." "Yeah," said Ozenk with relief, "the thing was getting to me."

"Now you know how it feels," said Basil, handing back the Uzi and looking down at the lifeless creature at his feet, blood trickling from its mouth, "You should hope an Arab puts a bullet between your eyes when you're *in extremis*." He was serious, he had never killed an animal in his life, not even a chicken, and what he had done did not leave him with a good feeling. How much different was it, he wondered, to kill a human?

He saw more than one dead body in the next few days, Arab and Jew. The most gruesome sight was the pair of cars run over by IDF tanks, crushed nearly flat. There were four Arabs in one and two in the other, but he couldn't bring himself to verify the reported body count in the heaps of broken glass, twisted metal, and gore. The Arabs were caught trying to escape a counter-terrorist operation. They were suspected of being the same terrorists who ambushed and killed three from an army patrol the day before.

As told, the story didn't make sense. Terrorists would hardly have tried to run a gauntlet of Israeli tanks and troops in two small cars. The cars were left in sight of the village they had come from. Situated on a rise some two hundred and fifty meters away, the village's numerous demolished buildings indicated an IDF visitation. Again the story was that two large arms caches were found, RPGs, grenade launchers, explosives, detonators, enough Kalashnikov ammunition "to supply a battalion". The day before Captain Klug had given the unit one of his pep-talks, telling them they were up against a "fanatic enemy" who wouldn't be satisfied until "the last Jew in Israel was cold and dead", meanwhile cautioning them to forget what they saw, "because war was never pretty and anybody who tells you it is is a fool or a fascist." Israelis were a peace-loving people he declared, that is until they were pushed to the wall . . . "then look out!"

He had thought of sending postcards to his father and Olga. But after what he had seen, writing postcards would have been absurd. There was no use sending Beatrix anything, even if he could write what he felt. Klug may have been right in telling them to forget what they saw. People at home didn't want to hear about army atrocities, their concerns were victory and survival. It was immaterial how these were achieved, the less they knew the better. Nothing should trouble their patriotic asses.

The invasion was in its second week with still no response from the Syrians. In some areas the two armies were close enough to be within shouting range. It was a wary distance, neither adversary willing to be the first to provoke the other. Some pointed to the stand-off and said it proved the Syrians paper tigers. Others gave thanks for another day without the wider war they feared. Rumor had the Americans urging an Israeli drive to Baalbek and beyond. The Americans had nothing to lose. But the Israelis, closer to the action, knew not to push too far. Mounting a large counter-terrorism operation within sight of Syrian positions was a risky proposition, yet there were always those for whom going to the brink exercised a fatal attraction. So the operation was announced as a "reprisal" for the "approximately ten to twenty casualties" suffered by an engineering unit in a night attack earlier that morning. The terrorists had escaped, but army dogs had followed the spoor to the vicinity of the village where a part of Basil's unit was detailed. The others had been ordered to comb the countryside for the missing arms caches, the furniture and mattresses strewn in the village's dusty and rutted lanes evidence of an earlier, futile, house-to-house search.

In forming up he noticed Klug and his adjutant conferring with two men in a jeep, one of whom bore a familiar red beard. It was Eliezar Ben-Judah. He waited for Ben-Judah to show some sign of recognition, he was looking directly at him. But apparently other matters occupied the myopic Ben-Judah. In short order the conversation ended, with Ben-Judah's jeep pulling away, followed by elements of the original attacking force, the ones responsible for the broken china and splintered furniture lying in front of the houses.

Klug had his orders now. They were there, he said, to persuade the inhabitants of the village to be more forthcoming concerning the involvement of some of their numbers in the attack. Military Intelligence had interrogated the villagers for much of the morning, none were willing to talk. To induce cooperation, women and children were to be confined to their houses and the men held outside. Klug pointed to the makeshift compound surrounded by concertina wire, where about forty to fifty adolescent and adult males squatted, hands on head. Some rocked back and forth, as in prayer. Others shifted their feet, trying to distribute the pain. The sun was hot said an Arabic-speaking reservist, pointing to its position in the sky, "maybe it will make some of you grow smarter." They would stay put until the guilty came forward.

He hated these collective punishment ordeals. "Military Intelligence" should have had more sense than to saddle a reserve unit with such rotten duty. Judging from the faces of the other guards it was obvious they didn't like it either, particularly those squinting in the sun, the ones too cowardly or dumb to seek shade. Seeing a wooden chair lying in the dirt, he picked it up, set it against a shaded section of wall and sat down. His resourcefulness brought an immediate protest from two of the others, "The Captain better not see you like that," they warned. "The 'Captain' can kiss my royal ass," said Basil, "It's bad enough punishing them without punishing ourselves."

They had emptied one of the village's larger houses of tenants and converted it into a temporary interrogation center. By some process of selection, individual Arabs were removed from the barbed wire corral and taken into the house for further interrogation. Although they saw him sitting, they chose to ignore it. Meanwhile, the Arabs were showing the first signs of thirst, eyeing the guards as they drank from canteens. It was all part of the process.

They called out the next batch of Arabs — all youngsters — by name, "Mohammed and Rashid Silhawny, Feisal Dibashi". He suspected the youths were brothers or sons of the Arabs previously selected for questioning, Klug trying some "applied psychology" scheme hoping to exploit the family relationship. Yet if the goons from Military Intelligence could not wring information from the villagers in a morning of effort, Klug was unlikely to either, even with the persuaders of sun and thirst. After about an hour the youths were led back, one by one, to rejoin their brothers under the sun, to be followed shortly thereafter by the adults.

It was three o'clock and his wall, now no longer in the shade, was as uncomfortably hot as any place else. He drank his water out of sight of the Arabs squatting on the hard-baked dirt. They were feeling the heat more acutely now, some pointing forlornly to their mouths, eliciting cries of *"Mamnu! Mamnu!"* (Forbidden! Forbidden!) from the guards. One Arab, a stubble-faced old man, had abandoned the required squat and was sitting on the ground, legs extended, supporting himself with his elbows. Just then Basil saw Klug and his staff approach, their interrogation initiative stillborn. When Klug saw the old Arab not squatting, he exploded. This wasn't a tea party, he yelled, his face reddening, Israeli soldiers had been killed by these people. So the old man had a bad back? That was the object, everyone should have a bad back. "What's the matter, *khatyar* (old man), getting tired? Maybe you feel like talking now?",

421

shouted Klug, angrily striding over to the old man and kicking him in the back. "Where is your great Nafsi now, *khatyar?*," demanded Klug, planting a boot on the Arab's neck, "Where is your great Nafsi *now?*"

There was to be no exception. Young or old, the Arabs were to keep squatting. Klug detailed a lieutenant and sergeant to supervise compliance with the order. "Your sympathy is misplaced," shouted an irate Klug at the guards, reiterating that, "Israeli soldiers were killed by these people!"

He kept an eye on Klug, watching him as he stood by the communications jeep, laughing and conversing with his staff. It was a longshot, but he was looking for a chance to catch him alone. Meanwhile, inside their barbed enclosure the Arabs squatted, their faces skewed with pain. The heat from the sun had abated somewhat, but when night came they would illuminate the enclosure with floodlights. Klug was not giving up, Military Intelligence was expecting that information.

Finally, he had his chance. While the mess truck was ladling out the evening meal — beef stew served with a hunk of rye bread and coffee — he saw Klug set his tray down and walk toward the back of the village, to the so-called "pissing wall". He followed, taking a parallel route, one that led between two houses. It was perfect, Klug alone at the wall, the buildings concealing them from view. He caught him as he was zipping up. In an instant he was on top of him, his knee in his back, his hands around the bony skull, pushing the face into the dirt. "You going to call off your interrogation, Yahoodi, or will they find you here, face down in a Lebanese latrine?" His hand grabbed the short-clipped blond hair and jerked up, Klug was spitting dirt from his mouth and lips. He pushed the face down into the dirt again, harder, demanding, "Make up your mind, Yahoodi, I can't wait all night, you have two seconds." He jerked the head up, there was blood on Klug's lips, "Alright," whimpered Klug, "Alright." He grabbed Klug's collar and pulled him up, "You fell, you understand? You fell." Klug nodded meekly. "Next time, I'll kill you!"

He was among the first to go to Klug's aid when the unfortunate captain stumbled back to the mess area set up between the trucks. He made sure Klug saw him standing close by, his finger on the trigger of his Uzi. Of course, they were surprised to see their captain in such a deplorable condition, lips and nose swollen and bloodied. But they were even more surprised when he ordered that the Arabs be let go, that there was nothing more they could expect to get from them. The search details looking for the elusive arms caches, they were called in too. If they couldn't find the arms in a day of searching, maybe there were no arms to find. The apprehension of the terrorists was a task better suited to Military Intelligence. It had the training and the resources for it.

It didn't take Klug long to recover — less than a day as a matter of fact. Because it was the morning after the morning after that a Major Grundstein, adjutant to Colonel Shor, regimental commander, came into the unit's base camp and asked for "Basil Primchek". He had come to take him to the colonel, who was waiting for him. "You're accused of a serious offense," said the major, "should you not come along willingly, I am authorized to order your arrest . . . Bring your gear with you, Primchek, but leave your weapon. I don't think you'll be needing it anymore."

Colonel Shor was a big man, carrying some one hundred and twenty kilos on a large frame. His first question upon asking Basil to be seated was whether he had ever done any wrestling. As a young man Shor had been army heavyweight wrestling champion, "but that was a long time ago," he said, patting a large expanse of belly. "I probably couldn't wrestle my way out of a paper bag now. But you . . . you probably outweigh Captain Klug by thirty kilos . . . I talked to the Captain yesterday. He came here, told me the whole story, or rather, his story. I like to get both sides before I make a decision . . . So tell me, Primchek, why'd you do it?"

After he described the collective punishment ordeal and Klug's abuse of the old Arab, Colonel Shor asked, "But didn't you threaten to kill Captain Klug?"

"Yes, I threatened to kill him — hypothetically. I said 'next time' I would kill him. Obviously, I haven't made good on the threat . . ."

"But would you kill him?," pressed Shor.

"I don't know. Let him stop kicking old, arthritic men in the kidneys and then we'll see."

"I'm sorry," said Colonel Shor, "but that's no way to run an army. When it comes to discipline, we can't wait around for hypotheses to be tested, that's why we have a chain of command. You may not personally like your commander, in fact, you may hate him, but in war personal feelings have to be subordinated to the success of the objective. When you enter this man's army, you put away any differences you may have with your fellows and pitch in against the enemy. Now I'm not justifying what the Captain did. I believe your story, that's what complicates this matter. You know, I could put you up for court martial right now . . . but the issues of this case bother me. Mind you, I'm not saying Klug did wrong. But it's a gray area, it would make a tough judgment. And my job is to run an efficient fighting force, not a prosecutor's office.

"There's a lot in war that's not very pleasant — especially to people like yourself, not regular army. The enemy doesn't play by rules, yet it expects us to abide by them. Sometimes we can and sometimes we can't. Being in a combat situation can be rough on people. It can make you do crazy things, things you wouldn't think of doing under normal conditions. It's battle fatigue, everyone, even the strongest, is susceptible. In the present situation you're a menace to yourself *and* the army. So, if there's no objection from you, I'm sending you home . . ."

Two days later on the ride back to Jerusalem he was still mulling the experience. A year ago and he might have been under the illusion that he could take on the whole IDF along with its courts martial. But the system was clever, bending when it needed to bend. Ordinarily, attacks on officers by enlisted men merited an automatic conviction. They didn't want developing what happened to the Americans in Vietnam — actually one of the better kept secrets of the Vietnam war — officers killed by their men. It would mean Jews killing Jews, which perhaps was an unthinkable proposition, except for the fact that in war, the distinction between the enemy and the officer class was vulnerable and subject to breakdown, and once broken down, was difficult to restore. A perception by men that they had no interest in fighting a war declared by those separated from them by class, station, and institutionalized arrogance, and you had the beginnings of a mutiny, perhaps a rebellion. When that happened — God, country, duty were all so much garbage.

They were smart, they let him off easy. While it would have been simple to transfer him from a court martial in Lebanon to a jail cell in Israel, it might have provoked protest. They knew that in some way he was affiliated with the IPR. But the real obstacle was the Third Temple prize, no nation wanted to be seen as prosecuting its own myths. They had given the prize to the wrong man and it was too late now to demand it back.

It was intriguing, this rebellion idea. But nobody was going to shoot any officers, and there wasn't going to be any rebellion — not in the Israeli army. Israelis would go like wolves or sheep as the case may be, to kill and be killed for as long as the "Amalekite" menace existed. Jews were condemned to fight forever, expecially as they had chosen power as the solution to the problem of powerlessness. By attaching themselves to the world's greatest power they had acted out of historical and ideological necessity. As long as there was an America there would be an Israel.

They were all glad to see him back. With Ben-Judah at the front, they were free to be themselves. Ulrich Fesser asked whether the entire unit had returned with him. "No, just me," said Basil. "They know people like me can never be heroes, so they send us home where we belong." Olga gave him a proper handshake, then asked him into her office. "Well, this is a wonderful surprise," she said in her coolly professional manner, "But now I have a surprise for you." Olga reached into her desk, took out an envelope and handed it to him. The letter, from the Ministry, was dated the day before. "It was delivered by messenger yesterday afternoon," she said. It was a letter of dismissal, his dismissal, "outside commitments" the stated reason. "They work fast," he said, handing back the letter.

"What do you mean?," she asked, "You knew this would happen someday."

"That's not what I meant, but I'll explain later," adding in a whisper, "tonight." She didn't answer, she didn't have to.

He prepared the bedroom carefully, setting candles against the wall, putting Frank's *Psyché* on the turntable of his stereo. Although she was bound to regard the devices as a bit of theatre, there was no harm in creating, or even enhancing, a mood. Still, he wanted to avoid the excessive or obvious, thus the piece by Frank. It had a kind of wave-like sensuality without being too familiar or clichéd.

Olga apologized for arriving somewhat later than usual. She had been playing piano four hands with Nadezhda Ikrova and had lost track of time. But she knew something was afoot when he asked her to take tea with him in the kitchen, it was not his practice to indulge in preliminary *tete-a-tetes*. "So you want to tell me some of your war stories? Good, we don't talk enough as it is."

It was all for the best, said Olga over their cups. He

426

was back home safe and sound and could now devote himself completely to private practice, without the nuisance of having to attend to the prosaic duties of the Authority. On the other hand, he had a remarkable ability for getting into trouble. "I wonder if I'm doing right by associating with you," she said, "a man like you is positively dangerous."

He sat with her on the edge of the bed, arm around her shoulder, playfully probing the fleshy breasts and kissing her cheek. He had something to tell her, something he hoped she would give serious consideration to. "Olga," he declared, pressing his profile against hers, "let's emigrate."

"But I don't want to go to America," said Olga, drawing back and eyeing him with a look of amused sympathy.

"No, Olga, not America, *Russia*. Let's immigrate to Russia, together. Things are changing . . ."

"But I emigrated *from* Russia. Now I should go back?" He tried to explain, that they would take her back, they could make a life there, she could teach him Russian, they would get a job with the government somewhere, in the Caucasus, or maybe on the Black Sea where there was an ancient colony of Greeks, perhaps the descendants of Alexander's legion. They were letting people travel now. If the venture didn't pan out, they could always leave and go elswhere, Canada, New Zealand, wherever she wished.

Olga was unpersuaded. It was wrong, she complained, to expect her to decide such a serious subject upon such short notice, to spring it on her when she was at her weakest. The few times they met were too precious to permit the intrusion of "peripheral issues". His recent adversity was having an "exaggerated influence" upon his reason, he needed time to rest and recover from the effects of his experiences. The music was telling them something she said, pulling him toward her on the bed and opening her wonderful Russian thighs.

46

"Al-jihad al-muqaddas". It was a phrase he was to hear with increasing frequency wherever Arabs gathered, from the coffeehouses and streets of the city to the workers in his contruction crews. They were quoting Salim Nafsi who had used it in his oration at the state funeral of the two fallen "martyrs", pilots of a Soviet Il-76 advanced warning radar plane. Israeli jets, under a claim of self-defense, had penetrated Syrian air space and shot the plane down. Israel, the Defense Ministry said, could not allow the deployment of such an "offensive capability" against its forces. *Al-jihad al-muqaddas*, holy war, a pillar of Islam, a duty of the faithful, a concept conjuring up Islam's conquering caliphs and commanders, Omar, Abu-Bakr, Khalid ibn al-Walid, Amr ibn al-As, and half a millenium later, Salah ad-Din al-Ayyubi, the sultan who restored an empire and in the process regained Jerusalem from the crusading Franks. Yet, as Islam declined, so did its concept, the jihad, falling to its lowest estate in the modern era. Bandied on the lips of charlatans and patriots alike, invoked against the English, the French, the Jews, and by association, the Americans, it became a "cry of wolf", a slogan rather than a strength. But with Iran, and now Syria, taking up the cry, the concept of holy war was revivified. The Arabs he heard in the streets and coffeehouses — they weren't bandying phrases, they were quoting Salim Nafsi, the man who had proclaimed, "I am a Christian by religion and a Muslim by nationality." Sunnite, Shiite, Christian — Islam emcompassed them all. In the Lebanon, Egypt, Arabia, Palestine, they heard the call. It was an article of faith.

In America the Democrats had nominated Tancredo "Tank" Colonna for the presidency. Colonna, the son of Italian immigrants, was already notorious as the hard-charging, square-shooting, square-jawed executive who took over the helm of Derek-Benson, a near-bankrupt manufacturer of tractors and farm equipment, and by a combination of innovative farmer-to-factory credit contracts, hard-nosed efficiency, and luck — a three year run of drought among America's grain competitors had severely depleted world stocks and sent the price of wheat to record levels, enriching and reviving the American farm economy — restored the company to vigorous financial and operational health. Running under the slogan of "Tank's a lot!", he was billed as the "farmer's friend", as the man who had saved a city (Midlothian, Illinois, headquarters and main assembly plant of Derek-Benson), and twenty thousand American jobs. He had beaten the Japs at their own game, the marketplace. Now he asked for a chance to show what he could do against the Russians. Labor, capital, white, black, rich, poor, support for Tank Colonna ran wide and deep. After years of being bled white by help the rich and soak the poor Republicanism, the country needed a savior. If anyone could save it, it was Tank Colonna. Al Abel had perhaps said it best — "Tank Colonna was the kind of man that if you were a girl and you took him home, your dad would instantly respect him and your mom would want to bed him." It may have been faith, but people believed Tank Colonna. Because in addition to everything else, Tank Colonna delivered.

Of course, before being nominated, Colonna had paid his political dues, speaking across the nation to high and low, appearing in convalescent centers and at county fairs, telling people of his visions for America, passing out little brass pins fashioned in the effigy of a column, and emphasizing his resolve with a bone-crushing handshake for the men and a little peck on the cheek for the women. Miriam had written how, at a Madison Square Garden rally prior to his nomination, Colonna had proclaimed, "You don't have to be Jewish to love Israel." As if on cue, the band struck up a rousing *Stars and Stripes Forever*, and an emotional Samuel

Shames had jumped from his place on the dais and hugged Tank, crying into the microphone, "My landsman! My landsman!" Cornball or contrived, it still made great theater. Colonna had the presidency in the bag they said. In Las Vegas, his candidacy was made a five to one favorite.

Elections were also set for Israel. The "centrist concensus", the game of musical chairs played by the Israeli political establishment, had run its course. The electorate was restless, it wanted to see some movement toward a solution of the country's perpetual problems, most notably the "Arab problem". Yahoshoah Aharoni, the darling of the Greater Israel advocates, had finally gained control of his party, and was predicted to become the next prime minister. Politician, hero in each of Israel's wars, acclaimed for his ruthless manner in shutting down terrorism in the Gaza Strip, and for his concept that Palestinians already had a homeland in Jordan, Aharoni was far and away Israel's most popular individual. Indeed, had Israel had a presidential elective system based on a popular vote rather than a parliamentary system, he would have been prime minister long ago. But in politics there was such a thing as being too popular, and for Aharoni the result had been that his colleagues, reactionary as they were, had always agreed on one thing — that he should not be the nation's leader. Aharoni, it was said, had a fuhrer mentality and would become a dictator. However, the real basis for opposition to Aharoni derived from a reluctance to provoke the Americans — it was generally understood that they would not look favorably upon an Aharoni Israel. Regarded by the American establishment as a "wild card" and megalomaniac, Aharoni was not trusted to work within the confines of America's grand design for the region. Thus, behind the years of party maneuvering and exclusion, loomed the shadow of Israel's patron. Yet when asked at a recent press conference about its attitude regarding an Aharoni electoral victory, a spokesman for the State Department would only say that, "In line with the long-standing policy of non-interference in other countries' affairs, *a fortiori* an ally, the United States would have no comment."

In any event, the effect of the invasion was to strengthen the power of reaction. In the Knesset a two day debate took place on the "demographic problem", with right-wing members calling for a massive increase in the deportation of Arab troublemakers and terrorists. The government, emboldened by the lack of a Syrian response to its invasion of Lebanon, instituted a stepped-up campaign of harassment against the Arabs in the territories, creating an acute sense of desperation among the occupied. An example of that desperation was the attitude of Albert Haddad expressed at a meeting in Ramallah to discuss progress on Villa Haddad. Two days before, Haddad's wife, re-entering the West Bank after a trip to Jordan, had been strip-searched at the border. Although performed under the probing eyes and fingers of women soldiers, to Haddad the deed was virtually equated with death itself, "And my wife is a *doctura* with degrees from three universities!," he exclaimed. "She should not have to suffer this! I *pray*, I *pray* I live to see the day when the Syrians drive the Israelis into the sea. God bless Salim Nafsi, God bless him!"

Only a few weeks ago he would have deemed Albert Haddad's prayer for Nafsian deliverance a naive act of faith. Now it was definitely within the realm of possibility. Syrian might had been building slowly, tentatively. Now, like a Burma dawn, it was upon them, issuing thunderous challenges. Nafsi's Lebanese allies had gone on the offensive, harassing and harrying the Israeli withdrawal, subjecting Israeli forces to heavy rocket attacks. Air and helicopter rearguard action was taken, but it was a phantom enemy. Amon Amitai had described the rain of Katyushas on their homeward bound convoy as "thirty seconds of hell". Occurring only seventeen kilometers from the border, the attack called into question the policy of equating land with security. It was Syria's turn to send a message — Israel was back to the *status quo ante,* the invasion was a strategic failure that had accomplished nothing. Calling the Israeli withdrawal a "retreat" and another victory of Islamic arms, Nafsi declared the balance of power had shifted irrevocably to Islam, warning that an Israeli attack upon Syria would result in "the destruction of the Zionist state."

Meanwhile, within cannon range of the Turkish and Iraqi borders, the Syrians and Iranians staged their largest joint maneuvers ever, involving numerous army corps and tens of thousands of troops. The maneuvers were Nafsi's answer to what he charged was an American inspired plan to employ Turkey as "number two regional bully" in an attempt to intimidate the Islamic Alliance. "Intervention," warned Nafsi, would expose Turkey to being "the ground meat in a three-sided *shawarma"* (a type of Arabic sandwich). The metaphor of a three-front war, with Russia and Greece as the other adversaries, would not be lost on American militarists, one of whose cardinal tenets was that Russians laid awake nights scheming for ways to obtain a warm-water port. As quoted by the government controlled Syrian press, Nafsi ended his statement ominously, "At an appropriate time the Islamic Alliance shall terminate the criminal regime in Baghdad, putting the head of its tyrant on a pike. For us, the road to Jerusalem runs through Baghdad."

Beatrix Brunwasser came by one evening, ostensibly to solicit him for the latest IPR peace campaign. This was the last chance for peace, she declared in her grave fashion, once Aharoni got in there would be very rough going. The IPR and a coalition of other peace groups were planning a joint Palestinian-Israeli conference to deal with the outstanding issues dividing the two peoples. Bethlehem, a symbol of conciliation and refuge, had been chosen as the conference site. Holding the conference in a West Bank city would also symbolize the willingness of Israelis to take the first step.

Scheduled to be invited were academics, lawyers, scientists, labor leaders, artists, workers, and housewives, from both nations. That was where he could help she said, using his "credentials and socio-economic status" to impress invitees, influencing them to attend. Displaying the list of prospective conference delegates, Beatrix suggested he contact those with whom he thought he would have the most rapport.

Bringing together a selective group of liberal Jews and Arabs and putting them under one roof where their collective fears and frustrations could have a go at each other, seemed a dreary proposition. The delegates whould end up playing UN, passing resolutions and expressing good intentions. The making of peace, like war, was a state monopoly, one much too important to be left to people. Yet, with Beatrix at his side, the impulse was to say "yes", there was a definite "tugging at the heartstrings." Although putting on a good face, it was obvious she had her own personal peace mission to promote. She was still at the age when words, especially those spoken in anger, were invested with exaggerated force.

He ran a finger down the list stopping at Laszlo Korda, Naturalist, Conservationist. "I choose him," he declared. Searching the list for an Arab name, he settled on a Nabil al-Badanjani, Professor, Sociology, Haifa University. He liked the name's ring, he had never heard of al-Badanjani. "That's enough," he said, gathering a handful of Beatrix's wild, red locks and playfully pulling her head back, "one Arab, one Jew. I don't think I can stand more than that."

Some years prior, Laszlo Korda had been honored by the International Wildlife Association with its Conservationist of the Year award for his successful reintroduction of oryx antelope to Israel's Negev desert. Known for his work in the captive breeding of endangered species, he and his mate of fifty-one years, Kati, raised animals for captivity as well as release in the wild. Basil accompanied Korda for a tour of the facilities of the ten thousand hectare "laboratory" the government had given Korda for his noble experiment of attempting to repopulate Israel with all the animals mentioned in the Bible. The place brought to mind a royal menagerie. Gazelles, bustards, and onagers, the wild ass from which descended the common burro, pranced and strutted in separate, fenced breeding pens. Korda envisioned a time when the kilometers of fencing surrounding the reserve would be taken away and the animals permitted to run free, of one day reintroducing lions, wolves, and leopards to the area. The present predator-prey relationship had been skewed by two millennia of hunting and killing, the large predators exterminated first, followed by most of their prey. "The Romans," declared Korda, "every city in the empire was beating the bushes for animals for their games and circuses, the waste and slaughter were horrific", depleting the whole Meditteranean littoral and its hinterland of once thriving animal populations. "Where do you think Hannibal got his elephants?," asked Korda. The custom of animal baiting has persisted to the present, with domestic beasts such as bulls and prizefighters replacing those from the wild. However, claimed Korda, with the growth of humane societies and a more sophisticated appreciation of both animal and human life, people were beginning to attach an appropriate opprobrium to those entertainments.

Korda regarded a peace conference with Palestinians dubiously. "The peace sought by your conference organizers would eventually result in Israel being absorbed by a greater body politic. No, let me finish," he said, holding up a hand to stay Basil's response, "Even if we could reach an accommodation with the Palestinians, they are only part of the problem. What would protect us from the hostility of the others with their program of Islamicization and holy war? After Syria and Iran swallow Iraq, where do you think they will turn? You hear what they say, they want to expunge us from the face of the earth. No, my boy. You are young, you have the optimism of youth. If you had as many years

434

under your pate as this old relic (Korda patted his bald head), you would be less inclined to put your faith in such chimeras. What we call civil zation is really only a very recent development in the histc ry of the race, tens of thousands of years of savagery preceded us. It does not take much to stir the beast in this creature. The merest of pretexts and they are at each other's throats, killing, maiming. Any excuse will do — a different language, religion, color of skin, anything to justify the impulse to murder. No. For the foreseeable future, Israel must remain strong. Reason unavailing, strength must be our defense against fanaticism.

"I survived the Holocaust . . . only because I was lucky, one of the few. The victims, what do you think they would say if they could speak? Look around you," said Korda, making a panoramic sweep of his arm, pointing to the herds of grazing ungulates, to the aviaries of rare falcons and raptors, to the breeding pens where baby antelopes nursed, "My life's work. What Arab country would possess our solicitude for the animal kingdom? You, I, we are artists. We want to preserve the past — you as an architect, I as a naturalist. Look at their cities. Junk! Buck Rogers comic book architecture. These creatures, my children, what would happen to them? Fair game for rich bums with automatic weapons shooting them from Cadillacs and Mercedes, Moslem society has no tradition of animal welfare, no tradition! Where are their national parks? In all their lands they have nothing, nothing like this, reverence, reverence for the other forms of life.

"We Jews are heirs to a tradition — not of the prophets, that is made much too much of — but of the Enlightenment, the age of science. Our exposure is eastern yet we face the West. Check the Nobel laureates in science. Jews, out of all proportion! The only ones who have a chance to equal our representation are the Chinese, and that is only because they outnumber us a hundred to one. But even then it will be a century before they even begin to

435

narrow the gap. The Moslems . . . if they had the power I am sure they would plunge the world into barbarism. Medieval notions, purdah of woman . . ." Korda paused, as if suddenly conscious of restating the obvious, before concluding in a calmer tone, "I am a Zionist and a naturalist. For me, there is no conflict between them. You tell your friends, the organizers of this conference for peace, that Laszlo Korda has nothing against peace . . . It is only that he values freedom and civilization more."

They walked back to the main house where Kati Korda, a diminutive, sprightly woman in shorts and boots, waited with sandwiches and iced tea. It was an honor for them to host a famous architect she said, knowing that he was also an animal lover. She invited him to bring his friends out next time, they loved company.

Korda's point of view was typical. The oldtimers were too imprinted with the past to take chances on the future. Essentially, peace was hopeless. It was war or holocaust, there *were* no other choices. In spite of the moral inertia, who could say they were wrong? He thought of taking Olga to the remote and beautiful reserve, staying the weekend in one of the cabins the Kordas kept for guests. But lately, following his dismissal from the Authority, she had been even more guarded about being seen with him. Her caution extended to the telephone — he was not to use it to discuss personal matters with her. As a Russian she was sensitive to such things, "You know they're watching you?," she said. But there was nothing exceptional about Russia. All governments spied on their people, even the democracies — indeed, especially the "democracies".

For months he had been trying to persuade her to make a trip, some Mediterranean isle, Sardinia, Sicily, even Elba — who would recognize them in Elba? — but she had put him off. Now, with Nadezhda Ikrova having moved in with her, she was even more resistant. Either she would be going off someplace with Nadezhda, or saying she couldn't

436

leave her alone, that it was "unfraternal". He had met Nadezhda once, running into her and Olga at an outdoor cafe one afternoon. A pretty girl with black bobbed hair and a sexy, compact figure, she had emigrated from Russia about a year after Olga. She would have made a perfectly compatible travelling companion, but when he suggested she accompany them, Olga only smiled and shook her head. Naturally, he suspected them of being lesbians. But it was only a suspicion, he didn't want to be like those learned gossips who presumed to see a homosexual relationship in any close friendship among unwed persons of the same sex. In any case, he thought, so what if they were? He wished the friendship well, at the same time realizing that Nadezhda would be one more barrier in the way of inducing Olga to emigrate.

He met Nabil al-Badanjani in the University cafeteria. Slender and conservatively dressed, Badanjani wore paisley-shaped, French-style eyeglasses, and smoked American cigarettes, nervously puffing on them between spoken phrases. Given his area of academic expertise and peculiarly self-conscious minority status as an Arab citizen of a Jewish state, Badanjani was fully conversant with the issue. Of course there was discrimination he said, it was inherent in the nature of Zionism, "the very fact of not being Jewish was a deviation from the norm." He could understand that, the logic of a Jewish state favoring its own over "competing nationalities or sub-groups." As applied to him personally, discrimination meant that as an Arab academic teaching at an Israeli university, he would never be the head of the sociology department. He could accept that, just as he could accept the government's decision to exempt Arabs from military service. "Who wants to serve in their fucking army anyway?," he said, taking the last cigarette from a pack of Luckies, then crunching the empty pack in his hand and tossing it on the floor.

Other than the examples of "intrinsic discrimination"

437

cited, Badanjani described his life as not much different than that of his Jewish colleagues. He lived with his wife and two small children in university supplied faculty housing. They were saving their money, hoping someday to buy a small car. Of course, with the predicted coming change of political leadership, there was the element of uncertainty. "But we always had that. At home we speak Arabic so our children will learn the language. I don't think they will expatriate us, we being 'citizens' and all that, but with all this talk about the 'demographic problem' one never knows. I *am* an Arab you know, an Arab holding a Jew's job, I could find myself looking for work tomorrow. Physical labor I don't think I could take, I haven't the physique or the stamina for it. My family, we're good for bullshit, not work." Badanjani came from merchant stock, his father owned a shoe store in town. His brothers were also teachers. Another brother attended the University studying computer science. Badanjani compared their situation to the "colored" in South Africa. As Israeli citizens they had more privileges than Palestinians in the West Bank and Gaza, but they still lived under a system of *apartheid*. Yet, when he compared their situation to life in an Arab country, they were not so bad off. "Of course, in Gaza and the West Bank when we demonstrate, you sometimes shoot us. But here at least, the killings get reported in the press, even the American press. But in Jordan, where Aharoni says we belong, when people demonstrate, they bash their brains out with clubs and the press turns a blind eye, His Majesty is America's king."

Badanjani took a special interest in press coverage, he was an inveterate letter-to-the-editor writer. The Israeli press sometimes published his letters, "but the American press . . . never!"

When asked if attending the conference was worth the risk, ". . . the Shin Beth is sure to be well represented", Badanjani replied that he didn't care. The conference would give him a chance "to confront some of these 'liberal' Jews

who claim they are for peace yet go along with the government on all basic issues. So they fire me? Do they need an
excuse? That I attended a conference on peace sponsored by
'communists'? Tomorrow they could fire me for any number
of reasons. One has to do something. I have a family that I
would like to see survive, the next war could be hell. The
Iraqis have their poison gas and the Israelis talk of the
'nuclear option'. I ask you, where does that leave us?"

Later that afternoon he found a letter from Alison
Cleveland in his mail. He had written her months ago,
shortly after her interview with Nafsi, and this was the first
he had heard from her.

Dear Basil,
    You were right. Yours truly, cub reporter,
was fired. It's been almost three months now since
I walked into Bill Baker's office and was told I
wasn't "carrying my weight", that he was going
to have to let me go. Imagine, me not carrying
my weight! But don't think I went gentle. Before
I was through I called him a few choice ones.
Although I got him to admit he had gotten flak
about my interview with Salim Nafsi, he insisted
that wasn't the reason. They were cutting back
and I had the least seniority. Humbug!
    But that was only prologue. Wherever I went
in the news industry it was, 'we'll call you', or
'we're looking for someone with more experience.'
Even Channel 13 wouldn't have me back. My
former producer claimed it was too late to revive
my show, the schedule precluded it — in spite of
an audience survey they had done which supported
a revival. Becoming desperate, I tried some of the
soaps, asking for a bit(ch) part. It would have
entailed moving to Los Angeles but I was spared
that grief, I got the same runaround. I went to the

439

actors union and complained, only to be informed that the word was out on me, and that maybe I should go underground for the season and emerge after the storm blew over. So I moved out of the Dakota and took an apartment with my sister who's attending acting school looking to follow in someone's murky footsteps. The house we live in is owned by the Episcopal Church and is restricted to females only. The arrangement satisfies my mother who's glad I'm there to look after my sister. As you know, AIDS is rapidly overtaking crime for the city's number one anxiety.

I recently got a small part in an off-Broadway production. It's a play about Armenians and in it I wear a black wig. 'Who now remembers the Armenians?' Hitler was said to have said, and judging from the size of our audiences he may have been right. In fact, even without the wig, you might not recognize me these days. In the process of 'returning to my roots', I've cast off twenty pounds, cut my nails, and let my hair grow out to its natural color — brown (how would you know?).

The political situation being what it is, I've been wondering if at some point you may finally decide to transfer your operations back to New York, where, if I may say so, you will be among friends. As verification, please consider this letter the apology I was prevented from expressing that night in Jerusalem . . .

She was sending him an "all clear" signal. A few months ago and he might have dropped everything and gone off heart pounding. Now it was too late, he had been lucky, he wanted to keep what he had. He felt a little sorry for her but life was like that, people made selfish choices. If later they turned out to be foolish, well, that was too bad. Where was *she* when he wanted her? Of course, he would continue to correspond with her, they would always be friends. But who was she kidding? Her punishment was only temporary, she was part of the champagne and caviar set. She would succumb, they would forgive. It was only a spanking. Some big producer or wealthy angel would come to her rescue. One walk-on and they would be eating out of her hand. She was too beautiful and too valuable to stay punished for long.

47

The first sign that all was not right was the failure of the new American administration to honor a long-standing tradition and invite the head of the new Israeli administration to Washington. It was an extraordinary snub and because of it the Colonna administration received an extraordinary amount of criticism. Nevertheless, the administration held its ground, maintaining a taut, diplomatic silence. "There was nothing," said an administration spokesman, "nothing that time and the workings of diplomacy could not resolve to the satisfaction of all." Yet, it was well known that the United States regarded the deportations as "disturbing". The outgoing administration had even spoken to that effect in its final weeks of power, and, as everyone knew, American foreign policy was consistent and unchanging. Although it was still too early to tell, the possibility the world had another American "human rights" administration on its hands had to be faced. Israel's American supporters lost no time in setting the record straight. An intensive public relations campaign was launched with pictures of a smiling Yahoshoah "Hosha" Aharoni appearing simultaneously on the covers of American news weeklies. Inside were stories reviewing the great man's exploits on land and on sea, along with colored photographs of Aharoni *en famille* and at his ranch, including some of him feeding handfuls of hay to his prize Arabian stallion, Sultan Abdul Hamid. American TV news shows interviewed "Prime Minister Aharoni" from his Jerusalem office where he projected the image of a reasonable, if, as he diffidently described himself, "sometimes misunderstood man". After all, the American public had known about Aharoni for a long time, he was a hero. Now that they had a chance to really get to know him, he being the prime minister of a friendly country, a country in the forefront of fighting terrorism, they could see that he was really a very fine chap who was trying to do his very best in a very difficult situation. While he was not the world's most handsome man, he spoke English well, made a good appearance, and proclaimed sincerely his wish for peace. What was all the fuss about?

In Israel it was business as usual. Despite regular protests from Jordan and Lebanon (the two main "transit countries"), deportations of "terrorists and troublemakers" continued apace. Arabs in the occupied territories were fools to listen to the blandishments of the Syrians or the PLO. As Israel would not tolerate a hostile Jordan on its borders, it would not tolerate a mass of permanently disaffected Arabs within them. "They should know," said Anton Wassilinsky, the Russian emigré hero, "that any revolt instigated with the aid of an outside power would subject them to expulsion *en masse*. If Major Nafsi can hear my voice, and I pray he can, then I implore him to think of the many law-abiding Arabs who would suffer from a Syrian attack upon Israel. Not only would such a course cause the certain destruction of his brutal regime, but the process could very well result in the liquidation of the 'Palestinian question' he so hypocritically

442

champions, ending for all time the hopes of many Arabs for the autonomy promised them by Israel, yet denied them by their leaders. So don't commit collective suicide, Major. Send your legions and the legions of your fanatic ally against the Iraqis. There you have a chance. Here there is nothing but a graveyard for you all. This is Anton Wassilinsky and that's my point of view."

Wassilinsky was making a fortune. His book, *Memories of a Refusnik*, was a best seller in Israel, the United States, and Europe, and his American publisher had recently commissioned him to do one on his impressions of Israel. His radio commentaries, originally heard once a week, were now repeated three to four times a day, while his face was a permanent fixture on Israeli TV screens. Listeners were invited to write for Wassilinsky's commentaries, available in transcript or cassette. As with all popular political personalities in a democracy, people were talking about whether he would run for office. Indeed, Israeli satirists began to refer to him as "Anton Wassilinsky A.A.", the initials standing for "after Aharoni".

There was a long line at the military checkpoint ahead. The checks were now commonplace on roads leading in and out of the city, Israelis stoically accepting their necessity. In addition to a check of drivers' papers, soldiers regularly searched vehicles, pushing mirrors mounted on wheels underneath chassis, and guiding sniffer dogs through interiors and trunks of automobiles. Today the process seemed to be going particularly slowly. A burning midday sun aggravated the exasperation of drivers as they emerged from cars and trucks, swearing and trying to discover the reason for the delay. "Terrorist attack in Jerusalem!" hollered a trucker going in the opposite direction from the window of his cab. Basil switched his car radio to the news station — the main news item was the clash on the Syrian-Iraqi border, Radio Damascus was claiming Syrian forces had "wiped out" a company of Iraqis. He wondered if this was

443

the beginning of the long-awaited offensive or just a preliminary feint. The Syrians and Iranians had been massing
troops and supplies at the border for weeks. On this issue
he was definitely pro-Syrian. Nafsi was not alone in wanting
the head of the Iraqi tyrant on a pike.

While the media was honoring the news blackout,
others were not. The word passed down the line was that
the bombing in Jerusalem was only one of a number of
bombings that morning, Israel was being hit with an organized campaign of terror. That explained the excruciating
slowness of the checkpoint, where soldiers were probing
engines, removing and deflating spare tires, hoisting cars
with highlifts. The country was fighting back with all the
means at its command — rigorous and blanket searches
employing the latest state-of-the-art technology. The soldier
handler of the German shepherd sniffing through his car
knew of two bombings — a synagogue in Jerusalem and
one in Eilat with tourists being killed. "If you can," said the
soldier, "I'd avoid city center. We have checkpoints all over.
Traffic is a mess."

He decided to go to his father's house and pick up his
mail, avoiding for the present the Arab quarter where police
and army presence was likely to be heavy. On the way he
was stopped twice, once at another checkpoint where the car
was searched again, and later by two soldiers at an intersection leading to his father's street. After checking his papers,
they told him people were being asked to stay in their
houses during the search for the terrorists. No, the more
talkative of the two said, they didn't know what synagogue
had been hit, they only knew what they were told.

His father's car was parked on the street. It was
unusual for him to be home at this time of day, but if he
had to pick a day to be home this was it. Running into one
of those interminable check-points was enough to make
anyone turn around and go home. Inside no one was about,
but he noticed that the door of his father's bedroom was

closed. Assuming the old man was napping, he went into his room, collected his mail, then stopped in the kitchen for a beer. It was there he saw the purse on the table; it was Ayesha's. Ayesha — gentle, roly-poly, reliable Ayesha, their faithful Arab maid. As far back as he could remember, she was there. A widow now for almost twenty years, she was like an aunt to him. He never would have believed it because he never would have suspected it. But it made sense, a widow and a widower, only the quaintness that attached to their coupling made it seem so bizarre. He had wondered what his father did for sex. Now he had the answer, or at least a partial answer. He took a swig of the beer, poured the rest down the drain, then hid the bottle. It was best to leave quickly. That way their secret might at least be ambiguous, they must have heard him come in. Now they heard him go out, closing the door in simulated haste. Bless them he thought, there was hope after all.

The soldiers had done their job well, the streets in the Arab quarter were deserted. He left his car at the curb and went up to the door. Opening it, he heard music. He didn't remember leaving the radio on, but it was that kind of day, he wasn't sure of anything anymore. Nevertheless, his suspicions were aroused. Burglary was always a possibility — a false burglary, the Shin Beth breaking in and leaving listening devices. Olga's warning came to mind — they were watching him. He wondered if they were dumb enough to suspect him. But dumbness was irrelevant, any degree of subversion made one suspect. He regretted not having Bogorodov install an alarm system, the peace of mind was worth the cost. Stepping into the salon, his heart jumped at the sight of the seated black-bearded figure, 9mm machine pistol in hand, its silencer equipped barrel pointed at him. The porkpie hat, long hair, wild black beard and black frock coat — it was uncanny. The eyes, the dark-rimmed orbits, the long, powerful, prophetic fingers — all was clear now. "What's the matter," said Bustanji, putting the pistol inside his coat, "don't you think I could be one of your Bnai Azadoi Beshallim? Or a *Khakite*? You should have changed the locks if you didn't want company."

Although redundant and he had about as good an idea as he was ever going to have, he asked it anyway, "What are you doing here?" Bustanji got up and went over to the radio, raising its volume, "Just listening to the radio. I *love* to listen to the radio. I'm waiting for an important announcement. It just might make my day."

They talked in the kitchen while waiting the government's release of what Bustanji termed "the day's body count". Basil wanted to know what to do in the event the police came. "Act natural," said Bustanji, "Your visitor is 'Rabbi Israel Golkevitz' of Neve Yacov, and has the papers to prove it. But I wouldn't worry too much, they're too arrogant to remember me. What did I ever do? To them I was just another harmless Arab."

Bustanji inquired of his mother and sister, how they were getting on in the "hell of lies", how often they wrote. Basil opened a drawer and took out a packet of letters from Sumaiya. Bustanji leafed through the envelopes, checking the postmarks. He hadn't time to read them, he just wanted to be sure his sister had not forgotten "her manners or her origins." At the mention of his brother the eyes misted and he wept, unashamedly, as he spoke.

Finally, at four o'clock, news of the bombings was announced. There had been incidents in seven Israeli cities, leaving at least eighty dead and scores injured. A bomb planted on the beach at Eilat had killed a party of Swedish tourists. The explosion that tore through the Torah and Land's Jerusalem temple during morning prayers killed eighteen and injured fourteen, five critically. In what Torah and Land adherents were calling a "miracle", their leader, Rabbi Benjamin Khak, escaped harm by being temporarily out of the city. The government blamed Syria, Iran, the PLO, or a combination of all three and promised reprisals — "at a time

446

Israel shall choose." In the meantime, it vowed to "cut off the heads of the perpetrators of these bloody deeds."

"Listen to them," exclaimed Bustanji, "they think by killing us they will have their satisfaction. There are millions of us. War is a matter of ratios. At one time it was one hundred of us to one of them. Then it was fifty, twenty, ten. Today the ratio went the other way."

The question had been bouncing around in his brain, it would have been a fantastic coincidence. "Khalil, did you have anything to do with the Maudlin attack?"

"No. I think that was Hizbollah . . . But I would have liked to have been the driver of that ambulance!"

Later, their dinner was interrupted by a pounding on the door. "You get it," said Bustanji with a nod, "you're the man of the house now." At the door an army lieutenant demanded his papers. "You are Jewish?," inquired the lieutenant solicitously. A positive response elicited an apology, "We are sorry, sir, but there has been a terrorist attack and my orders are to search all residences." Two privates followed the officer into the house. At that point Bustanji emerged from the kitchen, demanding in a loud, angry voice, "Is this the best you can do? Bother pious Jews when they are thanking the Lord for their daily bread? Who is your commander?" The privates retreated back to the door as the lieutenant sputtered an apology to the manifestly holy and outraged man. "Go and search for your terrorists elsewhere!," yelled Bustanji, shaking a great fist in the air, "they are probably a hundred kilometers away by now!"

The privates did not have to be told, they were already outside. Following them, a chastened and chagrined lieutenant reiterated his apologies for the "mistake".

"That was close," whispered Basil as they sat down again, "you're a good actor."

"Not close at all," replied Bustanji, getting up and turning on the radio, "You should see when it's really close." Bustanji invited Basil to feel the lining of his coat. "No," he said, "it's not Arabic bread. Plastique. 'Zyclonite.' From Czechoslovakia. It's a new development, a veritable wonder explosive. Light, powerful, and most importantly, completely odorless, outwitting the smartest Jewish dog. There's enough in this lining to have blown our little party out there into many unidentifiable pieces."

"And you were prepared to kill us all?"

"It doesn't pay for us to be taken alive — the torture you know. Naturally, I would have hated to do such a thing in my own house. However, I was confident I could handle the situation without resort to such desperate measures. I hope you don't feel put upon. In war 'innocents' sometimes get in the way. But it's all for a good cause. Besides, from what I understand, you should be prepared to go gracefully. You've had your share of thrills."

"Is that so? And what, may I ask, are you basing that on?"

"Never mind. Let's just say I have good intelligence."

The next morning, after a nervous automobile ride (he sweated blood when, outside of Tel Aviv, they were stopped briefly at a checkpoint manned by about a dozen mean-looking Sephardic troops. But again, one look at the "rabbi" and it was *passe partout*, the soldiers waving them on after perfunctory looks through the car's windows) he dropped Bustanji off near the huge Kings of Israel square in Tel Aviv. "The Lord bless thee, and keep thee," intoned Bustanji in a loud voice as he got out of the car, "The Lord lift up his countenance upon thee, and give thee peace!" He watched as Bustanji, in the bright morning sunshine, walked away, covering ground rapidly with his long legs, finally disappearing into the crowd. He would probably never see him again.

48

The first rockets hit the outskirts of Jerusalem early Sunday morning, one week after Easter. Approximately one hour before, in a pre-dawn strike, powerful multiple warhead missiles, of a type not known to be in the Syrian arsenal, exploded at airfields throughout Israel, neutralizing many and wreaking havoc with air defense systems. The Islamic Alliance, in a daring and well coordinated attack, had sent thousands of trucks, some driving all night, across the desert and into Jordan, overthrown in a simultaneous, pre-planned coup. The first waves of Islamic troops, attacking on a broad front and utilizing heavy firepower, had breached Israel's Jordan River defenses and were engaging Israeli units on the West Bank. A force estimated at 200,000 men, spearheaded by some 2,000 tanks, was rolling toward the Arab towns of Jenin and Nazareth, cutting off and isolating thousands of Israeli troops and pioneers in the Golan Heights. The main body of the Jordanian Army, now under Islamic command, buttressed by Iran's Third and Fourth Army Corps, had smashed across the Wadi Araba below the Dead Sea and was advancing north, destination Jerusalem. Lebanon, as if on signal, had erupted. A powerful assault upon Christian positions was in process, supported by Islamic air and ground forces. Another salient, believed to be the main Islamic thrust, had taken Jericho, and reinforced by Syrian artillery units, was also advancing upon Jerusalem. The Israelis, fully mobilized, were counterattacking on all fronts, launching their own stock of missiles against strategic and industrial targets in Syria, and sending what remained of their air force in desperate waves against the relentless Islamic advance. But the first minutes of the war had been crucial. Israel needed help.

It was to news of war in the Middle East that

Americans awakened on Sunday morning. It was big news, bigger than anything since the elections, when Tank Colonna won in a landslide. By a natural coincidence, the seven hour time difference between America and the Middle East saved newspaper editors the embarassment of missing the beginning of the biggest story of the year. In America newspapers published but one edition on Sunday. News editors held up presses pending latest developments, and when they could hold them no longer, published. Meanwhile, taking up the Sunday news slack, were the more flexible resources of radio and television, with stations periodically interrupting regular Sunday morning programming for news bulletins on the fighting, some featuring military analysts and active or retired military officers armed with maps and pointers giving brief two-minute overviews on the positions of the belligerents. In churches throughout the nation, Christian worshippers bowed heads in prayer for the land wherein once dwelled the Prince of Peace. Other, more fundamentalist Christians, prayed for the victory of the Jews, for it was written, Israel was the Promised Land and the fulfillment of divine prophecy. Millions more, believers and non-believers, disquieted by the news that the Soviet Union had placed its armed forces on maximum alert, prayed the war would not spread, engulfing the world.

President Colonna had cut short a weekend at Camp David and was at the White House. All Sixth Fleet units had been ordered to the eastern Mediterranean. The 82nd Airborne Division at Fort Bragg and the United States Marines at Camp Lejeune, North Carolina had been mobilized for possible combat. Military leaves had been cancelled. The President had met with the Joint Chiefs. American military units in Europe had been put on full alert in the event of a Soviet move into Turkey and the Balkans. SAC, the Strategic Air Command, the United States' Armegeddon in the sky, had been on full alert all along. It was Sunday, and in the welter of reports and rumors — some fact, some fiction — verification was impossible. If a crisis atmosphere had been created, it was no fault of the White House. A spokesman for the administration issued a brief statement: The President and his advisors were monitoring the situation closely and were prepared to take all possible measures to protect United States interests and the lives of Americans and their dependents in the area affected by the hostilities. Meanwhile, night had fallen in the Holy Land, and with the baseball season in full swing, a series of Sunday doubleheaders were being played in the major leagues.

It was Lester Kayam who first notified Shames of the attack in a one AM telephone call. Kayam was excited, he had just finished talking with Washington. They were alerting everyone to the situation early so they would be organized to swing into action first thing Monday morning. Shames was the first person he had relayed the news to. "Pass it on," said Kayam, excusing himself in order to notify the rest of the people on his alert list.

There were many more calls that night, incoming and outgoing. The house of Shames was a kind of unofficial communications center and Sam Shames was a rock, a rock of Israel. People were calling from around the country, California, Las Vegas, Florida. Some, in shock, sought reassurance. Others wanted to know what they could do to help. Although the news so far was sketchy, from all reports the attack was a major one and the Syrians had bloodied some of Israel's best. The missile attacks on the airfields were particularly distressing. Israel had always commanded the air. This was a new situation. Everybody had been taken by surprise, not only Israel. The attack had been expected against Iraq, the news had been saying that for months. Where were our spy satellites on this one? It didn't make sense.

"C.I.A. disinformation" railed Shames to his interlocutors. Now they had gone and deceived their own ally! He was of a mind to call C.I.A. headquarters in Langley, Virginia, but friends counseled patience, "Three o'clock in the morning on a Saturday night was a hell of a time to be calling the C.I.A."

After a final conference call, Shames dressed, took a bite of breakfast and entered his silver Mercedes 300 XL sedan. On the road it was dead time (the lull in traffic between the last Saturday night drunk and the first Sunday morning churchgoer) and this morning Shames' customarily heavy foot was heavier yet. The car's digital speedometer read one hundred and ten miles per hour as it sped down the Merritt Parkway, its lights blinking to warn the odd car and truck ahead of its approach. Sure it was fast Shames told himself, but the Krauts regularly drove their Mercedes a hundred and twenty on the autobahn for no apparent reason, while his was a true emergency. But the excuse was unnecessary, he didn't see a police car until he crossed the Triboro Bridge into Manhattan and got on FDR Drive where he slowed to a tolerable ninety miles per hour. It was ridiculous but here he was, a Jew, driving a German car. Der Fuhrer would roll over in hell if he knew what purpose the car was being put to that morning. It was those bums in Detroit, it was their fault he had to buy a Kraut car, they had abandoned the automobile market to the Germans and Japs, too fucking stupid and greedy to make a good automobile. The last good car made in America was the 1942 Lincoln Continental.

The news issuing from the car's soundaround speakers was not encouraging. They either didn't know what they were talking about or they were quoting Radio Damascus. It was impossible for Israel's defenses to be so weak that the Arabs were threatening Jerusalem. It was psychological warfare, lies, that was what they were good at, lies and poison gas. Bums, that's what they were, lying bums.

Shames left the car on the street in front of the Woolworth Building and ran up to the entrance, pulling then

452

pushing the door. In his haste he had forgotten it was Sunday. He started pounding, stopping only when Henry, the weekend maintenance man, came running from his place behind the elevators.

"Mister Shames, what brings you out so early, sir?"

"Duty, Henry, duty," answered Shames. "Say, Henry, there's going to be a meeting in my office this morning. A lot of people will be coming up. So let 'em in will you? Here's a little token for your troubles." Shames pressed a fifty dollar bill into the man's hands.

"Yessir, Mr. Shames! *Yessir!*"

The Israeli ambassador's statement made to the horde of reporters camped outside the White House gates was on the front page of every morning daily in the country: "I have just come from a meeting with the President. I informed him that early this morning the State of Israel was attacked by the combined forces of four Islamic nations — Syria, Iran, Lebanon and Jordan, the last mentioned country overthrown in a bloody coup only this morning. I am proud to report that my country is resisting this dastardly and unprovoked act of aggression with all the means at its command. Our morale is high, our spirit strong. The people and government of Israel are confident that with the support of its allies and freedom-loving people throughout the world, they shall repulse and severely punish the aggressors." A photograph of a helmeted Prime Minister Yahoshoah Aharoni meeting with his chiefs of staff underscored the urgency of the crisis. Reporters armed with binoculars watching the White House gates and porte cochere counted the comings and goings of scores of the powerful and influential, including the Joint Chiefs (twice), the French and English ambassadors, the Russian ambassador, the Secretaries of Defense, State and Treasury, and a host of assorted senators and representatives. Some of the hardier journalists had been on vigil for over twenty-four hours. The rain that had begun falling late Sunday made their task that much more miserable, but newsgathering was like war, while the cannons sounded no one slept.

While darkness brought a halt to the Islamic advance, artillery bombardment continued through the night, striking fear and panic among soldier and civilian alike. Taking the brunt of the enemy's fire were the West Bank settlements. The new suburbs around Jerusalem — French Hill, Pisgat Zeev, Neve Yacov, Gilo — were particularly hard hit. By Monday morning fires, fueled by thousands of incendiary rounds, were raging in the rubble of destruction. Hospital wards overflowed with thousands of civilians, the dead and dying, victims of burns from the terrifying phosphorus ordnance. Although each side employed its biggest guns, the Islamic artillery, being closer and better positioned, was taking the heavier toll.

In the air Syrian jets ranged freely, flying solo or in twos and threes, striking at armored columns and troop concentrations, leaving air defense to the seemingly ubiquitous mobile anti-aircraft batteries, the ones equipped with a secret weapon undergoing its first tests in battle, and according to returning Israeli aviators, proving devastating. Called the *Chuhl* (Swarm) and jointly developed by the Russians and Syrians, it was a heat seeking missile fired in salvos of twenty at attacking aircraft. Previous defenses against heat seeking missiles were ineffective against the smaller but more numerous projectiles, any one of which usually found its mark in a jet's engine. The weapon's effect was to force pilots to unleash their ordnance from great distances, preventing close-in attacks against armor and troop movements. Thus, on day two of the war, Israel's air force, formerly master of the sky, was reduced to a purely defensive capacity. Out-planed, out-gunned, and out-manned, the situation was becoming desperate. There were rumors of resorting to a diplomatic solution. But the overtures, made through the Americans, were ignored. The Islamic Alliance was moving on Jerusalem, its strategy to cut the country in two.

On TV morning news shows correspondents spoke from Israel giving the latest tally of plane and tank losses, while in the background puffs of smoke marked the falling of a shell or bomb. This time there was no censorship. The shells were falling on Israel and gaining sympathy was more important than some short term rule of military security. In the United States, politicians appeared grim as they condemned the sneak attack of the Moslems and raised the eventuality of future American involvement. A group of leading congressmen emerging from a meeting at the White House was particularly close-mouthed, excusing itself from saying more for reasons of security. While supplying reporters in the White House press room with the latest developments at hourly intervals, the administration, repeated a press spokesman, did not want "to create a crisis atmosphere." The United States was monitoring the situation and the President was being kept fully informed.

Samuel Shames was in his office early Monday. They had agreed the day before to press for a diplomatic solution, the cease-fire. Shames had opposed it, arguing that it was unrealistic, the enemy had achieved too much, a "lucky punch" was the way he described it to his fellows. It was close but his side had been outvoted. The majority was concerned with public relations. To be seen at this stage as too strident for Israel could be counter-productive. It was better to wait, let the Gentiles lead, then push. That way they were holding the high ground of reasonableness, of conciliation.

The majority was cautious but history was on its side — no Arab army had ever gone more than a week in the field with Israel without collapse. The Arabs were sprinters, not long-distance runners. They would wait one more day, the outcome was still too close to call. In the meantime they had been assured that Israel would be resupplied.

Shames had been impressed with the assessment of

Professor Sheldon Kaufman. Kaufman, professor emeritus of Judaic and Oriental studies at Princeton, had warned against reliance upon recent historical parallels. The army attacking Israel was no "mere Arab army," declared Kaufman, it was "a Moslem army." Furthermore, argued the professor, this was a "jihad", the first genuine one in memory. Moreover, they were underestimating the Iranian input. The "ideology of Shia Islam was paramount."

They were wrong thought Shames, dead wrong, as he surveyed the placement of the colored pins on the large map of the United States, set up on an easel in his office. The yellow pins stood for key men; blue, cultural institutions; and red, economic institutions. It was all part of a plan, a contingency plan, a plan he had been developing for years, secretly, in his imagination, the kind of plan one prayed never to have to implement, a last resort. The others were aware of it now, they had gotten a glimpse of what he was doing with the large map and colored pins, they were in touch with many of the same people he was, they were contemplating some of the same things. But they were afraid, afraid to carry it out. They needed a leader. In times of crisis the Jewish people produced leaders. This was no time for modesty, leaders led. His position, his standing in the community, his whole life had prepared him for this moment. He thought of Joshua, of his hero, Zeev Jabotinsky. He heard his people calling. He was ready.

Shames' telephone buzzed. Washington was calling reported Tatiana, the receptionist. Shames had been trying to get through to Tank Colonna all morning to no avail. Shames' satisfaction that the President was responding to his calls turned to disappointment when he recognized the voice on the line — it was Marvin Rattus, co-chairman of "The Committee of Fifty", a group composed of the heads of the major Jewish organizations. "Colonna won't see us!," exclaimed an agitated Rattus. "No appointments for the duration of the crisis!"

456

"You're there to talk about the crisis! Didn't you tell them that?," replied Shames, exasperated.

"Of course," said Rattus, "they said they were sorry, but if they saw us they'd have to see everybody. We even showed up at the front gate of the White House and demanded to see the President . . ."

"What happened?"

"They wouldn't let us in. You know if we had somebody inside, somebody inside Colonna's inner council . . . But who do we have? Does this guy *have* any Jewish friends?"

"Yeah, I know," said Shames, "I've been trying all morning to get through to him myself. Listen, you just keep buttonholing those congressmen. I'll handle the escalation from this end."

Later that afternoon White House spokesmen gave confidential assurances of help on the way — the Sixth Fleet, marines, the Seventh Armored Division in Germany, secret mobilizations. The Laborite British government was reported to have mounted an expeditionary force of British marines, destination Jordan, their lost colony. Some from The Committee of Fifty indulged in congratulations, the pressures they had helped set in motion were beginning to have an effect. Others, dubious, wanted their assurances direct from the mouth of the President. Pictures of the fighting were coming in now, horrendous images of burned Jews, victims of the savage Islamic bombardments and incendiarism, photographs released by the Syrians showing the thousands of Israeli prisoners taken in the Golan heights, their hands clasped behind their heads, shepherded by guards brandishing automatic weapons. Remembrances of the Holocaust were unavoidable. It was a holocaust, the task now was to avert a greater holocaust. A momentum for intervention was building up, now was the time to go with it.

Throughout the nation governors and mayors proclaimed Tuesday Rally for Israel Day, following the lead of

457

the Mayor of New York who declared an unpaid holiday for non-essential city employees. Private employers, unhampered by public considerations, gave employees the day off with pay, urging attendance at the demonstration. Claiming they were faced with massive absenteeism, Wall Street firms announced they would be closed for business on Rally for Israel Day, suspending trading in the nation's stocks and bonds.

In Washington people began arriving the night before the rally, filling all available hotel space. Latecomers were routed to outlying motels or accepted the hospitality of local synagogues and churches, sleeping on pews and folding cots. Fleets of chartered buses from New York and New Jersey carrying Orthodox Hasidic Jews rolled into town early Tuesday morning, rendezvousing on the Washington Monument mall. Two busloads of "Gays for Israel" pulled into the parking area and disgorged placard-waving men and women wearing identical white T-shirts emblazoned with a blue Star of David. A dispute was averted when the gays agreed to take up a position at the rear of the demonstration. It was a fine day for demonstrating, warm and balmy with nary a cloud in the sky. A strong rank and file union representation was expected, as well as union leaders from around the country, come to speak and join the many other dignitaries from all walks of life. It would have been a shame if the rally's organizers permitted controversial issues such as homosexuality and lesbianism to divert attention from the crisis at hand. Jews were liberal people but when the whole nation was watching you had to be careful, you put your best foot forward. The Rally for Israel was an American demonstration, a demonstration for democracy, for freedom, for humanity.

In the Oval Office President Colonna was closeted with his National Security Advisor, Alexander Van Zell. Colonna joked he had picked Alex Van Zell for his height — at six feet four Van Zell stood out in a crowd. Actually,

Colonna prided himself on his ability to judge people, to pick the best man for the job. "Only the best" he had promised during the campaign, "only the best" would serve in his administration. Invoking the name of Franklin Delano Roosevelt, he recalled how the great patrician assembled a "brain trust" to guide and inspire a demoralized nation out of its worst economic morass in history. A country was like a corporation he said, bad management and it could fail. Like Roosevelt, Van Zell was a son of privilege, a scion of the Hudson River aristocracy. He had gone into government service directly from Princeton, serving out a career in the back corridors of the State Department. When the big boys had a problem or wanted their facts straight about some remote region like Outer Mongolia, Byelorussia or Dahomey, they applied to Alex Van Zell. Seventy years old and five years past retirement age, they had kept him on. Alex Van Zell was one of those rare individuals without whose expertise and experience organizations crumbled, an indispensable man. Now, after a lifetime of supplying facts to intellectual inferiors and board room bums on sabbatical, he was being solicited for his opinions by the President of the United States.

Responsibility weighed heavy upon Alex Van Zell's slightly stooped shoulders as he stood before the President's desk reporting the latest developments in the crisis. The Syrians had drawn a line fifty nautical miles out from the Mediterranean coast. Air and naval forces breaching the line would be met by "the full might of Islamic rocketry." The Egyptian Third and Fifth armies were rolling toward the international border, its American equipped air force leading the way, engaging Israeli squadrons over Sinai and the Negev. The Saudi air force, angered by the Israeli downing of a billion dollars worth of AWAC reconnaissance planes, had rebelled and placed itself at the disposal of the Islamic Alliance in "the final battle against Zionism." The Russians were warning the Western Alliance not to intervene. "The chickens are coming home to roost, Mr. President," said Van Zell, "the chickens are coming home to roost. We've been on the line with General Helmamy all morning. There's nothing they can do — even if they wanted to. The streets of Cairo are filled with Moslem Brothers crying for arms to fight the Israelis. The Arabs smell blood. They've waited a lifetime for this moment. There's no calling them back now."

Tank Colonna stood up. He had dealt with conflict before. They had called him to Derek-Benson in the midst of a long strike that threatened to destroy the already wobbly company. He had been firm but fair. At first the workers balked at his proposals, calling him "corporate scab" and "Wall Street wolf". But eventually he won them over, settled the strike and saved the company. The rest was economic history. He thought back to Franklin Delano Roosevelt, how he would have responded to the situation. Roosevelt was his ideal. He often referred to Roosevelt and his administration in his speeches, harkening to a perhaps imaginary spirit. He wanted to be in that tradition, the tradition of a president for all America. He recalled his cement mason father seated beside their Philco console radio, listening to the news of FDR's death, removing his eyeglasses and wiping them with his handkerchief. He was too young to feel the same emotions but he knew his father was crying and he understood why, the President was dead, President Roosevelt was dead. Later he came to know Roosevelt better, to know that he was a politician like any other American president — expedient, deceptive, manipulative. Presidents and leaders were not angels, angels were in heaven. Firm but fair, he reminded himself, firm but fair.

Tank Colonna gazed out the window over the White House lawn to Pennsylvania Avenue and saw black. Thousands of black-garbed Hasids and other Jewish cultists filled the street, spilling over from Lafayette Square, a surging, moving mass of protest, a black sea of protest. The demonstrators were chanting and carrying placards. The placards were too far away to read, but the chanting carried and Tank Colonna heard it — "Israel dies while Colonna lies! Israel dies while Colonna lies!"

It was America and people had the right to peacefully protest but Tank Colonna was angry and he spat out his anger in bursts of contempt and resentment, "Look at those fucking kikes! Why can't we send the Park Police down there?"

"Mr. President, there are at least a hundred congressmen out there not to mention an unknown quantity of stage and screen personalities . . . 'Sticks and stones', Mr. President, 'sticks and stones'. " Alex Van Zell was a moderating influence, he knew what precipitate action could do. He remembered how Nixon had sent the police against Vietnam demonstrators. It was government thuggery at its worst. Van Zell had opposed the Vietnam war from the beginning — not like most of the others who got their peace credentials from the American Embassy at the fall of Saigon. But who was listening to him in those days, an obscure research staffer in the basement of the State Department? John Kennedy and his brother Bobby, busy with orgies in the White House, arrogant, *nouveau riche* brats spoiled by the easy availability of power and glamor. Johnson — he wasn't fit to be president of Texas. Alex Van Zell had a duty to protect the President, to avoid a scandal that could weaken presidential authority at a critical moment in history. There was also his own place in history to consider.

There was a loud buzzing from the telephone monitor on the desk. Alex Van Zell picked up the receiver and put it to his ear. He had dreaded this call, ever since the first reports of the Islamic attack. "The Israelis have informed us they're prepared to exercise the nuclear option," declared Van Zell, relaying the information on the line. "We have until noon our time to intervene with air and ground forces . . . Inaction on our part will be taken as assent for them to go nuclear . . ."

461

Tank Colonna gritted his teeth and glowered at his National Security Advisor, then exploded, "Not on my watch they don't! Not on my watch! Get Knoop and Cutting in here!" Alex Van Zell opened the door to the outer office and summoned General Lowell Knoop and Admiral George Archibald Cutting, Chief of Staff and Naval Chief respectively. He had kept the two officers parked outside the Oval Office since early that morning for just this contingency. The commanders knew what was expected of them, but in matters of such gravity a direct order from the Commander-in-Chief was the only prudent course. In rapid succession Colonna issued his orders, exercising his constitutional prerogative as Commander-in-Chief of the armed forces of the United States — "Tell the Israelis help is on the way and that we're steaming in. Inform the Russians of what we're trying to do and make sure they tell the Syrians not to target our ships and planes. I want that reactor obliterated! I don't care how many passes it takes, make that rubble bounce! Do you hear? Bounce! And tell them we'll hunt them down! That if just one nuclear missile explodes we'll hunt them down! I don't care where they go, we'll hunt them down!"

A presidential counsellor has a duty to support the president, to back up his decisions, to reinforce his judgments. Alex Van Zell waited while General Knoop and Admiral Cutting, having their orders, went their respective ways, then spoke up. "Mr. President, I commend you for a courageous action, and, if I may say so, as one who has served this country under many presidents, an action long overdue. When the facts surrounding your decision are disclosed — and I believe they must at our earliest opportunity — I am confident you will have the overwhelming support of the American people, if not their undying gratitude. And in the unhappy event the plan should fail to dissuade the Israelis and there is a resort to the nuclear option, the action you have taken will at least be a contribution toward persuading the Russians of our good faith in attempting to contain the conflict. If, God forbid, Israeli missiles land on their soil, it may be our best hope against their retaliating in kind."

Tank Colonna pushed his chair away from his desk and stood in front of the window again. The front ranks of the demonstration had a salt and pepper look now. A younger and brasher element had come to the fore, its contribution to the ongoing medley of insult a loudly impudent chant of "Colonna, Bullona! Colonna, Bullona!" They were after him, after his presidency. Some were already calling for his head, talking of "impeachment". They were from the group of political opponents that he called the "lunatic fringe", but it didn't matter, they had power and influence, they could kill him politically as well as physically. He needed to fight back, to hit them before they had a chance to get organized, to put out the fire before it became an inferno. Meanwhile, behind him, Alex Van Zell, in his scholarly, sequential manner, was relating possible political repercussions from the "tilt", " . . . recent studies show support for Israel emanates from a relatively small number of older, philanthropic Jews. If this group makes the adjustment the others will follow. For the majority of American Jews Israel has always been a peripheral issue. Who in his right mind believes Jews are in danger of persecution in this country?

"The real problem will be Congress. Thanks to those political contributions it's now more Zionist than the Zionists. With Israel out of the picture there will no longer be a motivation for giving. Wealthy Zionists will be searching for new outlets for their philanthropic energies and Congress is unlikely to be one of them. That demonstration out there, that's only one of the first symptoms of the withdrawal syndrome. I suspect Senator Brainard won't lack for allies on this issue."

At the mention of Brainard's name Colonna whirled around, his face livid. "Get Guy Impastato in here!," he

463

ordered, "We'll see who's going to run this country!"

Alex Van Zell hesitated, Lord Acton's famous saying about power surfacing in his encyclopedic mind. The association was unavoidable, but Mussolini had started out as a reformer too. The first assassination was always the hardest, the others came easy. He did not want to see the country go down that road, "Mr. President . . . I trust there will be no rough stuff. In my opinion, any such action at this stage would be decidedly premature."

"Don't worry, nobody's going to get hurt."

Gaetano Impastato — the young, 36 year old, highly intelligent, Hollywood-handsome, former head of New York City's anti-drug strike force, holder of graduate degrees in history and anthropology from Cornell and Yale, Colonna's personal choice as C.I.A. director. Impastato was that new breed of cop attracted to law enforcement for the animal thrill of the hunt, the hunt for the underworld's biggest and most dangerous game, the international drug dealers. Suave, broadly cultured and articulate, Impastato was as much at home in his private box at the Metropolitan Opera (bought for him by an anonymous admirer) as chatting with society matrons at a benefit for the handicapped. Samuel Shames knew Guy Impastato. He had introduced him to his steady companion, Trilby Danzig, Broadway's reigning queen of song, at one of his Woolworth Building bashes. The story was that the drug bosses had offered Impastato fifty million to retire from law enforcement but that he had contemptuously rejected it, saying they could never compensate him for his satisfaction in seeing them put behind bars for the rest of their "unnatural" lives. Everyone knew Gaetano Impastato was incorruptible, the figures proved it. During his tenure the consumption of drugs in New York City had dropped by over thirty percent. So what did it matter that some of this success was attributable to the growing number of known drug kingpins found floating in the East River? The big drugsters were afraid to get within fifty miles of the Big Apple, they knew what could happen if they were caught. There were complaints, a couple of Latin American countries and the usual whining by civil libertarians, but no one was listening. Drug dealers having no respect for the law, why should the law have respect for them? People demanded the same success for their own cities. New York was cited as an example, a hope, that the drug problem, so long a drag on the nation, was indeed ameliorable. From around the country, delegations of law enforcement officials came to New York to learn first hand the reasons for New York's success. So when Tank Colonna came into New York during the campaign, he requested Guy Impastato be given responsibility for his protection. He wanted to meet the young miracle worker, it was evident he had some good ideas, ideas the nation might profit by. The two men took an instant liking for one another, the first night staying up until four AM in Colonna's Waldorf Astoria presidential suite discussing national and international problems — how best to limit the spread of AIDS, the loss of the nation's soil and water, overpopulation, species and forest destruction in the Third World, international cooperation to prevent ecological disaster. The discussion, as they say in diplomatic parlance, was full and frank — except for the matter of nuclear war. Guy Impastato did most of the talking on that issue. A presidential candidate could not be too prudent when discussing the nation's security, especially when his discussant was a proponent of unilateral disarmament.

They had expected Colonna to select a C.I.A. director from the "intelligence community". They even presented him with a list of names to assist, as they said, "in the selection process." Colonna's announcement he was nominating Gaetano Impastato touched off a small earthquake in Washington. "The C.I.A. was no place for on-the-job training," critics wailed. Al Abel contributed to the chorus of complaint with a column mockingly entitled, "*Who* is Gaetano Impastato?" Senator Brainard, a member of the Senate

465

Foreign Intelligence Committee, quickly lined up a coalition of reactionary Western and Southern senators to oppose the nomination. Some of the party bigwigs advised Colonna to withdraw the nomination, to throw Impastato to the congressional wolves, he couldn't afford a fight with Congress so early in his administration. But Alex Van Zell warned him to go all the way with Impastato. Van Zell knew what the others only suspected, that Colonna was an idealist, a reformer, that he wanted to take on the military-industrial complex, to get the troops out of Europe, Nicaragua, the Philippines, to take the country out of the death business once and for all. The Japs had done it Colonna argued privately, and look where they were. But, countered Van Zell, Japanese capitalism had been persuaded to take such a course only after a crushing military defeat, "a defeat etched upon the Japanese consciousness in the ten thousand degree inferno of two atomic bombs." The C.I.A. was the most powerful institution in America, with powerful allies inside and outside government. Like the military-industrial complex, it was an outgrowth of the Second World War, they both shared the same ideology and goals. The C.I.A. was the military-industrial complex's watchdog, it would kill to protect it. And when the C.I.A. killed it was with impunity, nobody touched the C.I.A. In the final analysis it was the C.I.A. that defined the limits of American politics. If there was one appointment that was critical, it was director of the C.I.A.

It was at an afternoon news conference a week before the confirmation hearings that Colonna struck back. The people opposing Gaetano Impastato were, he said, "the same people who used to call us wop to our faces but now call us wop behind our backs." The statement threw the news conference into turmoil with half the reporters rushing out to call in the story and others, not trusting their ears, replaying tape recorders. "Colonna Cries Foul" and "Bigotry Behind Impastato Opposition Says Colonna" blared late editions, capitalizing on the news with provocative headlines. Colonna's statement was an exaggeration, but in the circumstances an inspired exaggeration. There had been references of the usual tasteless variety such as "Mafia" and "godfather", but nothing outside the acceptable context of American political commentary. But now there was a disturbing new category to add to the list of infamous American political practices — "wopbopping". People were troubled, they had believed prejudice was a thing of the past, that it had been overcome. Fair play was the American way. Everyone agreed that slurs on a person's race or national origins had no place in American life, it was wrong. Especially was it shocking in regard to Italians, the fastest rising star in the American firmament who, sociologists agreed, had finally come into their own. Impastato's detractors hastened to add their voices to the outcry, declaring their admiration for the "great contributions" Italians had made to the nation, undoing with fulsome phrases an inheritance of decades of bigotry. America they said, was discovered by an Italian, named after an Italian. What could be more American they asked, than Joe DiMaggio? Their only object, they explained, was to secure the best man for the position, someone with "foreign intelligence experience", a "track record". But it was too late, Colonna had stolen the advantage, the momentum was against them. When people saw the handsome, tweedy Impastato stand to take the oath and heard his measured and sonorous replies to questions, there was an outpouring of sympathy and admiration for the wonderful young man who had been so unfairly traduced. People were proud to have such a man in government. That was the great thing about America they said, that it could attract such outstanding individuals to public service. On that same day a barrage of pro-Impastato articles heralding his accomplishments written by reporters sympathetic to the administration appeared in newspapers across the country. At the hearings Gaetano Impastato gave all the right answers to all the right questions. After three days the opposition gave up, they had lost. The outcome was summed up by the statement of a senator, one with a heavy representation of Italian-Americans in his state. A vote against Impastato, he said, would have meant he "could never go home again."

Guy Impastato's helicopter landed on the White House lawn. It was a form of transportation he preferred to avoid, helicoptor crashes were implicated in numerous assassinations. But today was an emergency, a double emergency. Alex Van Zell left the two men alone. It was that kind of relationship, like father and son. Impastato was Colonna's Praetorian Guard, the protector behind the throne, the person charged with watching for plots and cabals that hatched, like roaches, in the filthy corners of American capital. Colonna told Van Zell to give them fifteen minutes. That was all the time he would need.

At about the same time, somewhere in the Mediterranean off the coast of Israel, two hundred heavily armed fighter bombers, the United States Sixth Fleet's entire complement of warplanes, took off from carrier decks, the late afternoon sun behind them, their orders to destroy Israel's Dimona reactor. "Operation Delilah" had been in the secret contingency hopper for years, now its time had come. The Russians knew of the attack's time and place, they had been informed. It was assumed they would alert their agents inside Israel. Their intelligence on the location of Israel's nuclear missile stock was superior to that of the United States, it had to be. Tiflis, Yerevan, Kiev, perhaps even Moscow, tens of millions of Russia's people, were within striking range of the Israeli missiles. The Russians were haunted by an Israeli "nuclear Masada". The Soviet Union stood against Zionism, it was the main supplier of Syria, the Jewish state's archenemy. "American ruling circles" had played a cynical game in permitting Israel to build a nuclear arsenal. Those guilty of an attack upon the territory of the Soviet Union would not go unpunished. Nations were

468

responsible for the consequences of their intent.

Meanwhile, outside the White House, the demonstration continued, a holiday atmosphere prevailing. People sang "We Shall Overcome", "Michael Row the Boat Ashore", "Joshua Fit de Battle o Jericho". Speaker after speaker, their voices magnified a hundred-fold by the powerful amplification system, assailed the Colonna administration's do-nothing policy, vying with each other in the militancy and fieriness of their words. Yet for all the marching, praying, blaring of trumpets and stamping of feet, when four o'clock came round the walls of the White House still stood. Nor had there been any of the expected dramatic announcements — that the Moslems had pulled back from Jerusalem, or the United States had intervened in force, turning the tide for Israel and freedom. For that the faithful would have to wait for the morrow because now they were footsore and hungry, they needed to conserve their strength for the rally's climax, a four hour ABS-TV special, "Artists for Israel", to be simulcast from New York and Los Angeles immediately after the evening news, the program the fruit of the organizing genius of Samuel Shames.

Shames, hoping to pull a coup, had tried to recruit Trilby Danzig for the extravaganza, but Guy Impastato had already called her and suggested she not participate. The merits of the issue were immaterial she told Shames, "Italian men expected their women to be loyal." Trilby or not, the evening was billed as the greatest assemblage of entertainment talent ever brought together in support of a cause. In what was claimed as the greatest simultaneous viewing audience in history, hundreds of millions of viewers the world over forsook a good night's sleep and stayed up to watch. A succession of top Hollywood stars acted as hosts as performers fiddled, fluted, twanged, banged, danced and sang their hearts out. One spot featured ten leading concert pianists on a single stage playing Chopin's *Military Polonaise*. Four rock bands, one in England, played *Hava Naghila* simultaneously. The effect was stupendous. No one had ever done anything like it before. The program climaxed with a live performance of the chorale from Beethoven's *Ninth Symphony* direct from the stage of the Metropolitan Opera. Interspersed with the music were clips of the bombardment of Jerusalem and its burned and battered victims, followed by footage of Jews emerging from Warsaw Ghetto sewers, hands raised, surrendering to Nazi stormtroopers. Schiller's inspired *alle Menschen werden bruder* (all men shall be brothers) poetry took on a special poignancy seen against the faces of the two Huns, the Moslem and the German. At the chorale's final *allegro* tuxedoed men and gowned women were on their feet, shouting, weeping, crying. From the great red curtains a spotlighted Samuel Shames emerged expecting to say a few words in summation and gratitude, but in the emotional high a shouted "NEXT YEAR IN JERUSALEM!" was all that was possible. At that moment no one could say whether the day's efforts would have the desired effect. Nevertheless, it was a tremendous catharsis.

That night, at approximately four-thirty in the morning, a powerful explosion blew out the side of the First Methodist Church in Yonkers, New York, destroying a 19th century John La Farge stained glass window. Almost simultaneously, eight hundred miles away, another explosion rent Atlanta's Shiloh Baptist Church, reducing the apse of the landmark stone structure to rubble. Taking credit for the bombings as "a protest against Gentile complacency in the face of Jewish annihilation" was the Jewish Fighters for Freedom, the JFF, a clandestine right-wing organization, implicated in the harassment of Russian embassy personnel and acts of terrorism against American critics of Israel. Reports said the JFF had left its calling card, large spray painted "We shall smite thee hip and thigh!" and "Never Again!" slogans on the outside walls of the damaged buildings. Churchmen, Jew and Gentile, rushed to denounce the acts. "Terrorist blasphemy . . . insanely criminal . . . utterly at odds with the Judeo-Christian tradition," they replied to early morning interview calls of newspaper and TV reporters. Although quick to condemn the outrages, Jewish leaders cautioned against making too much of them. Rabbi Judah Quicksilver, the prominent theologian and philosopher, urged people to see them as "isolated incidents in a train of Jewish pain and trauma", further stating that the Jewish community stood ready to take full financial responsibility for the acts of its members, "misguided and unconscionable though they be". In the midst of the expressions of shame and outrage, security was not left neglected. Guards were dispatched to synagogues and Jewish owned businesses alerted to possible acts of sabotage or arson. The Shiloh Baptist Church was a Black church and people were angry, blaming the Jews for failing to control their miscreants. In a replay of the sixties, a self-styled black revolutionary group vowed vengeance. Old resentments began to resurface, economic, political, resentments over Israel and South Africa, the Arabs and Islam. Black leaders had been humiliated, made to do public penance for uttering the word "Hymie", branded as anti-Semitic and shut out of the media for daring to profess a position antagonistic to Israel, to Zionism. Only two days before in a debate on intervention on the floor of the House, Lorenzo Jefferson, the former all-pro defensive guard, took near-violent umbrage at the remarks of a Jewish congressman who made a point to remind his Black colleagues that the Arabs were involved in the slave trade. A furious Jefferson had shouted, "We don't need you to tell us who our slavemasters were, we know damn well who they are!" The Speaker of the House gavelled him out of order and two Black colleagues rushed to restrain his 275 pound bulk, but the point had been made — Blacks were tired of being patronized by Jews.

471

Al Abel's column carried an eyecatching heading that morning.

BLOOD AND SAND (Syrian style)
Producer: Soviet Communism
International
Director: Major Salim Nafsi
Writer: Nikolai Lenin
Rated X — Contains scenes of
excessive violence. World
condemnation and outrage advised.

The theatrical title with its quaint list of credits was a reference to the coup that overthrew Jordan, bringing the resources and territory of the desert kingdom under the sway of the Islamic Alliance. Drawing upon his extensive network of intelligence and diplomatic sources, Abel revealed how the Syrians, by appealing to sentiments deeply held by all Arabs concerning religious and political unity, had seduced key elements of the Jordanian establishment, mainly army and police, to revolt. The plot was based upon a proviso that the lives of the King and royal family would be respected. Once in control, the promise was ignored, the Syrians slaughtering the royal family to a man, permitting only Queen Fatima, the King's Italian bride, and her young children to escape. The article went on to describe how the King and his court were roused from their beds, assembled in the throne room of the Royal Palace, and one by one, the King first, "executed in the time-honored communist method — on their knees with a bullet in the back of the head. At the same time, perhaps deservedly, surely poetically, died the Jordanian traitors who in betraying King and country had thought to mitigate their treason by demanding as a price for their pact with the Devil, the life of their King. The arrest and execution of the duped quislings was ordered by Salim Nafsi, who demonstrated once again that he is an able if unimaginative student of Soviet communist history. Only when the murdered King's last sympathetic subject is eliminated will this bloody-handed Soviet satrap be satisfied. Only then will he be secure in his sultanic proclamation, 'The Hashemite Kingdom of Jordan is no more.' "

It was another blood bath, some said in the thousands, the bodies buried in the desert. How many only the sands knew, the Syrians weren't talking. But now the story was in Al Abel's column, a column eagerly awaited by millions of faithful readers, syndicated in one hundred and eleven newspapers, and written by a man known as "the writer's writer", the "conservative H.L. Mencken". As columns go, "Blood and Sand (Syrian style)" was one of Abel's best, lean, direct, with just the right degree of overstatement. On any other day the column's regicidal revelations would have been front page news. How often was a king killed? They were a vanishing breed, so few of them were in existence. But this morning the church bombings were the major news story, displacing even the war as the number one news item. The TV early morning network news shows were full of it, coming back to it time and time again, showing the damaged churches, the painted JFF slogans on the walls. The Jewish Fighters for Freedom had taken credit for the bombings but — the announcers and newspeople took pains to explain — the JFF was a fringe group, not representative of the Jewish people at all, no, not at all.

Despite the media's diligent disclaimers, the news profoundly disturbed Samuel Shames. He already had a problem with Al Abel's column. He knew Al Abel, not intimately, but on a social basis, running into him at Jewish and Democratic party functions. Shames was repelled by Abel's philosophy. In America they called it conservatism, but how could the slaughter of Nicaraguan peasants, the use of poison gas, opposition to environmental regulations, how could that be "conservatism"? It was more like Nazism. Abel was for those things and others — like the anti-abortion freaks, the right-to-lifers. It was sickening. Shames had been a little

473

queasy about calling Abel, but in a time like this you ignored differences and made common cause, even with schmucks like Abel. Shames had thought to coordinate with Abel, to get the maximum publicity for the cause. "Don't worry," Abel had told him, his next column was "going to be a bomb", it would "blow the lid off Washington." Shames was disappointed. Abel's column dealt more with the Soviet menace than the plight of Israel. Who cared about the death of some bum of an Arab king? He should have written about the Moslem bombardment, its savagery, the targeting of civilians, the burning flesh from phosphorus shells. Abel's tunnel vision had squandered an opportunity. Shames regretted ever contacting Abel, he should have listened to his stomach, not his head. Conservatives were assholes. He had gone to bed happily exhausted after the "Artists for Israel" TV special and now he had to wake up to this embarrassment. This tsuris he did not need.

Shames' first act upon arriving at the office was to call a meeting of the firm's employees. A telephone pool was organized to contact leading opinion makers — corporation heads, university presidents, TV producers, news editors, politicians, people who determined what the nation heard and thought. There were follow-up calls to make to allies, to reestablish contact with supporters cross-country. Now was the time to consolidate support, to prepare it for even higher levels of action. The secretaries, draftsmen, journeyman architects, they went about their assigned tasks with enthusiasm. Shames was the boss and a good one. They liked and respected him, they were loyal. Except for Miriam Scheine. She refused to be part of the mobilization effort, thought it "presumptuous and demeaning". She said so too, in front of everyone. Shames didn't let on at the time, but after the briefing he went to Miriam's office and told her to empty her desk drawers and get out. Nearly ten years with the firm and he told her to get out. It bothered him to do what he did, but in war a commander could not brook defiance

— especially when committed in public — there had to be discipline. His argument with Elliott Chase was the most wrenching though. They fought over the office's mobilization and Miriam's firing. When the shouting was over, Chase said he was going home, that he had "been waiting for this day". That his own partner would say such a thing to him, that he had "been waiting for this day", a Jew waiting for "the destruction of Israel" — that was the unkindest cut of all. When he thought about it, it hurt him, hurt him deeply. But he couldn't let it throw him, make him break his stride. He thought of Zeev Jabotinsky again, the battles he must have gone through in his struggle to lay the foundations for the Jewish state to come; Moses, when he came down from the mountain and found the Children of Israel worshipping the golden calf. Backbiting, lapses, forsaking friends, criticism, these were the leader's lot. A leader had to be above all that. He had to chair a meeting, this was no time to be going soft.

Clenching his fist in response to his determination, he strode through the open door of his office. Lester Kayam, Marvin Rattus, Sidney Falk, Rabbi Judah Quicksilver, and several other cohorts were already there waiting. The outside grayness of a steady rain falling against the Gothic windowpanes accented the grim, wake-like atmosphere prevailing in the room. The Rally for Israel at the White House, the "Artists for Israel" show, they had no words for those events. It was as if they had never happened, never occurred. The bombings, something had to be done about the bombings they said, the guilty parties apprehended and brought to justice. Rabbi Quicksilver announced the consensus — "The JFF must be cast out of the Jewish body." There was no time to spare, the Committee of Fifty and the American Rabbinical Council were ready to issue a statement of "disassociation" to the press, "before the fires of anti-Semitism could be ignited."

It was a panic. Shames saw Lester Kayam looking up

475

at him, a bewildered expression on his face, it was obvious he was in over his head. They were a bunch of fat cats, strangers to adversity, a crisis and they collapsed. He threw them a stern look of contempt, then sat down and picked up his telephone. "Get me Joe Rudy," he ordered, in the next breath assuring his confederates, "I'll get to the bottom of this." Retaking their seats, they waited expectantly while the call went through. "Joe, Sam Shames . . . Fine, Joe . . . Yeah, thanks, Joe, every little bit helps. Listen, Joe, I'm busy here, I don't have much time to talk, but these JFF dummies, is this how they pay us back for our support? They've got to have rocks in the head. Maybe we should put out a contract on the bastards." Shames' eyes narrowed, he was listening now, "You sure of that?," he asked, the aggressiveness gone out of his voice.

"What did he say?," they wanted to know when Shames put down the receiver.

"He said they said they didn't do it." There was a stunned silence as the reality of the situation sunk in. Men given to a lifetime in public relations and public speaking could only look at one another, leaving Samuel Shames to enunciate the common sentiment, "That dago sonofabitch! That rotten son-of-a-*bitch*!"

Before they could recover from the one shock, three of their fellows, latecomers, burst into the office delivering two more, "The Moslems have broken through . . . they've broken through the Jerusalem defense lines!," cried one breathlessly, "They're fighting house to house!" "We just heard it on the radio," added another frantically, "they detected high levels of radioactivity over Japan!"

The news hit the room with the force of a Katyusha rocket. "The Arabs have introduced atomic weapons into the Middle East!," cried a shaken Sidney Falk. "You mean the Russians," corrected Rabbi Quicksilver, "the Syrians are only their Cossacks. This is a pogrom that shall live in infamy!" A general free-for-all ensued with the meeting becoming a chaos of shouting, gesticulating men, men racking their brains for some scheme, some resort, one last gimmick to win over American public opinion for Israel. "Moslems killing Christians, we can work with the Vatican on that!," exclaimed Sidney Falk in the manner of one hitting upon a panacea. But Shames was opposed, reminding the group of the price paid by Israel for its last flirtation with the Vatican — a humiliating rejection of Israel's claim to Jerusalem. "They're all Romans under those skirts," said Shames, "you can't trust them."

"We've got to target the Arabs," insisted one faction, "they're the enemy! They control ninety percent of the world's oil." Another faction, the majority, agreed, but wanted the focus to be the threat of Russian communism. One man, a writer and publicist with long experience in such things, suggested running a full page ad in tomorrow's major dailies entitled, "Can We Allow the Russians to Take the Middle East and Not Lift a Finger to Stop Them?" No, said others, ads wouldn't work. People didn't read, especially long, full page ads telling them to send telegrams to their congressmen. A university academic's suggestion of nation-wide teach-ins was turned down for the same reason, too little and too late. Direct action was the only way, perhaps a sit-in of the Senate spearheaded by a joint Judeo-Christian contingent of clergymen. The suggestion of a sit-in at the UN drew a sneer and a snide comment from Shames, "Great idea, they hate us there."

"Alright, Mr. Smart Guy, maybe you have a better idea," said an exasperated Marvin Rattus. "Remember, it was your idea to lay siege to the White House. We blew our wad on that one. Figure where it got us. All it did was antagonize Colonna. Now no matter what we do we're damned."

The scent of rebellion in the air, Shames moved quickly to reassert his authority. Drawing up to his full five foot five inch height behind the massive Italian Renaissance desk, he looked each man in the room in the eye and told it like it was, "I shouldn't have to say this, but the only reason we're this far is because of me. When I proposed the Rally for Israel there wasn't a man in this room who wasn't for it, *one hundred percent!* So don't come here now with your twenty-twenty hindsight and blame me because for obvious reasons it didn't work according to expectations. Since when did Jews depend on the Goyim for their existence? If we had to rely on their good will we'd all be dead now. And that goes for Israel too. Jews made Israel, not some Judophiliac American president signing some paper proclamation in Washington, D.C. They were all johnny-come-latelys, even Truman, coming around only after we showed them what we could do, *Jews* could do. Israel was born in blood and tears and sweat and will endure in blood and tears and sweat. If the Holocaust has taught us anything, it's that.

"You see that map over there?" Shames pointed to his war board studded with the tri-colored pins. "Well, that's our support system. You can all walk out of here right now, but I'm sticking with Israel. As long as Jews are being slaughtered by the combined forces of six Moslem nations I'm going to be in there pitching, Colonna or no Colonna. As far as I'm concerned the war isn't over until the last shot is fired!"

It didn't have the polish of the words of an Abba Eban, or the stylistic finesse of an Elie Wiesel appeal, nor was it likely to go down in history as one of the great fighting speeches of all time — and not because it was unrecorded. But as the expression of one man's sincerity, love and devotion, there was no doubt, at least in the minds of those assembled in that room high up in the upper reaches of the Gothic majesty of the Woolworth Building. It was the kind of speech that took away the opposition's breath, albeit temporarily. The concepts and tenets proclaimed were so basically true and shared by all that answering it was impossible. It was the kind of statement that in a Black church would draw cries of "Hallelujah!", or "Amen, brother!" But these were Jews, men of the world, men who prided themselves upon their ability to analyze, to square the logical circle, practical men, men of affairs. They wanted to believe, but could not.

The meeting had reached an impasse. Still, no one wanted to be the first to move for its adjournment. So they waited, hoping for something or someone to release them from the sense of discomfiture and guilt they felt sitting there under Shames' stern and relentless gaze. They were being tested these men, many of whom had spent their entire adult lives "in the trenches" for Israel. Their commitment, the very quality that defined them as Jews, was being challenged. It was unfair.

The buzzing of Shames' telephone console caused all eyes to focus on the console's blinking red light. Ordinarily, incoming calls were held up during conferences. But Shames' secretary knew this was no ordinary call, it was from Lionel Beaufort. Shames was delighted, he could not have asked for a more prestigious reinforcement. "Lionel! I'm glad you called. We're having a little problem — by the way, I've got the conference speaker on so we can all hear you — some of the boys are letting the news unduly affect their judgment. I've been trying to tell them . . ."

The distinctive voice of Lionel Beaufort interrupted, "That's why I'm calling, Sam . . . Sam, I'm releasing my people from their commitments. It's over, Sam, there's no use going on." Shames' jaw dropped, it was a shock. "We're shifting our resources to relief, there will be hundreds of thousands of refugees . . . "

"But Lionel, you can't do this! I've got the Boston Symphony lined up, the Los Angeles, Chicago, the Philharmonic. They're not going to play! The markets, we're shutting down the markets! We can shut this country down if we want!"

"Sam, listen, it's a tragedy, I know. But Jews have experienced adversity before and prevailed. You don't put all your eggs in one basket."

There was desperation in Shames' voice, "Lionel, I'm begging you. Hold off, a few more days. Israel will come back, she always has. It was a lucky punch, a sneak attack . . ."

"Sam, you don't seem to understand. This isn't the Pollard case. You're fighting the President of the United States!"

"Lionel, I'm telling you, you're making a mistake."

"That's it, Sam. I only called as a courtesy. You can do as you please."

"You're making a mistake, Lionel, you're making a mistake . . ." But Lionel Beaufort was beyond reason, he had hung up. Shames was still holding onto the receiver as a wide-eyed Lester Kayam stood up and exclaimed, "Lionel Beaufort! He's the tallest tree in the forest, Sam."

"That lousy, Roman sonofabitch! That double-crossing, Roman sonofabitch! I endorsed that sonofabitch. Never trust a Roman! It was a lucky punch, a lucky punch! . . ." But the men in his office were not interested in hearing Shames' rantings. They were gathering up their papers and brief-cases. They were leaving.

They were close now, close enough for him to hear the throaty cries of *"Allahu Akbar!"*, the valedictory Moslem gunners gave their shells as they shot from the breech. They had added mortars to their arsenal, supplementing the rain of Katyushas that continued to whine overhead, at times with squall-like intensity, to explode against distant targets. He knew all of them now, rockets, shells, bombs, mortars, the explosive payload each carried, knew the intervals between their whines and the thud of striking a target. He was a veteran, a survivor of the bombardment of Jerusalem. He had been hiding for four days, ever since they came for him early Sunday morning. He knew something was awry, they had never come for him in a truck. He ignored the pounding, waiting until they drove away before turning on the radio and having his suspicion confirmed. The telephone had rung twice that morning but he hadn't dared answer it. In the days following he had plenty of time to think about the calls, whether they were from people he was trying to avoid, or his father, Olga, Beatrix. The next day, when he finally decided to call them, the line was dead, completely dead. So in the meantime he worried, about where they were, whether they were safe, how his father and Olga would react to his refusal to report. Especially Olga. He had never discussed politics with her, never had to, their minds always seemed to be on the same wavelength, even when she was posturing or playacting. But now, as he made his way toward her apartment, he wished he had. He stayed close to walls while darting in and out of doorways, now running, now walking, trying to avoid presenting a target for a potential sniper. He still hadn't seen any troops, neither Israeli nor Islamic, and in the early morning twilight he hoped they hadn't seen him.

A bedraggled mongrel promptly fled at his approach. With only an occasional hit, the Old City was remarkably intact, a testament to the care the Moslems had exercised in avoiding it with their ordnance. By contrast, most of the New was in ruins. Seen through the morning haze, the fires and rising columns of smoke recalled images of a Biblical destruction, of a Sodom and Gomorrah.

He had made it to Olga's door and began rapping on it with the big Turkish door knocker. There was no response. But he hadn't expected one, people were in basements or shelters. He bolted across the street, knocking and pounding on the door of Olga's neighbor, finally calling out her name, "Mart Jalil! Mart Jalil!"

"Who is it?," replied a voice in Arabic through the door. "It's Basil . . . Bawzil Bey!," he cried, using the name the Arabs knew him by. Mart Jalil, an aged widow, opened her door, the expression on her face seeming to ask, "Where is your gun? Where is your uniform?", as if the place of all young Jews was naturally in the army. "I'm looking for Olga," he blurted, "Do you know where she is?"

"*Ya wayli*!," exclaimed the old woman, putting a hand to her face. "They came Sunday night, men with guns, *Yahood*, and took her and Nadezhda! We do not know where she is!" Mart Jalil took hold of his arm to pull him inside. "No," he protested, stepping back, "I have to find her. She may need help."

He began running again, detouring around the burned-out vehicles, fallen masonry, and barricades of earth and rubble clogging the streets. There was little chance of his being arrested as a deserter now, the soldiers he saw were too preoccupied dodging mortars to pay attention to civilians running through the streets. Various scenarios on Olga's abduction played in his mind — whether it was some kind of vigilante press gang bent upon dragooning bodies for a last ditch defense battalion, or just some women to care for wounded. He wondered if he was the issue again, if he had put her at risk from Rabbi Khak's forces, or some other band of diehards applying guilt by association and settling private scores in the chaos of battle. Although he tried not to, he thought of Aziz Bustanji, consoling himself with the fact that Aziz was an Arab, whereas Olga was an emigré Russian, the elite of Israeli immigrants, and that an attack upon that group would be contrary to the settlers' basic belief structure.

He still had a kilometer to go to reach police headquarters when he heard a command to halt. Stopping and throwing up his hands, he turned and saw four Islamic soldiers pointing their guns at him. In their flaring fiberglass helmets and lapped body armor they resembled Japanese samurai warriors or giant insects. "*Inta Yahoodi ow Arabi?*" (Are you a Jew or Arab) demanded the closest. "*Amerkani*" he replied, having previously decided to declare himself American, realizing that with his name and command of

Arabic, he would never pass as Arab. Displaying outdated US Immigration Department papers, he was on his way to the "Moscobiyya," he said in English and halting Arabic, to inquire about his girlfriend who had been abducted from her home by a band of armed men. How much the soldiers understood he didn't know, but the expressions on their faces were not such as to inspire optimism. "Passport! American passport!," barked one of them. In the circumstances he could only shrug his shoulders, provoking an accusatory "*Jasoos!*" (spy) from his irate interrogator. Poking him with their gun barrels, they prodded him through the doorway of a nearby building, pushing him to the floor. Two Israeli soldiers already there regarded him with silence.

He sat until one of his captors signaled him to get up, kicking him in the leg for good measure. Outside, about a dozen Israeli prisoners stood in line, hands folded behind their heads. Suddenly, a blow in the back catapaulted him against another captive, the collision nearly knocking over both of them. One of the Moslems had struck him with the butt of his Kalashnikov. "*Yallah*" (let's go) ordered the brute, and he found himself obediently moving out with the others.

It is said a drowning man's life passes before his eyes, but no such memorial to dear life projected before his, as he trudged behind the moving line of captives, hands on head, taunts of the Moslems and rattle of automatic weaponry in his ears. His thoughts were of regret, regret he had ever returned, that he hadn't left when he had the chance, that he had let Olga persuade him otherwise. He had been too easy, always giving way to her whims. He should have made her emigrate, if necessary forced her to leave with him. But no, to attempt to use force to impose one's will upon another was absurdly stultifying. It was his fault, he should have initiated the process by securing the necessary papers, documents, plane tickets. She would have followed, she would have had to. Now he was paying for his sensibilities as she

483

might be too. In a few minutes it would all be over. He recalled past massacres, of Arabs shot down in their tracks as they came in from the fields, seated at their dinner tables, without warning. They would be seeking revenge, for then and now. Perhaps his execution would be Nazi-style — stood in front of a pit and mowed down. He thought he preferred that way, to have advance notice of the bullets. Suddenly, in the midst of his macabre reverie, he felt a violent jolting about his neck and he was jerked stumbling from the line. Regaining his balance, he looked up at the face behind the arm gripping his collar. It was Bustanji, in the uniform of an Islamic warrior, his formerly luxurious rabbinical beard now a trim Muslim mode. "Allah be praised!," exclaimed Bustanji in his mocking fashion, his hand still holding fast his prisoner's collar. Before more could be said, the march halted and the soldiers who arrested him were confronting Bustanji, pointing to the "jasoos" at his side. Basil watched as Bustanji, in Arabic and Farsi, argued with them, then checked the captives' identities, making sure none were high-ranking officers. The discussion over, he heard Bustanji order — "Finish with them!" He grabbed Bustanji's arm, "You're not going to kill them?," he protested, "They're prisoners!"

"Maybe you'd like to join them?," retorted Bustanji, his eyes flashing angrily. "It's still not too late you know. I can tell them I was mistaken when I said you were 'our spy' . . ."

Interrupted by signals from his radio, Bustanji placed it against his ear, repeating the latest developments, "They have blown up the Dome of the Rock . . . Our forces have taken the Moscobiyya . . ." They jumped into a military vehicle along with three other Moslem soldiers, snaking through streets highlifts were still in the process of clearing. Despite the continued bombardment and gunfire, some close by, people began surfacing on the streets, waving white handkerchiefs and long-hidden Palestinian flags at them as they passed, the first harbingers of the jubilation to come. "One of the few satisfactions of war," remarked Bustanji.

At the Moscobiyya they were met by grim-faced soldiers, men from the assault group, witness to the carnage within. "They killed them all," said one, "the bodies are piled up in the cells." Inside they passed some Israeli bodies near the building's entrance, soldiers and police killed in the assault. In a large basement detention room Syrian army photographers were taking stills and filming the grisly scene, while medical personnel fingerprinted bodies. "Political prisoners," said one of the medics, "both Israeli and Arab." He noticed Bustanji looking anxiously up and down the row of cells. He didn't know who saw the blonde hair first but both made it over to the cell at the same time. Olga's body lay on top of Nadezhda Ikrova's, her arms still around her friend's shoulders. Part of her skull had been shot away and pieces of brain adhered to the cell's walls. He knelt down and closed her eyelids, touching the lips for the last time. "Olga Shalansky and Nadezhda Ikrova," declared Bustanji, "I worked with them. We shall bury them in the Tomb of the Russian Martyrs!"

The truck stopped in front of the Moscobiyya and began unloading bodies, the dead and wounded, remains of a band of Israelis ambushed near the Old City. Witnesses had placed them in the vicinity of the Haram ash-Sharif about the time the Dome of the Rock was dynamited. Occasionally one of the bodies would cry out when it struck the pavement. One such was an Israeli with a bushy red beard. Eliezar Ben-Judah had lost his glasses and in the bright sun his eyes squinted trying to get a bearing on his surroundings. He cried out again when soldiers roughly lifted him to his feet, his long arms dangling useless and bloody at his sides. Bustanji conferred with a group of officers, then ordered the soldiers to take Ben-Judah into the Moscobiyya for interrogation. Five minutes later Bustanji emerged from the building, a look of disgust on his face.

" 'Captain Eliezar Ben-Judah, Israeli Military Intelligence.' Otherwise your former associate will say nothing," reported Bustanji. Bustanji removed his pistol from its leather holster and handed it to Basil. "They're waiting for you inside. Save the people the trouble. Go in there and blow his brains out!"

An hour ago and he might have hesitated. But now he took the proffered pistol, put it under his belt, and climbed the stairs of the Moscobiyya. An Islamic officer standing in the lobby pointed to an office on his left, "In there," said the officer.

Ben-Judah was slumped in a chair against the wall, blood from a wound dripping down his fingers onto the floor. "Eliezar!" cried Basil, taking the pistol from his belt and drawing close for the benefit of the myopic Ben-Judah, "it's Primchek!"

"God damn you, Primchek!," cursed Ben-Judah, catching sight of the black automatic pointed at him, "I figured you for one of them. Go ahead, shoot, I don't care. Shoot me like we shot your fucking Olga. She was a whore, Primchek, a communist whore!"

His first shot was from the hip and passed through the left side of Ben-Judah's neck, provoking another spasm of raving, "I have seen her riding in cars with Arabs, Primchek. I have seen her with Arabs . . ." Ben-Judah's head snapped back from the force of the bullet then fell forward. He put the pistol on safety, walked out into the lobby, giving a kind of backhanded salute to the solemn-faced Moslem soldiers. Outside, he handed the pistol back to Bustanji. "Thanks for the satisfaction," he said.

EPILOGUE

There was no surrender. The "Zionist entity" was a bandit state, possessed of no rights an Islamic nation need respect, not even that of surrender. The Israeli nation was dissolved, its wealth "reappropriated" for the benefit of the land's former and present Arab inhabitants. Israelis were placed under a rigorous curfew, their lives and property subjected to the ancient law of war — woe to the vanquished. Israeli military and political leaders, bureaucrats, police, members of the power structure, were arrested and summarily shot. No trials, no appeals, none were necessary. Mere participation was proof of conspiracy. There was no defense. Moslem priorities were "repatriation and reparations", not reconciliation.

A few succeeded in escaping, but only those who fled early, before Moslem forces sealed the borders of Israel and Lebanon. Moslem boats and helicopters patrolled the coast, interdicting and sinking vessels irrespective of their human cargos. Traffic in "boat people" was forbidden.

In Lebanon separatist elements paid dearly for their collaboration with the enemy. Lebanese allies of the Islamic Alliance and contingents of Iranian Revolutionary Guards descended upon Christian Lebanon, laying waste villages, slaughtering those who resisted. For more than a hundred years the West, invoking a common Christian kinship, had intervened in the region's affairs. Even Jewish Israel had asserted the shabby hypocrisy. But now no self-annointed defenders of the faith rushed to protect "the Christians", no mighty imperial armadas sailed the coast spewing fire and death. The "Lebanese question" was being settled for another hundred years — by Islam.

His father was one of the thousands missing and presumed dead. His burned-out car was found in Maale

Adumim, parked behind the three story tenement in which the bakery leased commercial space. The bombardment had reduced the building to a heap of rubble. The new suburban developments surrounding Jerusalem had been hard hit from the start. On the other hand, their home suffered only minor damage — a few broken windows and cracked walls. But the clinic, his one purely individual architectural contribution to the city, was badly damaged. The tile roof bordering the open courtyard had been blown away, and sections of the facade carrying the sculptured frieze were shattered beyond repair. Bustanji promised to "some day" reexecute the sculptures, but his present occupation of chief of Islamic intelligence for Jerusalem suggested the day would be long in coming.

For Beatrix Brunwasser, the war and its aftermath was an opportunity to work for a dream. Before the shooting stopped she had offered her services as a translator to the invaders. And, with other IPR operatives, she was involved in the first tentative efforts at de-Zionization. Her father had been briefly arrested then released, his name put on a list of those permitted to emigrate in exchange for the payment of reparations. A typical scientist, ideology had relevance only as it related to his work and its rewards. According to Beatrix, whether he stayed or left was immaterial, living anywhere else was unthinkable. These were "exciting times, revolutionary times," she exclaimed with her characteristic enthusiasm.

Bustanji had placed him with a committee of engineers and architects charged with damage assessment and coming up with a plan of reconstruction. The committee's temporary head was a kindly Iranian mullah, Hojatoislam Nasrollah Tabrizi, who, while not an architect, brought a fervent religious confidence to the solution of problems. An example of this was his immediate importation of a team of skilled Iranian tilemakers to study the replication of the destroyed Dome of the Rock's tiles. Shortly thereafter, in a public

490

ceremony giving thanks to God for restoring Jerusalem to Moslem hands, the Saudi ambassador pledged his nation's treasury to the mosque's reconstruction.

Tabrizi, a religious scholar (a professor of law at the University of Qum), had seen the design for the Third Temple. Impressed, the good mullah made some representations and arranged the morning's meeting with the great man himself, Salim Nafsi. While Basil had no advance notice of the meeting's agenda, he was quite sure Nafsi wasn't going to order the building of the Third Temple. In any event, it wasn't every day one had an audience with the *Rais*. He recalled Alison Cleveland's interview, still the only one Nafsi ever granted a Western correspondent. He had received a wire from her a few days before — after the restoration of outside communications — and immediately wired back a succinct reply, "Reborn in Jerusalem". There were reports of a meeting between Gaetano Impastato and Nafsi in which the Syrian was said to have given assurances that the Islamic Alliance had no designs on the oil fields of the Gulf (it had enough of its own), nor plans for further conquest (it had enough problems). Tending to support these assurances was the recent military coup in Iraq, an effect of the Islamic Alliance's stunning battlefield victory over Israel. While the Iraqi tyrant's head was not put on a pike as promised by Nafsi, his body was thrown to the mob which reportedly tore it to pieces.

Outside of his political persona, not much was known about Nafsi, Syrians were not in the habit of publishing details on the private lives of their leaders. He had heard that while a student in Moscow Nafsi had a Russian girlfriend, but that she had died, tragically, of cancer it was said. So they had something in common.

He saw the busload of troops parked near the Damascus Gate. The rear window was open and his eye was drawn to the overly feminine face of a soldier waving to a small group of well-wishers. Projecting from the helmet

491

were the familiar strands of bright red hair. She saw him too, calling out his name, excited by the opportunity to be seen by him outfitted for battle. She showed him her Kalashnikov, saying they were going to the Galilee to wipe out pockets of resistance from diehard Jewish zealots. He asked the Syrian officer in charge to look out for her, telling him she had a tendency to be reckless of danger. "Don't worry," replied the officer, "we won't let her out of our sight." At the sound of the bus' engine she reached out and took hold of his hand, pressing it to her face. "I told you! I told you the Jewish and Arab people would live in peace together one day! I told you!," she cried as the bus pulled away.

At the Damascus Gate his contacts, two Syrian army officers, were waiting in a faded blue Mercedes. They drove down the Via Dolorosa, then along the city wall to St. Anne's Church where a quartet of soldiers manning a guard post at the base of the great stone structure waved them through. His escorts at his side, he entered the church rectory and climbed a flight of stairs to a large, second story anteroom where soldiers worked at desks. He waited until one of his escorts emerged from Nafsi's office and announced he could go in. Nafsi was standing behind a desk, a large map of Palestine on the wall behind him. Of medium stature, he possessed the soldier's trim physique. His face was shadowed by a dark bristle of unshaven hair extending upwards over gaunt cheekbones. With its thick, black Syrian moustache and sloping brow, it bore a faintly primitive, almost Neanderthal cast. There was a natural austerity about the Syrian, the type best expressed by the serious scientist or pious divine. This was a Savonarola, a scourge sent by God to redeem, in spite of itself, his people; a man, who, defying the impossible, united a disparate East, the ancient and the modern, in the process erasing boundaries and altering history, making the gnomes who drew the maps and wrote the books scramble to mark the changes. In the presence of such a person, a sense of expectation, of destiny, was inevitable.

"You are wondering why you are here," said Nafsi, retaking his seat. "You are here because your reputation precedes you . . . You will design the Tomb of the Russian Martyrs. In this project you shall report to me directly. For reasons of state it shall enjoy the highest priority. And yes, you will direct the reconstruction of Jerusalem." Nafsi's tone was peremptory, like an order for battle, as if there wasn't the slightest possibility of a demurrer or refusal. Basil rose, intending to shake Nafsi's hand. But Nafsi's hand was raised, he was not finished. Syria, he said, was a poor country. Reparations would pay but a fraction of the costs of reconstruction. The rest would have to come from outside sources — Muslims, Christians, Jews, the world over. Solicitation of funds would be a a major responsibility of the director. The fact that he was a Jew was as it should be, merely coincidental. Nevertheless, cautioned Nafsi, it was natural that in the wake of war a period of moral reaction would follow, all the more in a war defined as religious. There were bound to be moralistic excesses. "But we are not afraid of them," he said. "A little morality will be good for this people spoiled as it is by a culture of indulgence. A puritanical Islam will help provide the moral grease for the passage of a time of hardship. And that is to the good, because Islam is in our blood, our emotions, it will not easily be purged. I am a Christian, yet when I hear the Muslim call to prayer, I am touched.

"On the other hand," continued Nafsi, placing a hand on the Uzi machine gun lying on his desk, "they will be 'waving the flag' of Islam against us. We are in a time of uncertainty, surrounded by conspiracies, internal and external. A bomb, a bullet, and one is gone. Should that happen, don't wait for the knock on the door. If I go, you go. However, I wouldn't be overly concerned. I didn't get this far because of a charmed life, my enemies know I am a

493

veteran conspirator. I'll probably be around for a while yet." Nafsi came from around his desk. "Good luck!," he exclaimed, grasping Basil's hand. "Maybe I should wish you the same," responded Basil.

Following expressions of gratitude and loyalty, he had a favor to request of the Syrian, "In the event you decide to do another interview with the Western press, you might consider Alison Cleveland again. Naturally, she'd like the opportunity. They pretty well buried her after the first."

"Certainly," said Nafsi. "See Baghdash on the way out. He's our director of press relations."

He met Bustanji for dinner in a local restaurant that evening. His mother and sister were coming home. He also had an apology to make. "You remember what I told you when you asked about my sister? . . . It has been bothering me for a long time. Everytime I think about it I am ashamed. Naturally, we would be proud to have you . . ."

"That's alright," said Basil, mercifully interrupting his friend's effort at expiation, "you underestimated me . . . But you couldn't help it."

They called it a tomb, but it really was a temple, a temple to an obscure Russian goddess, the only temple he would ever build, if he built it. Despite Nafsi's warning of a coming Islamic reaction he put his visions on paper, inspired by memories of soft pelvic lines and flowing breasts, incorporated in the fluid arching pilasters projecting at intervals over the helmet-shaped structure. He had to realize these people had never heard of the Renaissance. On that score they were five hundred years behind, twenty-five hundred if one counted from the Greeks. He could only hope that by the time the tomb was built, Nafsi would be powerful enough to shoot its critics. If not, they could shoot its creator.

Of course, Olga would not be alone. More than a dozen other Russians would share the tomb. Besides

494

Nadezhda Ikrova, he was surprised and saddened to discover that his "security expert", Viktor Bogorodov, was another. Bogorodov had been killed in a raid on Eshkol airport, a top-secret atomic weapons dump of Israel's strategic strike force. He had been wiped out with his band, but not before wiping out Eshkol's atomic capability. Bogorodov was a *nom de guerre*, his real name was Vassily Koutamanos. He wasn't even Jewish.

He appointed Patrimoine Architectural consultant to reconstruction. Two days later Bernard Gluckmann was in Jerusalem, having recruited a team of scholar scientists and preservationists, a group Gluckmann jokingly referred to as "the second Napoleonic expedition". In his white linens and splendid Panama hat, the bearded Gluckmann fast became a familiar figure on the streets of Jerusalem, guiding colleagues through the more heavily damaged areas, pointing out the sites of former landmarks, now destroyed. The team from Patrimoine Architectural was tangible evidence that at least one important sector of the "international community" was involved in the city's reconstruction.

Once his appointment became known, he found himself with a great number of "friends", many of whom he had never met. They would stop in unannounced or call his headquarters in the Old City, offering congratulations, "incidentally" inquiring whether a post could be found for them somewhere. Even architects from Mordechai Levy Associates visited, shamelessly soliciting his favor. It made sense, *he* was the government now. Architects existed in a state of suspended animation. All construction had been frozen by the Moslem conquest, there was absolutely nothing for them to do. Even the stock exchange was unavailable to fill the empty hours. There was no stock exchange. It had been converted into a vegetarian cafeteria.

He received his newfound friends civilly enough, asking each to submit examples of their work. Afterwards, he would pull out a lengthy pad of paper and ostentatiously enter their names on a list of previous applicants. If their work was particularly obnoxious, he would inquire whether the applicant had experience in architectural conservation. Negative responses elicited advice that emigration might be the most practical option. Of course, a waiting list existed for that also. But application could be made to the "Samuel and Myra Shames Jewish Rescue Foundation." It was doing "great work in buying emigration rights for deserving applicants." It may have been heartless and arbitrary, but that was the way the world worked. He owed them nothing.

So when his secretary rang and said a young woman wanted to see him, he gave it no particular significance, thinking it might be some Palestinian student referred for a summer job. "Send her in," he said, getting up and walking around his desk, intending to put the young visitor at ease. He was surprised to see that his visitor was really an old friend, a very old friend. He hadn't seen Rachel Aboulafia for over a year, since the night at Fagan's with Alison Cleveland. "Well," he said, "I must say this is a pleasant surprise. How are you, Rachel?"

"My father sent me," she replied, giving his hand a hesitant shake and averting her eyes, "He said you might be able to find me a job." The Arabs had seized her father's trucks and she had lost her job at the hospital, the family resources were running thin. Her formerly flat abdomen bore a noticeable hump, an increase the cotton maternity smock she was wearing exaggerated more than concealed. He opened a folding chair for her and asked if she were married. "No, the child I am carrying is Raffi's. He was killed in the war."

Seeing her in such a stupid condition made him realize how hopelessly primitive she was. He could have asked why she hadn't obtained an abortion, but the answer was obvious. Mentioning it would have been useless, the world must have one more bastard. He was sorry for her but that was all. "I'm sure with the numbers of wounded there must be plenty of openings for nurses here or in Tel Aviv. I'll do some calling around . . . But you understand you'll be working with Arabs. That means some of those quaint notions of yours will have to go."

Rachel gave a nod of the head, as if she had already resigned herself to the unpleasantness of the change. His gesture of assistance seemed to have given a boost to her confidence because she rose and stood there, gazing down at him, her lips slightly parted. The pelvic expansion was incidental, she was the same brown-skinned sexual animal he remembered. "That's alright, Rachel," he said, " . . . you can go now."

He was leaving from Sidon in the morning, taking the boat to Cyprus. He was rendezvousing with Alison Cleveland in Paphos, at the Hotel Sappho. She had chosen Paphos because of its legendary reputation as the birthplace of love. "Aphrodite was born in the spume of its sea" she had written on the Italian watermarked paper. Her message could have been a sonnet, poetic without poetry's pretense. One did not have to be superstitious to appreciate such sentiments and such paper.

He reread the telegram in his hand:

ARRIVING IZZEDIN QASSAM AIRPORT TOMORROW. SEEK ENTRE TO OFFICIALDOM FOR IMMIGRATION NEGOTIATIONS. HOPE YOU CAN HELP.

It was signed "Sam". He telephoned the Al-Aqsa Hotel and reserved a room for Shames, the one he used to use for assignations. Rooms were at a premium in the city, most of the larger, mainline hotels had been shelled into rubble. He scribbled a quick note — "Called out of town official business. Room reserved for you al-Aqsa Pension. Walking distance Wailing Wall. Next week in Jerusalem. Basil" He called in his secretary and told her to give it to Shames when he came.

497

That night while packing he rummaged through his store of treasures for some little thing to present Alison. The embroidered Palestinian purse Sumaiya Bustanji had made to give to his mother was where he had left it, wrapped in tissue paper in a small box. "Sumaiya wouldn't mind," he said to himself, "No, she wouldn't mind at all."